MEG GARDINER

Mission Canyon

Meg Gardiner

Hodder & Stoughton

First published in Great Britain in 2003 by Hodder & Stoughton
A division of Hodder Headline

The right of Meg Gardiner to be identified as the Author
of the Work has been asserted by her in accordance with the
Copyright, Designs and Patents Act 1988.

1 3 5 7 9 10 8 6 4 2

A CIP catalogue record for this title is
available from the British Library

ISBN 0 340 82250 3 (hardback)
ISBN 0 340 82251 1 (trade paperback)

Typeset in Plantin Light by Palimpsest Book Production Limited,
Polmont, Stirlingshire
Printed and bound in Great Britain by
Clays Ltd, St Ives plc

Hodder & Stoughton
A division of Hodder Headline
338 Euston Road
London NW1 3BH

Mission Canyon

Also by Meg Gardiner

China Lake

For Tani Goodman

For their help with this novel I thank Paul Shreve, Sara Gardiner, MD, Bill Gardiner and Suzanne Davidovac; and for service beyond the call of duty: Mary Albanese, Adrienne Dines and Nancy Fraser.

One

People ask me whose fault it was. Who caused the accident? Where did the blame lie – on reckless driving, blinding sunlight, a sharp curve in the road? Hidden in their questions is a deeper query. Did Jesse bring it on himself? Was he careless? Perhaps he rode his bike into the middle of the road. Perhaps he insulted God. Maybe that's why he won't be walking me down the aisle, they imply.

What people want to hear, I think, is that the accident was fate, or foolishness. The hit-and-run killed Isaac Sandoval outright. It left Jesse Blackburn paralyzed and broken on the hillside, struggling to reach his friend's body. And people want me to tell them *yes*, it was the victims' fault. Jesse should have done something different, should have looked over his shoulder or flossed his teeth every day. What they want me to tell them is *no*, of course it could never happen to you. They want reassurance, and I can't give it to them.

When they asked me whose fault it was, I always said: the driver's. It was the fault of the man who sat behind the wheel of a satin-gray BMW, arcing up a narrow road into the foothills of Santa Barbara, with one hand on the steering wheel and the other caressing the hair of the woman whose head bobbed above his lap. It was the fault of the man getting the blow job. It was the fault of the guy who got away.

That's what I always told people. Until now.

'There's going to be security,' Jesse said.

'Don't worry, I can handle it.'

Jesse stared out the window of the car at the Santa Barbara Museum of Art across the street. Sunset was painting the white building orange. Guests were arriving, and their costumes glittered as they climbed the steps to the entrance. Jesse drummed his hands on the steering wheel.

'You can't hesitate,' he said. 'Straight in, do it, get out. If there's any trouble—'

I put my hand on his. 'I know how to crash a party.'

He gave me a glance – blue eyes cool, mouth askew, the patented Blackburn Wry Look. 'Evan, this isn't a Brownie sing-along.'

'Trust me. It's an art museum. The guards care about keeping the paintings inside, not about keeping people out.'

'Don't count on that,' he said. 'And your wig's crooked.'

I straightened it. 'You just want to do this yourself. You'd love to stick it to Cal Diamond with all his colleagues looking on.'

'Absolutely.'

But we both knew that Diamond would spot Jesse coming a mile away, even though he had on faded jeans and an old USA Swimming T-shirt, and didn't look like a lawyer. With his youth and good looks, the brown hair he hadn't cut in months, and his hardware, Diamond couldn't miss him. So the job was mine.

I struck a pose. 'How do I look?'

He gazed at my costume: frosted white lipstick, hoop earrings as big as grapefruit, the black wig rising on my head like a hair volcano. The sequined pink mini-dress came from a vintage clothing store, the white vinyl boots from my closet, relics of a year misspent on the high school drill team.

'Perfect,' he said. 'Very I-Dream-of-Jeanie.'

'It's supposed to be Diana Ross.'

He eyed my Irish complexion skeptically.

'Fine. Diana O'Ross,' I said.

He handed me the summons and complaint, and held up a snapshot. It showed a man in his fifties, bald with unruly eyebrows and snappish teeth.

I said, 'He even looks like a swindler.'

'Yeah, and I hear that tonight he'll look like Zorro. So watch out for his whip.' He flicked his finger against the snapshot. 'And for his wife.'

The photo showed Mari Vasquez Diamond standing next to her husband, looking much younger than him, all sinewy bronze limbs and long fingers curled around his arm. She had set her dogs loose on the last process server who approached their door.

'Her Dobermans won't be here tonight,' I said, getting out of the car. 'I'll serve him, Jesse.'

I crossed the street. The lights of the city were coming on, a glittering spray below the green folds of the mountains. The sky was streaked with jet contrails flushing pink in the summer sunset. Ahead, guests were going into the museum. Bogart, Cleopatra, the Pope.

Sashay, I told myself. Act as if you have an invitation to this benefit. Attitude is everything.

Cal Diamond was all attitude. He acted the business wizard, and investors shoveled money into his software company, Diamond Mindworks. He cooked the books, plundered the company pension plan, and built himself a Spanish-style hacienda fit for a conquistador. But Diamond's life was about to come tumbling down, because his investors had hired Jesse's law firm to sue him for fraud.

The problem was, Diamond had been evading service for weeks. Jesse was getting pissed off. And when he got pissed off, he got ruthless.

It was one of the things I loved about him.

He knew that Diamond wouldn't miss this charity fundraiser – his company was one of the high tech firms sponsoring it. This was our best chance to hit him with the summons.

I climbed the steps toward the museum entrance. A woman with a clipboard stood at the door, checking names against the guest list. She wore tiny square eyeglasses and brown lipstick. When I approached, she assumed a knowing expression and pointed at me with her pen.

'Let's see. Jackie Kennedy?'

3

'Score half a point for the correct decade. Who's in charge here?'

Her pen hovered in the air.

'Yoo hoo,' I said. 'Do you work for this museum?'

Her mouth puckered. 'Certainly.'

'Well, you're about two minutes from disaster.' I pointed over my shoulder. 'One of your guests is circling the block looking for a parking spot. He's dressed as the Lone Ranger, and he's hauling a horse trailer.'

'You can't be—'

'Serious? Do you want to wait until he rides through the door into the Greek Antiquities, shouting, "Hi Ho, Silver?"'

She blinked, looking up the street, and said, 'Wait here.'

She scurried down the steps. I walked inside.

Two minutes: I figured that was all I had before she came after me. I breezed into the foyer, past a string quartet, and into a central gallery. Above the skylight a Gauguin sky unrolled, dense blue. People stood in clots, drinking and preening. It was a tech crowd, here to raise money for science and engineering scholarships. Most were baby boomers costumed in polyester and nostalgia. I saw Sonny and Cher, and Darth Vader. But I didn't see Zorro.

I worked my way around the gallery. Talk caromed off the walls. In my head I heard my dad's voice. *Thousands of dollars for law school and you're serving a summons yourself?* A waiter handed me a glass of Chablis. *You hated practicing, but love the dirty work. What are you thinking?* I pushed through the chiffon-and-Spandex forest.

And ran straight into Cal Diamond's wife. Lady Doberman.

Her ruby necklace spelled out *Mari*, but could have read *trophy bride*. I guessed her to be about forty. She was as thin as a paper cut, wearing a strapless black evening gown and showcase breasts. Wow. What a geometry problem for the nerds in the room – calculate volume and density, accounting for the molecular mass of silicone. Her sable hair was sculpted high on her head. Her long fingers were coiled around a glass of red wine.

4

She was talking to a sandy-haired man, and I started to veer away, anxious to avoid her. But the man called to me.

'Where ya going, Gidget?'

He was slouching against a pillar, with an insouciance so cool that he must have practiced it before a mirror. His costume was a black turtleneck, houndstooth jacket, and tight jeans. He eyed me as though I were an hors d'oeuvre.

'Surf's up. Stick around,' he said.

Mari Diamond stood as straight as a scalpel, swirling her wine glass. 'She's not actually going for Gidget.' Chill gaze. 'I hope.'

I nudged past her. What a queen bee. She was ready to sting me, just for diverting a man's attention from her. In my head I now heard Jesse's voice, saying, *Don't, Delaney. Holster your tongue and back away from the bait.*

'After all,' she said, 'Gidget was a teenager. Talk about missing the mark.'

Okay, blow my attitude knob off the control panel, why don't you?

I heard myself say, 'You should know.'

'What?'

I pictured Jesse slapping his hand against his forehead. I told my feet to move. I said, 'You're not exactly prom queen material, yourself.'

She froze. 'You did not just say that.'

'Sure I did. I'm too old to take cheap shots from snotty socialites. Excuse me.'

'Don't you walk away.' She thrust out an arm, blocking my path. 'What's your name?'

'Diana Ross.'

Her nostrils dilated. Her jaw didn't move. 'Who is this woman?'

She looked to her companion for support, but his face was bright with amusement.

'She's our Baby Love.' Smiling at me. 'And I'm Steve McQueen.' He gestured to her. 'This is Maria Callas.'

'Charmed,' I said. 'Will Maria be singing tonight, or just hissing at the guests?'

His laugh was full of appetite. 'Dueling divas. I love it.'

And he did. He wanted some of what I was dishing out to her. He could have worn a sign saying, *spank me.*

But Mari Diamond's fingers were white on her wine glass. 'If you're from Diamond Mindworks, you're out of a job.'

She turned and swished away. Raising her hand, she snapped her fingers, signaling somebody. I saw Clipboard standing at the edge of the crowd, her tiny glasses shining as she scanned the room. Mari Diamond was beckoning to her.

Damn. I dove into the crowd. I was almost out of time.

And I saw, in the center of the gallery, a masked character in a black cape and gaucho hat. He was grinning broadly, looking care-free, indifferent about the people he'd bilked, the elderly investors and hourly-wage workers whose life savings he squandered. I took the summons from my purse.

An older man stepped up to shake his hand. His hair looked like an upturned white scrub brush. If his suit was a costume, he had come as an undertaker.

I knew him. Everybody in the room knew him. He was the big man here, and not just because he was a head taller than most people. He was George Rudenski, the CEO of Mako Technologies, main sponsor of tonight's benefit. But I didn't have time for protocol; I had to butt in on him. Mari Diamond was talking to Clipboard, pointing in my direction. I had to do this, right now.

Steve McQueen grabbed my arm. 'What's your rush? Those guys are old farts. Come talk to me.'

'Another time.' I swung out of his grip.

I approached Zorro. 'Cal? Is that you under that mask?'

Pressing a hand to his chest, he bowed and said, 'Señorita, Zorro never reveals his identity.'

George Rudenski looked at me. I had interviewed him for an article on cyber-security that I wrote for *California Lawyer* magazine, and he was trying to place me. His eyes were penetrating.

'Forgive me. Are you with Mako?' he said.

'No, I'm with the Supremes.'

For all I cared, he could out me as a freelance legal journalist, or itinerant lawyer, or for planning to wear white at my wedding. But he knew my connection to Jesse, and if he mentioned it the game would be up.

He gave me a concentrated stare. 'Evan.'

I was out of time. I raised the summons toward the man in the mask.

'Are you Cal Diamond?'

That's when I heard, near the entrance, a whipcrack. I looked up. Strutting through the door was another Zorro.

Laughter bubbled through the room. The first Zorro set hands on hips, consternated at the sight of his double. I felt sweat breaking out on my forehead.

A woman's voice called out, 'There she is.'

Clipboard was butting through the crowd, with a security guard right behind her. She shook her finger at me.

'You. You're in big trouble.'

Looking back, I see how many of the pieces were present, even then. But they were scattered, camouflaged, like leaves swirling across the ground on the wind, and at the time I didn't know what I was seeing. It was the last moment before events started assembling themselves into the nightmare.

Near the entrance, a man let out a shout. The security guard raised a finger to his earpiece, listened, and started running toward the door. Clipboard watched him go, confused. Or maybe wondering if the Lone Ranger really had shown up. She shot me a suspicious look.

A second guard ran through the crowd. My cellular phone rang, and stopped, and that sent a tickle up my neck. I turned to leave.

George Rudenski put his hand on my arm. 'Why are you looking for Cal?'

'It doesn't matter.'

'Are you here to ambush him?' His calm eyes now had heat

in them. 'Tonight is about raising money for disadvantaged kids, not about getting yourself a scoop.'

He had it wrong, but just about right. Turning from him, I ducked toward the door before Clipboard could stop me. I felt small.

Outside, I found tumult. Two cars had tangled in front of the museum. A white minivan was up on the sidewalk, and a blue Audi had sideswiped a mailbox.

The guards were running toward it. It was Jesse's car.

I rushed down the stairs, fighting fear. The minivan driver was walking toward the Audi, waving his arms.

'You call that driving?' he shouted. 'You pulled out right in front of me.'

A security guard reached the Audi and yanked open the driver's door.

'Get out of the car.'

Leaning in, he grabbed Jesse's arm. I wanted to slap him.

Jesse wrenched loose. He was talking on his cellphone, had the earpiece in, hands free.

'—South on State Street,' he said. 'Right now, as we speak. Five eleven, brown hair, blue dress shirt and khakis.'

The guard reached for him again.

'Don't touch me.' He elbowed the guard, and locked an arm over the steering wheel so the man couldn't pull him out. Into the phone he said, 'Yes, on foot.'

I breathed. He was okay, I saw. And he was talking to the police, but not about this fender-bender.

I said, 'What's going on?'

The minivan driver turned on me. 'You know this guy? Where'd he learn to drive, clown college?'

Jesse looked up. His eyes were fiery.

He said, 'Brand's here.'

His voice was like a falling blade. The guards, the minivan driver, the shouts and jostling elbows, faded to static. My palms tingled.

'Where?' I said.

He pointed toward the corner. 'Headed down State Street. Hurry.'

He didn't need to say anything else. I ran.

I sprinted down State Street. People were thick on the sidewalk, their faces cheery in the sunset, backed by palm trees and music tumbling from clubs and restaurants. I weaved and dodged, holding onto my wig, looking frantically around.

Five-foot-eleven, brown hair, blue dress shirt and khakis. That described dozens of men on the street. It didn't begin to cover Brand.

Franklin Brand was the man who drove his two-ton, 325 horsepower car into Jesse and Isaac Sandoval. He was the coward who left them ruined on the ground. He was the fugitive who fled Santa Barbara the night of the crash, the bastard who'd spent three years enjoying himself on a foreign shore while Isaac lay cold in the dirt and Jesse fought to reconstruct his life. He was wanted on a felony warrant for vehicular manslaughter, and he was here, now, somewhere among the throng.

A woman stepped into my path. I banged into her, called out, 'Sorry,' and kept going.

Franklin Brand was the executive who, on an evening like this one, took his company car for a joyride up Mission Canyon. Rounding a curve, he came up behind Isaac and Jesse. They were powering up the hill on their bikes, training for a triathlon. Brand didn't see them until it was too late. The skid marks only started after the point of impact, when he braked to keep from plunging over the edge himself.

At the corner a red light stopped me. Cars streamed past. I looked up and down the cross street. Traffic eased and I ran across the intersection, knocking into people, muttering excuse me.

The day after the crash, an anonymous caller phoned the police and identified Franklin Brand as the driver. The police asked the caller how she knew it was Brand at the wheel. Her answer, recorded verbatim in the police report, was succinct.

'Because I was with him. I had his cock in my mouth at the time.'

She told the cops where to find Brand's car, abandoned and burned in the hills behind the city. But Brand had a passport and he had money offshore, plenty of it. Millions. By the time a judge issued an arrest warrant, he was in Mexico City. The trail died there.

What in hell he was doing here, tonight, in downtown Santa Barbara, I didn't know. But I could not let him get away.

Down the street, I saw a blue shirt swinging through the crowd. My breath caught. His hair was brown and he had on khakis, was the right height. I closed on him.

I remembered seeing Brand's photo in the paper after the accident: pasty skin and budding jowls, a bored look. Ahead, the blue shirt turned, and I caught a glimpse of the man's face, stained red by a neon sign. I slowed, squinting at him.

A feeling like icy water dripped through me. The eyes, the cast of the mouth. It was him.

I hesitated. Should I perform a citizen's arrest? Yell, *Stop, in the name of love?* He picked up his pace.

Call the police, that's what you do. I dug in my purse for my cellphone.

Two college students stumbled out of a Mexican restaurant, singing drunkenly. They lumbered into me and knocked the phone from my hand.

'Oh, man,' said one, staggering. 'Dude, look what you did.'

I bent down, grabbing the phone before they accidentally kicked it. Standing back up, I looked around. Where was Brand?

Ten feet ahead – there, blue shirt standing at the curb. He raised his arm and, with that universal urban gesture, hailed a taxi. A yellow cab swung to a stop. I couldn't believe it. In Santa Barbara, taxis come along as often as Santa's sleigh.

He was grasping the door handle when I dove on him.

I hit him from behind, hard enough to knock his feet off the curb. We bounced off the taxi and tumbled to the sidewalk. My wig fell over my eyes. I heard his breath blow out, felt my knee hit the concrete, heard the sequins on my dress clicking as I scrambled on top of him.

He squirmed underneath me.

I yelled, 'Call the cops.'

I pushed the wig out of my eyes. Beneath me the man stared back.

His hands were up, gesturing surrender. 'Take it – take the damn cab. I'll get another one.'

He was at least fifty-five, with a pencil mustache and aristocratic Latin looks. His wig was just as crooked as mine. It wasn't Brand, not by a mile.

Mortified, I climbed off him, apologizing, helping him up. He fumbled with his toupee. I brushed dust from his shirt.

'I'm sorry,' I said for the fifteenth time.

He waved me off. 'Go away.'

Teeth clenched, I started down the street again. My knee was bleeding. I limped along, looking at the crowd, trying to ignore their stares.

After ten minutes, I stopped. I had lost him.

Two

When I jogged back to the art museum two cops were talking to Jesse, and they didn't look happy. He was out of his car, sitting in the wheelchair. The sky had softened to velvet blue. The security guards watched from the museum steps, and the minivan driver had backed his vehicle off the sidewalk. The usual forces had been at work. The wheelchair cleared space the way a magnet repels polarized metal. It also worked as a mute button, shutting people right up. But the resulting hush was never empty; pity and discomfort lingered on the twilight.

And Jesse, typically, had seized the silence. Apparently he had defused the other driver and convinced the guards to back off. The police officers stood with arms crossed, listening to him. Disability as stun gun: knock people off guard, gain the upper hand. He was a born litigator.

I heard him say, yeah, he pulled out without signaling. The van swerved, and he swerved, and the mailbox got the worst of it. His fault, but Brand took off and he had to follow him.

'And every second, he's getting farther away. If you'll give me the ticket, you can go find him.'

His face was luminous with anger. Then he caught sight of me, and a dismaying expression ignited in his eyes: hope. I trotted up, shaking my head. His shoulders dropped.

The shorter cop was a brunette built like a stove. She said, 'Ma'am, this gentleman claims he saw an individual who's being sought by the police.'

'Franklin Brand,' I said. 'He's a fugitive wanted on a manslaughter warrant.'

'So we hear. You saw this individual?'

'Heading down State toward Carrillo.'

Her partner half turned and spoke into his portable radio, calling in the information. The radio squawked.

Jesse pointed at my bloody knee. 'What happened?'

'Never mind.'

The cop eyed my costume. 'Is the rest of the Mod Squad still chasing the suspect?'

'Yeah. Just follow the groovy theme music, you can't miss them.'

She could have battered doors open with that face. Time for me to dial down the attitude.

Jesse said to her, 'Chasing the suspect should be what you're doing.'

He gripped the push-rims of the wheelchair. His hands, in his half-fingered gloves, looked bloodless.

The cop ripped a ticket out of her citation book and gave it to him. 'The Postal Service will contact you about the mailbox. Next time, watch for oncoming traffic.'

'We done?'

Without waiting for a response, he spun and headed for his car.

He'd barely started the engine before he got on the phone again, calling Chris Ramseur, the police detective who handled the hit-and-run investigation.

'Tell him to call me. It's urgent,' he said. Hanging up, he looked my way. 'Did you serve Diamond?'

'No. There were two Zorros.'

'Damn.' He pulled out. '"You saw this individual?" They think I'm seeing ghosts.'

'Chris won't.'

He swung onto State, a brazen illegal turn. 'Brand walked across the street right in front of my car. He stared straight at me.'

The image gave me a chill. 'Did he recognize you?'

'Didn't give me a second glance. No, he was going to the museum.'

We looked at each other.

'Mako,' I said.

'The ghost that won't stay dead, no matter how deep I bury it.'

Before Franklin Brand was a fugitive, he was a vice president at Mako Technologies. He was a star player at the company, which designed cyber-security systems for corporations and the government. When he was charged with the hit-and-run, Mako panicked. It tried to divorce itself from the crash. Executives expressed shock at the charges. They disputed Brand's guilt and convinced others to dispute it, persuading their insurance company to deny claims under Brand's policy.

That left Jesse up the creek. He was critically injured and flat broke, a law student facing a six-figure medical bill that Mako's insurer refused to pay. The future looked brutal.

'I saw a life selling pencils,' he once told me. 'Or worse, sitting on a corner holding a cardboard sign. *Hungry, toss food.* I had nothing to lose. I loaded and fired with everything I had.'

He threatened to sue the insurer for bad faith denial of liability. Then he called George Rudenski at Mako. He talked to him about Isaac's death, and his own spinal cord injury, and about Mako giving Brand a $65,000 car to play with. He explained that when he sued the insurance company, Mako would be a co-defendant. Then he mailed Rudenski photos of the accident scene. Color photos.

Forty-eight hours later, the insurance company agreed to square things with Jesse and with Isaac's brother. Rudenski had put it right.

'Mixed emotions' barely described Jesse's feelings toward Mako Technologies.

He said, 'Brand was following somebody to the museum. He's trying to get in touch.'

'Why would he risk coming back here?'

'Think about it.'

I thought. Stupidity. Love. 'Money.'

'That's my guess.'

'You think he has unfinished business with Mako?'

'Yeah. That means so do I.'

He drove slowly, looking at people on the sidewalk. Light washed across his face and shoulders, gold and red pouring over his skin, flashing in his eyes.

'He stared me in the face, Ev. Straight at me, and he didn't react. He didn't know who the hell I was.'

He claimed he'd put it all behind him. No good looking back, he said. Life's a crapshoot. Eyes front, 'cause the future's the only place you can go.

Acceptance, they call this.

He was a remarkable person, accomplished and savvy, a first-class smart-ass who made me laugh and kept me honest. He took everything the world threw at him and hit it back, hard and clean, straight down the line. The year before, he had saved my life. He was handsome, and brave, and I loved him. I was going to marry him in nine weeks.

And right then, hearing the pain in his voice, I knew. It wasn't true. He accepted nothing, as long as Brand remained free. Everything had just changed, for him, and for me.

I said, 'Turn around.'

'Why?'

'Go back to the museum. It's time to start finishing some business.'

He let me out and I climbed the museum steps, knowing that Clipboard would never let me back in. She stood guarding the door, clicking her ballpoint pen as though tapping out Morse code. *Supremes invading. Send air support.*

'Simmer down. I'm just looking,' I said.

I stared past her shoulder into the foyer. I didn't see George Rudenski. But I did see Steve McQueen finishing a plate of canapés. I rapped on the door and waved at him. He came outside, licking his fingers.

'Back for round two with Mari Diamond? This will be rich,' he said.

'I need your help. Could you tell George Rudenski that Evan Delaney wants to speak to him?'

'Oh?' He jammed his hands into his jeans pockets and stepped too close. 'And he'll break away from this shindig on your say-so?'

'Tell him it's about Franklin Brand.'

His suavity flickered. He gazed past me down the steps, where Jesse was maneuvering out of the car.

'Why don't you tell me about it? I'm Kenny Rudenski.'

Swing and a miss, strike three. First Zorro, then the Brand lookalike, now this.

'Sure,' I said, 'when you get your father.'

His gaze ran over me. 'You're a pushy thing. Lucky for you, I like that.'

He went inside and I jogged back down the stairs. Jesse was locking the car.

He said, 'Do you know who that was?'

'I'm sorry. I blew it.'

Kenny Rudenski was the Mako executive who bleated loudest about Brand's innocence after the accident. I remembered a newspaper quote in which he speculated that Jesse and Isaac had been drinking before the crash. This was going to be unpleasant.

'Forget it,' Jesse said. 'George will be stand-up.' He nodded toward the museum. 'And we've got flak at twelve o'clock.'

George Rudenski was walking down the steps, as straight as a flagpole. Behind him came Kenny, scurrying to catch up, and at Kenny's side was a woman in her late thirties. With her crimson suit and shocking fall of silver hair, she looked like a banked fire that could flare up at any moment. She was Harley Dawson, Mako's attorney.

I said, 'I'm on it.'

I aimed myself toward George, ignoring the others. 'Sorry to pull you away.'

He nodded and shook Jesse's hand. 'What's this about Brand?'

I said, 'I just chased him down the street.'

He stilled. 'You're sure it was him?'

'Dead certain,' Jesse said.

'Son of a bitch.'

Harley Dawson strode up. 'I knew it, Evan. You came here to serve a summons, didn't you?' She nodded at Jesse. 'How's it going, Blackburn? You enjoying work with the militant wing over at Sanchez Marks?'

Jesse raised a fist in salute. 'Power to the people, Harley. You still like greasing the wheels of power?'

'Yeah, it's caviar for the soul.' She pointed at George. 'Anything to do with Franklin Brand is a legal issue. Let me take this.'

George said, 'He's back.'

Harley blinked. She had freckles and elfin eyes, delicate features overcome by the hard stare and tense mouth. Which now hung open.

I said, 'Here's the legal issue, Harley. People at Mako have to hear that if Brand shows up, or phones, or flicks spitwads through the window, they need to call the police. Immediately.'

Jesse said, 'That means within thirty seconds.'

'Make it ten,' I said. 'Wait too long, you'll tick off the cops, and they'll start using terms like harboring a fugitive—'

Jesse said, 'Obstruction of justice, conspiracy—'

Kenny shook his head. 'Unbelievable. Blackburn's still trying to blame Mako for his life.'

George gave him a scolding look. 'Kenny, this isn't the place.'

'No, Dad. Frank's back, and the first thing this guy does is complain to you. Must be time for a fresh handout.'

Jesse said, 'Kenny.'

Kenny stared at the wheelchair. 'Hey, life sucks, how about cutting a check?'

'How about this,' Jesse said. 'How about I hand you your ass. On a serving platter, with a sprig of parsley stuck between the cheeks.'

George's face mottled. 'Gentlemen, enough.'

Kenny raised his eyes and glared at Jesse. 'I'd like to see you try, and—'

'*Enough*. Our guests are waiting. Please go and entertain them.'

George turned to Jesse. 'This is a matter for the authorities, and will be handled accordingly. You have my word.' Eyeing Harley, he said, 'I'll speak to you privately.'

He walked away.

Kenny stared at Jesse. His jaw muscles were bulging. He was rubbing his fingers against his palms as though they were greasy. Harley nudged him, trying to get him moving.

He looked at me, wiping his palms on his jeans. The McQueen cool returned.

'It's okay. I respect that you're standing up for the guy.'

He touched my elbow, rubbing it with his thumb. Harley nudged him again. Shaking her off, he left.

Jesse watched him go. 'And he's in line to take over at Mako? Hope you like bankruptcy law, Harley.'

He rocked back, spun a 180, and headed off. Harley pursed her lips.

'Crap-o-rama.' She ran a hand through her icefall of hair. 'This incestuous town. When a skeleton falls out of a closet, it hits someone you know. You can bet on it.'

'Mako's getting a second chance here. Don't let them screw it up,' I said.

'Great. Professional advice from a gal dressed like Ginger in *Gilligan's Island.*'

'Go talk to George. He'll do the right thing, especially if you remind him to.'

'Tell you what. I'll do my job, and you do yours.' She nodded in Jesse's direction. 'You need to rein that boy in.'

I must have looked incredulous. 'Jesse is not the problem here.'

'He should watch his words. He could regret tussling with Kenny.'

All at once, I felt acutely angry. 'Kenny needs worming.'

'I know, he can be—' Uncertainly tugged at her mouth. 'Intense. But he feels passionate about Mako and he's loyal to his friends.'

'Intense? No.'

'Okay, he shouldn't have spoken the way he did. That was—'

'Revolting? Odious? Stop me when I hit the right adjective.'

She held up her hands. 'I get your point.' She tilted her head back. 'Let's blow this gig. Want to? Get a beer, go dancing, play poker. I'm sick of being a bitch.'

I nearly laughed. We'd been friends for years, and her impulsiveness always amused me.

'Kid, I never tire of watching you spin on that dime. But not tonight.'

She sighed. 'No, I guess not.' She started walking backward toward the museum. 'So, are the rumors true?'

'Lies. A vast conspiracy of lies.'

'There's a story going around, you're getting married.'

'I heard that, too,' I said.

Her mouth curled up. 'He's a lucky guy.'

'Damn straight he is.'

She waved, and I walked away. Jesse was waiting by his car, watching traffic cruise by. He had a predatory look in his eyes.

I touched the back of his neck. 'Want to come home with me?'

He shook his head. 'I have to tell Adam.'

His tone of voice told me he'd rather eat glass.

I said, 'Do you want backup?'

'Yeah. I'll sing melody, you take the harmony. We'll do the whole lousy song.' He unlocked the car. 'The Your Brother's Dead and His Killer's Back Blues.'

'Three years and three weeks. Brand just missed the anniversary of the accident.'

Adam Sandoval leaned against a windowsill, staring out. He lived on the Mesa, a hillside neighborhood overlooking the ocean. Sunset flickered red on the water.

'He isn't here to lay a wreath. What brought him back?'

'Money,' I said.

He was supernaturally still. His quiet, I knew, should not be mistaken for tranquility.

'He has money. It's more than that,' he said.

A breeze blew through the window, billowing his white linen shirt. He was barefoot, and his khakis hung loosely on him. The only item that didn't look careless was the crucifix. It hung directly over his heart, as though placed with an awareness of force and balance worthy of a physicist, which he was.

'The arrogant bastard. Showing up at a public event as if nothing's wrong, as if three years on some beach washed the stink off of his guilt.'

He turned from the window. He had a rugged face. His eyes brimmed with melancholy light, a sorrow that faded but never disappeared, even when he smiled. He wasn't smiling now.

'This is sickening,' he said.

Jesse said, 'No. Trying to contact people from Mako, out in public – that will get him caught. This is excellent.'

'If you believe that, why do you look like you've been punched in the face?'

Jesse sighed.

I said, 'Because he's been trash-talking with Kenny Rudenski.'

Adam looked surprised. 'That's going straight for the jugular.'

'Of course,' I said. 'His business card reads 1-800-RIDE-THEIR-ASS.'

Adam gave him a sardonic smile. 'Did he look you in the eye?'

'He can't,' Jesse said. 'He has a congenital impediment.'

Adam pushed off from the windowsill and shrugged across the room. The house was furnished with one sofa, two computers, and bookshelves cluttered with Ludlum, Tony Hillerman, Aquinas, and the collected lectures of Richard Feynman. The whole place smelled like chile verde. Adam was a post-doc at the university, and it showed.

Jesse said, 'Let Brand be arrogant. It doesn't matter, because nobody in town's going to get close enough to poke him with a stick. That's why he was standing outside the museum like a beggar.'

'Or like a stalker,' Adam said. 'He wants something, and he wants it bad.'

Standing by the bookshelf, he gazed at an eight-by-ten photo in a pewter frame. His face was wistful.

It pictured him, Isaac, and Jesse – the unholy trinity, they called themselves. It was taken at the NCAA national swimming championships, plainly after a win, and in victory they looked glorious. Adam was almost goofy with delight. Isaac wore a puckish grin and was holding up his index finger for the camera: we're number one. He was the wild man, so furious in the water that they called him the Washing Machine. He tattooed their winning time on his ankle afterward.

And Jesse looked ecstatic. He had draped his arms across the Sandovals' shoulders, pulling them to him. His hair was bleached gold from chlorine, his body rippled with power from head to toe. It was the way he looked when I first met him, when his blue eyes and athletic grace knocked me flat on my butt, astonished at my own desire.

He still had the lithe build that gave him such fierce beauty in the water. His shoulders could carry almost anything, and since the accident they'd been carrying the weight of concern for Adam. I heard it in the words he chose, the care in his voice. I knew why. He thought that between them, Adam had suffered the heavier blow.

He said, 'Whatever Brand is after, he's taking risks, and that's why he's going to get nailed. He'll fuck up.'

Adam looked at him. 'Once more, with feeling.'

'He'll blow it. Because that's what fuckups do.'

Another caustic smile. 'You're such a cheerleader.'

The light muted and the ocean took on a silver sheen. Shadow brushed Adam's face.

I said, 'What do you think Brand wants, if it isn't money?'

'Revenge,' he said.

I must have looked startled. 'Against whom? Mako?'

'The woman. The anonymous caller who phoned the police and turned him in.'

'You think he was stalking her at the museum?'

'Yes.'

Jesse said, 'You think she works for Mako.'

Adam nodded. 'And I think people at Mako know who she is,

because office affairs are never truly clandestine. But nobody has ever come forward. Nobody has the backbone.'

Jesse gave me a glance. We were thinking the same thing: Adam had been working this out for a long time. He lived with this, constantly.

Adam said, 'If you want to get in Mako's face, I'll get in it with you. But be prepared for them to land on you like a hammer. George Rudenski may be a nice guy, but Kenny's a schemer, and he'll set the tone.'

'Screw Kenny, and screw Mako. They're just the levers we use, to get to Brand. Eyes on the prize, buddy.'

Adam nodded and stared out the window at the ocean. Jesse gave me a look: time to go.

He touched Adam on the elbow. 'I'll talk to you tomorrow. You okay?'

'Yeah.'

We started toward the door. Adam said, 'One thing, *jefe.*'

Jesse glanced back over his shoulder.

'You're taking action against a killer. There's going to be a reaction.'

'I remember my Isaac Newton, Dr Sandoval. Equal and opposite.'

Adam said, 'Be careful, man.'

In Hope Ranch, the landscaping lights were on at Cal and Mari Diamond's estate. They illuminated the palms and the flower beds where red camellias grew as big as fists. They spotlighted the arches and balconies of the house, Casa Maricela. And they cast shadows at the edges of the property, where the young woman walked outside the wrought-iron fence, dragging a metal baton along the railings. She waited for the noise to bring the dogs.

Her name was Cherry Lopez. She was twenty-four, but with her wiry frame people took her for a teenager. She kept her hair cropped short and dyed it gothic black. A tattoo ran like a cable from her ankle up one leg, coiling around her thigh, across a hip and over her ribs, eeling around her breast and up

22

her neck. It ended behind her ear, with a viper's head sinking its fangs in.

The baton rang against the railings. 'Here, doggies. Got a surprise for you.'

And now they came, two Dobermans racing across the lawn in the dusk, ears flat against their heads. Cherry reached the gate at the top of the drive. The dogs charged it, teeth bared, barking. The sound annoyed her. They were bigger than she expected, mean-looking things.

She didn't want to do this. This was aggro. She shouldn't even be here, but their timing got thrown off at the museum because of the chick in the pink dress and the guy on wheels, variables they hadn't factored in. Mouthy chick, but she wasn't the big problem. The plan had bugs, face it. But she knew what would happen to her if she backed out now.

'Here, Fido.'

She stuck the baton through the gate. One of the dogs lunged forward and grabbed it in its teeth. Cherry pressed the switch. The dog jerked and fell to the ground.

The second dog kept barking and jumping at the gate. Man, the noise was provoking her nerves. Up at the house, a light came on. Cherry looked over her shoulder, down the driveway to where the Corvette was parked. Inside it glowed the red tip of a cigarette, or maybe a joint. Mickey was watching. She had to finish the game, or pay the price.

She jammed the baton through the railings again, hitting the second dog in the chest. It mewled and quivered and dropped to the ground.

There, quiet. That was better.

She examined the baton. It delivered 300,000 volts and only cost $64.99. Not bad. Bought off the Net, and, the sweetest part, with Cal Diamond's own credit card number. Technology wins again.

Reaching into her back pocket, she pulled out the envelope. Diamond would wet himself when he saw the photos. She dropped it through the railings and rang the buzzer by the gate. Giving the stunned dogs a last look, she walked down the driveway to the car.

Climbing in, she smelled the weed. Mickey sat behind the wheel, still wearing the stupid Zorro hat. Zorro with long blond hair, right. He took a hit and held the smoke in his lungs.

She said, 'I did it.'

He blew out the smoke, turned, and hit her in the cheek with the flat of his hand.

'You didn't put the tape over the video camera in the gate.'

Oh, man. 'I forgot. The dogs were barking, and—'

He hit her again. Her fingers curled around the shock baton, and loosened. Not now. It wouldn't be worth the punishment.

He started the Corvette. 'But who gives a shit? It's your head on the chopping block.'

Cherry looked at him. 'Yours too.'

'Nah.' He dropped it in first. 'You're on camera. I was never here.'

Three

Jesse dropped me at home, his face troubled. The mountains shouldered a starry sky. I went through the gate toward my house, a cottage at the end of a deep garden. My friends Nikki and Carl Vincent live in the Victorian house along the street. It's a comfortable neighborhood near the Santa Barbara Mission, crowded with old houses, overgrown oleander, oak trees, the scent of star jasmine and the shouts of kids at play. But I felt disheartened and restless.

Through the Vincents' kitchen window I saw Carl at the sink, washing baby food out of his pinstriped shirt. The kitchen lights pinged off his owlish glasses. On the back porch in the rocker, looking carved from mahogany, Nikki sat nursing Thea.

She caught sight of my pink sequins. 'Who have we here?'

'Condoleezza Rice.'

A deep laugh. 'And I'm the Prime Minister of Sweden.'

I sat down on the porch steps. 'Franklin Brand's in town. Jesse's ballistic.'

'Oh, my God.'

I told her about it, realizing as I talked that I felt cooked. When Thea finished nursing, I held out my hands.

'Let me see this girl.'

Nikki handed her to me. Thea was nine months old and robust. She wrapped her pudgy thighs around me and patted my sequins. I smiled at her.

Nikki said, 'Heard from Luke?'

He had been gone since Christmas. I felt my stomach pinching, a familiar ache.

'He's good,' I said. 'Playing baseball. Learning subtraction.'

She watched me. 'Evan, you are permitted to say that you miss him.'

But I couldn't say it, because the words would rub off the scab over my heart and start it bleeding again.

Six-year-olds can sure leave a hole when they go home.

Luke was my nephew, my brother's little boy. He lived with me for a year while Brian's fighter squadron was overseas, and later because Brian's estranged wife joined an extremist religious sect – violent zealots who tried to poison me and who nearly killed Brian to get their hands on Luke. It was a nightmare. But so far I was healthy, and Brian had recovered. So Luke had gone home, and that was good. Still.

I kissed Thea, and handed her back. 'Say a prayer for Jesse.'

'Didn't think he believed in the power of prayer.'

'He doesn't. That's why he needs us backing him up.'

In the morning the sun cut through the shutters, painting stripes across the patchwork quilt on my bed. I stretched and rolled over. I could hear birds singing outside, and a garbage truck rumbling up the street. The air promised heat.

Nothing inspires me more than summer days, but I lay pinned by thoughts of Franklin Brand, thoughts of failure and foreboding.

I got up, headed into the kitchen, and turned on the coffeepot and the *Today* show. I never used to watch breakfast television, but a quiet house now unsettled me. All my tidy self-sufficiency, my Scandinavian furniture and Ansel Adams prints, my whole single-girl leitmotiv, had paled. I wanted mess. I wanted kids. I missed Luke.

While the coffee brewed I checked my calendar. My schedule was busy: I was working on two appellate briefs, had a steady gig doing research for a local law firm, was editing my new novel, *Chromium Rain*, and preparing to give a seminar at the East Beach Writers' Conference. Together it added up to my car and mortgage payments, and a lot of freedom. If I closed the shutters I could even work wearing nothing but my Diana Ross wig and a crazed grin. I've never done that, but might, someday. Maybe when the killer asteroid reaches our atmosphere and everyone else is busy downtown, looting.

My morning was free. I could try again to serve the summons on Cal Diamond.

Briefly I glanced at the pile of papers on the dining table. It was the wedding mound: invitations, notes on the caterer, the photographer, music. . . . Just looking at it made my heart race and my head pound. I was excited, felt overdue, and wasn't ready, not even close. The mound begged for attention, but I poured myself a cup of coffee and headed for the shower.

Half an hour later I climbed into my Explorer and aimed it toward Diamond Mindworks. I was wearing a khaki skirt, turquoise blouse, and loafers. Forget pretense. I planned to burn the go-go boots.

The company was in Goleta, a sprawling suburb that hosts most of the area's high tech industry. The coastal marshlands carried the scent of salt water to my nose. A jet glinted on final approach to the airport. Beyond the runway, on a bluff above the Pacific, sat the University of California, Santa Barbara, my alma mater.

The jet flared and came in, thrust reversers roaring. I drove into a business park, past imported coconut palms, toward a sleek building with smoked blue glass and curving white lines. It looked like a cruise ship cutting through the lawn.

I slowed. An ambulance was parked outside the entrance.

I parked, headed into the lobby, and stopped. The receptionist slumped at the front desk, crying into the phone.

'. . . just now, oh, God . . . right here in the office . . .'

I stood, summons clutched in my hand.

'. . . no, no warning, when she walked in he just—'

She looked up. She had a chubby face and oil-gusher hair. Mascara was smeared across her cheek. A plaque on the desk said 'Hi, I'm Amber Gibbs.'

I said, 'I need—'

'We have an emergency. You'll have to come back.'

Somebody, I thought, was dead here. And I did a shameful thing.

'I have a delivery for Mr Diamond.'

A paramedic pushed through the door into the lobby, carrying a heavy equipment case. The phone rang. When Amber picked it up, I followed the paramedic down a hall. Hearing Amber call, 'Wait . . .' I kept going behind the paramedic, turned the corner, and found the hallway full of people. They huddled staring at an office door with a brass nameplate. *Cal Diamond.*

A man near me was muttering, 'Did you hear it? The crash was awful loud.'

A woman said, 'The way she screamed. My lord.' She shook her head. 'Who'd ever believe I could feel bad for Mari Diamond?'

I felt a sick chill, and a horrible image formed in my head. The summons hung in my hand. I knew I wasn't going to be serving it.

The office door opened and the crowd fell silent. Two paramedics came out, hauling a stretcher. I stared at it. The stretcher rolled by. Strapped on it, face swaddled in an oxygen mask, was a bald man in his fifties. Unruly eyebrows tangled above his waxy face.

I heard a woman saying, 'Everyone, go home. We're shutting the building.'

Standing in the office doorway, dressed in a pink-and-lime green suit, holding a Chihuahua under one arm, was Mari Diamond.

Nobody moved. The little dog cringed in her grip, vibrating like a tuning fork.

She said, 'For my sake. Go. Now.'

She looked like a bud vase wearing perfume and kitten heels. People began shuffling away, and she saw me. Her eyes were as bright and brittle as light bulbs. Her mouth tautened.

She pointed at the summons. 'Is that the lawsuit?'

Heads turned.

'Is it?' She was walking toward me.

'Yes,' I said.

She slapped me in the face. I felt surrounded by sharp light and heat.

'Cal's had a heart attack,' she said. 'Because of that. You nearly killed him.'

Four

Jesse threw his pen on the desk and said, 'Oh, no.'

'Straight to cardiac intensive care,' I said. 'They don't know if he'll survive.'

He pinched the bridge of his nose. Behind him the sun spilled through his office window. The mountains packed the view, pulsing green in the heat beneath a blue sky.

'Poor, rotten bastard,' he said.

In the hallway his boss scudded by. He called to her.

'Lavonne. Cal Diamond's had a heart attack.'

Lavonne Marks hovered like a Jewish mother and had a Philadelphia accent that hit your ears like bricks. She was an old campus radical, which is why Sanchez Marks was nicknamed the militant wing. She shook her head.

'Hold off on serving the summons. He isn't going anywhere.'

'About that,' I said. 'There's a minor problem.'

I told them about Delaney v. Vasquez Diamond II: Gidget Gets Bitch-Slapped. I explained how I left Diamond Mindworks at a run, repeating, *Don't smack the wife.* Mari was frightened and hysterical. Don't get indignant. Don't hold it against her. I could hear the Chihuahua yapping all the way to the lobby. And Mari, shouting: 'I'm calling my lawyer. They'll run your tits through a paper shredder.'

Jesse said, 'That's absurd.'

'She's in the mood for absurdity. Expect a phone call,' I said.

Lavonne said, 'I hope you don't in any way feel responsible for this. It's not your fault. And – my God, where did that come from?'

Her eyes had gone as round as coins. She was looking at Jesse's computer. The screen was displaying the image of a penis the size of a bratwurst.

Jesse raised his hands. 'Shoot, oh. I don't know. Lavonne, sorry.'

He started stabbing at the keyboard. His face had paled.

'The web browser opened on its own. I didn't do this,' he said.

'I hope not. I didn't think this was your proclivity, Mr Blackburn.'

With each key he hit, a new image popped up, more explicit than the last. He tried to quit the program and a dialog box appeared.

Do you have a tiny penis? Click YES or NO.

He tried to click NO. The button jumped around the screen, playing keepaway.

'Stupid practical joke . . .' He clicked YES.

Another box appeared. *Shall we send you more photos?* Click. A third box. *Shall we forward them to your boss?*

'What is this?' he said.

Lavonne frowned. 'It's an intrusion.' She headed for the door. 'I'm getting our IT guy.'

Jesse tried again to quit.

Shall we send photos of you?

He stared at the screen. The cursor blinked.

We can. We have them, Blackburn.

'This is screwed.'

He tried to quit again. Nothing happened. He reached around to the back of the computer and yanked out the Ethernet cable, disconnecting from the Internet. A new dialog box appeared.

You can't stop this.

He hit the power key. The computer died.

'I believe you, Jesse. I do,' Lavonne said.

The IT guy concurred. Jesse's computer had been breached. The firm's firewall should have stopped the porn photos from getting through, but didn't. He ran a virus scan on the laptop but found nothing.

'Probably a worm,' the IT guy said. He scratched his chin beard. 'Came to you randomly, and your machine may have sent it on randomly. Check with people on your e-mail list, see if any of them are having this problem.'

'But it referred to me by name,' Jesse said.

'Your e-mail screen name's j.blackburn. The worm probably picked it up automatically.'

Jesse shook his head. 'I don't like this.'

'Nobody does. Fortunately, you're the only one at the firm who's been infected.'

'If it happens again?'

The IT guy shrugged. 'Let me know.'

The 911 dispatcher took the call at ten-thirty that night: disturbance at Harry's Plaza Café. The manager reported customers fighting outside the restaurant. It's turning ugly, she said. Shouting and shoving and yeah, there goes, guy's throwing a punch.

By the time the patrol car drove up, it was over. The manager came out the door, pointing.

'Two of them already split. Fat man in droopy jeans and a skinny girl with black hair. Laurel and Hardy.' She hooked a thumb toward the restaurant. 'It's the one inside I want you to get rid of.'

He was leaning on the bar, nursing a Jim Beam and busted knuckles. When the cops walked up, he tossed back the bourbon and put the glass down.

'There's no problem here, officers. I wanted to finish my drink. I'll go.'

They escorted him outside and asked to see some ID.

'I told you, there's no problem. I'm leaving.'

He tried to walk away. The officers noted his sharp clothes, the cologne, his torn knuckles and rabbity eyes. They insisted on seeing an ID.

He huffed, but finally handed it over. A British Honduras diplomatic passport.

The cops examined it, glanced at each other, and asked to see another ID.

'No.' His nose was rising. 'I have diplomatic immunity.'

'From a country that no longer exists? I don't think so.'

And what do you know, not only had his California driver's license expired, it had a different name on it. They ran it, and the warrant showed right up.

Out came the cuffs. 'Franklin Brand?' they said. 'You're under arrest.'

Five

The news came the next day, right after the weirdness.

I bumped into Harley Dawson at the county law library. She asked me to meet her for a drink after work at the Paradise Café, and she was sitting by the window when I walked in. She waved and brushed her silver hair back from her face.

When I sat down she said, 'Hey ya, babydoll.'

Sunshine was falling through the venetian blinds, and in the stark light she looked like a character in an old film noir. It was the sense of solitude she exuded, and the flinty edges, the jagged energy.

She said, 'You'll be happy to hear that George Rudenski is circling the wagons at Mako. People won't blow their noses without calling to check with me first.'

'Good.'

'No, it's a pain in the ass.'

'Is that why you wanted to get together, to tell me that?'

'Not at all. Though I do inform you that the hornet's nest is now stirred up. You can put away your poking stick.'

'But it's so shiny, and sharp,' I said. 'For example. How well did you know Franklin Brand?'

'Oy vay.' She leaned back. 'Not well. He didn't return phone calls. Did golf course deals.'

'Have you ever wondered if the anonymous caller works at Mako?'

'The gal who liked sucking on Brand's spermsicle stick? No, I haven't.' The sun shone on her freckles. 'Want to go to Del Mar this weekend? They're running the Oaks. Afterwards we could get in eighteen at Torrey Pines.'

I laughed. 'Harley, you know I don't gamble, and the time you tried to teach me to play golf I hit you on the head with a putt. A weekend away sounds great, but pick a secondary target.'

'Vegas. You could catch a show.' She shrugged. 'Can't help it. In the blood.'

Her father had been a high roller, and she spent her childhood in casino coffee shops and along the rail at Santa Anita. But I wondered if her yen for company meant she was having one of her periodic tussles with loneliness. I was about to ask, when a waiter came to the table with an ice bucket and two champagne flutes.

'What's this?' I said.

Harley looked coy. 'Time to kick off the wedding party.'

The waiter put the champagne bottle on the table. I saw the label.

'You're kidding.'

'You want something more upscale?' Harley said.

'No, Dom Perignon is fine.'

The waiter popped the cork and poured, and I wondered, as always, at Harley's extravagance. Though we were good friends, this was still a lot to splash out. But she was impulsive, and generous, and I knew she liked fine things.

She hoisted her glass. 'Here's to true love.'

'Cheers.' I raised the glass and drank.

I have a rube's palate. The last champagne I'd drunk was at my cousin's wedding in Oklahoma City, and I think it had an oil derrick on the label. But oh. This.

This wasn't champagne, it was an epiphany. I knew I should drink it, destroy the bottle, and bang my head against the table until I got amnesia, because otherwise this is all I'd want to drink, ever, and then I'd go bankrupt.

'My God,' I said.

Harley raised her glass again. 'And here's to unconventional love affairs.'

I held the bubbles on my tongue, deciding how to reply. 'If you're talking about the age difference, I don't consider it a big deal.'

'Me neither. We both like 'em young,' she said. 'And different.'

35

I said, 'And how are things?'

'Things are fine. Things are sublime. Choirs of angels sing me to sleep at night.' She brought her glass up, stopped. 'Wait. Are we talking about my sex life?'

'Yes.'

'It's status quo. Shit flambé.' She drank her champagne. 'I have as much of Cassie as she can give me, and that's just the way it is. It's – what does Jesse call it?'

'An FFL.' Fucking Fact of Life.

'You got it, sister.'

I didn't know Cassie, Harley's lover. I only knew what Harley told me: she played on the women's tennis tour, and was fearful of coming out as a lesbian. From the light in Harley's eyes when she spoke her name, Harley was hooked.

She said, 'Talking of FFLs, how's your boy handling Brand showing up?'

'He's focused. And he's not a boy, Harley.'

Her eyes quieted. 'Sorry, you're right. He's twenty-seven, and older than most men are at fifty. My fault. I think of my biz law students as kids, even years later.'

Harley occasionally taught an undergraduate class at UCSB. Jesse had taken it, and, I gathered, so had Cassie – for extra credit.

She was pouring herself another glass of champagne when the door opened and Kenny Rudenski walked in. Scratch that. Kenny paused in the doorway, giving everyone in the bar time to admire him. He was wearing a motorcycle jacket, khakis, and heavy boots. The outfit was straight out of *The Great Escape*. He held a motorcycle helmet under one arm. He smiled and strolled to the table.

'Harley.' He beamed at me. 'Gidget.'

He spun a chair around backwards and sat down, straddling it. He set the helmet on the table as if it were a war trophy. Bring me the head of Steve McQueen.

He leaned my way. 'I owe you an apology. The other night, I didn't know you had a thing going with Jesse Blackburn. Sorry if I made things uncomfortable for you.'

36

I looked at Harley. Had she set this up? She was staring at her champagne.

I said, 'Thank you. But Jesse's the one who deserves the apology.'

'Loyalty. I like that.' He pressed his thumb against a knot in the wood of the table and massaged it. 'Anyway, I didn't mean to get so hot.'

'All right.'

His thumb worked the wood. He saw me looking at the helmet.

'Old love. Raced motocross in my wild youth. You like motorcycles?' He nodded out the window. 'Mine's parked up the street. You want, I'll take you for a ride. I'm perfectly safe, no bike crashes, I promise.'

I stared him straight in the face, thinking, did he just say that?

I said, 'I'm taking a poll. Why do you think Franklin Brand has come back?'

'To clear his name? What do you say, one spin around the block. I bet it's been a long time since you were on a bike.'

'You're still hawking the line that Brand didn't do it? Who do you blame, the Mossad?'

Harley looked up. 'Don't answer that, Kenny.'

'Why shouldn't I?'

I said, 'Yeah, why shouldn't he?'

'Evan's a legal journalist. That's how she met your father, interviewing him for a magazine article.'

He said, 'She's not interviewing me. We're just jawing.'

She set down her glass. 'All communications with the press are to go through my firm. I'm not kidding.'

He grinned. 'You like to strap on real clangers, don't you, Harley?'

Her cheeks pinkened. 'Save it for the locker room, would you?'

The grin spread. 'Hey, it's okay. Don't get your jockstrap in a twist.'

I stared at him with bewilderment. Were these jibes meant to tease Harley about her sexuality, or about lawyers? Were they meant to impress me? Or were they a mental tic, equivalent to Kenny grabbing his genitals to make sure they were still there?

He got up from the table, saying to Harley, 'If she's a writer, it means Blackburn has unlimited bandwidth to tell his side of the story. Maybe it'd be good to let me even things up.' He winked at me. 'Last chance for that ride.'

'No, thanks.'

'Your loss. Catch ya later, Gidget.'

He took the helmet and headed back through the bar toward the restaurant.

My mood had dried and curled up at the edges. 'Harley, what was that all about? Did you set it up for him to stop by?'

Her hand went through her hair. 'I thought it would be a good chance to cool down the rhetoric, let Kenny get back on the right footing.'

'Rhetoric? That was innuendo, and it was rough.'

'It's okay. If you haven't noticed, nothing in life ever goes right for more than ten seconds at a shot. It's why lawyers earn such a handsome living.' She held out her glass. 'Pour me some more champagne.'

When I left the Paradise, I drove to Jesse's house. The sandstone on the mountains glowed gold under the sun and thunderheads burled into the sky. The inland valleys were getting lightning.

Jesse lived on the beach, down a drive that curved between Monterey pines. The house was pale wood and glass, with a cathedral ceiling and a wall of windows facing the surf. When I drove up, Adam Sandoval's Toyota pickup sat on the driveway. I found Jesse and Adam sitting outside on the edge of the deck, wearing surfer swim trunks, warming their feet in the sand. Breakers frothed up the beach.

From the back, from a distance, Adam and Jesse looked similar. Swimmers' shoulders, rangy limbs, California skin tones. Only closer could I notice the differences – Jesse's scars, and the stillness in his legs. The injury had taken almost all the movement and sensation on his right side, and about half on the left. He could walk, barely, with braces and crutches. He got to the water by scooting backward on his butt.

I crouched down behind him, slipping my arms around his neck. His skin was hot from the sun. He tilted his head back and I kissed him.

He said, 'Adam's been showing me his new dive gear.'

He nodded toward a mask, fins, and a spear gun. Adam was accomplished at spearfishing, did it free diving. He cooked the catch pretty well, too.

Jesse smiled. 'The diving off Kauai is spectacular. There's still time for you to get your Scuba certification before we go.'

I kissed him again. 'Good try.'

'Honestly, you'd love it.'

'No, you love it. Bottom line, I'm not spending my honeymoon in flippers.'

'But flippers are my favorite turn-on.'

Adam stood up. 'You kids.'

Jesse said, 'Adam agrees that my porn outbreak at the office was probably caused by a computer worm.'

'Charming experience, isn't it?' Adam said.

I said, 'Explain to me exactly what a worm is.'

'It's malicious computer code, similar to a virus. It replicates itself and spreads without your control. It might delete files, or send documents on your hard drive to random addresses it generates.'

'So Jesse's computer may simply have had an unlucky address?'

He found his crucifix and slipped it around his neck. 'Could be.'

'Then let's hope that's the end of it.'

'Yeah,' Jesse said. 'Except our IT guy couldn't find any evidence of a worm on my machine.'

The breakers crashed and ran toward us, hissing over the sand.

Adam picked up an envelope of snapshots. 'Look what I found. Photos Isaac took. I hadn't seen them before.'

I leafed through them – casual shots of Isaac at the beach, and with girls in bikinis, and at the computer startup where he worked. They looked prosaic, full of sunny normality. Right before the light snapped off.

'They're great,' I said, handing them back.

With care, he returned them to the envelope. 'I finally started going through his things. Boxes his colleagues packed up from work. Until now, I just couldn't . . .'

Pain pinched his face.

Jesse pulled the wheelchair close. Hands on the edges of the seat, he hoisted himself up.

'Tell her the rest,' he said.

Adam rubbed his fingers across his forehead. 'I found something perplexing. Notes Isaac made about a problem at work.'

Isaac had worked at Firedog Inc., an Internet firewall company. He was a programmer, an athlete-geek like Adam, and when he died Firedog lost its scrappy spirit. Eventually, when the market imploded, they sold their technology to investors and closed up shop. One of those investors, I recalled, was Mako Technologies.

'Going through Isaac's things, I found a scratch pad with Mako's phone number and notes about a hassle of some kind. It sounds like Mako was on his back about some missing paperwork.'

In the back of my mind I heard Harley Dawson. *This incestuous town.* Everybody knowing each other, dealing with each other, hurting each other.

'But it seems like more than paperwork, it seems like . . .' He looked at Jesse.

'Missing records,' Jesse said.

Slowly, I turned toward him. He didn't look perplexed. He looked grave.

'And it took you five minutes to tell me this?' I said.

That's when the doorbell rang. It was the police.

I opened the front door. 'Hello, Detective.'

Chris Ramseur, Santa Barbara PD, looked surprised. 'Evan. Long time no see.'

He had the face of a jaundiced English teacher, thoughtful and canny. His tie and oxford-cloth shirt looked weary. I ushered him in.

'I have news.' He stared at Jesse and Adam coming through the patio doors.

'Chris,' Jesse said.

Ramseur gazed unblinking at Jesse's chest, as though looking at his legs might be dangerous, like Lot's wife taking that fatal glance back at Gomorrah.

He said, 'I wanted to tell you in person. We got him.'

Jesse looked as though the floor had dropped away beneath him, clear to China. Adam put a hand on his shoulder.

'Brand was arrested after a fight outside Harry's. And you'll love this, he tried to bluff his way out of it with a fake diplomatic passport from British Honduras.'

'Belize?' I said.

'Yup. Anybody can order one of these out-of-date passports online and use it to impress women at cocktail parties. You just can't claim diplomatic status with it.'

Jesse still looked dumbfounded. I took his hand.

'So now his lawyer's bitching that the officers arrested him while he was arranging to turn himself in,' Chris said. 'He's ranting about the statute of limitations, habeas corpus. Oh, and that Brand's innocent.'

Jesse said, 'When's the arraignment?'

'He'll be in court tomorrow. Are you up to it?'

This time his gaze did go to Jesse's legs, and jerked away.

'Up to it?' Jesse said. 'You couldn't stop me with a bullet.'

We celebrated, drove to the harbor and hit Brophy Brothers. Jesse took his graphite crutches so he could get up the stairs to the bar, and we sat on the balcony while the music hopped and the crowd jostled, waitresses swerving between the tables. Below us in the marina, the commercial fishing fleet rocked on water gone purple with shadow. Beyond the breakwater the ocean shimmered in silver light.

41

Adam got drunk quickly, a light drinker knocking back tequila shooters. I didn't ask him any more about the missing paperwork, because his mood had lifted to sweet heights. He started talking physics with intoxicated passion. But I knew what Jesse was thinking: there's no such thing as coincidence.

Adam was explaining time dilation using a shot glass and salt shaker. 'Accelerate toward the speed of light, and time passes more slowly.' He held the shot glass like a space ship. 'You hit light speed, you're going so fast through space, you have no speed left to move through time.' He looked at us crookedly. 'See? At light speed, time doesn't pass.'

He turned the glass to reflect the sunset off Jesse's hand. 'Light never ages. Look at it, *jefe*. That shine there, it's eternity.'

When we got up to leave he hugged me and put his hand over his heart.

'Maybe this rock will go now. This stone, that sits in my chest.'

'I hope so,' I said.

Jesse got to his feet, pushed up and set the crutches. He was six-foot-one and I loved to see him tall. Loved it when he leaned against me. It felt like dance time, a Hollywood hold, and its rarity gave me a pang. Adam wasn't fit to get behind the wheel so I drove his truck home for him, and rode with Jesse back to the beach house. In the car, I asked him about Isaac's notes.

He said, 'I haven't seen them, but they say something like, "What shares?" and talk about doublechecking that everything had been sent to Mako.'

'What do you make of it?'

'Mako invested in Firedog the way they did in a bunch of startups. Angel funding, cash in exchange for a chunk of stock. It sounds like Mako couldn't find the Firedog stock certificates and Isaac was trying to figure out where they were.'

'And you're thinking what I'm thinking?'

'That it isn't a fluke. But I don't know what it is.'

The tires hummed over the road. I said, 'Why does Adam call you chief?'

'*Jefe?* A play on my name, I guess. And because I captained the team.'

He wouldn't say the obvious: and because Adam looked up to him.

At his house, I put music on, Marvin Gaye. Jesse took a Viagra, which, if it wasn't a miracle, came close. It had given him back a reliability in lovemaking that he thought he'd lost because of the spinal cord injury.

We went to the bedroom and turned off the lights. Jesse knew what I wanted and let me have it, standing by the window, moonlight hard white across his face. I unbuttoned his shirt, pulled my own shirt over my head, and wrapped myself against his smooth skin. He swung an arm around my back. His eyes were dark, smile on his lips, his mouth coming down and kissing me, a long, hard, old-fashioned kiss. My heart hammered and my loins ached.

He pulled back. 'You looked like this our first night.'

'Naked and smelling like tequila?'

'Enchanting.'

'It was dark,' I said.

'Let me flatter you, Delaney.'

I kissed him again. He wouldn't be able to keep his balance much longer.

'You made me breathless,' he said. 'You were magical.'

Nothing beats the mountains on a summer night, the city laid out like a blanket of diamonds below, the stars blazing, this man I craved, actually wanting me.

It felt like high school. Leaving a party with a guy, going for a drive. We were working together at a local firm that summer, me practicing and Jesse on summer break from UCLA Law School. When I asked him why he didn't have a date for the party, he looked downcast. He said he was a lonely teenaged broncin' buck with a pink carnation and a pickup truck . . . which made me think he was sad about a lost love, some college sweetheart who had let him down. And endeared him to me all the more.

Nobody around, night and the sharp scent of chaparral, the stars turning down until they sank into the ocean. The breeze fresh on my shoulders when he peeled off my blouse, his mouth on my skin. Me fumbling to unbutton his jeans while we grappled against the tailgate of his pickup.

'Some magic,' I said. 'I had the word *Ford* etched on my back afterward.'

'You never complained. To the contrary, you complimented me. You said I had a prizewinning butt.'

'Is that so?'

'Ass of the Decade,' he said. 'Words I cherish.'

I smiled at him, smelling the ocean on his skin, feeling his heart pound in his chest. The mountain was a singular event. Just that once, before he got hurt.

He said, 'You miss it?'

Oh, damn. His hands were on me, his eyes on me, his hips pressed against mine, swaying now, his wiring short-circuited, nothing to be done about it. No lies to tell, because he had a sharp ear for insincerity, and I hated the truth.

'Of course I miss it.' I ran the back of my hand across his cheek. 'But I don't miss you, babe. I have you.'

I wasn't saying it. How I desired him right now, as he was. And how I fought the wish that he was whole, that we could recapture it, just once. It killed me.

He said, 'Lie down with me.'

We moved to the bed and I lay next to him.

I started working my lips up his chest, kissing, teasing his skin with my mouth and teeth and tongue. Saturate him with sensation in the places he could feel it. I lifted his arm and kissed the inside of his wrist, working my way up to his neck, his face. His mouth.

He said, 'I love you, Evan.'

'Shut up and kiss me.'

At first I thought it was the wind that woke me. The Monterey pines were scratching against the roof. The clock said two-fifteen.

44

But it was Jesse, dead asleep beside me, breathing hard, his hand clenching the blanket.

Talking in his sleep. 'No. Help him. Don't . . .'

I shook him by the shoulder. He was hot, his forehead damp with sweat.

'Jesse, wake up.'

His eyes flicked wide and he grabbed my arm. 'Don't you leave—'

'Hey.' I pressed my hand against his shoulder. 'It's me.'

Recognition squared away on his face, and he let go of my arm. He stared at me, but even in the dim moonlight I could tell he was seeing something else entirely.

'Jesus Christ.' His chest rose and fell. He covered his face with his hands. 'It was the crash. The noise wouldn't stop, and the light kept spinning. And Brand was standing over me, this big man without a face, staring down to see if I was dead.'

I wound my arms around him and stroked his hair.

'Then he went to Isaac, but he wouldn't help him, he just walked away.'

'It's over,' I said.

But like the night, the dream would return.

He dropped back to sleep before I did. About three a.m., I got up for a drink of water.

The house was built around an open plan, the living room, dining area, and kitchen all one space under the cathedral ceiling. His laptop was on the dining table, and I could see the screen from the kitchen sink. He had been online earlier, and the computer was still connected. Seeing it, I felt a twitch.

The screen was displaying a color photograph. I walked to the table. It was a News-Press archive photo, showing Jesse standing on the starting blocks at a swim meet. He looked voraciously confident, with all the certainty of bulletproof youth. Below the photo flashed the words, *You have a message waiting.*

This was wrong.

I looked toward the bedroom door. He was exhausted, and I

45

knew if I woke him again, he wouldn't sleep for the rest of the night. I stared at the screen. I could leave it alone. I could shut down the computer. I couldn't stand it.

I clicked on *message waiting.*

Jesse Matthew Blackburn:
 You've had an amazing life. How'd you like for people to read all about it? How'd you like them to know everything? Everything.
 Do you want your woman to know? Think she'll stay?
 We don't either.

I felt as if I had bitten down on aluminum foil.

Don't turn that dial, bucko. We'll be right back.

There was only one possible meaning to this, and the earlier intrusion. It was a threat.

The web browser quit. Boom, it disappeared, and the computer froze. When I rebooted and opened the browser, the History page had no reference to the site.

I headed back to bed. But I didn't sleep.

Six

The day dawned cloudy. Jesse dressed in silence, putting on a white dress shirt with a blue suit. The maroon necktie whipped as he knotted it. He could barely get down a cup of coffee, though I drank almost a whole pot.

'Write down the message, word for word. I'm taking this to the police,' he said.

I held my coffee mug, feeling chilled. 'What did they mean by *everything?*'

'Somebody's threatening to blackmail me.' He packed the laptop in its case. 'And you know who I think it is? Kenny Rudenski.'

He looked up, eyes fierce, and saw my anxious face. His expression softened.

'Ev, you're not actually worried that they have something on me, are you?'

'No.' I ran a hand through my hair. 'Yes.'

'Like what?'

'Sex and drugs and rock'n'roll, baby. You're a red-blooded Californian, you tell me.'

He gave me the wry look, and took my hand. 'I've never been a Puritan, but I don't do stuff that's illegal, immoral, or fattening.' He tugged on my hand. 'I never took steroids, didn't cheat on the Bar Exam. That business with the circus pony, the tabloids exaggerated the whole thing.'

I rolled my eyes, relaxing.

'They're trying to freak me out. What I need to do is figure out how to trace the message path, so the next time, the cops can get on them.'

'Next time?'

'When they tell me they want me to shut up, or back off. Just watch.' He grabbed his car keys. 'Let's go. The arraignment's in half an hour.'

The county courthouse was a white fortress designed along the lines of an Andalusian castle. Adam was waiting outside. He wore Dockers and sandals, the academic-casual look not hiding the lines of tension in his face. Not hiding the hangover, either. He had on sunglasses and was trying not to move his head.

He said, 'I don't know how I'm going to look at his face.'

'Just stick with me,' Jesse said.

Upstairs in the courtroom, we took a seat on the hard benches. Jesse sat in the aisle, leaned on his elbows, and stared at his feet. A minute later Chris Ramseur joined us, dressed in his usual jacket, checked shirt, and knit tie. Seeing him warmed me. Detectives rarely attended arraignments, but Chris was invested in the case. More than that, he cared.

Soon the courtroom door clattered open, and Sheriff's deputies herded the shackled prisoners up the aisle, a conga line of the dead-eyed and defiant. Their blue coveralls stank of sweat and strong detergent.

And finally we saw him, toward the end of the line. Adam's hand gripped the bench behind my back. Jesse sat up straight. Brand walked past us, his gaze jumping around like a flea. He looked angry. He looked tired and dirty. But above all else, Franklin Brand looked rich.

He was tanned. He was smooth. He actually looked younger than in photos. He could have posed for the cover of a Yachts R Us catalog.

Jesse said, 'He's had plastic surgery.'

When the judge called his case he was unchained and walked through the gate to stand at the defense table. His attorney was a man named O'Leary who stroked his skull repeatedly, as if hoping to find hair there. The charges were read out.

Vehicular manslaughter. Reckless driving causing great bodily harm. Hit and run. Flight to avoid prosecution.

At the recitation of each charge, the judge said, 'How do you plead?'

And Brand said, 'Not guilty.'

I glanced at Jesse. He was barely breathing.

The prosecutor requested five hundred thousand dollars bail. Even I, no criminal attorney, knew that was high, but Adam hunched toward me, his face a fist.

'Is that all?'

O'Leary asked for fifty thousand dollars, the guideline amount for vehicular manslaughter. The prosecutor piped in again, talking about the multiple counts and Brand's risk of flight, and the judge raised his hand.

'I've heard enough. Bail is set at two-hundred fifty thousand dollars.'

That was it. The talk went on, but we were through. Jesse spun to leave and I stood up to follow him.

Adam said, 'They're letting him go.'

He was on his feet, gripping the bench in front of him. The judge looked up.

'Two-hundred and fifty thousand dollars won't keep him in town. This is wrong.'

The judge banged his gavel. 'Order in the court.'

'Are you insane? Two-hundred fifty K is nothing. The man is a millionaire.'

The judge clacked the gavel. The bailiff pushed through the gate toward us, his face like wood. Chris urged Adam toward the aisle, but he held onto the bench. Brand kept his eyes front. He was picking his fingernails.

Jesse said, 'Adam, come on. It's all right.'

Adam turned to him, mouth wide. After a long second, he let go of the bench and hurtled from the room.

Jesse caught him in the corridor outside. Adam was pacing in circles, holding his head. I heard him say, 'Isaac—'

Chris said, 'Evan.' He was writing on a business card. 'This is the name of someone at Victims' Assistance. Encourage Adam to call her.'

'Right.'

'This is only the start of a long, hard process. He needs to get a grip.' He looked at Jesse. 'How about him? He's going to have to testify.'

'Don't worry about Jesse,' I said, and my mind tripped over the word. *Testify.*

Adam was gesturing, arms wide. His voice bounced off the walls. Then the reporters came at them, calling out questions.

'Mr Sandoval, what do you think of Brand's arrest?'

'How does it feel to see your brother's alleged killer face to face?'

Adam froze. Jesse swiveled, putting himself between them.

'Is justice finally being served?'

'Any comment on today's proceedings?'

Jesse said, 'You bet I'll comment. Just a minute.'

He looked at me, and I read his eyes: get Adam out of here. I grabbed Adam's elbow and hustled him down the stairs. At the bottom he shrugged me off and strode outside as though desperate for oxygen.

He said, 'They're letting him go. They're letting the bastard go.'

His hands were shaking, and I didn't think from the hangover.

'How can Jesse stay so calm? *Comment?* I don't want to comment, I want to stand Brand up against a wall and drive into him with a cement truck.'

He bent and put his hands on his knees. Immediately he straightened again, hurried toward a trash can, leaned over it and threw up.

After a minute he wiped his mouth with a handkerchief. 'Sorry.'

I put my hand on his back. He was sweating.

He said, 'Can't we protest the bail order? If Brand gets out, he'll disappear.'

The anguish in his voice helped make up my mind. 'We can't keep him in jail. But we can follow him to make sure he doesn't try to skip town again.'

He looked at me quizzically, before it clicked. 'Yes.' Almost instantly, he looked lighter. 'Of course. But, around the clock? We have to work, and—' He checked his watch. 'Oh, I have to get to campus, I have a seminar.'

'Go. I'll take the first watch.'

He took both my hands in his. 'Thank you.' His eyes were red, his face haggard. 'Thank you.'

He was halfway down the block when Jesse and Chris came outside. I told them he had gone to the university. Chris looked pensive.

Jesse put on his wraparound sunglasses. 'I told Chris about Isaac's hassle with Mako over the missing paperwork. And about the blackmail threat on my computer.'

I said, 'The threat. What if they want to dissuade you from testifying against Brand?'

They both looked at me. Jesse swore. Chris nodded at police headquarters, across the street from the courthouse. 'Come on back to the station with me.'

'Give us a minute,' I said.

'Sure.' He sauntered out of earshot, head down, looking like an absent-minded professor lost in thought.

Jesse said, 'You're going to tail Brand, aren't you?'

'Until I'm convinced he isn't hitting the road.'

'Great. I'll join you as soon as I can.' He looked toward the courthouse. 'It will be hours before he posts bond. In the meantime, they'll probably take him back to the county jail.'

'So I'll get a cup of coffee, and watch to see if the deputies put him back on the bus with the chain gang.'

He nodded at Chris, idling up the street. 'Just remember, his desk overlooks the courthouse. Stay out of his line of sight.'

'I thought he was on our side.'

'Evan, the only people on our side are us. Count on it.'

Seven

The coffee was a mistake.

I spent the afternoon parked across from the county jail in Goleta, sitting in the back seat of my Explorer, playing office. I caught up on phone calls, dug business receipts from my glove compartment, and ate a bag of peanut M&Ms for lunch. I outlined the seminar I planned to give at the writers' conference: conflict. Ha, easy. Follow me, class. Observe, and take notes. And I worked on *Chromium Rain*, the chapter where the heroine escapes from the ruins of Cheyenne Mountain, Colorado. I kept an eye on the jail and the county Sheriff's headquarters next door to it. I didn't want a curious deputy tapping on my window to ask why I was writing about blowing up NORAD.

And the coffee had run through me. I needed a bathroom. I looked at the jail, hoping that if Brand came out, it would be soon.

Did he plan to skip? I didn't know. Despite Adam's alarm, the idea of forfeiting $250,000 might deter a millionaire from running. Not to mention the thought of getting a bounty hunter after him. Moreover, I still believed Brand was in Santa Barbara on unfinished business.

By three o'clock I was squirming. I needed relief, but Adam hadn't phoned. When my cellphone finally rang, I grabbed it and said, 'Hello?'

I think that's what I said, but it may have come out as *Grrr*, because my brother said, 'Well, aren't you a bundle of sunshine.'

'Brian.' I fidgeted on the seat. 'How's D.C.?'

'Humid. So sticky that to stand up, I have to scrape my butt off the desk chair with a spatula.'

He was at the Pentagon. It was a customary stop on a fighter pilot's journey up the ranks in naval aviation, but he chafed at the desk job. The Pentagon could no longer be considered dull, safe duty, but it wasn't an F/A-18.

'Listen, Ev, I'm calling to give you a heads up. Company's coming.'

'Really? Great, Bri, I can't wait to see you and Luke—'

'Afraid it isn't us. It's Cousin Taylor.'

My spirits, momentarily elevated, dropped. 'You're joking.'

'Sorry, Sis. The Hard Talk Café is bringing her mouth to your town.'

Across the street, a black Porsche Carrera pulled up at the jail. The driver got out, and I sat up straight. It was Kenny Rudenski.

Brian said, 'I just talked to Mom. Taylor's husband is being transferred. The oil company's sending him to a rig in the Santa Barbara Channel.'

Kenny smoothed his hair and went inside the jail. I scrambled over the gearshift into the front seat, feeling a ping from my bladder. Dropped into the driver's seat, stuck the key in the ignition, and stopped.

'Wait. Taylor is *moving* here?'

'There you go again, making that growling sound,' Brain said.

Kenny came out of the jail with Franklin Brand. I started my car. Even at this distance I could see that Brand didn't seem cheerful. His face looked stiffer than a boxing glove. Wordlessly he and Kenny climbed into the Porsche.

'I'll call you back, Brian.'

The Porsche pulled out. I let it go, waiting for a silver Mercedes SUV to pass before I fell in behind it, letting it screen me from Kenny's view.

The Porsche got on the freeway and headed west into Goleta. When he pulled off so did I, keeping the Mercedes between us. The light was turning red but Kenny didn't stop for it. The Porsche gunned onto Patterson. I braked, blocked by cars ahead in both lanes, peering past traffic to see which way Kenny was going. The Mercedes SUV was stopped next to me in the right

53

lane, and I saw the driver and passenger doing the same thing as I was.

Looking at the Porsche.

The passenger was a wiry young woman with whippet's limbs and cropped black hair. She was craning her neck. The driver was a rotund man whose glasses nestled in skin the color of pancake batter. His double chin hung like a gourd below his beardlet. The woman pointed at Kenny's car. The driver spun the wheel and maneuvered the Mercedes onto the shoulder, around the cars in front of him, and made the turn.

They were following him, too. For a moment I felt a bizarre competitive urge, and I started to spin the wheel and follow. But cautious brain cells awoke and kept my foot on the brake. *Wait. Watch.*

The light changed and I turned onto Patterson. Ahead, the Porsche bounded around another corner and accelerated out of sight, the road bending beyond an avocado orchard. The Mercedes followed.

So did I, speeding past the orchard, a fire station, new houses going up on what had been farmland. I hit another intersection and played the odds, going straight, into a commercial strip of shops, motels, and restaurants. I saw neither Kenny nor the Mercedes. Anxiety balled in my belly. I couldn't lose Brand again.

I stomped on the brake. There was the Porsche, under the portico at the Holiday Inn. The marquee out front announced LOBSTER BUFFET $9.99 and WELCOME GARCIA FAMILY REUNION. I turned in, parked, and watched the Porsche in the rearview mirror.

Brand got out, slammed the car door, and walked into the lobby of the motel. The Porsche drove off, engine revving.

I waited.

I didn't see the Mercedes following the Porsche. I didn't see it in the parking lot. I didn't see the choppy-haired woman or the fat man strolling into the lobby.

I win.

Pulling on a baseball cap and sunglasses, I got out and headed for the lobby.

I pushed through the doors into the Holiday Inn. Brand was standing at the front desk talking to a clerk, his back to me. I walked past him.

He said, 'Messages?'

'Your room number?'

'One twenty-seven.'

Sometimes you get lucky. He was checked in. He was expecting messages. I walked over to a rack loaded with tourist brochures, picked one, and slipped a pen from my back pocket. I wrote *127* on the brochure.

I stood there for a few seconds longer. If I didn't get to a bathroom, I would have a blowout. I glanced over my shoulder. Brand was standing at the desk reading message slips. The bathrooms were along a hallway to my left. I thought about it. What if this was an elaborate ruse on Brand's part? He could be planning a getaway. Perhaps Kenny Rudenski had only pretended to drive off. Perhaps he was circling the block, preparing to pick Brand up by the laundry bins.

And perhaps I should have read the skulking manual before following him. Page one: pee, *then* tail.

I couldn't wait any longer. Turning my face away from Brand, I hurried for the restroom. I pushed through the door and saw that rare ladies' room jewel, the vacant stall. O frabjous day. I locked the stall door, jammed my bag on the coathook. My eyes were watering but I was about to burst into song, maybe rip loose with an aria from *Tosca* in joy.

Outside the stall came footsteps, and feet appeared, wearing Doc Martens. A woman's hand reached over the top of the stall door, fumbled around, and grabbed my bag off the coathook.

I yelled, 'Hey—'

But she was gone.

It was a classic bit of thievery. I hurried as best I could, zipped up, ran from the stall and out into the hallway.

Right into Brand.

I swallowed a gasp, feeling my pores open. He was solid, a big man marbled with weight beneath the cashmere sportcoat. He smelled jail-sour and had shaved badly. Graying stubble patched his jowls.

His head snapped around. 'Watch it.'

His eyes were a strange calico green and brown, almost kaleidoscopic, and rank with anger. Brushing me aside, he headed out toward the pool.

My vision was thumping. Dumb seconds ticked off, until I ran outside too, looking for the woman in Doc Martens. The motel was built around an interior courtyard, with a lawn and tall palm trees and a turquoise swimming pool. Kids were playing, sunlight flickering on the water. Brand walked toward the far side of the courtyard. He had a keycard in his hand.

The woman wasn't there.

Screw it. I ran back inside, to the lobby, and out the main door.

My bag was sitting in a planter, half open. My wallet was nearby. I checked: all cash, my driver's license, Social Security card, and credit cards were gone. So was my cellphone.

Out on the street, a silver Mercedes SUV roared away from the motel.

I went back in the lobby and told the desk clerk to call the police.

The manager came to the front desk, apoplectic with embarrassment.

She said, 'We're terribly sorry about this. Your stay will be complimentary, ma'am.'

It was the thinnest of silver linings. 'I was just about to register. The name's Delaney,' I said. 'Do you have anything near room 127?'

Eight

The East Beach Writers' Conference was the official name, but the event should have been called the Fiction Smackdown. It was two days of controlled chaos, organized by a gang of writers who suppressed their neuroses and jealousy just long enough to book the hotel conference center. At noon the next day I arrived to give my seminar. The hotel looked out across Cabrillo Boulevard at beach volleyball courts, Stearns Wharf, and the pinprick sparkle of the ocean. The sky flew above like a taut blue sail. I was already in a bad mood.

I had spent the morning canceling my credit cards and arranging to get a duplicate driver's license. The bridal shop phoned to tell me they'd lost my measurements and I should come in for another fitting. And, the *pièce de résistance*, Jesse called with the news that Mari Vasquez Diamond was threatening to sue him, me, and Sanchez Marks for intentional infliction of emotional distress.

And I had stayed up most of the night, peeking through the curtains of my poolside room at the Holiday Inn, watching to see if Franklin Brand did anything. He didn't. He kept the curtains drawn. He received no visitors. When I walked past his door I heard the television droning. The only activity along his wing of the motel was in the connecting room next to his: Maintenance was working on a leak in the ceiling. After three a.m., espresso couldn't keep me alert. Eventually, fretting over who stole my things, and how the thieves were connected to Brand, couldn't either.

Now Adam Sandoval was taking a turn on watch. I left him in the motel room, looking grimly refreshed, working through coffee and a box of his brother's mementos.

So I walked into the conference room tired and crabby, to make my debut as a teacher. I wet my thumb before passing out a sheet of lecture points. Twelve people sat around the table, staring at me. They were a mix: women, men, tie-dye, pinstripes, slickness, reticence, looking for enlightenment, or at least craft, listening and interrupting and taking notes as I talked about story structure. To my surprise, I enjoyed it.

No, I loved it. At the end of two hours I found myself hoarse but invigorated. I could get used to this, I thought.

Gathering up my things, I noticed two students lingering in the doorway, a couple in their forties. The man offered his hand.

'Tim North. Excellent seminar.'

He had an English accent and a brisk handshake. He was trim, with cool eyes and a mutt's face. From his carriage, I took him to be ex-military.

I hoisted my backpack over my shoulder. 'I'm glad you enjoyed it. You didn't say a word during the session.'

'Observing and assimilating,' North said.

He was tightly wound, as if he was ready to spring. His accent was broad, his features . . . malleable. I got the feeling that he wasn't among the usual aspirants.

He gestured to the woman. 'My wife, Jakarta Rivera.'

Her smile gleamed. 'It was everything we hoped it would be.'

Her voice was patently made in the USA. She was African American, more stylishly dressed than the average Santa Barbaran, and had a ballerina's physique: deceptive fragility covering pure muscle. She looked as sleek as a Maserati.

She reached into her bag for a copy of my novel *Lithium Sunset*. 'We're fans.'

'I'm flattered.'

I led them through the door. I sensed that they wanted something – for me to read their screenplay, or to give them my agent's name. We stepped onto a patio where coffee and snacks were set up. The sun was intense. The tile floor radiated heat, and the potted plants throbbed. I took a peach from the snack table.

'We have a proposal for you,' North said, and looked at his wife. 'Jax?'

She was selecting an apple, examining it for bruises. The diamond in her engagement ring looked as big as the grapes on the table. It matched the stud earrings she wore, and the solitaire stone in her necklace, all shatteringly brilliant.

She said, 'We want to hire you.'

Halfway through biting into the peach, I stopped. 'To do what?'

'To ghostwrite our memoirs.'

This was not what I was expecting, and she knew it. She regarded me with the cool and intense gaze of a cat. I felt pinned.

North said, 'We'll pay you far more than you're earning in your current publishing contract.'

'Now I am truly flattered,' I said. 'But I have no experience as a ghostwriter.'

Rivera said, 'You do journalism, though. You know how to interview people, and how to portray them insightfully.'

North said, 'And frankly, you know how to write about men. A bloke wouldn't mind having you put his thoughts on paper.'

Rivera said, 'And we do know a bit about you. We like what we've seen.'

'What's that?'

North said, 'You stood up to that religious terror group last year. Really, you bloody well sorted them out. That impressed us.'

Disquiet wriggled up my back. 'I don't regard that as résumé material.'

His wife said, 'Honey, you should.'

I looked at her. 'Who are you?'

North said, 'Miss Delaney, we wish to engage you to write our memoirs. We will pay you a hell of a lot of money to do so.'

My disquiet was turning to apprehension. 'Don't be cryptic. Tell me who you are and why I should spend one minute of my life writing a book about yours. What do you do?'

'We're retired,' he said.

'Sorry. Find yourself another girl.' I started walking away.

'Wait,' Rivera said. 'Tim didn't tell you what business we're retired from.'

She waited until I looked at her. Those feline eyes pinned me again.

She said, 'Espionage.'

Jesse wiped his hands on a napkin. 'Say that again.'

'I laughed at her.'

'And walked away.'

'They were a joke,' I said. 'I didn't waste any more time on them.'

'Weird joke.' He drank his iced tea.

'So what did Chris Ramseur say about the computer harassment?' I said.

'He went into deep thinker mode. He'll investigate.'

The waitress bustled by, putting the check on the table as she passed. It was nine p.m., and the restaurant at the Holiday Inn was nearly empty.

'How's the lobster?' I said.

'Tastes like chicken.'

Around the corner in the banquet room, the Garcia family reunion was revving into high gear, with slide shows and laughter at the dessert buffet. In the cocktail lounge, a tenor turned up the vibrato on the Hammond organ.

Jesse said, 'If he sings "Memory" one more time, I'm getting a flamethrower.'

I rubbed his hand. 'I'm on duty now. Go home.'

He paid his $9.99 for the dinner and we left the restaurant. Outside, I kissed him goodnight, and put fifty cents in a vending machine for a Snickers. Feeling lonely at the thought of sleeping alone, I put in another fifty cents for a Payday.

I was mulling the York Peppermint Patties when I saw Brand's door swing open. My pulse jumped into fourth gear. He came out and I followed him to the parking lot. When he drove away in a gold rental car, I followed him.

He drove through Santa Barbara to Montecito, eventually turning toward the beach and pulling in at the Biltmore, the *grand dame* of local hotels.

At the entrance he handed his car keys to a valet. I parked on the street across from the seawall. The beach was dark. I heard breakers drumming onto the sand and saw the oil platforms offshore, lights winking in the salt air. Walking up the hotel driveway, I noted the preponderance of good tailoring on the people coming out the entrance. Brand would fit right in, wearing that cashmere jacket. I was wearing a faded Pendleton shirt of Jesse's, and my cords had a hole in the knee. I inhaled some attitude and decided to pass myself off as an eccentric novelist. Or a lumberjack.

I went through the door into burnished light and the scuff of Italian leather soles on terracotta tile. A jazz pianist was playing in a lounge where huge windows faced the ocean. I strolled in and sat down, attempting nonchalance, as though I was waiting for someone. Ernest Hemingway, possibly. I tried to look for Brand without seeming to look.

'Hi, can I get you something to drink?'

The waitress had a zesty, gosh-life-is-great soprano. I ordered a Coke. She nodded and turned away, stopping for a man who was passing by.

He had a slow stride and a face like a Bowie knife, sharp and narrow. His blond hair fell in rings to his shoulders, but there was nothing feminine about him. With the black clothes and brown goatee, he looked like a rock star, or George Armstrong Custer. His eyes had a dark buzz, like black static. He held a longnecked beer bottle in his hand.

The waitress gave him space. It was as if he was emitting feedback, like a poorly grounded electric guitar. He headed to the far side of the room, where Franklin Brand sat in the corner holding a glass of whiskey.

The blond sat down across from him. He slouched back,

stretched his legs out, started talking. Brand put down his drink. As he listened, his posture stiffened.

The pianist was gliding through a downhearted piece. No way could I catch their words. Blondie seemed relaxed, crossing his legs, drinking his beer. Brand, however, looked as though a flaming dog turd had dropped in his lap. When he spoke his jaw was tight, and I could see his teeth.

My Coke came. I drank, watching.

The chair next to me scraped backward. I saw a jacket and checked shirt, knit tie. Waspish expression. Chris Ramseur sat down.

'What are you doing here?' he said.

'Watching Brand and his new dance partner. Lean back, you're blocking my view.'

'What is wrong with you? Did you bump your head and start confusing your life with an episode of Charlie's Angels?'

'Who's blondie?' I said.

He bent toward me. 'I know this is personal for you. But you need to go.'

'He and Brand aren't hitting it off. I doubt they're going to slow dance.'

Chris tapped his fingers on the arm of his chair, and stared at me. 'Have you ever considered a career in law enforcement?'

'Seriously?' I set down my Coke.

'You're smart, you're tenacious, and you care about putting criminals away. Come in any time and pick up an application.'

'Thanks, Chris.'

'But until you start cashing a city paycheck, keep your nose out of police business.'

He took my elbow and stood up. Pulling me along, he walked out of the lounge, through the lobby, and outside. The jazz faded.

'You can let go now,' I said.

He kept walking. 'Where are you parked?'

I said nothing. He led me down the driveway. Behind us the windows of the lounge glowed gold.

'Okay, you've made your point. I—'

He raised a finger. 'Don't.'

I stopped myself from replying. His eyes, beneath the flint, looked troubled. All at once, I knew he wasn't peeved about me keeping tabs on Brand. This wasn't about turf. My mouth turned dry.

I said, 'I just blew something, didn't I?'

'Go home, Evan.'

He released my arm with a nudge and stood in the driveway, ready to stop me from heading back inside. Over his shoulder I could see Brand and the blond through the windows of the lounge.

'Chris, I'm sorry,' I said. 'I'm going.'

And I meant to. Except that Brand slammed down his glass and stood up, stabbing his finger at the blond, and started to stalk away.

The blond raised his hand, holding something between his index and middle fingers, something thin and round and shiny. Brand stopped. The blond threw the object on the table.

'Chris,' I said, pointing at the window.

But by the time Chris turned his head, Brand had dropped back onto his seat and slipped the object into his jacket pocket.

'Goldilocks just gave him something,' I said.

'What was it?'

'I don't know.' It occurred to me. 'Could have been a disk.'

'Get out of here,' he said.

He started up the driveway toward the hotel, taking out a cellphone and punching numbers as he went. I walked to my car, got in, and watched.

Chris didn't even get inside the hotel. The blond sauntered out, hands loose at his sides like a gunfighter ready to draw. Chris walked past him, his head bent into the cellphone, feigning disinterest. The blond handed the parking attendant a ticket. A minute later he climbed into a Corvette and drove off.

I waited. Brand came out within the minute, and I followed his gold rental car back to the Holiday Inn. In my room across the courtyard from his, the message light on the phone was blinking. Jesse had called.

I reached him at home, told him about the Biltmore, and described the blond.

'Sound familiar?'

'Not remotely.'

'Jesse, Chris Ramseur yanked me out of there. Something's going down. I think I just stuck my nose into a police operation.'

'Brand's mixed up in something that Chris didn't tell us about?'

'Yes. Possibly because he thought I would stick my nose into it.'

I peered out the window. The lights in the empty pool reflected ripples on the palm trees. In Brand's room, the curtains were part way open. I could see him inside, pacing back and forth. He was talking on the phone.

I said, 'Brand got something from blondie, maybe a computer disk. I think he went to the meeting to get it.'

I noticed the room connecting to Brand's, where Maintenance had been repairing a leak. The door was propped open with a chair. My adrenal glands did a pirouette.

'Oh, my. The room next to Brand's is open,' I said. 'I can go in and listen through the connecting door.'

He made an exasperated noise. 'Hold your horses.'

'Excuse me? When have you ever wanted me to do that?'

'Just wait,' he said. 'Do you see the police anywhere?'

'No.'

'Are you wearing quiet shoes?'

'Yes.'

'Don't knock anything over when you go in.'

I started to reply, and experienced a karmic moment, a confluence of desire and opportunity. Brand opened the door of his room. He had an ice bucket in his hand. He flipped the deadbolt so the door couldn't close while he strolled to the ice machine.

64

'I can get into Brand's room,' I said. 'I'll call you back.'

Jesse was shouting when I hung up.

I hurried out. From my side of the courtyard I could see the ice machine. It was in a breezeway around the corner from Brand's room, about fifty yards along the courtyard. Give him twenty seconds to walk there, ten more to fill the ice bucket and head back around the corner. Call it thirty seconds.

And what could I do with that time? Perhaps only unlock the connecting door to the next room, giving myself access later. But perhaps more.

Brand was no longer wearing his cashmere jacket, the one where he'd pocketed the blond's shiny object. I could – what, steal it? Burn it? Eat it?

Examine it. Borrow it. If it turned out to be a computer disk I could download it onto my laptop, then return it. Whatever the object was, the police were interested in it. And they didn't have it. It was small, and valuable, and could easily be hidden or destroyed. If I didn't get it myself, the police might never. I could get my hands on it to make up for throwing a wrench into Chris's evening.

Boy, I could rationalize for Team USA. I ran on tiptoe past the pool toward Brand's room. He was still walking toward the ice machine, his back to me. I reached his door, gave him a last glance, and went inside.

The room smelled thick with cologne. The television was droning. The cashmere jacket hung over the back of a chair. I hesitated. Technically, I wasn't committing burglary, or even breaking and entering. But I was about to commit theft.

I reached into the jacket, slipped my hand into the satin lining of the inside pocket, and pulled out the object. I held it up. It was a miniature disk about the size of a business card.

There was a knock on the door.

Every bit of my body seemed to jump, including my hair. The door started to open. I jammed the disk into my own shirt pocket.

'Housekeeping.' A maid peered in. 'The towels you wanted.'
'Right.'

I felt as if I was erupting in hives. And they were spelling out T-H-I-E-F across my forehead. When she walked to the bathroom I sped out the door, dodging her laundry cart.

I heard voices along the courtyard. Peripherally I saw Brand turn the corner and head this way. A woman was with him. She wore a jacket with the collar turned up, and had her hair tucked under a cap. Her face, from this distance, was indistinct.

Quick decision: I ducked into the connecting room, past the chair wedging the door open. Inside, the lights were off. I could smell damp and mildew. A fan rattled on the floor, drying the carpet. I considered pulling the chair inside and closing the door, but that might draw attention to the room. With the lights off and curtains drawn, no one could see me in here, anyway.

I slunk to the doorway connecting this room with Brand's. Gingerly I opened the door on my side. Through the second door, on Brand's side, came the sound of voices. Who was she? Lover, mother, stockbroker? Was she the woman from the hit-and-run? The droning of the fan obscured their words.

I stepped closer, and kicked a wastebasket. It banged into the wall.

I held my breath, hearing my heart pound in my ears, half expecting Brand to yank the door open. But after a few seconds I heard the voices again. The fan clattered. I pressed my ear close to the door, trying to decipher their words.

Brand's baritone. '. . . so how dare he—'

Her mumble.

'—a king-sized prick. Pulling this on me.'

Her laugh. Words. Unintelligible.

'. . . won't think it's so funny when—'

I listened, heard the TV, and music, and – barking. Was that a Chihuahua?

They stopped talking. I heard a clicking sound. Brand or the woman had opened the door out to the motel courtyard. Was she leaving? I strained to hear.

Behind me, the chair propping open the door was kicked into the room. The lights flipped on. I spun around. Brand loomed in the doorway.

Nine

I lunged away but didn't get two feet. He barged into the room, a bearlike mass. The door slammed shut. He grabbed my arm and flung me at the bed. I tripped against the corner and tumbled to the floor, landing on my back. I tried to get to my feet but he pushed me down on the carpet and pressed a hand over my mouth.

'Who are you?' His calico eyes were jittering. 'Did Mickey send you? Are you one of his flunkies?'

I squirmed and kicked and worked my lips apart and bit him.

'Christ.' His hand flew off my mouth.

I screamed.

'Don't do that, don't.' His fingers groped at my face again.

I yelled but with the fan clamoring I didn't think anyone could hear me. He reeked of cologne. His hand closed over my mouth and nose. I clawed my fingernails into his arm but he didn't budge. His ring pressed into my skin, a pinkie ring with a diamond as big as a computer chip.

'Who are you working with?'

One shot, I thought – I had one shot to talk my way out of here. Or at least to talk him off of me, so I could grab for the phone. I called upon the god of attitude to pump up the impudence and keep it coming. I pounded on his arm.

He shook my face. 'I take my hand off and you scream again, I'll hurt you. I'll break your jaw. I'm not kidding.'

I blinked assent. He took his hand away.

'God, that cologne stinks. What is it called, Putridity? Get off of me, the smell's getting in my clothes.'

His face puckered.

I said, 'Kathleen Evans, *Los Angeles Times*.'

He blinked. 'You're with the press?'

'And you're toast.'

He blanched. I felt his breath on me.

'Two choices,' I said. 'One, you keep this up, and the headline reads Death Driver in New Assault.'

His hand hovered near my jaw. His eyes were sour. 'And two?'

'We go to the bar and you give me your side of the story.'

'You want an interview?'

'Uncensored, your own words.'

He guffawed. 'You're kidding. What, Franklin Brand, My Story?'

'Yes.'

'How I lost my job, how my wife divorced me and now my so-called friends wouldn't cross the street to blow their nose on my shirt. That's what you want?'

He wasn't letting me up. I tried to gauge how far it was to the phone, and he saw me looking. He reached over and ripped the cord from the wall.

He stared at me. I prayed that the mini-disk wasn't sticking out of my pocket.

'Forget it,' he said.

'Then give me a comment about the hit-and-run. Do you have any words for the victims?'

A blue vein was squirming on his temple. 'No. No comment from the death driver. No comment from the millionaire fugitive heartless perpetrator.'

'Why did you come back?'

'You don't have a clue, do you? You are so far off base you can't even see the ballpark.'

My plan wasn't working. He believed my cover and was still holding onto me. My chest tightened with fear.

I said, 'Tell me about your meeting tonight at the Biltmore.'

His lips parted. I had caught him off guard.

'What got you so upset?' I said.

'Shut up.' The vein wriggled. 'It doesn't matter. You'll see. You'll all fucking see.'

I heard the sound of a key going into the lock. The door opened and a maintenance man gaped at us from the doorway. He wore a green uniform with a name patch that read *Floyd*.

He said, 'What's going on?'

'Help me.' I fought to get up, but Brand didn't move. 'Get him off me.'

'I thought I heard screaming.'

And like smoke, Brand's anger evaporated. His eyes cooled. 'Sorry it got loud. She's a little drunk.'

'No, help me,' I said. 'Please, get me out of here.'

Floyd looked back and forth between us, as if deciding whom to believe. He said, 'This ain't your room. You got to leave.'

Brand's voice had turned smoother than oil. 'She told me this was her room. Said she's here for that family reunion.' He raised his hand toward Floyd. It had a twenty-dollar bill in it. 'Honest mistake on my part. Can we square it away?'

I said, 'Call the police. For godsake, he ripped the phone out.'

Floyd looked at the hole in the wall. He scowled, and grabbed the twenty, and said, 'Get out, both of you.'

Finally, I felt Brand relent. I jumped up and bolted for the door. It wasn't until I was in my car and halfway home that I started crying.

Blocking a doorway can be harder than it looks.

'You're not going to the motel,' I said.

Jesse faced off against me in Adam Sandoval's front hallway. He was ready to push straight through me. His face looked like a hurricane.

'Move,' he said. 'I'm going to whip his ass.'

Behind him in the living room, Adam pretended he wasn't listening. He sat at one of his computers, dinking with the mini-disk.

I stood my ground. 'This is why I didn't tell you.'

And Jesse might not have found out that Brand attacked me, if

70

my computer had been able to play the mini-disk. But my laptop couldn't handle it, so we brought it to Adam. Who welcomed me in and said, 'What happened to your lip?'

Brand's diamond pinkie ring had scratched my face. Jesse got a good look at me in the light, and I didn't know how to lie to him.

'Once I report the assault, the judge will revoke Brand's bail,' I said. 'He's going back to jail. Do you want to share his cell?'

'Yes. Make it me and Bubba and a bar of soap and a crowbar.'

I thought he could pull me off my feet and pitch me over his lap to get past. I thought he could probably do Brand significant damage, before he ended up on the floor, or in the ER. I knew I loved him for wanting to protect me. I had to stop him.

'If you put a fist into Brand's face, he's going to figure out exactly who I am, and where the mini-disk is,' I said. 'Hold fire. Let's see what's on the disk, and I'll call Chris Ramseur.'

His shoulders were tight, his eyes cold blue. His voice quieted.

'He could have hurt you.'

And that was the truth of it. I felt the tears welling up again, fought them.

'Ev?'

'No, I'm okay.' If I cried, nothing would stop him. 'We've misjudged Brand, all these years. We thought he was a coward, fleeing from what he did. But he's dangerous. He's into something bad.'

Adam said, 'It's running.'

Jesse gave me a look aching with frustration. We went into the living room. I hoped the mini-disk would be worth the risks I took to get it.

Adam hunched at the computer. 'It's a CD.'

He typed, so fast that the keys clicked like a Geiger counter. He opened a directory and scrolled down a list of files. I stared over his shoulder.

'Spreadsheets, accounting data, e-mails . . .' He stopped scrolling.

Jesse said, 'Whoa.'

71

'They're Mako financials,' Adam said.

He opened a file. It looked like a record of disbursements from Mako to other companies.

'Accounts payable?' I said.

Jesse said, 'The amounts look awfully big for that . . .' He read. 'It's a list of companies Mako invested in.'

Adam stared at the screen. 'Angel funding. This is their development fund, money going to small firms Mako bought into.'

I read the names of the companies. PDS Systems, Segue, Firedog –

Of course Firedog would be there, Isaac's company. But seeing it sent a *frisson* down my spine.

'What's in these other files?' I said.

They were labeled *Grand Cayman* and *Bahamas*. They were bank records for accounts in the name of FB Enterprises.

'You think?' I said.

We huddled around the computer, and started peeling back the layers. There were e-mails from Brand to various bankers, and records of deposits and transfers he made. The money invariably went first into the Bahamas account and from there to the Cayman Islands. But where did it come from in the first place?

I looked at my watch. We'd been at it an hour.

I said, 'We have to get this to the police. Wait much longer, they'll think my whole story is fishy.'

Adam said, 'Let me download it first. I'll print it, and also e-mail it to both of you.'

He typed, hit Send, jumped up, and ran into the guest room. We heard him rustling around.

Jesse ran a hand over his face. 'Why has all this stuff been compiled on the disk? And why did this guy at the Biltmore give it to Brand? What's the point?'

Adam came back in with a bulging cardboard box. 'More of Isaac's things from the office.'

He began unloading papers and folders on a table. I stood and stretched, feeling grungy. When I inhaled, I smelled Brand's

72

cologne on my shirt. Excusing myself, I went to the bathroom to wash up.

I craved a shower, but settled for splashing cold water on my face. In the guest bathroom I let it run over my hands, and scrubbed my skin. The scrape from Brand's ring looked minor. My face looked as exhausted as I felt. I came out and sat down on the guest bed. Just for a minute.

When I heard voices raised in the living room, I realized I had fallen asleep. I sat up. Outside, the eastern sky was graying with light. How long had I been out? Finger-combing my hair, I walked back to the living room.

Papers covered the desk, coffee table, and floor. Jesse was stretched out prone on the sofa with a printout in his hands, looking weary. Adam stood in the center of the room, clutching a stack of papers.

'Evan, look at what I've found.' He shoved the papers into my hands. 'From Isaac's desk. God, why didn't I go through it years ago?'

I flipped through them – memos, phone message slips, scratch paper with hand-jotted notes. I glanced at Jesse. From the look in his eyes he knew what the papers contained, and he didn't like it.

Adam pointed to a sheet of binder paper. 'Look.'

I saw it; a single word. *Brand.*

Adam said, 'Isaac knew Franklin Brand. He knew him. He knew him.'

I said, 'You're telling me—'

Adam gestured toward the papers. 'If you read through those, you can follow the sequence of events.' But he was too agitated to let me read through them. His eyes looked wired. 'Do you know what Brand did at Mako?'

'I'm not sure—'

'Finance. Mergers and acquisitions. He would have negotiated Mako's investment in Firedog. Seven hundred thousand dollars Mako put in, cash for stock.'

I glanced at the papers again. There were references to *shares* and *stock certificates*, with question marks doodled near the words.

I said, 'And Isaac—'

He bustled to the coffee table. 'We laid it out in order. Jesse cross-referenced the stuff from the mini-disk with Isaac's notes.' He pointed. 'Mako's initial investment is here.' He showed me the printout of the angel fund data. 'But look here. The next year. The angel fund lists another investment as going to Firedog.'

I took the printout and started reading. Adam hovered by my shoulder. I saw the entry on the spreadsheet: Firedog . . . $500,000.

He said, 'The money never got to Firedog.'

I followed the trail they had laid out. Half a million dollars was listed on Mako's accounts as going to Firedog. Shortly thereafter, the Bahamas account for FB Enterprises registered a half-million dollar deposit, on the same day as $200,000 transferred from an entity named Segue. The next day, $700,000 was transferred from the Bahamas account to the Caymans account of FB Enterprises. I looked at Adam, and at Jesse.

Jesse said, 'Follow the trail down the rabbit hole.'

I looked at Isaac's jotted notes. *What shares? All sent.* These were the notes that had piqued our interest in the first place.

I said, 'Let me get this straight. You're saying that Brand stole investment money that should have gone to Firedog?'

'I'm saying that he *told* Mako he was arranging additional financing, in exchange for another chunk of stock. But he never gave the money to Firedog. He kept it.'

Another note. *Brand – shares/his action item.*

I said, 'Isaac was double-checking on the actual, physical transfer of the stock certificates from Firedog to Mako.'

Jesse said, 'Somebody at Mako called Isaac and asked why they hadn't sent the shares over. That has to be it.'

I said, 'And Isaac said, what shares? Because they hadn't done a second round of investment with Mako?'

Adam said, 'Yes. They should have been in a vault somewhere. But they weren't.'

Brand. Brand. Brand.

I said, 'You think Brand stole the money?'

'Yes.' His chest was laboring up and down. 'I think so because Isaac thought so. He thought Brand was embezzling money from Mako.'

Jesse said, 'Half a million dollars worth.'

My mind ran off into the bushes, digging, sniffing, running ahead and out of control. Isaac was a young guy, not the top man at Firedog; a programmer handling other duties because the company was so small. The messages on his doodle sheets showed that he tried many times to get hold of Brand, without success. His calls and e-mails weren't continuous, but they were persistent.

You don't have a clue, do you? You are so far off base you can't even see the ballpark . . . Was this what Brand meant?

I stared at the papers assembled on the coffee table. Back to the records of the accounts labeled FB Enterprises.

'Hang on. Is there any evidence that FB is actually Franklin Brand?'

Jesse rolled on his side and sat up. 'Yeah. Account records.' He stretched for some papers and handed them to me.

I read the details – account numbers, instructions for transferring funds through a correspondent bank in New York, owner and co-owner information. The owner of both accounts was listed as Franklin Brand.

I was awake now, but still I almost missed it. I did a double-take. I sat on the arm of the couch and showed the data to Jesse.

'The names.'

Co-owner of the Bahamas account was C.M. Burns, and of the Caymans account, Bob Terwilliger.

'It can't be,' Jesse said. 'C.M. Burns? C. Montgomery Burns?'

'And Bob Terwilliger.' Simultaneously we said, 'Sideshow Bob.'

Adam said, 'What?'

Jesse said, 'You don't watch enough TV. They're cartoon characters.'

'From The Simpsons,' I said. The room seemed to shift

75

beneath me. 'He faked the names. The accounts are fraudulent.'

The rest of the implications fell into place on their own.

I said, 'Brand was embezzling from Mako.'

'And Isaac stumbled onto it,' Adam said.

Brand stole the money, and Isaac found out. Maybe he didn't even know what it was he'd found out. But he kept pestering Brand about it. He started dragging it into the daylight. He would have exposed Brand.

Jesse said, 'The hit-and-run. He ran Isaac down deliberately.'

Adam's face looked desperate. 'Brand murdered him.'

Ten

Chris Ramseur hung up the phone. 'The lieutenant's on his way.'

He stirred chunks of non-dairy creamer into his coffee. Behind his head, the morning sky was a square of gray light outside the window. He was staring at the stack of papers Adam had slapped down on his desk. The mini-disk was in his hand.

He shook his head at me, his eyes crackling with energy. 'You couldn't leave it alone, could you? You stole this from Brand—'

'Borrowed.'

'—stole this from Brand, you hand it to me on a platter, and expect applause.'

I held out my hands. 'Cuff me, Detective.'

He sighed and threw his coffee stirrer into the trash. 'There's no chain of custody, no proof of where this disk came from, beyond your word.'

'That disk contains enough evidence to prosecute Brand for theft, fraud, and tax evasion.'

'And murder,' Jesse said.

'It reads like the prosecution's exhibit list. Don't you believe me?'

'I believe you,' Chris said. 'But I feel a year-long migraine coming on.'

Adam said, 'But you can get corroboration from the banks in the Caymans and Bahamas, and from Mako. You need to get over there and lock down their computers. Get a warrant or whatever you do.'

'Dr Sandoval—'

'Their system will contain records of Brand's fraud. Even if he

77

wiped his hard drive, Mako will have backups or a server that keeps their records. But you should hurry, because if he gets wind that we're on to him, his friends there might try to destroy the proof.'

Chris said, 'We? Your surveillance is off. Kaput. Finito.'

Adam said, 'No. Brand might decide to run.'

'We're on it.'

A deep voice said, 'Detective,' and Lieutenant Clayton Rome walked up to Chris's desk. 'What's going on?'

Rome was crisp, buffed, growly – a man who presented himself as though he were a police motorcycle. His buttons and belt buckle gleamed. His black hair gleamed. His teeth gleamed. He listened to Chris explain the situation, and stared at us, rubbing a finger alongside his nose.

'Okay, we'll take it from here.' He gestured at me. 'You give a statement about the assault at the motel?'

'It's being typed up,' I said.

'And you're done playing vigilante?'

'Certainly.' I avoided Chris's eyes.

Rome looked at Adam. 'I'm sorry about the loss of your brother. We'll give this our complete effort.' He sighed at Jesse, and patted him on the shoulder. 'Hang in there, son.'

He walked away. Jesse let his condescension go without comment.

I said, 'The blond man at the Biltmore, the one who gave Brand the mini-disk. What does he have to do with all of this?'

Chris stared at the disk for a moment. 'Mickey Yago.'

'Pardon?'

He looked up. 'The blond's name is Mickey Yago. He's from L.A., and he's a career criminal. He is not a person you three want to have any contact with.'

Jesse said, 'What kind of career criminal?'

'Narcotics, porn, extortion. He's sly, and he's violent, and he doesn't work alone. Stay away from him.'

I crossed my arms. We were all staring at Chris.

I said, 'Who does he work with? Franklin Brand?'

78

'That's under investigation. I'm telling you this to help you protect yourselves.'

'At the motel Brand asked if Mickey sent me, if I was one of his flunkies,' I said. 'Who are Mickey's flunkies, Chris? The fat man and skinny girl in the Mercedes SUV, who stole my wallet?'

Chris tapped his pencil against the desk.

I said, 'You have any more names for us to stay away from?'

'Fine. Win Utley and Cherry Lopez. These are all people you should be vaccinated against, I'm not kidding.' His face looked strained. 'Brand killed your brother, Dr Sandoval, and he – Jesse, he did this to you. Now you bring me evidence that perhaps he did it intentionally.'

Adam said, 'He did.'

'My point,' Chris said, 'is that Brand may be more dangerous than we thought. And he may be connected to people who regard violence as ordinary business.'

My mind jumped forward on the playlist. *Porn. Extortion.* 'Is Mickey Yago involved with the attempt to threaten Jesse?'

Chris pointed a finger at me. 'A warning, Evan. Brand may come after you for the disk.'

'You think he'll find out who I am?'

'I would take the possibility seriously.' His eyes were solemn. 'Be wary.'

After signing my statement, I walked out into the gray morning. Across the street, the white walls of the courthouse blended into the gloom. I felt as though I'd grabbed an exposed electric wire.

Jesse and Adam were waiting on the corner. Adam was running a hand across his short hair, staring at the sidewalk.

When I walked up I heard him asking, 'Will Ramseur follow through?'

Jesse said, 'Yeah, because I'll pester him.'

Adam gazed into the distance. 'I can't . . .' He fingered his crucifix. 'I have no words to tell you how – appalled I feel that—'

'Stop.'

'You were injured so bad because Brand went after Isaac.'

'It's a bitch, buddy. Life's a bitch. And Franklin Brand is her suckling dog. But my injury is not your fault. Don't you dare blame Isaac, or yourself.'

Adam looked at him, and clearly did not believe it. He walked away.

'I'll drop you at home,' Jesse said. But he didn't.

We drove in silence. The ashen sky weighed on us. The stereo was playing *Riding With The King*. Clapton and B.B. King, dueling blues guitars. The car bounced over dips in the street, Jesse driving just over the limit. His car had a big engine, a guy's engine, and he drove smoothly. But too fast today.

I didn't speak. He needed company, not conversation. He drove toward the mountains. They rose, massive and dark, into the clouds. We drove by the Old Mission and on past Rocky Nook Park. The live oaks stretched overhead, gnarled and dark. I knew where we were heading. To Mission Canyon. The place we never went, the pain he never spoke about.

We crossed Foothill Road and broke out of the clouds into sunlight, throbbing greenery, the sandstone shining on the mountains, the sky above La Cumbre Peak a lacquered blue. The road split and started climbing along the west flank of the canyon. After a few minutes the houses died out. Below us, oaks and sycamores lined a creekbed littered with boulders. Down the canyon it was a million-dollar view to the Botanic Garden, the city and the sea, with the cloud layer unrolling over the coastline like wool. Jesse slowed.

'Right here, Isaac passed me. He goes, last one to the top buys the beer.'

We were going to trace their final journey together.

'It was a gorgeous day, a hell of a day. It's a mile up the canyon to this point, and we were pumping, really gunning it. Jesus, Isaac went balls-to-the-wall. Always.'

The road climbed steeply. The hillside rose on our left and fell away sharply to our right, through tall grass down to the creekbed. There was no guard rail.

Jesse pulled over and cut the engine. An unsettling quiet flowed around us.

'I pulled ahead of him by a couple of feet,' he said. 'Twenty-four inches, that was the difference between us. The only sound was our breathing, and the pedals turning. Until we heard the BMW.'

I rested my hand on his shoulder.

'High revs. The engine was just screaming, he must have been redlining it. I always thought it was because Brand was too busy getting blown to shift, you know, she was leaning across the stick. But that wasn't it. He was accelerating at us.'

His hands gripped the steering wheel, knuckles white.

'The noise, it just filled me up. And it was – bang, I went into the windshield.' His muscles were rigid. 'He hit us so hard it blew my shoes off. I don't think they ever found them. And Isaac had a necklace, a crucifix Adam gave him. Just gone.'

He looked toward the edge of the road.

'I went over the side, into the air for what felt like forever. I hear this sound, and realize it's me, hitting the ground. I'm going ass over ankles with the bike, just going over and over. Until I blacked out.'

He clutched the steering wheel.

'When my vision came back I was face down on top of the bike. Dirt up my nose and grass in my mouth, I knew I was hurt and it was bad. I lifted my head, and saw Isaac. He was just uphill from me, on his back. His arms were thrown out from his sides. He wasn't moving, his face was turned away. I called to him. I tried to get up but couldn't, kept calling his name. His head, he, all this blood—'

He pulled off his sunglasses.

'I saw, thought I saw his hand move. Was sure. He was fighting. I tried to get to him and I—' He squeezed his eyes shut. 'Just wanted to hold his hand. Tell him he wasn't alone, hang on. He was six feet from me, right there.'

He fought for his voice. 'And I couldn't fucking move.'

He backhanded his fist into the door. 'Brand put me in the dirt with a broken back, and Isaac died alone.'

He hit the door again, and fumbled for the handle, shoved the door open, and swung his legs onto the pavement. He wrangled the wheelchair from the back seat and hopped on.

I got out. We were parked at the edge of the hill, and I watched my step. I walked around the car to see him sideways on the road, gripping his push-rims to keep from rolling downhill. I looked at him with alarm.

'Jesse—'

'Don't, Evan.'

God, how I hated this. I bit my tongue, kept my hands at my sides, didn't step toward him. He let nobody push him, ever.

He set his shoulders and swung around, cutting an S-curve, working uphill to get around the car. He aimed for the side of the road and I followed. I heard an engine up the hill. He headed off the asphalt onto the shoulder, stopping near the drop-off. I watched to see that he set his brakes. A pickup truck curved past, heading downhill.

I knelt down next to him. 'Don't punish yourself.'

'You don't understand, I'm not talking about guilt, I'm talking about what Brand did to Isaac. He stole the only solace he could have had, at the final moment of his life.'

He stared over the edge, his eyes cobalt in the sunlight.

'I hate him, Evan.' He pressed his fist against his heart. 'So much that it gives me chest pain. It's like this *thing* inside me, a snake, with teeth, and it crawls and chews on me.'

I put my hand on his arm.

'I thought I was past it, I truly did. Told myself life's short, don't waste it on anger. Hatred only gives him power. And I didn't want him to have any power over me. But.' His voice trailed off. 'But he did it intentionally. If I see him again, if I get close to him, I don't know what I'll do.'

He shook his head, as though pushing away the thought. Exhaled.

'Adam's the one we have to worry about. You saw him outside the police station, that look on his face.'

'Like the guilt train had derailed inside his head,' I said.

He ran a hand through his hair. 'He's always had trouble with what happened to me. Now it'll be ten times worse.'

I held onto his arm.

'Half the time he thinks it's horrible that I got my ticket punched, no exchanges, no refunds, lifetime guarantee. The other half he sees me and thinks, why can't that be Isaac?' He looked down the hillside. 'I can't walk, big deal. I'm here. Isaac isn't. And I agree with him. I am so goddammed glad to be alive. But how could I ever tell him that?'

I had no answer.

'Keep your ears open. He won't talk to me but maybe he'll talk to you.'

'I don't know.'

'Evan, he loves you like a sister. You didn't know that? Because you love me. You make me happy, and he thinks the world of you because of that.'

'Oh, Jesse.'

He touched my face. 'You do, you know.'

Raising an arm to his face, he wiped his eyes on the sleeve of his T-shirt.

I said, 'Can we continue this conversation in the car?'

'Too much catharsis for one day? Yeah, fine.'

He flipped off the brakes. Half-consciously I put a hand out in front of him. He gave me a wry look.

'Planning to throw yourself in front of me if I start to go over the edge?'

'Something like that.'

He spun sharply. 'Don't worry. Once was enough.'

He pushed onto the asphalt, and I felt myself easing down. Until he swung out into the road.

'What are you doing?' I said.

He looked up and down the hill. 'What do you see?'

'You in the middle of the road, with no way to evade oncoming traffic.'

'My point exactly.'

My toes were cramping. I looked down the hill. The road bent

83

around the mountainside. With the trees, brush, and curves, I couldn't see anything until almost the bottom of the canyon. I thought about the hit-and-run: Jesse and Isaac taking off after work and heading out to ride through wooded back roads.

'Brand tracked you down,' I said.

'Exactly. But how the hell did he know where to find us?'

Eleven

'Let me get the chair,' I said.

He started to protest, but, perhaps seeing sweat on my upper lip, acquiesced. He transferred to the driver's seat and I put the wheelchair into the back. I barely got in before he jammed the car in gear and pulled out.

'Brand tracked us. He hunted us down.' He drove uphill, looking for a place to turn around. 'How? Did Isaac mention we were going riding to people at work? Maybe Brand called Firedog and they told him.'

The road twisted upward for a quarter mile and dead ended. He turned around.

'He must have watched Isaac leave work, and followed him. He waited until we cleared downtown, until we got into the hills, when nobody else was in sight.'

His voice was returning to normal, but he was now consciously ignoring the callousness of the facts: Brand knew all along that Jesse was riding with Isaac, and didn't care.

'And there's a big piece of the puzzle I don't understand.' He gave me a stark look.

I gave it back. 'The woman.'

'You got it.'

Mystery number one. Who was the woman in the car with Franklin Brand?

'What did she do after the crash? She certainly didn't leap out and try to help us. And what does that tell you?' he said.

It hit me. 'That she was Brand's accomplice.'

'From the start.'

That's when his cellphone started ringing. It was in the glove compartment. I got it and answered, 'Jesse Blackburn's phone.'

'Jesse Blackburn's boss,' Lavonne Marks said. 'Jesse Blackburn's late.'

I cringed. 'Hold on.'

'No time. Tell him to get his keester into the office, pronto.'

I ran out to the curb in front of my house with clothes for him: a button-down shirt, a sports coat, and a tie. He was two hours late for work and didn't have time to drive home, didn't even have time to get out of the car and come inside to change.

I saw him pulling off his T-shirt. My neighbor Helen Potts, watering her plants with a hand-held sprinkler, gave him the gimlet eye. When I opened the driver's door and she saw him, bare-chested, the sprinkler veered wildly. Maybe she thought his jeans were coming off next.

I handed him the shirt. He whipped it on and started buttoning it up.

'Lavonne's going to kill me.' He stretched his neck to do the top button on the shirt. 'Tie.'

I handed it over. He looked at it, said, 'Tweety Bird?'

'The alternative was a Happy Face. With a bullet hole through its forehead.'

He started knotting. 'You're confiscating my joke ties?'

'As a public service.' I handed him the jacket.

He threw it on the passenger seat and fired up the engine. 'I'll call later.'

The tires squealed. I watched him go, thinking that Lavonne would understand. She would grumble at him, because Sanchez Marks was her pride and passion, built up over two decades from the sole practice she started as an ungainly girl from Philly, barreling her way into Santa Barbara's genteel legal fraternity. She demanded excellence from everyone at the firm, most of all herself. But she wouldn't kill Jesse for being late, not today, for beneath her brisk intensity lay a soft spot for his heart and tenacity.

I ran my fingers through my hair. A grab-bag of fears rattled in my mind. Biggest was the thought that Brand had confederates. If he was working with Mickey Yago and if they wanted to intimidate Jesse, how far would they go?

I turned toward my garden gate. As I did, a sports car cruised up the street, honking and flashing its headlights. It was a little red Mazda with Oklahoma plates. An arm poked out the driver's window, waving.

I stood rooted to the sidewalk. She'd already seen me. It was too late to run, and if I dove into the hedge, Helen Potts would rat me out.

The car pulled up and a woman jumped out, squealing, 'Evan!'

It was my cousin, Taylor Delaney Boggs. She skipped toward me, arms extended, shivering her fingers like a Fosse dancer. Her nails matched the red paint on the Mazda.

She said, 'Hello, darling.'

That's darling, rhymes with marlin.

And she was on me, gym-strong arms rocking me back and forth, one-two, like a metronome. Her Talbots ensemble was crisply pressed. Her honey-brown highlights rose above her scalp like solar flares riding a trail of hairspray.

Her nails gripped my shoulders. 'Look at you, Californian to the last inch.' She smoothed a lock of hair away from my eyes. 'This is such an adorable little hairstyle. It looks like you . . . jumped out of a plane.'

'When did you get in?'

'Night before last, drove from Oklahoma City.' She stared at me with eyes the color of blueberry pie. 'You don't sound surprised to see me. Who told?'

'Brian.'

She stamped her foot. 'Spoilsport.'

Jesus, rapture me, I thought.

'Ed Eugene's working seven-on, seven-off on one of y'all's offshore platforms. It's amazing you can see them from the beach. After all this time with him commuting to the North Sea, now I can go and wave to him.'

She tilted her head. Waiting. 'Well? Aren't you going to ask me in?'

I felt myself gesturing toward the garden gate, heard my voice inviting her in. I was trapped. Whatever I said, whatever she saw, would be reported to my family within twenty-four hours. But I had no reason to refuse. When I was seventeen, I'd told her I had leprosy. So I'd used that excuse right up. She was the nosiest, talkiest woman west of the Mississippi, and she was moving onto my turf.

Walking along the path, she pointed at the Vincents' house. 'Who lives there?'

'My college roommate.' Telling myself, don't volunteer information. Name, rank, serial number, soldier.

'How sweet,' Taylor said. 'And she lives in that big old place all by herself?'

'With her husband and baby.'

She nodded, storing the fact away, saying, 'Speaking of babies, Kendall's only five months along and she's gained forty pounds.' Kendall was another cousin. 'But you know what Aunt Julie says. When Kendall's pregnant, buy stock in KFC.'

She paused for breath, smiling at me. 'And what about you?'

So there we had it, a new record: from *hello* to *when will you breed?* in under two minutes. I opened the French doors and ushered her inside.

She clapped her hands. 'Well, isn't this just as cute as can be?'

Here was the trouble with Taylor: while she was the world's biggest gossip and buttinsky, she had a witchy ability to shield her own life from scrutiny. There were no scandals in her past, no teenage peccadilloes, no story about her barfing at Grandma and Granddad's fiftieth anniversary picnic. No, that would be me. She had gotten straight A's. She starred in school plays. When she came out, it was as a debutante, not a lesbian. She had a church wedding, and if her husband had a hick name, so did my male cousins, and if his job left grease under his fingernails, well, honk if you love the oil business, that's what made Oklahoma great. Taylor had no flip side. Nobody told stories about her. We had a gossip gap.

She stopped near the kitchen, examining an Ansel Adams print. 'It's kind of stark. Real outdoorsy. But you always were a tomboy.'

She continued perusing the room. I felt my angst meter rising, and I scanned the room too, trying to stay ahead of her. No anarchist literature lying around. No Star Trek stemware. What else . . . argh, the wedding mound. I couldn't let her get hold of my wedding plans. I stepped in front of it, but the thing had grown so large I couldn't block her view. I couldn't remember the last time I'd touched it. I was at the point where I dreaded reaching into the center of it, for fear I'd let oxygen in and it might spontaneously combust.

She looked toward my bedroom door. 'Ooh, let's check out your boudoir.'

What could go wrong there? What couldn't?

But she was already through the door. She stopped, said, 'Oh.'

She was staring at my bed. It was made. No socks hanging from the bedposts, no drool on the pillow.

'It's Grandma's quilt,' she said. 'You have Grandma's quilt.'

'Yes, she gave it to Mom, and Mom gave it to me.'

She looked at me with an unusual expression on her face. Her lipstick was cracking. 'I told Grandma I wanted it. She knew that. Everybody knew that.'

'Taylor, I—'

She looked away, waved her hand. 'Never mind. It's just a shock, is all.'

Over a *quilt*?

Spinning on her sandals, she hurried back into the living room, and that's when she saw the photos on the mantle. There was one of Brian, smiling from the cockpit of an F/A-18 Hornet, and another of me hugging Luke. And one of Jesse, a great shot, a close up of him in the sunset, grinning. She picked it up. And here we went, on the Tilt-a-Whirl.

'Is this your fiancé?' Her forehead crinkled. 'Why . . . he's very handsome.'

89

'I think so.'

'My goodness. But he's—'

She peered hard at the photo, and actually tipped it up and down. I knew she was trying to imagine what the rest of him looked like. I had an urge to clutch the photo to my chest, protecting it. She was going to say it, I knew she was . . .

'But isn't he handicapped?'

I felt like screaming. 'He has a spinal cord injury.'

Illumination. 'So he wasn't born that way.'

'No, he—' I stopped myself from saying *had an accident*. 'He was hit by a car.'

'And you're fixing to marry him anyway.'

'Yes. No. I mean, not "anyway".'

She looked at me, and I knew without a doubt that back in Oklahoma she had speculated about me, and my wedding plans, at length. She and my girl cousins, Kendall, Cameron, Mackenzie, a bunch of successful women whose names sounded like counties . . . and how had the discussion run? *What is up with Evan? Did she hit thirty and turn desperate?*

She touched my arm. 'Bless your heart. You are really a special lady.'

'I'm lucky. He's a great guy.'

'Listen to you. I'll bet you just give him the courage to keep on living.' She examined the photo again. 'But, getting married. Have y'all checked it out with doctors and everything?'

It. Don't respond . . .

But her blueberry eyes looked eager. 'You know.'

. . . she'll take your words and repackage them as ammunition . . .

'Hon, I'm talking about marital relations.'

I lost it. 'You mean, can he do it?'

'You don't need to put it that crudely.'

'But that's what you mean.'

'Why are you so touchy? It's a perfectly understandable question.'

'Really.'

'Everybody naturally wonders—'

'*Everybody?*'

My blood pressure shot up so fast, I'm surprised my eyeballs didn't burst out and smack her in the cheeks.

'Tell everybody that we do it ten times a day. I have to guzzle power drinks to keep my weight up. We keep a fire extinguisher beside the bed so the freakin' sheets don't catch fire.'

The look on her face was both shocked and lascivious. 'Well.'

That's when the phone rang, rescuing me. Or so I thought. It was Harley Dawson.

'I just got a call from Mako Technologies,' she said. 'Adam Sandoval's at their office, causing a riot. Get over there and help calm the situation down, girl.'

Twelve

I pulled in to Mako Technologies in Goleta, hoping I wouldn't find a fistfight in the parking lot. I knew Harley had called me hoping a friend could convince Adam to leave, rather than having security guards drag him away. And she thought getting Jesse over there would only add fuel to the flames. I was still sputtering about Taylor's remarks, the lurid glow in her eyes . . . *Everybody naturally wonders.* Her curiosity was ravenous. Even as I rushed her out of the house, she asked, 'Who was on the phone? Who's in trouble? Is it Jesse?' And as I jumped in my car, she said, 'We'll talk. I'll take you to lunch tomorrow. Someplace nice, so spruce yourself up.'

I ground my teeth together.

Mako's headquarters spread across several buildings in a business park. With their mustard-colored walls and exterior struts painted white, they looked like shoeboxes held up by slide rules. The parking lot shone with new cars.

No fight. So far, so good.

I pushed open the door into the lobby. The walls were decorated with posters advertising Mako's products – 'Tigershark: security against hacking, viruses, and insider threats' and 'Hammerhead: protecting your infrastructure against intrusion.' Photos portrayed Mako's history: men with slicked-back hair standing next to electronic boxes, surrounded by cabling and other slickbacks in lab coats or military uniform. There was none of the trendy aspiration of Diamond Mindworks.

However, behind the desk was something directly out of Cal Diamond's company: the receptionist. It was the girl with the pudgy cheeks and unruly black hair, who had been crying on the phone the day Diamond suffered his heart attack. She was drinking a Slimfast shake and eating a glazed donut. Her 'Hi, I'm Amber Gibbs' plaque sat next to a Beanie Baby frog.

I said, 'I'm looking for Dr Adam Sandoval.'

'The professor guy? Okay.' She started punching buttons on a phone console. 'But I don't think you'll have to go looking. You can follow the noise.'

My teeth started to grind again. Past the front desk I saw a security door with a keypad. It had a window, and down the hallway on the other side I saw secretaries at their desks and men chatting by a vending machine. Amber spoke on the phone and hung up.

'It'll just be a minute,' she said. 'Can you tell me what is up with him? He came in saying he had to see Mr Rudenski Senior about a murder.'

'Yep, I'll bet. Can I go back and find him?'

'Who got murdered?'

'His brother.'

'Oh.' Her mouth blossomed. 'That's horrible.' She blinked several times. 'Did it happen here at Mako?'

'No.' I looked at her frightened face, realizing she was new, and may not have known the flurry about Brand. 'Is this your first day here?'

'Yeah. Diamond Mindworks laid me off.' She shrugged. 'It's okay, things are getting weird over there. The donuts are gone, and the Coke machine. I'm like, hello, the donuts didn't make Mr Diamond go cardiac, do we all have to suffer?'

Then I did hear the noise, coming from beyond the security door. Men's voices raised in anger. I looked through the window and saw Adam in the hallway, arms in the air, talking at Kenny Rudenski. I heard him mention Mako's computer records. Kenny pointed a finger and Adam swatted it away as if it were a buzzing fly.

I said, 'Amber, unlock the door. Now.'

She froze. 'I don't know . . .'

'Come on.' I peered through the door. Adam was yelling. Kenny crossed his arms. He looked starchy in a white shirt and designer tie. His expression combined recalcitrance and condescension. I pounded on the door. Adam frowned at me and kept talking.

'Evan.' Harley came into the lobby, her heels hammering the linoleum. She was sculpted into an Armani suit, swinging a handbag as small and sleek as a blackjack.

'Be nice if we could stop Kenny and Adam from coming to blows,' I said.

She looked at Amber. 'I'm Harley Dawson, Mako's counsel. Open the door.'

Amber jumped up. 'Yes, ma'am.'

She came around the desk and punched a code into the keypad. Harley opened the door and we went in.

Adam was saying, 'You can't brush me aside.'

Kenny shook his head. 'I'm not. But you can't just barge in here and commandeer our records.'

Harley walked toward Adam with her palms up, trying for conciliation. 'Dr Sandoval.'

Kenny raised his hands and backed away from Adam. 'Here you go, amigo. Put your demands to our attorney.' He looked at Harley. 'He claims we've been sitting on proof of murder for three years.'

Adam said, 'I've told his father, it's all in your computer systems, proof that Brand killed my brother deliberately.'

Harley said, 'That's a strong accusation, sir.'

'It's the truth.'

She shoved her silver hair away from her face, and looked around. Several secretaries, the cluster of men at the vending machine, and Amber were watching us as though we were an amateur production of *Cat on a Hot Tin Roof*.

She pointed at Kenny. 'In your office.'

We marched past his wide-eyed secretary into a corner office that faced the beach and university. It had sofas and soft lighting and an ostentatious desk. Adam stalked in and planted himself in the center of the room. He was not going to be moved until he was ready.

94

Harley said, 'Dr Sandoval, I'll look at any documentation you provide, and—'

'I've already given it to the police. I want Mako to pre-emptively protect their records so nobody can tamper with them.'

Kenny said, 'Data protection is our bread and butter. Why don't you dial the intensity back down into the visible spectrum?'

Harley's nostrils were wide. She was struggling to maintain her composure. 'You've already been to the police?'

I said, 'That's where you take evidence of a crime, counselor.'

She looked from me to Kenny. She said nothing, but her aura was emanating *crap-o-rama*.

Adam said, 'I'm talking about doing the right thing. You shouldn't have to wait for a warrant, or a subpoena, you should stand up.'

Kenny said, 'You have nothing to worry about. Mako has severed all ties with Franklin Brand.'

A golf club was leaning next to the desk. Kenny picked it up and took a swing. Watching him work on his grip in the face of Adam's righteous grief, I decided that if Adam took the club and bent it around Kenny's neck, I would put my finger on it so he could tie it in a bow.

I said, 'I saw you give Brand a ride from the jail to his motel the other day.'

Harley said, 'What?'

I said, 'Did you put up his bail bond?'

Harley said, 'Don't answer that.'

Kenny ignored her. 'No, I didn't.'

I said, 'Why did Brand look so unhappy when you dropped him off?'

Harley pointed at him. 'Don't. This conversation is finished.'

She looked tighter than a highwire. For a second I felt remorseful. She was on the verge of losing control of the situation. But I'd just caught Kenny in a lie.

Kenny said, 'He wanted money.'

Harley hissed out a breath.

I said, 'Why?'

'Because he's a butthole.' Backswing, stroke, follow-through. 'He claims Mako owes him his annual bonus for the year he disappeared.'

Harley said, 'Why didn't you tell me this?'

'I told Dad. It wasn't a legal issue, it was greed. I told Brand to piss off.'

Adam looked as though he was having trouble swallowing. 'Why did he come back? What does he want?'

'I don't know.'

'You know who the woman was, don't you? The anonymous caller, she's from Mako, isn't she?'

Harley said, 'Kenny, don't even speculate.'

He took another swing. 'I'll tell you what I think. I think there wasn't any woman in the car with him.'

The same thought had occurred to me, but that's not why his statement surprised me. 'When did you concede that he was the driver?'

He shrugged. 'Three years on the run? At some point, denying it started sounding lame.'

Adam said, 'I thought he was your friend.'

'So did I.' He stopped swinging the club. 'But he's a leech. He latches onto things and sucks them dry. I'm talking business, friends, women.'

I said, 'Do you think the woman was an ex with a grudge?'

'Here's what I think,' he said. 'The caller was some chick he tricked into picking him up after he set fire to his Beemer. You know – hey, baby, the car broke down. Can you come get me? She shows up and he smells like smoke and gasoline. Later she hears about the hit-and-run, puts two and two together. Decides she doesn't like being made a—' he snapped his fingers. 'What do you call it, Harley?'

'Accessory after the fact,' she said.

'He's a user. Capital U. And I ought to know, since I'm the idiot who brought him onboard at Mako.' He shook his head. 'Never hire somebody more ambitious than yourself. They'll stick the blade between your ribs, every time.'

I tasted acid in my mouth. Kenny thought this was about him. If he felt any anger, it was at being betrayed by Brand. I saw no evidence of sympathy for Isaac.

His phone rang. He answered it, talked. 'Dad wants to see us, Harley.'

Adopting a serious expression, he turned to Adam. 'Brand's caught in the court system. And the police have all the information you turned up. It's out of our hands.'

His gaze settled on Adam's crucifix. 'Mexican silver, right?' He reached out, took it between his fingers, and started rubbing it. 'Looks like you got a higher power you should be calling on right now.'

Adam raised a hand and removed the cross from Kenny's fingers. His eyes looked like arrowheads.

He said, 'Let's go, Evan.'

We walked out of the office. Kenny's voice followed us.

'Light a candle, doc. That's what you should be doing. Saying Hail Marys.'

Outside, Adam stalked toward his pickup truck. He carried himself as though he was expecting a punch, ready to clench a fist at the slightest provocation.

'Pray to the Virgin. Treating me like a campesino, thinking I wouldn't know I was being insulted.' He wheeled on me. 'And what were you doing here? Did you think I was going to tear the lobby apart, or pour gasoline over myself and strike a match?'

'Please, that's not it.'

'Franklin Brand murdered my brother. I cannot repeat that word enough. Murdered. Murdered. I am not overreacting.'

'I know you're not.'

'I'm not suffering a breakdown, or going fuzzy-headed. To the contrary, I'm seeing things with astounding clarity.' His hands clenched and released. 'Don't worry about me. Take care of Jesse. He needs you now more than ever.'

'Of course I will.'

'He was run down and left to die because Brand was after Isaac.

He was treated like litter.' He put a hand to his forehead. 'It's ghastly.'

He looked toward the beach, the university sitting on the bluff in the distance.

'George Rudenski is going to look into things,' he said. 'For what that's worth.'

'That's good.'

'Not good enough.'

Cue the straight line. 'What would be good enough?'

He looked at me. 'Brand's head on a pike.'

Half a second after I started the Explorer, Amber Gibbs bounced through Mako's front door. She looked like a kid set free for recess. I started to call to her and changed my mind, not wanting Mako people to see me asking her questions.

She unlocked a blue Schwinn from a bike rack and pedaled away toward the shopping center up the road. I beat her there, and was waiting when she puffed in and dismounted. When she strolled into Jerry's, I was behind her.

Diners crowded the Formica tables. The TV in the corner was showing the Dodgers game. While Amber read the menu on the wall, I ordered a taco. I sat down and heard her tell the counterman, 'Burrito, two tacos, large pintos with extra cheese. And a Diet Coke.'

She turned around to find a seat.

I said, 'Pull up a chair.' She sat down at the table. 'You're having quite a first day on the job.'

'No lie.' She smoothed her unruly hair.

'How do you like Mako so far?'

'It's complicated. There's all these departments, and two mister Rudenskis, and an internal computer network with a million security rules.'

I tried to look sympathetic. 'Well, cyber-security is Mako's business. Didn't Diamond Mindworks have security rules?'

'If a reporter phones, hang up,' she said. 'And if anybody comes in looking for Mr Diamond, tell him he's gone for the day.'

'Be glad you don't work there anymore, Amber.'

Her forehead crinkled with confusion.

'Lucky you got another job so quickly,' I said.

'Mrs Diamond put in a good word.'

'Mrs Mari-with-the-yapping-Chihuahua Diamond?'

'For all of us who got laid off.' She played with her hair. 'I know what you're thinking, she's scary. She is. But, because of the circumstances, she did it.'

'What circumstances?'

The counterman called our orders. Amber's selections took up three-fourths of the table. Her burrito was a glistening package the size of a cat.

I said again, 'What circumstances?'

'The divorce.'

My taco looked magnificent, with the shredded chicken and salsa and cheese. I didn't even take a bite.

'Whose divorce?'

'The Diamonds.'

'When did this happen?'

'The day of his heart attack. That's what they were yelling about in his office before he collapsed, I heard.'

I put my taco down. Thinking – but I'm the one she slapped that day. Or maybe just the last one she slapped.

Amber twitched on the plastic chair. 'What you told me, about your friend whose brother died? What's going on with that?'

'He was run down and killed by Mako's former VP of business development.'

She put a forkful of burrito in her mouth. 'Who?'

I looked around and saw a pile of newspapers on a table. I got them, riffled through, and found a photo of Brand at the courthouse. She looked at it, chewing.

'I know him,' she said.

'You do?'

'He's the dog guy.'

I watched her chew. 'What dog guy?'

'Who gave Caesar to Mrs Diamond.'

She took another bite. I waved my hands.

'Her Chihuahua,' she said.

'How do you know this?'

She wiped the corner of her mouth with a napkin. 'I took some papers to the Diamonds' house one time. He was there, and Mrs D was all gushy over this puppy, about the size of a shaved mouse. She said he gave it to her. He—'

Her face went stark. She was looking over my shoulder, at Kenny Rudenski standing in the doorway.

He hooked a finger at me. 'Come on, Gidget. Let's go for a drive.'

The last bit was the easiest, though the road was steep and curving. With the hairpin turns Kenny had to slow the Porsche, and I could keep him in sight. It had been tougher following him on the freeway, because he liked to gun the Porsche in and out between cars, as if daring me to keep up. His vanity license plate read 2KPSECUR – to keep secure – which fit with Mako's work but not with his driving.

'Follow me,' he'd said. 'I'll tell you whatever you want to know.'

I wanted to know about Franklin Brand, and Kenny's connection to him.

We were now north of Foothill Road and winding upward toward the mountains. The tall grass was yellow in the ravine below. Avocado orchards unrolled green across the foothills, and La Cumbre peak stretched toward the sky. Houses clung to the slope, huge places with jutting balconies. Downshifting around a switchback, I watched the Porsche brake and turn into a driveway. I followed.

Kenny's villa was a Mediterranean fantasy of palms and gold stone, nestled between the road and the ravine. The view took in the city and the Channel Islands. The ocean was a carpet of light, sapphire brilliant.

He climbed out of the Porsche. 'You stuck to my tail. Not too shabby. Come in, we'll have a drink.'

Next to the front door was a plaque with the name of the house. *Mistryss*. He unlocked the door and I noticed the security camera mounted above the frame. Inside he punched a code into a beeping alarm panel. We walked into an atrium with a skylight, marble floor and spiral staircase, and from there into a vast living room with white carpeting, a Steinway grand, and Warhol prints bright on the walls. The back of the house was a solid wall of glass facing the ravine. Outside were a swimming pool and expansive lawn.

'Want a beer?' he said.

'Club soda's fine.'

'I thought you'd be more fun than that.'

'I need to drive back down the hill.'

'I have Chardonnay.' He got himself a Beck's. 'Or something stronger, if your tastes run along another line.'

Another line? Did he mean cocaine?

He said, 'We're going to spar, you need something to put you in the mood.'

'Spar? I left my mouthguard at the gym.'

'Verbally. Like back at the office.' He opened the Beck's. 'I'll start. Don't pump my employees for dirt. Ever.'

'I don't work for you, Kenny.'

'Anything you want to know, ask me personally. The muff diver isn't here to stop me from answering.'

My mouth felt sour. 'Ah, *sparring*. Insulting my friends, you mean.'

'It's no secret about Harley. She's self-professed. A lioness, and she likes her meat fresh. She teaches that class at the university so she can trawl for students.' He pointed the beer bottle at me. 'Were you her student?'

He was standing too close again, getting that thirsty look on his face.

'No,' I said. 'And I've changed my mind. Make it champagne.'

He snorted. 'Taittinger okay?'

'Sure,' I said, pretending I knew what the hell it was.

He went into the hallway and unlocked a door. I heard him trotting down a staircase, realized I was in a house with an actual wine cellar.

I gazed around. Framed photos stippled the walls, eight-by-ten glossies of Kenny with athletes, TV stars, and stuntmen. Other pictures showed him motocross racing, dirt bikes skidding through a turn, flinging dust.

Also framed was a glossy magazine article titled 'Santa Barbara's Most Eligible Bachelors.' Kenny's photo showed him posed against the hood of his Porsche. The copy gushed, describing him as the 'scion of the Mako technology empire.' It skimmed over a divorce, and turned maudlin. 'But Kenny's life isn't all power lunches and glittering charity balls. He has a sensitive side, and it has been brushed with tragedy.' It mentioned the death of a high school girlfriend, quoting Kenny: 'When I lost Yvette, I withdrew into my studies. Even today, I tend to shield myself with my work. It will take a special lady to hold my attention.'

No, I thought; it will take an antimatter lady to repel your relentless flirting.

And then I felt callous. I wondered if losing this girl was what turned Kenny toward risk-taking. Death sometimes did. Maybe that, rather than overweening ego, explained his fascination with motorcycles and fast cars. The braggart, the daredevil persona, hiding the fearful boy desperate to feel in control.

I wandered further around the living room. The Warhols overlooked a collection of sports memorabilia: display cases filled with auto racing souvenirs. There was a crash helmet signed by Dale Earnhardt. A pair of driving gloves, with the label: *Ayrton Senna*. And a Nomex driving suit with an illegible signature. The label said, *Mark Donohue, Indianapolis* 1972.

I heard footsteps coming back up the stairs from the cellar, the door shutting and a key turning in the lock. A moment later a cork popped, and soon Kenny came into the living room carrying my glass of champagne.

He found me looking at his memorabilia. 'You like auto racing?'
'I don't know much about it.'

He handed me the champagne and gestured to the display cases. 'Mark Donohue was an Indy Five Hundred winner. Senna, had to be the greatest Formula One driver ever. Dale Earnhardt was a NASCAR legend.'

I noticed the past tense. I looked at the displays again, getting a funny feeling.

'They all died on the track, didn't they?'

He touched each case in turn, tracing his fingers up and down the Plexiglas. 'Donohue, practicing for the 1975 Austrian Grand Prix. Senna at Imola, 1994. Earnhardt – what can you say? Bought it on the final lap of the Daytona 500. February eighteenth, 2001.'

This champagne, too, was spectacular. What had I been drinking all my life, dishwashing liquid? Kenny stared at the Senna display for a moment longer, his fingers working on the Plexiglas.

'They're all race-worn items. Primo, primo stuff.' He turned on a boyish smile, but I didn't think his primary interest in these things was financial.

I looked around. 'Now I understand all your security precautions.'

'Hey, security's my business.' He waved a hand around the room. 'Camera's on you, right now.'

Another sour note. 'So much for privacy.'

'Privacy is dead, Gidget. We're in the era of total surveillance.' He drank his beer.

'All hail Big Brother.'

'Sweetheart, corporate America is Big Brother,' he said. 'Know how much technology exists to invade your privacy? Start with web cookies tracking the sites you visit. Smartcards with ID chips. Biometric software that performs voice or retina recognition. Cellphones that work as personal trackers. Parents who want to microchip their kids so they can know where they are every second of their lives.'

'You trying to scare me, or give me a sales pitch?'

'I'm asking, do you think these things are threats, or conveniences? You want absolute privacy? Of course not. It would be a nightmare for national security, law enforcement, public health, and free speech.'

He stood back and took a long draft of the beer.

'You're good, Kenny.'

'You bet your bottom dollar. That's why I'm VP of Marketing.' He finished the beer and threw the bottle in a wastebasket. 'Okay, the ballbuster isn't here. What do you really want to know?'

'When did you find out that Brand was embezzling money from Mako?'

'A month after he skipped town.'

He couldn't have sounded more casual. He ambled to the bar and got another beer.

He said, 'I take it you're talking about the Firedog thing. What happened, your buddy the professor figure it out?'

'In essence.'

'What, it turns out his brother kept records?'

'Didn't Mako?' I said.

'Yeah, but you can guess. Frank cooked the books. He set up a fake round of investment funding in Firedog, and gifted it to himself. And when a clerk in our treasury department got finicky and called Firedog to ask where their share certificates were, the prof's brother—'

'Isaac Sandoval.' Blessed Mary, couldn't he remember Isaac's name?

'Yeah. He pestered Frank about it. So Frank counterfeited the certificates and handed them in to Mako's treasury.'

'How did he expect to get away with it?' I said.

'He used the angel fund like a three-card monty game. Now you see it, now you don't, now it's over there. And he was a VP at Mako. Nobody questioned him.'

'You're going to tell the police all this, I presume.'

'No. This is a private conversation.'

I felt my face heating. 'Private?' I looked around at the air, indicating the security camera he claimed was monitoring us.

'If the authorities ever got hold of the record of this conversation, it would show us saying and doing exactly what I want it to. So if you quote me, I'll deny it.' Thirsty smile. 'Unless you'd like to continue this discussion over dinner.'

I put down my champagne. 'No, thank you.'

'Your loss.' He was still smiling. 'Sure you don't want something stronger than Taittinger?'

Again with the innuendo. Did he mean drugs, or sex? 'I'm sure. Thanks for the drink.'

I headed out the front door. I heard music coming from an upstairs window, and looked up at a balcony. Someone was sitting outside, a young woman from the look of the bare feet propped on the railing. I couldn't see past her knees, but caught sight of an unusual tattoo. It looked like a black snake running up her leg.

Kenny stood in the doorway. 'Call me, Gidget. Anytime. I'm always happy to talk.'

When I got home, I called Harley Dawson.

'What, precisely, is wrong with Kenny Rudenski? Does he have an extra chromosome? He wanted to discuss Isaac's murder over dinner.'

'I know, he's incorrigible,' she said. 'Listen, he isn't a bad guy, but he's up to his neck in what's about to become very nasty publicity for Mako.'

'He has a funny way of handling pressure. Using death as a pick-up line.'

'This is going to trash Mako's reputation. George Rudenski grew his company by building secure networks for defense contractors and outfits like the NSA. How's it going to look that he didn't know one of his VPs was sticking his hand in the cookie jar, right down the hall from him?'

'Do you mean Kenny didn't tell his dad about the missing stock certificates?'

'He thought he could handle it by himself.'

I held tight to the phone, saying nothing, hearing dead air on the other end. Did Harley realize what she had just done?

'Evan – I didn't mean to say that.'

She had just violated attorney-client privilege, telling me about private discussions with the Rudenskis.

'Please . . . oh, shit.' She breathed into the receiver. 'Just – can you just forget I ever said that.'

But the genie was out of the bottle. 'Unless I'm asked.'

'Damn it, cut me some slack here.'

'Harley, what is going on with you?'

'It's this Brand garbage. Christ on a pony, the SEC's going to land on Mako. Shareholders will file class action lawsuits.'

'Excuse me?' I couldn't believe what I was hearing. 'This "Brand garbage"? We're talking about the murder of a young man.'

There was a long pause. 'Please, Evan. Please, forget it.'

I didn't know what to say.

Jesse took a break for lunch around one thirty. He headed down to the market on the street corner. There were tables on the sidewalk. The owner went out periodically and asked the homeless man not to shout religious slogans at passing cars. Jesse got an Italian meatball sandwich and a salad.

He decided to eat at a table outside, in the shade, rather than go back to the office. Get a few minutes to himself, think. He took off his half-fingered gloves and picked up the sandwich.

The fat man was sitting at the table next to him. He was dressed in black. Reeboks, bulging jeans, T-shirt. His round-rimmed glasses looked as if they'd been nudged halfway into his eye sockets. The chin beard was a just ginger squiggle below his lips. He looked like a helium-balloon version of a French intellectual. Inflatable Sartre.

He caught Jesse's eye. 'Can I borrow your pepper shaker?'

'Sure.'

Jesse leaned forward to pick it up. When he did, the man reached out, grabbed the wheelchair, and pulled him backward to his own table.

'The hell are you doing? Stop.'

The man dropped a manila envelope in his lap. 'Some photos for you.' He stood up. 'We'll be in touch. Bon appetit.'

Inside, the deli man heard Jesse raising his voice, and went to the door. He saw the fat guy hunkering away and Jesse looking at something from an envelope, maybe pictures. Jesse pinched the bridge of his nose. Then he ripped the pictures up.

Thirteen

The dog guy.

Amber Gibbs called Franklin Brand the dog guy. At the Holiday Inn, I had thought I heard a Chihuahua. Mari and Cal Diamond were divorcing, just when Brand turned up in town. One plus one plus one equaled . . . what? I needed to know. And, given Amber's volubility and apparent lack of discretion, I needed to cultivate her as an inside source. I phoned Mako.

She answered, 'I listen to Santa Barbara's hottest hits on KHOT FM!'

A radio deejay chattered in the background, promoting the station's phone contest.

'Amber, Evan Delaney. We were talking at Jerry's.'

'Oh, right.' She cleared her throat, started over. 'Mako Technologies.'

I rubbed my eyes. 'You were telling me about Franklin Brand being friends with Mari Diamond.'

'Yeah, and now it's creeping me out. He killed a guy and I was in the same room with him.'

How blunt should I be? Silly question. 'Was Mrs Diamond having an affair with him?'

A pause. 'I hadn't thought about that.'

She went quiet, maybe engaging her brain in thought neuron by neuron. I sat down at my desk and logged onto my e-mail account.

I said, 'What do other people at Mako say?'

'I don't know.'

'If you hear, would you let me know?'

'Sure. I—' In the background, the radio was urging listeners to call in. 'Gotta go. I'll talk to you later.'

My e-mail program chimed. I had a message from Jakarta Rivera and Tim North.

It was a proposed book contract. They offered me a fee upfront plus a big chunk of any publishing advance and generous royalties. They wanted their names on the cover, but offered me *as told to* credit. The price was good, the terms all reasonable. Then they signed off with this teaser:

We're talking twenty-four years combined work with the Company and the SIS, plus a decade in private espionage. The real deal, stuff that was black and wet and deep. Come on, we know you're intrigued.

Apprehension weeviled up my back again. Black work? Wet work? If they weren't scamming me, if they were indeed the real deal, they were bad. I deleted it.

I stood up, feeling disturbed. Needing to shake out the bugs. I changed clothes and went for a run.

I angled past the Mission, standing formidable against the mountains in the afternoon sun, and headed up the hill on Alameda Padre Serra. I pumped my arms, felt my quads whining. This part of the run I consider penance; it absolves me of pride, lust, gluttony, bragging, and the clothes I wore in the eighties. Maybe even of encouraging Amber to gossip. Burn, quads, burn.

I ran for forty-five minutes. When I finally stopped in front of Nikki's house I bent over and propped my hands on my knees. Rivulets of sweat ran down my face.

Nikki came running out her door with Thea on her hip. 'Jesse came by ten minutes ago, looking for you. Something's lit a fire under him.'

A nut of worry hardened in my stomach. 'Thanks.'

In the house, I reached him on his cellphone.

'I'm on my way to Goleta.' He was talking on the hands-free set, raising his voice over the sound of the engine. 'The shit's hitting the fan. Brand's lawyer knows the cops are looking at the hit-and-run as murder. O'Leary called me, telling me to back the hell off or be sued for harassment.'

'That's absurd.' Sweat stung my eyes and I wiped it away.

'The point is, O'Leary called Adam and threatened him the same way. I had a phone message from Adam. He sounded berserk.'

'Where are you going?' I said.

'To the Holiday Inn. I'm afraid Adam's on his way there to confront Brand.'

I grabbed my car keys. 'It's room 127. I'll be there in fifteen minutes.'

'I'm pulling off the freeway now. Pray I'm not too late, Ev.'

The Sheriffs were at the Holiday Inn when I arrived, two cruisers parked with their lights flashing. I skewed into a parking space and jumped out, running between buildings into the courtyard. My knees felt wobbly.

Ahead on the walkway, a crowd stood outside room 127. I saw Jesse. Tweety Bird smiled a bright yellow smile from his tie, but his face was colorless.

He said, 'It's a mess.'

The door to Brand's room was propped open. I couldn't see inside, but I heard a deputy saying, 'You have the right to remain silent—'

Jesse had heard the tires screech as he swung into the Holiday Inn. He saw Adam's truck near the lobby. He parked and got out, thinking, slow, I'm too slow. He pushed up the ramp and headed for the courtyard. Going along the sidewalk, looking for Brand's room.

And what was he going to say if Franklin Brand opened the door?

Here it was, three years in the making, and still a surprise. Don't punch him, he decided. Not right off.

The courtyard was quiet, the pool empty. The only person in sight was a maid pushing a laundry cart. He counted the room numbers.

127. He stopped, and knocked. 'Brand. Open up.'

He rapped again, harder, and the door moved. He realized that it hadn't been completely shut. He nudged it open.

'Hello?'

He pushed it further open and smelled a metallic smell, heard the sound of labored breathing. The light caught Adam leaning against the wall inside. His face looked sick. He was staring at something Jesse couldn't see, blocked by the door.

Jesse's mouth felt dry. He couldn't believe what was in Adam's hand. A baseball bat.

Adam looked at him. 'It's not. I didn't. Jesse, don't—'

But Jesse shoved the door open. It hit the wall and bounced back. He stopped it with his hand.

'No, Jesus, Adam.'

Lying on the floor beyond the bed, under tangled sheets soaked red with blood, was a body.

Jesse ran his fingers through his hair. A moment later, a deputy said, 'Move back,' and came out of the motel room leading Adam by the arm, with his hands cuffed behind his back. He looked lost.

Jesse said, 'I'll get to the jail as soon as I can.'

Adam tried to nod, tried to open his mouth, seemed unable to do either. He just looked at Jesse over his shoulder as he was led away.

A deputy approached. 'You went in the room?'

'Just as far as the doorway.'

'Touch anything?'

'I pushed the door open.'

'The crime scene people will need to get comparison prints. Don't go away.'

Jesse had been trained the same way I had in lawyering: don't volunteer information, don't run off at the mouth, especially not to the police, and don't repeat hearsay. But he looked at the deputy and said, 'Adam told me he didn't do it.'

'Rightie-o,' the deputy said, walking away.

Fourteen

It was eleven when Jesse came home. The surf was crashing onto the beach, phosphorescing in the night air. He looked exhausted and sad.

I got up from the sofa. 'I saved you some Thai takeout.'

'Thanks, Ev, but I'm just not hungry.'

He unknotted his Tweety Bird tie and flung it on the kitchen counter. From the fridge he took out a bottle of cranberry juice and poured a glass.

'Feeling okay?' I said.

He pressed his knuckles into the small of his back. 'Just staying on top of things.'

Paraplegics were prone to urinary tract infections. The cranberry juice helped prevent them.

He said, 'I went to the jail.'

I waited.

'Adam insists he didn't murder Brand. He says he went to the motel to talk to him. Says he couldn't hold it in anymore after getting that snotty phone call from Brand's lawyer.' He finished the juice. 'He admits taking the baseball bat. He says when he got there the door was open. He went in and found the body.'

I said, 'Do you believe him?'

He rubbed his eyes. 'I do. But who am I to the cops? He's royally screwed.'

He headed out onto the deck. I followed him. The air had cooled, and moonlight shimmered on the ocean. Up the coast, the city lights rimmed the harbor like gold coins.

'What the hell was he thinking?' He looked out at the water. 'He's the most disciplined person I know. I've seen him do workouts that could be outlawed as torture under the Geneva

Convention. He argues theology with me until my ears bleed. He has a Ph.D. in physics from Cal Tech and he's a post-doc at UCSB, where the profs have been snatching Nobels like dog biscuits.' He shook his head. 'And he takes a baseball bat to the motel. Stupid, stupid, stupid.'

I rested a hand on his shoulder. He pulled me onto his lap and put his arms around my waist.

'How'd it all get so screwed up?' he said. 'No, forget that. Brand's dead and that's just fine.'

A wire of shock ran through me. He felt me tighten.

'I know that sounds cold. So be it.' He stared at the breakers. 'I wouldn't admit how I feel to anybody but you.'

I knew he was talking about trust. I brushed a lock of hair off his forehead.

He said, 'I'm sorry I never talked with you about these things, all these years.'

'You don't have to apologize, Jesse.'

'Yes, I do. I know there's been a black hole, topics that were off limits. But I couldn't find a way . . . that was such a bad time, so dark. Even thinking about it gave me vertigo, like a void was ripping open and if I spoke it out loud, I'd fall in.'

His hands were tight on my waist.

'You still feel that way, don't you?' I said.

'Hanging onto you so I don't slide down, right now.'

I wrapped my arms around his shoulders. He closed his eyes.

'Thanks for putting up with me,' he said.

'Don't say that.'

'Let me talk. Thanks for coming to see me when I was in the hospital. And for coming to rehab.'

'Ssh.'

'No, it's important. Tough times sort people out. You find out who you can count on,' he said. 'And I could count on you and Adam. You were there.'

Cold water ran through my heart. As Jesse never spoke about the crash, I never mentioned how some of his friends treated him afterward. They disappeared. I didn't talk about it because he didn't need my anger, and he rejected pity in the most withering terms.

And rehab was a difficult place to visit.

I first went a month after the hit-and-run. It was evening, and I took him a submarine sandwich and a couple of beers. When he saw me coming up the corridor, he reached for the grab bar that hung above him and started pulling himself up. I tried a smile and failed. He was in a body brace, and his left leg had leg rods and pins drilled through his skin into the bone. Under the bedside lamp his face looked pale and thin. He must have lost twenty-five pounds. The man next to him on the ward was a quadriplegic with a halo brace screwed into his skull.

I said, 'Thought you might be hungry.'

He worked to sit up straight. I watched, and he watched me watch.

He said, 'And for my next trick, I'll drag my ass off this mattress onto the floor.'

The next time I went, I approached the door and saw a man standing by the bed with his back to me. He was wearing a UCSB Swimming T-shirt, and he had Jesse's dark hair, height, and honed physique. Longing overcame logic, and I said, 'Wow.'

Adam turned around.

I stopped in the doorway with witlessness dripping down my face. Cue mortification. Jesse said, 'Over here,' and I saw him sitting next to the bed, in the wheelchair.

Thinking about it made my teeth ache. But that was the moment when he took charge and showed us how it was going to be.

He said, 'Either of you have today's newspaper?'

Adam and I looked at each other. I said, 'No, why?'

'You look like a couple of lost puppies. I want to roll up the sports section and spank you both across the nose until you stop it.'

Now Jesse leaned his head against my shoulder. I didn't like his show of gratitude, didn't think I should be congratulated for sticking with him.

I said, 'Hey.'

He looked up, and I kissed him. The waves lapped at the sand beyond us.

'I love you,' I said.

'You're not just saying that because you already bought the wedding dress?'

'No, I'm saying it because I've ordered five hundred canapés. I'm in deep.' The breeze stirred and I felt goosebumps, a spooky prickle. 'We are in deep, aren't we?'

'Jesus, yeah. How the hell I'll get Adam out of this, I don't know.'

He let out a hard breath. 'Ev, I have to tell you something else. The people who've been threatening me made contact today.'

'Oh, my God. What do they want?'

'I don't know yet, beyond jerking me around. They didn't specify.'

I tried to read his face in the moonlight. 'Jesse?'

'I don't know, Ev. But I think it's going to get worse before it gets better.'

Cool air rushed across my arms. 'Let's go in.'

Back inside, I locked the doors, closed the shutters, and we headed to the bedroom. While Jesse went to brush his teeth I started undressing. I felt tired and at sea. But, shimmying out of my jeans, I decided to shut the door on anxiety and sadness, at least for the next eight hours.

I went to the stereo and selected an album, Aretha Franklin. In the bedroom I dimmed the lights and stripped down to my bra and panties. When Jesse came out, I was kneeling on the bed with the covers turned down, as if I were Rita Hayworth.

He had a wistful look on his face. Understanding that this was going to be a concerted effort, R and R from the combat zone.

He said, 'I haven't taken any Viagra.'

'It's okay. Come here.'

He slid over onto the bed. I unbuttoned his shirt and pulled it off.

He tilted his head. 'You know, in the catalogs women wear underwear that matches.'

'You read women's underwear catalogs?'

'For the political commentary. Is there any reason your panties are inside out?'

I pushed him down and straddled him. 'Yeah, I'm a sexual outlaw.'

'Who?' He smiled. 'Can I play, too?'

'Sure. You like politics, how about President and First Lady?' I worked on the top button of his jeans. 'Or Che Guevara and the peasant girl?'

'Excellent. But for once, I want to be Che.'

I was laughing when I lay down on top of him and pressed my mouth on his.

It was midnight when the phone rang, and Jesse was having another nightmare. I fumbled for the light and reached across him to grab the phone from the nightstand. I ended up lying on his chest, feeling his heart pound against my own. His skin was hot. I picked up the phone.

It was Adam.

'I've been released,' he said. 'I'm sorry, I don't have any money for a taxi. Could one of you give me a ride home?'

In the morning I went with Jesse to the police station, wanting to find out from Chris Ramseur what had exonerated Adam. I asked for Chris at the front desk, and got a look. The receptionist said, 'One moment,' and phoned Lieutenant Rome.

Clayton Rome walked as though he were growling. His belt buckle and cufflinks gleamed. His face looked as though it had been smoothed into a frown with a belt sander.

He said, 'What the hell's going on?'

Jesse's guard went up. 'We wanted to speak to Detective Ramseur. Adam Sandoval was released from jail last night, and we wondered—'

'You're a piece of work.'

'Excuse me?'

Rome's nostrils were flaring. 'You wondered what?'

'What cleared him.'

'You were at the crime scene before any of us. You tell me.'

'What's going on?'

Rome's hands were drawing into balls. 'Forensics and pathology exonerated Dr Sandoval. The baseball bat wasn't the murder weapon. The pattern of blood spatter didn't fit with the cleanliness of Sandoval's clothes and shoes. And there's something else.'

I said, 'What?'

'It wasn't Franklin Brand.'

In the background a phone rang.

'It was Detective Ramseur.'

Jesse put his hand against the desk, bracing himself. The room became bright, and I heard a buzzing sound.

Rome had turned to wood. 'And you and Sandoval were in the room with his body when the Sheriffs arrived. I hope you're parked outside. You can save me the trouble of getting a search warrant to go through your car.'

Fifteen

By the disorganized haze in Jesse's eyes, I knew his shields were down. He handed Rome his car keys. I went outside and phoned Lavonne Marks.

She swooped into the station like a crow, telling Jesse, 'You're in shock, and this is nothing but harassment. So shut up.'

And she was right. The police had no intention of arresting Jesse. He was taking the brunt of their rage and grief at the death of a comrade. When we left the station, they made him run the gauntlet, glaring in silence as he headed past.

When we got outside, Lavonne said, 'All right. Tell me what they think.'

Jesse rubbed his forehead. 'They think Adam and I are dirty. We were at the crime scene, and Brand's gone, and Rome thinks those facts are connected.'

'Is that it? Nothing specific?' she said.

'Rome thinks that Isaac was in on Brand's embezzlement scam, and demanded a bigger cut of the proceeds. He thinks that's why Brand killed him.'

I said, 'That's outrageous.'

'I know.'

Lavonne said, 'Why does Rome think that you and Adam Sandoval were part of this imagined conspiracy?'

'Because Mako paid us off.'

A darkening rage seeped over my vision and thoughts. 'The insurance settlement – Rome thinks Mako paid it to you as hush money?'

'From his questions, that's the only conclusion I can draw.'

Lavonne said, 'He was trying to spook you. Don't let him.'

'Too late.' He looked up at me, his eyes awash with uncertain light. 'I can't believe it was Chris, and I didn't know. I saw his hand . . .'

He pulled his tie loose and unbuttoned his collar.

Two men in suits strode past us, heading into the station. They had confidence in their stride, as though everyone would move out of their way, as though they were the offensive line of the Chicago Bears. One of them, a man about my age, leaned forward, as if leading with his nose, sniffing. His gray suit hung large on his reedy frame. He looked at us with assessing eyes.

After they passed, Jesse said, 'They're feds.'

Lavonne stared back at the building. 'Yes.'

'I don't think that's a coincidence. What—'

She held up a hand. 'Not here. You're in trouble, Jesse.'

That evening I sat on my porch watching the western sky. The horizon was stained purple and pierced with the evening star. I felt sadness winding like a cord around my chest.

Chris, I thought. A sweet man with a tart edge, he believed in Jesse, and me, and the cause of justice. I didn't know him, really. I only knew that he went to Franklin Brand's motel room, and died violently.

The news overflowed with the headline: *Police Hunt Cop Killer.* But that was backward. The roles had switched. The hunters had become the hunted.

And Brand was out there. I went inside and locked the door.

When Jesse phoned and said, 'Can I come over tonight?' I told him, 'You don't have to ask.' I surveyed my tired clothes and dirty hair, and decided I'd better shower before he came. I took my boom box into the bathroom and turned on music I knew would sustain me, Beethoven's Ninth Symphony. Went straight to the Ode to Joy. Standing under the shower, I leaned my arms against the tile and listened with my eyes closed, letting the water hit my face.

I didn't hear the bathroom door open. A breeze, a strand of cold air unraveling through the steam, brought my attention.

'Jesse?'

119

I smelled cologne. I opened my eyes. Franklin Brand was standing in the center of the bathroom.

His calico eyes were wide, pupils big and black. They were staring at me through the clear plastic shower curtain.

His voice was flat. '*Los Angeles Times*, you told me.'

He held up the framed law school diploma that hung above my desk.

'Liar.'

The tremor started in my legs, like a high wire vibrating. It crawled up my back and along my arms. I stared, frozen.

'I should have known,' he said. 'Lawyers are always at the bottom of it.'

He threw the diploma in the wastebasket. I heard the glass crack.

'You stole the mini-disk. I want it back.'

The water stung me. I couldn't seem to move, just shake. Oh, Jesus.

'Who are you working with? That gimp?' he said. 'What does he want, money? He can join the crowd.'

He had taken down a cop. Killed Chris before he could draw his gun, reduced his head to bone and pulp. My teeth chattered. The music rose, the orchestra soaring.

What could I do? What could I use to protect myself? Soap, shampoo? For the love of God, a loofah?

'Turn off the water,' he said.

A razor. I had a razor. My Lady Godiva safety razor, advertised not to nick even if you sawed it back and forth across your wrists. How in hell could I do this?

'Turn off the water, I can't breathe.' He twisted his neck, pulling at his collar. His shirt was covered with dust. He pulled down the collar of his shirt and I saw a red welt on his skin.

I slid my hand toward the razor, leaving the water blasting. Maybe the steam would drive him out of the bathroom to catch his breath. And maybe I could get a piece of broken glass from the diploma and use it to hold him off.

'Get out of the shower.'

'No.' My voice sounded ninety years old.

'Get out or I'll get you out.'

He took a step. My fingers clawed for the razor. It fell through my soapy hand, hitting the tile. The blade bounced loose. I stared at it, my heart racing, the tremor shaking my legs.

Brand stared at it. 'That was stupid.'

He slapped his palm on the shower curtain. His diamond pinkie ring flashed in the light. I jumped. Clamped my teeth together, but the moan still escaped.

'I want the disk. Where is it?' he said.

I couldn't tell him the police had it, because once he thought I couldn't help him, he'd kill me. Only one thing to do now. Get past him. Two steps, going, going, gone, I had to get outside, and do it loudly.

'I'll get the disk. Move back. Don't touch me.' I stuck a hand out past the shower curtain and grabbed a towel, whipping it around myself.

'You think I'm going to rape you?' He was right outside the shower, filling the view. 'That would be poetic justice. Turnabout's fair play.'

Christ, have mercy. My mouth found words.

'I know everything,' I said. 'About the mini-disk and the money, and Mako. Firedog, and I'm not the only one. The cops know.' I was babbling, talk erupting like the goosebumps on my skin. Anything to keep him back. 'The D.A., everybody. I told them all. I know about Mari Diamond—'

'No.' The vein on his forehead was popping.

'—and Kenny Rudenski knows—'

'Rudenski? You told him?'

'I—'

His neck was purple. He yanked open the shower curtain. I shrieked and put up my hands.

'Tell him, if I go down, I'm taking him with me.'

He reached for me. Beethoven's chorus filled the room. I shrank back against the tile wall. Wet sounds rolled from my throat. I tried to shove him away, but he closed his hand around my wrist.

Behind him, in the doorway, I saw Jesse.

Six-one never looked so tall. He stood balancing himself against the doorjamb. He was holding one of the graphite crutches like a jousting lance, tightening his hand on the grip. He had taken the rubber tip off the bottom, exposing the hard composite. He was going to ram Brand with it. He would only get one shot. After that, he'd probably fall over.

He said, 'Get away from her, motherfucker.'

One shot, and he wanted to put it in Brand's eye.

Brand turned his head. Jesse drove the end of the crutch at his face.

It hit him square in the nose. He grabbed at his face, letting go of me. Blood streamed from between his fingers. I saw Jesse tipping forward off balance, thought he was going down, but Brand roared and charged at him. He knocked him backward out of the doorway into the bedroom.

They crashed to the floor with a clatter and a terrible crack that I thought was Jesse's head hitting the wood.

Move.

I leapt out of the shower and ran into the bedroom. They were on the floor. Brand's nose was pouring blood. He had Jesse's shirt twisted in his fists and was shaking him up and down, knocking him into the floorboards.

I said, 'Stop it.'

I picked up a lamp, yanking the cord from the wall socket. I brought it down on Brand's back. He collapsed on top of Jesse, but almost instantly looked up at me. His eyes were ugly.

'You want it, you're going to get it.'

He tried to climb up. Jesse held on and said, 'Ev, get out.'

I turned and ran into the living room. I saw the mess, everything tossed out of my desk. The glass broken in the French door. I heard Brand's footsteps behind me. He came flying through the doorway.

Right into Nikki, who had the fire extinguisher.

She let loose with it. Powder shot out, whitening his face. He started yelling.

We heard the siren, and so did he. Spitting and wiping his eyes, he barreled out the French doors.

Nikki plunged out the door after him. 'Thea, God—'

Holding the towel wrapped around me, I went to the doors and saw Brand's cashmere jacket flapping as he dashed through the gate to the street. The siren grew louder, a block away now.

Brand was running away, not going after Nikki's baby. I rushed back to the bedroom. Stopped in the door, my heart booming.

'Oh, Jess.'

He looked up. 'Are you all right? Did he hurt you?'

He was sitting on the floor, rubbing the back of his head. I dropped to his side and he gathered me in his arms. Soon I heard Nikki coming in, and felt her wrapping the quilt around me. The shuddering wouldn't stop.

Jesse held me, stroking my hair. 'I'm sorry,' he said. 'So sorry.'

'Brand knew my name, and where I lived. I can only think of one person who would have told him, and that's Kenny Rudenski.'

The cops wrote it down. Nikki brought me a refill of Jack Daniel's. I huddled on the sofa with the quilt gripped around my shoulders. Jesse stood by the door with the police officers.

'Whatever Brand's into, Kenny's into it with him,' I said.

'Yes, ma'am,' the officer said.

I drank the Jack's. I couldn't seem to make myself get up off the sofa. I knew I had to do something, but I didn't want to leave the quilt. The officers said goodbye and Jesse walked them out.

When he didn't come back, I knew where he had gone.

He drove to Kenny's house. Got out, muttering under his breath, seething with an anger that could have burned the night sky. He rang the bell. After a minute he pressed it again. Finally a man's voice tinned through an intercom.

'What do you want?'

'Let me in, Rudenski.'

'Collecting for charity? Sorry, I already gave at the office.'

Jesse heard him laughing. He looked around and saw the video camera mounted above the speaker.

He said, 'You told Brand how to find Evan. You sicced him on her. You're not going to get out of this one.'

'How are you doing that?'

'Doing what?'

'Standing up.'

Jesse looked at the camera. He sucked in a deep breath and spit on it.

Kenny said, 'You really are pathetic, you know.'

The intercom clicked off.

At eight the next morning, under a sky the color of cement, I walked into Mako Technologies. Amber Gibbs looked cozy behind the front desk, blowing on her hot chocolate, reading *Cosmopolitan* magazine.

'I'm here to see Kenny Rudenski,' I said.

'Junior? He isn't in yet.'

'Then get his father.'

'Okie-doke.' She reached for the phone.

'His secretary will try to blow me off. Tell her that's a mistake. This is urgent, and George will get angry if she sends me away.'

Her brow gnarled, but she called and repeated my words. 'Pop's coming.'

'One other thing.' I pointed to her *Cosmo*. 'You don't want the CEO to see you reading an article titled, "It's Length *and* Width That Count!"'

She was still blushing when George strode into the lobby, pulling on his jacket. With his height, it was like having a telephone pole come at me.

He said, 'Let's walk.'

Outside, he stalked away from the parking lot, past employees pulling in. The gray sky weighed on us. George's gaze was cooler than the air.

'Your summoning me begins to pall, Miss Delaney.'

I trotted to keep up with him. 'Brand broke into my house last night. He threatened me and fought with Jesse.'

Eyes front, face grim. 'Were either of you injured?'

'Bruises.'

'This is distressing news. You've informed the police?'

'Yes. But Brand escaped.'

He kept up the brisk pace. Sprinklers misted the lawns of the businesses along the sidewalk.

'Harley Dawson tells me your heart is in the right place,' he said, 'But I don't see why you insist on giving me a first-hand account.'

'Because Brand gave me a message for your son. And I quote: Tell Rudenski if I go down, I'm taking him with me.'

He stopped and put a hand on my arm. 'What the hell is that supposed to mean?'

'What do you think? It was a threat. And it implies that Kenny is involved in Brand's criminal activities.'

'That's a reckless accusation.'

'Brand's words, not mine.'

'Of course it was a threat. To smear my son and ruin this company.' He started walking again, shoulders tight. 'How can you be so gullible?'

'Excuse me?'

'Taking at face value the words of a murderer.'

'The police didn't consider me gullible when I told them.'

'What are you doing?' He stopped again. 'Are you planning to write an exposé? Do you want to tar Mako with the same brush as Diamond Mindworks, make high tech sound like a bunch of thieves? I won't let you.'

'That's not it, George.'

He spread his arms. 'Look around. What do you see, wherever you look?' He gestured at the surrounding business parks. 'Electronics. Aerospace. Defense engineering.' Pointing toward the university in the distance. 'Molecular biophysics. Computer networking. Do you have any idea how instrumental people here have been in developing the wired world?'

'You don't need to lecture me.'

'I was in the Computer Science Department when cyberspace came into existence. This campus was the third node on the Internet. We took this planet online.'

His craggy face took on a hard metallic sheen.

'Next week I'm flying to Washington to meet with the Secretary of Homeland Security. I'm testifying before the House Armed Services Committee about cyber-warfare. These things, young woman, are matters of import. And I refuse to let you help a bitter SOB like Franklin Brand shoot down my business.'

He turned back toward Mako's office, stopped, and pointed at me.

'How dare you accuse Kenny of complicity in Brand's schemes? How dare you help a criminal try to destroy my son?'

'To protect the man I love.'

The finger hung in the air a moment longer, but the electricity left his eyes. He started walking again.

I said, 'George, I'm not trying to ambush you. But we're talking about a cop killer who has a connection to Mako.'

'I'll see you to your car,' he said.

'I still want to talk to Kenny.'

'No. You are not going to snoop around my company.'

Was he in denial, or was he covering up? He didn't want to hear it. Not about Brand, not about Mako, and especially not about his son.

I said, 'Tell Kenny what Brand said. Tell him I want to speak to him.'

But I was talking to his back as he walked away.

The rest of the morning I worked at the law library, hunching over treatises, chewing through my pencil. When I came out the cloud cover had gone. The breeze was warm, the sky dazzling. Sunlight flashed off cars in traffic, and people walking along the street looked confetti-colorful. I walked down to the Coffee Bean and Tea Leaf.

I was waiting to pay when Jakarta Rivera put coins on the counter.

She said, 'My treat. Consider it a down payment on Chapter One.'

'Thanks, but no need. I'll give you the first line, free.'

Carrying the paper coffee cup outside, I started up the street. She followed.

I said, 'There once was a girl from Nantucket, who told such big lies I said—'

'You're a hoot, you know?'

'My life's a laugh riot. So I don't need new jokers adding humor to it.'

'I was in the D.O. for nine years. Taipei, Bogotá, Berlin.'

'You were a CIA agent.' The *yeah, right* was implied.

'And you knew exactly what I meant. You're confirming our judgment.'

She slipped on a pair of Chanel sunglasses. Her silk sweater and animal-print skirt had a gaiety and stylishness, accentuating her dancer's figure, that made me think of Paris. She was far beyond most Santa Barbarans in terms of refinement, and she did it with a dab hand that said: I'm the finished article.

'D.O. – Directorate of Operations,' I said. 'Every Tom Clancy fan is up on acronyms like that.'

'Not everybody's brother flew Hornets, doing Test and Eval at China Lake.'

Anger started tightening my spine.

'Not everybody's father had black clearance working on weapons projects for Nav Air.'

'Whoa.' I put up a hand.

She walked with her shoulders thrown back, chin up, passing through the pedestrian crowd like light through a window.

'Want to know more?' she said. 'You go to Mass more often than you tell your boyfriend. You give blood. You believe in marriage, and the lone gunman theory, and in the projection of American naval power in defense of democracy. You know which end of a shotgun does the business and for a civilian you're fairly cool under fire. You're sleeping with a T-ten paraplegic yet you regularly refill your prescription for birth control pills, which makes you an optimist. Your permanent record shows great academics, spotty deportment. And in case you're wondering, you don't have an FBI file.'

She glanced at me. 'But Jesse does.'

At that, I squeezed the coffee cup too hard and the top popped off. I flinched as it slopped out on my hand. Shook it off. When I looked back up, she was gone.

I headed straight to Sanchez Marks. I was stepping into the foyer, with the mahogany paneling and the ficus trees, when Lavonne came scurrying by. Her eyes were intense.

She waved. 'Come with. I just received some information Jesse should hear, and you as well.'

'Strange, that's what I was about to say.'

She shot me a look. We headed to Jesse's office. He was talking on the phone, taking notes, but ended the call when we came in.

Lavonne said, 'I just spoke to Cal Diamond's attorney. Diamond's out of Intensive Care, and his law firm will accept service of the lawsuit.'

Jesse tucked his pencil behind his ear. 'That's a surprise.'

'Here's a bigger one. He claims Sanchez Marks has a conflict of interest. He wants you off the case.'

'Why?'

'Diamond's filing for divorce. He's going to make a stink about his wife committing adultery. With Franklin Brand.'

Jesse gaped at her, and at me, and back at her.

She said, 'The divorce is neither here nor there, and the conflict of interest claim is monkeywrenching, a maneuver to wrongfoot us. But the news about Brand—'

'We have to tell the police.'

She nodded, grim. 'We may have found Brand's companion from the night of the hit-and-run. The anonymous caller. Mari Diamond.'

I said, 'And if she's still in touch with him . . .'

Jesse reached for the telephone. 'She may know where he is.'

I raised a hand. 'Wait. There's something else.'

I told them about Jax Rivera's remark. He went quiet.

'This relates to those FBI agents we saw heading into the police station,' he said.

Lavonne's mouth pinched. 'Leave me to do the talking to the police.'

She scuttled away. Jesse stared out the window at red tile roofs and the green swell of the mountains.

'Ev, this Jakarta Rivera character.'

'Yeah?'

'Watch out. She has the stink of the real about her.'

Kenny showed up at my house an hour later, lunchtime. I was out at the curb saying goodbye to the home security salesman, telling him I wanted to buy the burglar alarm but how about throwing in booby traps and some artillery? Nothing big, maybe a twenty-millimeter Vulcan cannon, the kind the Navy puts in its F/A-18s.

He pulled up in the Porsche. He had the engine revving. 'Get in.'

When we drove away, Helen Potts, standing at her mailbox, scowled at us.

'You're trying to jam me up,' he said.

I saw nerves and anger, his mouth sour beneath the sunglasses, his hand goosing the gearshift back and forth.

I said, 'You told Brand I had the mini-disk, didn't you?'

'He's a pathological liar.'

'Even if he is, it isn't my place to protect you from his lies.'

'Little Miss Semtex. Blowing crap in all directions, not caring who gets hit.'

He rumbled up the street. My hair batted in the wind.

'You shouldn't mess with me, and neither should Blackburn,' he said.

'You're angry that I told your dad.'

He upshifted. 'You have no idea the pressure I'm under.'

'Daddy's little boy.'

'Gimpy's little bitch.'

I glanced at him, disbelieving my ears. He raced up Laguna Street.

'The rose garden's up ahead,' I said. 'Pull over, we'll take a walk.'

'No.' He downshifted. 'You need to see something.'

We headed around corners and onto Santa Barbara Street.

He said, 'You're messing in places you shouldn't. Don't ever speak to my father about me again.'

'I'll do what I need to, Kenny.'

'He doesn't believe in me. No matter what I do, I can never live up to what he thinks I should be,' he said. 'And he's looking for an excuse to hang onto power at Mako. You're giving it to him.'

'Sorry, but that's not my problem.'

We passed First Presbyterian and turned onto State Street.

'You tell him I'm buddying with Brand? You tell him I'm a screwup yet again?' He adopted George's brusque basso. 'Kenny, get inside and entertain the guests. Kenny, get your finger out of your nose. Kenny, you can't be a stunt man. You can't race moto-cross, it'll make the family look trashy. You can't do anything.'

He ran a red light, looking at me. 'How'd you like to grow up with that?'

'How'd you like to slow down?'

We were weaving ever faster through the weekday traffic. I leaned back in the seat, holding onto the door. Kenny's face, behind the even features and movie-star hair, was acidic.

'But he forgets. My sainted father, Mister Save The Nation, he forgets. I may have hired Frank, but Dad's the one who promoted him to VP.' He screeched around the corner onto Hope. 'Well, ha. After the hit-and-run, Dad had to face the fact that he backed the wrong horse.'

We squealed into the driveway at Calvary Cemetery. Greenery arose along our left. The drive curved between silent lawns, trees shading the graves, the markers flat against the ground.

I said, 'Anytime you want to tell me what we're doing, I'm listening.'

'Here.'

He pulled to the curb, killed the engine, and got out. Trying to regain my composure, I followed him up a rise. What had I been thinking, riding along with him? Anger and high performance German engines were a bad combination.

He stopped near the top of the hill, under a spreading tree.

'What do you think I have to do with Brand? Honestly. I want to know,' he said. 'Give it to me, right in the gut.'

I tried to read his face.

'Don't try to figure out how to play it. Just tell me,' he said.

So I did. 'I think you're his majordomo,' I said. 'I think you're his errand boy. I think you've been in on the embezzlement scheme almost from the start.'

'Go on.'

'I think you've been trying to squelch Jesse from the moment he found out Brand was back. I think you're the one who's behind this computer harassment campaign against him.'

'Is that all?'

'I think you're Franklin Brand's toady.'

He stared at me, his face pinched. 'You read about Yvette. The girl who died.'

'Yes.'

He pointed at the ground behind me. The gravestone had her name on it.

'The driver was two times over the legal limit,' he said. 'Yvette was thrown out and the car flipped over on her. Nearly cut her in half.'

I read the name, putting it together. Yvette Vasquez.

'She was Mari Diamond's sister?'

He nodded. 'The driver ran, left her. She was seventeen.'

'I'm sorry, Kenny.'

He knelt next to the grave marker, rasping his fingers over the letters carved in the stone. 'Brand deliberately ran over your lover. He smashed the Sandoval kid's head like a melon. And he ran.' He looked up. 'Do you think I would have anything more to do with a bastard like that?'

I looked in his eyes, wondering if, in his crude way, he was talking truth.

He brushed off his hands and stood up. 'You know I don't hold any truck with your boyfriend. He turned the crash into his winning lotto ticket. But it doesn't make what Frank did okay.'

The wind brushed me. 'You had me going there.'

'What?'

'Until you started slagging Jesse off, you had me feeling sorry for you.'

'Wake up and smell the scam, sister. He uses his handicap as a stick to beat people with. He's using you. You do everything for him, even argue.'

I told myself not to mouth off, not with someone so angry and manipulative, but my own anger had reached boiling point. 'It doesn't bother you that Mari Diamond had an affair with Brand?'

'That's sex. That's different.'

'Pardon?'

'Did you ever get a good look at Cal Diamond? Banging Frank was probably the only thing that kept Mari sane.'

I blinked. 'My God, you're low.'

'Mari's head is screwed up and has been since Yvette died. Marrying that geezer, that proved it. And she needs lots of sanity, constant infusions. She doesn't need to apologize, and neither do her lovers.'

'You're telling me that you—'

'Don't say sloppy seconds. She's too classy.'

'But you're her lover, too?'

'Bullseye for the crip-fucker.'

I slapped him in the face.

He flinched and drew a breath. 'I've been waiting all week for you to do that.'

'You're a pig, Kenny.'

He smiled. 'At last. Now at least I know you have some real emotion in there. You're not just Blackburn's lackey.'

My hand was stinging. I wanted to hit him again.

'I'm out of here.' I started to walk away.

He put a hand on my arm. 'So you're going to judge me for screwing Mari when you have your own kinky thing going on?'

'I cannot begin to dignify such garbage with a response.'

'This is really getting you hot, isn't it?'

'Let go.'

'Hang on. Why don't you give me a shot? It would be fun.' His tongue tapped against his teeth. 'You want, I could even pretend to be like him. I'd like to see you when you're really turned on.'

'Stop.'

I tried to twist away from him. He gripped me around the waist, and here came his thigh, nudging between my legs.

'Come on,' he said. 'You know we'd be awesome.'

I pushed him away. My vision was thumping. I turned and ran down the hill, and heard him behind me by the grave, laughing. I reached the road and kept jogging toward the cemetery office. After a minute I heard the Porsche start up. Kenny cruised up alongside me and rolled down his window.

'The invitation remains open,' he said. 'But if you mention this, to anyone, Mari will have you for lunch. She'll rip out your kidneys and serve them to her dogs.'

He pulled away.

I got a cab, wanting nothing more than to get home and scrub myself with a hard brush. But when I opened the gate I saw my cousin Taylor sitting on the doorstep. She had applied so much hairspray that she should have been wearing a warning sticker: *keep away from open flame.* She was sorting through my mail.

She held up an envelope. 'I didn't know you had a gold card.'

I took it from her. 'What's going on?'

She stood up, brushing dust from the seat of her shorts. 'We're having lunch today. Remember?'

I drooped. 'I'm sorry, I forgot. Give me a minute, I'll go spruce myself up.'

I took her to Café Orleans, on the promenade at Paseo Nuevo, and we sat outside having po' boy sandwiches and iced tea. I felt perturbed and dirty from Kenny's come-on. But Taylor seemed oblivious, talking about her job, her blueberry eyes sparkling.

'Countess Zara lingerie, you've heard of it. I rep for the Dazzling Delicates line. I settle in, I'll gin it up here.' She gazed at passing shoppers. 'Y'all could surely use some pizzazz. And underwiring.'

I stared absently. What did Kenny want to accomplish with his cry-and-grab act? If he thought he would get either sympathy or sex out of the encounter, he was perverse. He had subverted himself. His behavior was self-sabotaging.

'What?' I said.

'This new book you're writing, is it like the last one? Missiles and mutants?' She was fluffing herself, adjusting her watch and bracelets, checking her manicure. ''Cause you know what would be great. Fewer bomb runs, more love scenes.'

'In this one the heroine conducts a running gun battle up in the Rockies.'

'Oh. Mountains, well, heights are good. Cliff scenes scare the dickens out of me.'

'She's not on a cliff, she's in the tunnels at NORAD.'

'Heights are better. Could she climb up on a roof to escape? I'd read that, even with the mutants.'

'No. My heroine would never run up on a roof. Nobody runs up on a roof to escape. No roofs.'

She frowned. She sipped her iced tea, and dabbed at her lips with a napkin.

'Going back in time, then. She could meet a Highlander and have his baby.'

I didn't hear the rest. For all I know, she outlined an entire trilogy. I was sinking into despondency, picturing life with Taylor as my self-appointed muse. It so depressed me that after lunch I went on a minor shopping spree, replacing my stolen cellphone with a shiny, happy little model that promised me text and games and a mobile positioning system that could alert the fire department if I needed help. Then I bought a two-pound box of See's chocolates.

She was driving me home, still talking about underwire or NORAD, when her own cellphone rang. I dug it from her purse and answered for her.

'Who's this?' The man had a twangy Oklahoma voice.

'Ed Eugene? It's Evan Delaney.'

Silence lay there like raw liver. 'Let me speak to my wife.'

I remembered him: a stringy man with a bland face and a magpie's quick dark eye.

'She's driving,' I said.

He made a noise known to parents of teenagers as the *duh, stupid* sound, and said, 'Hold the phone up to her ear.'

Sourly, I did it.

'Hi, hon,' Taylor said. 'She's showing me around . . . we're by the beach, look, we're waving at your platform . . .' turning to me, saying, 'Wave.'

I waved at the oil platforms in the channel.

She glanced at me. 'He wants to say hi.'

I said hi again, and he said, 'So, who all went to lunch?'

'Taylor and I.'

'Really? You sure you didn't introduce her to some of your men friends?'

My God, he was checking up on her. Instantly, strangely, I felt protective toward her. 'We're doing girly things.'

But he had hung up. I looked at Taylor. She was keeping her eyes on the road.

She said, 'Poor baby. He gets so lonesome out there, he's desperate for every last detail.'

Either she didn't get it, or was deliberately not getting it. 'Everything all right?'

'Peachy keen.'

But from that point, she turned quiet. It wasn't until she dropped me off that she said, 'I almost forgot. While I was waiting for you to show up, a man came to see you.'

'Who?'

'An FBI agent.'

I stared at her.

'He showed me his badge, and left a business card. Here.'

She took it from her purse and handed it to me. Beneath the FBI seal, it read, Dale Van Heusen, Special Agent.

She picked at a cuticle. 'Why on earth would the FBI want to talk to you?'

Why did the FBI want to talk to me? After Taylor dropped me off I stared at Dale Van Heusen's card. I picked up my phone and dialed.

'Jesse Blackburn.'

'Guess whose radar just painted me,' I said.

I told him, and he said, 'Be a good citizen. Call and find out what he wants.'

He said goodbye, and I dialed Van Heusen's cellphone number. His voicemail kicked on. I was leaving a message when Nikki knocked on the door. I waved her in.

She said, 'I met your cousin.'

'Sorry.'

'She wants to throw a bridal shower for you.'

'What? No.'

'Wants it to be a big surprise. She wanted the names of all your friends.'

I was waving my hands. 'Unh-unh. Noooo.'

'Wanted me to let her inside so she could check out your address book.'

'Oh, God. You didn't, though.'

'But you did. I saw her coming out with you earlier, right?'

I spun around, looking at the desk, where I kept the address book. I couldn't see it. I scrounged on the desk, looking under papers and books. It wasn't there.

Jesse couldn't put it off any longer. It was nine thirty p.m. and the grocery store would be closing soon. He had no coffee, no milk, no eggs or oranges or shampoo or Raid bug spray to disperse the trail of ants that had been marching across his kitchen counter for the last two days. Mundane life demanded attention.

He backed into the parking space five minutes before closing time. He was the last customer in the store. He paid the lackadaisical checker and headed out into the darkness.

He turned down the curb cut and was unlocking his car when the silver Mercedes SUV pulled in and parked next to him. Right next to him, putting him between the two vehicles. A man got out. It was the fat man, Inflatable Sartre.

'Told you we'd be back.'

Jesse gauged it. The man stood in front of the SUV's open door, blocking his path back toward the store. The Mercedes itself blocked the view of the checker inside. Sartre hitched up his jeans and stepped toward him.

One-on-one, okay.

Jesse backed up, toward open space behind the cars. Sartre strolled forward. He must have weighed two-fifty but his arms had the muscle definition of french fries.

He said, 'You're in a tight spot, bucko.'

Not that tight, Jesse thought, just a few more feet and I'll have room to swing, room to move into sight of the checker in the store.

The Corvette drove into the parking lot, stopping right behind him. Mickey Yago got out. Jesse felt it, the vibe like a dog whistle or a feedback loop, painful and electric. Yago sauntered toward him, blond ringlets swinging in the breeze.

He said, 'Going somewhere?'

Sixteen

I was cleaning out the refrigerator when Jesse called.

'Ev, I need a hand.' His voice sounded thin.

'What's wrong?'

'I'm, ah. Shit.'

My hand squeezed the phone. 'Where are you?'

'Parked in front of your house.'

I threw the phone down and ran outside. The Audi had angled to the curb, facing against traffic. I opened the door and leaned in.

'Jesus, you're bleeding,' I said.

'You'll have to get the chair. My hand's bunged up.'

I looked at his wrist. Gingerly he turned it over, trying not to rotate the joint. When I reached to touch it, he shied away. The dirty scrapes on his palm and elbow matched those running down the side of his face.

I said, 'You fell.'

'I met Mickey Yago.'

I found it hard to breathe. Fear and anger wound themselves around my chest.

'Is your wrist broken?' I said.

'No. But putting weight on it hurts like hell.'

I retrieved the wheelchair. Getting out of the car proved awkward for him, and when his hand hit the door frame he hissed through his teeth. His wrist was visibly swollen, sprained at the least.

I said, 'How did you drive?'

'Screaming.'

He tried to grip the push-rim and gave up. Tried to push with his left hand alone and veered to the right. He closed his eyes, took a couple of breaths.

'You're going to have to do it,' he said.

The chair had no handles. It wasn't meant to be propelled from behind. It was supposed to be another set of legs. I knew he had to feel humiliated. I wrapped my hands around the low seatback and started toward the house.

I said, 'You going to tell me?'

'Yago arranged a welcoming committee at the grocery store. Tub o' lard supreme, black clothes, wussie chin beard. Drives a Mercedes SUV.'

'Win Utley.'

We reached my front door. Inside, I steered into the bathroom. He turned on the water and started rinsing his hand in the sink, while I got hydrogen peroxide and gauze pads. His white shirt was covered with dirt and what looked like food.

I said, 'What's all this?'

'Milk and tomatoes. Utley went for me when I threw my groceries at him.'

He fumbled with the gauze and with the spool of medical tape, tearing it with his teeth. Gently I took it from him and started fixing a bandage.

'He went for you?' I said.

'I think it was the cantaloupe that hurt him. Or maybe the bottle of bleach.'

The bandage went on. He winced.

I said, 'Let's go to the Emergency Room, have this wrist looked at.'

'I'm not spending the evening at the ER.'

'What if it's broken, or dislocated?'

'It isn't.'

'You don't know that. You look like you fell hard.'

I smoothed his hair back from his face, examining the lacerations on his cheek and forehead. He took my hand and lowered it to his lap.

'Evan, I'm not made of glass.' His eyes were hot blue under the lights. 'I didn't hurt the wrist hitting the ground. I hurt it hitting Utley's face.'

I looked at him. 'How many times?'

He nearly smiled. 'Once. He walked right into it.' His face sobered. 'He responded by giving me a big shove. Would have just sent me backward, but Yago was standing right behind me and he flipped me over.' His voice ebbed. 'He put his boot down across one of my arms, and Utley knelt on the other one. They pinned me.'

The image of him spreadeagled on the asphalt caused my stomach to squeeze.

'What do they want?' I said.

'Let's get out of the bathroom.'

With his left arm he tried to back up, swerved into the tub, said, 'Suck.' I did the backing, and got into the living room. I crushed some ice cubes in a baggie and gave it to him.

He wrapped it around his wrist. 'Okay, fine. I'm going to physical therapy in the morning anyway. I'll get the PT to check it out.'

The physical therapist was not a doctor, but I knew this was the best I could hope for. I did not mention the word 'x-ray.'

I said, 'What do they want?'

'Money.'

'How much?'

'Two hundred thousand dollars.'

I stared. 'My God.'

'And they want it in forty-eight hours.'

I sank down onto the sofa. My vision was throbbing. 'Why?'

'Because they're extortionists, Evan. That's their game.'

'You have to tell the police.'

'I have. After Yago and Utley drove off, the clerk in the grocery store saw me in the parking lot. He called the cops.' He ran a hand through his hair. 'But Lieutenant Rome already thinks I'm mixed up with Brand. He'll consider this demand from Yago as more proof of a falling out among thieves.'

The wind was picking up. I heard the bushes shimmying outside. I felt an awful premonition, a sense of foreboding.

'And if you don't get the money? Then what?'

He adjusted the ice pack on his wrist, not responding. The dryness in my throat worsened.

'What's the *or else*?' I said. 'If you don't pay them, do they tell me "everything"?'

'There is no everything.'

A gulch seemed to be forming in my stomach. 'Jesse, it doesn't matter. Nothing you tell me could shock me, or turn me away from you.'

'Do you trust me?'

'Yes.'

'Then trust me.'

We gazed at each other. I said, 'Of course.'

'They didn't specify the consequences. They just said I wouldn't like it.'

I stood up. My nerves were crawling. I wanted to bite the furniture, to scratch holes in the walls.

I paced. 'Why you? Why now?'

'Yago thinks I owe him money.'

'Say again?'

'He told me he wants his money. And if he can't get it from Brand, he'll get it from me.'

'Whoa, whoa.' I waved my hands. '*His* money?'

'Apparently so. Which makes me think Brand owes Yago money.'

'Two hundred thousand dollars?'

'Could be.'

'Why do they want the money from you? What do you have to do with it?'

'I don't know. Because I got the settlement from Mako? Because I have a house I can mortgage or a portfolio I can liquidate?'

'Not in forty-eight hours.'

'Of course not. And I wouldn't do it anyway.'

My stomach was knotting. 'That makes me think they don't expect you to make the deadline.'

'Which means they're planning to hit me with something else. Something worse.'

'Oh, my God. Jesse, what did you tell them?'

'To shove it up their ass with a ski pole.'

I waited, knowing there was a punchline.

He said, 'Yago told me I'd be hearing from them again. Utley was complaining that I'd hurt his face, saying what a bastard I am, but Yago was calm. He just ground his heel into my hand and walked away.'

I could hear him breathing. I didn't say anything.

'Utley kept moaning that I'd bruised him, he pulled off his glasses and patted his cheek. He started kicking the groceries. They were spilled all over the asphalt. And as he was walking away I told him, hey, asshole, you forgot something.'

'What?'

'He turned around. He had his glasses off, and he couldn't see, I guess. So he stepped back toward me, squinting.'

'And?'

'That's when I sprayed him with the Raid.'

He spent the night, feeling embarrassed every time I had to assist him. Squeezing toothpaste onto the toothbrush. Taking his socks off. Taking his jeans off. Going to the bathroom. He felt . . . disabled. *Really* disabled.

We had been through all this at the beginning, of course. The day he was released from rehab we went out to dinner and he stared across the table at me.

And said, 'So, are we going to do this?'

'This. I presume you mean . . .'

'Sex. Us.'

The sun was on him. I looked at his blue eyes, his handsome face. In just a few months all the youth had been scoured from it.

He said, 'Fucking Fact of Life number one. I can't walk worth shit and don't know if I ever will. If that's too much—'

I stood and leaned across the table and kissed him. Feeling crazy, thinking I was jumping off a cliff, hearing a plate hit the floor and shatter. Knowing I wanted him no matter what.

'My place,' I said.

Sitting on the edge of my bed, he unbuttoned my blouse. 'I have to just say it, Evan. I have an incomplete spinal cord injury. It's not as bad as it could be but I still got the full menu. Can't move or feel much. Muscle spasticity. Bowel and bladder and sexual dysfunction.'

'I know we aren't in Kansas anymore, Toto.'

'And we missed the exit for Oz, way back.'

My knees started shaking. 'So, where are we?'

His hand slid around my waist. 'Lie down. Let's find out.'

We'd spent three years making our way. And now it was the beginning all over again, with the issue that never disappeared. He was dog tired, so I got him some Ibuprofen and a new icepack, and helped him into bed. But I felt fried, scorched with anger. I went into the living room, put on *The Matrix*, and poured myself a drink. On the coffee table I spread out the printouts of the files from the mini-disk. I wanted to take a hard look at the data.

I stared at the printouts. This information had come primarily from Mako's files, but also contained the bank records for Brand's FB Enterprises accounts. The disk was a personalized record of Brand's transactions.

I looked at a list of companies and venture capital funds that Mako invested in. When Adam first analyzed it, we had all looked at Firedog. But other firms had received angel funding from Mako. They were listed here.

My breath caught.

There it was. *Segue.* $200,000 had been transferred from an entity called Segue into Brand's Bahamas account, and then moved, along with the faked half-million Firedog investment, on to the Caymans.

Two hundred thousand dollars. Brand had taken two hundred grand from this Segue account.

And it hit me full force. Brand didn't go to the Biltmore to get the mini-disk. He went for another purpose, and Mickey surprised him. The mini-disk was a bill. An invoice delivered to Franklin Brand by Yago, for money they thought he had taken from them.

Brand the embezzler. Brand the clever monkey, who had been moving money around as if he were a huckster running a game of three-card monty. Franklin Smarter-than-thou Brand, the idiot, had plundered Segue. He had ripped off some major league thieves. And now they wanted payback.

But he didn't have it. So they had decided to take it from Jesse instead.

Quicksand. We were sinking in quicksand.

When the phone rang the next morning I was dripping wet from the shower. Jesse was still asleep, my quilt runched around his ribs. I grabbed the phone from the nightstand.

His mom coughed. I heard her cigarette lighter flicking. 'Is my son there?'

I said, 'Hang on a second, Patsy.'

'Never mind, you just give him a message. Tell him his mother doesn't think he's funny.'

'Excuse me?'

'If I wanted garbage first thing in the morning, I'd go stare into my trash can.'

'Patsy, you've lost me.'

'I suppose that means you find it amusing, too.'

Jesse didn't open his eyes, but held up his hand for the phone. I gave it to him.

'Mom, what's wrong?'

His voice was rough with sleep, which no doubt gave Patsy Blackburn the image of her boy *in my bed*. I hoped the vision wouldn't drive her to take a nip before she went to work. No – she'd pull out the vodka she kept in the Evian bottle under the driver's seat, and drink while she drove.

'No, I didn't – I wouldn't do that,' Jesse said. 'Mom, let me check this out . . . no, I swear to you, absolutely . . .'

He listened, and opened his eyes. The look on his face was the one people get when the IRS calls them in for a tax audit.

'Evan had nothing to do with it. I don't care how much it looks like her, it couldn't be. Look, I've been having computer problems, somebody's harassing me, it's . . . no, I don't want to talk to Dad. Listen, let me—'

He squeezed his eyes shut again.

'Dad, yeah. This is a sick joke, I didn't have anything to do with— No. It's not her. I swear to God . . . Anyone can digitally alter an image to make it look like . . . yes, I'll tell you how I can be sure. Because Evan doesn't have a devil's head tattooed on her backside.'

I changed my mind. It wasn't Patsy Blackburn who needed a drink. It was me.

I paced back and forth next to my desk. 'This is contempt-ible.'

The e-mail had been sent to me as well as to Jesse's parents. And to God knew who else. It was from jesse.blackburn@fuckyou-verymuch.net. The message said, *How's this for stag night?*

'This is outrageous. It's defamatory.' I stabbed my finger at the computer. 'Not in a million years is my butt that big.'

Jesse stared at the screen, tilting his head. I slapped him on the shoulder.

'No, of course it's not,' he said. 'Your butt's perfect, optimum size, the paradigm butt against which all butts are measured. And this . . .'

The woman in the photo had my face, the grimacing face on my driver's license photo. The studded dog collar, thigh boots, and bare buttocks thrust toward the camera belonged to someone else.

He ran a hand through his hair. His wrist seemed more limber, less painful to him than it had last night. Or maybe this new problem was distracting him.

He said, 'Utley sent this because I sprayed him with the Raid.'

'And to tell you what they can do to you if they want,' I said. 'How do we put a stop to this?'

That's when Nikki knocked on the door. Her voluptuous lips were crimped tight.

'God, you saw the e-mail,' I said.

'No, Carl did. He's at the sink now, washing out his eyes. Woman, couldn't you at least have worn a thong?'

I sat down and put my head in my hands.

Seventeen

My e-mail inbox was crammed, and the message light was blinking on my answering machine. Seventeen messages.

My brother Brian expressed the prevailing sentiment. 'Jesse had better keep a cyanide capsule handy. It'll save me the trouble of killing him.'

I replied to everyone, even the wailers and shouters. The last person I phoned was Harley Dawson.

She said, 'A piece of advice. Never let the man keep the negatives.'

'It's fake, and don't you dare comment about the tattoo. I'm not in the mood.'

'Guess not.'

'Harley, the people who faked the photo are tied in with Brand and Mako.'

Dead silence on her end.

I said, 'I'm not shooting in the dark here.'

'Brand *and* Mako. No, I'd say you're throwing grenades in the dark.'

'Listen, Harley—'

'No, you listen. I talked to George Rudenski. I know you went out to Mako and threw accusations around. Threatening that Kenny's going to, what was it – go down with Brand?'

'That's what Brand told me.'

Now there was real anger in Harley's voice. 'Suggesting things like that will get you in trouble.'

'Why? Is Kenny dangerous?'

'Don't be asinine. You're making a slanderous accusation. And you're making it to Kenny's lawyer.'

'It's a caution, Harley. I'm asking for your help here. You

know Kenny's not right. He's . . . *off*. And he was a friend of Franklin Brand. He dislikes Jesse. So you tell me who's leaping to conclusions.'

Her voice sounded weary. 'Evan, don't. Just don't screw with Mako. It's not something you want to do.'

'Why?'

'It will only cause trouble. Take my word for it.'

Forty-eight hours, down to thirty-five. What could I do? Talking to the police wouldn't do any good right now, not with their current attitude. How I wished that Chris Ramseur was still here, and running the investigation.

Chris had been involved with the case from the start, doing the detective work on the hit-and-run. I sat down at my desk. Jesse had given me a copy of the police report and I flipped through it, recognizing Chris's attention to detail and occasional sharp comment.

Turning a page, I came upon information I had neglected before. There was a witness.

One witness, not to the crash but its aftermath: a man named Stu Pyle. He was a plumber who had been driving up the road looking for an address, and found Jesse and Isaac. He recalled seeing Brand's BMW racing downhill past him, just before he arrived on the scene.

I found Pyle's statement. He couldn't specify the driver's gender, much less identify any passenger. It had been three years. Was it worth prodding his memory?

I found his number in the Yellow Pages, Pyle Plumbing.

'The accident, I been through all that with the police I don't know how many times.' His voice sounded wet, as if he was eating a gummy sandwich. 'I talk about it anymore, you're gonna pay my hourly call-out rate.'

I felt the growl starting in the base of my throat. 'Bring your tool kit. You can tighten the pipes under my kitchen sink.'

When he arrived Nikki was there, and Thea, crawling on the carpet, eating crumbs. We had taken bets on what he would look like – on how thick his stubble would be, the diameter of the beer belly, and how low his pants would sink toward his butt. I put my money on cleavage.

'You Ms Delaney?' he said.

For a second I didn't answer. He was built like a juicy steak, with biceps almost throbbing in his shirt sleeves. His cheeks were spanky-pink and radiated musky aftershave. Nikki lifted an eyebrow and stifled a smile.

I said, 'The sink's this way.'

He hauled his toolbox into the kitchen. His thighs were tree trunks. He squatted down in front of the sink and ran his hand along the drainpipe. 'Feels dry to me.'

'Good. Now, about Franklin Brand.'

He twisted to look at me over his shoulder. His blue shirt pulled free from the waistband of his jeans, exposing a hairy lower back.

He said, 'I been thinking about that.'

'Excellent. I want to ask you about the passenger in his car.'

He had a wrench in his hand. He hunched his shoulders and his jeans started slipping down his waist. Nikki shifted behind me.

'My call-out fee gets your sink looked at. It don't work on my memory.' He stood up with a grunt. 'Memory takes over-time pay.'

'I see.' I frowned. 'And if I appeal to your sense of civic duty?'

'Civic duty got the cops busting my chops after the wreck. Give me a break.'

'Let me get this straight. You want me to pay you to talk about what you saw the evening of the hit-and-run?'

'I read in the paper the driver's out on bail, two-hundred fifty grand. Lot of money floating around this case. Why should lawyers and the bail bondsman get it all, stiff the eyewitness?' He hitched up his pants. 'You ain't even started bidding yet.'

'I don't believe this.'

'You want to know, the cops want to know, the driver will want to know.'

'The cops won't like that.'

'Let them put in an offer. Maybe make me a real good witness. For the prosecution, or else for the defense. Who knows? It could go either way right now.'

'Get out of here,' I said.

'I'll give you right of first refusal. Just 'cause you're so cute.'

He bent over for his toolbox, and the pants slid way down. There it was: the plumber's friend, America's other crack problem. My win.

'You heard me. Out.' I pointed at the door.

'Your loss, honey.'

'I don't think so. Your ass could use a good waxing.'

That afternoon, boiling with anxiety, I took a run. The mountains shimmered green and the sky curved above, flawless blue. Coming back past the Old Mission I heard the organ echoing out the doors of the church, and found myself detouring inside to listen for a minute. Sometimes a Bach fugue can give you the fortitude you need.

When I came out, the man in the gray suit was standing on the church steps.

'Ms. Delaney? Dale Van Heusen, FBI.'

His voice had the high insistent tone of a drill. The suit was too large, as though he wanted to look bigger than he was. I walked down the steps.

He came with me. 'Running gear in church? I didn't know that sweat and holy water mixed.'

'How can I help you?' I said.

He pointed to the Spanish fountain, and we sat down on the edge.

He said, 'This is how it's played. I ask you questions and you tell me what I want to know, in complete detail. Do that, and you'll have an easy time, a straight shot at getting home. Got the picture?'

Water dripped from the mossy fountain and koi swam among the lily pads.

I said, 'Why are you questioning me, Mr Van Heusen?'

'Agent Van Heusen.' He shot his cuffs. 'Shall I go over the rules again? You seem to be an intelligent woman, I thought you'd get it the first time.'

He had the face of a badger, unprepossessing and nasty behind the eyes. Deep in my mind I heard a high-pitched droning, an alarm. Part of me wanted to run, part wanted to dump him into the fountain, and part wanted to draw swords.

He said, 'How long have you known Jesse Matthew Blackburn?'

En garde.

'Three years and three months. Are you inquiring, or verifying?'

'How well do you know him?'

'You're joking, right?'

'What?'

'You must know that he and I are engaged.'

'He has a lot of money for someone in his twenties.'

I didn't respond.

He said, 'You weren't enticed by it?'

I almost laughed. 'Jesse's money is invested in his house. And mutual funds. And long-term disability insurance.'

'I see. Did he tell you not to talk to me?'

'No.'

He leaned forward and clasped his hands between his knees. 'Because I get the distinct feeling you're trying to protect him.'

'You're right. If you'd tell me why you're asking questions about him, perhaps I wouldn't feel so worried.'

'An honest citizen shouldn't feel worried about talking to the FBI.'

'Oh, please.'

He brushed lint off his trousers and straightened the crease. 'I'm sure Mr Blackburn has warned you to watch your words, and reminded you to stay in his corner. But ask yourself what he has to gain by letting you take the heat for him.'

'This is preposterous.'

'Before his accident, did you know his confederates?'

'Confederates?'

'It means associates.'

'I know what it means.' And what it implied. Accomplices.

'Who did he hang around with? The Sandovals?'

'Yes, of course.'

'What kind of activities were they engaged in?'

'Swimming, biking, running.'

'Anything else?'

'Drinking beer.'

'None of them were wealthy at that time, were they?'

'No.'

'Did Mr Blackburn have any other sources of income besides his salary?'

He thought Jesse and the Sandovals were in on Brand's scheme. That was clear.

I said, 'No. He saved his summer salary to pay for law school. During the school year he worked part time on campus.'

'Daddy didn't spring for his tuition?'

The droning sound was returning to my head, but now it was the hum of anger.

'Jesse's dad sells office supplies. He doesn't have the money to spring for anything.'

'Is that why his son wanted to become an attorney? Money?'

'You're not a lawyer, are you?' I said.

'No, I'm a CPA.'

An accountant. A man who added for a living, whose deepest dreams involved carrying the one to the tens column. What was he after?

He took out a notepad and thumbed through it. 'And during this time, Adam Sandoval was at Cal Tech, correct? Did he ever work at the Jet Propulsion Lab?'

'Not that I know of.'

'JPL is a NASA lab. If he had access to government computer systems, you should tell me.'

Computers again, with a new twist. I resisted the urge to say, ask him yourself. This rude interrogation would loosen Adam's screws.

He said, 'Why are you trying to influence the testimony of Stu Pyle?'

The plumber. 'I'm not. What did he tell you?'

'That you paid him to visit you.'

The top of my head felt hot. 'If he said that, he was trying to worm money out of the cops. He's conducting a testimony auction.'

'Testimony about what, precisely?'

'Identifying the woman in the BMW.'

'Ah.' He flipped through his notepad. 'And you believe her to be whom?'

I couldn't see the harm in telling him. 'Mari Vasquez Diamond.'

He looked at the notebook, and nodded. 'If Pyle is really trying to work that angle, he won't get far. We have independent confirmation that she was with Brand the evening of the hit-and-run. And you needn't pry into that any longer.'

Van Heusen reached into his jacket and handed me three photos.

'Do you recognize any of these people?'

The crop-haired girl, Win Utley, and Mickey Yago. My hair felt as if it was sizzling in the sun.

I said, 'The two men are the ones who jumped Jesse. The girl, I can't prove it but I think she snatched my purse. Why are you asking me?'

'Has Mr. Blackburn or Adam Sandoval ever spoken about i-heist?'

'No.' I thought about it, and nodded at the photos. 'Is that what these guys call themselves?'

'Their racket is stealing from people electronically. They commit blackmail via computer.'

'They've demanded two hundred thousand dollars from Jesse. He reported this to the police.'

'And what are they blackmailing him about?'

153

Touché. I had walked right into that one. Van Heusen was close to smiling.

I said, 'Lieutenant Rome told you about the demand, didn't he? That's why you're here now. It's because they roughed Jesse up.'

Van Heusen held up the photos. 'Mickey Yago headed a cocaine trafficking organization in Los Angeles, dealing to rich college kids and the dot bong crowd. He has now moved on to other enterprises.' He touched Win Utley's picture. 'This fellow worked for the IRS before Yago corrupted him.' The girl's photo. 'Cherry Lopez is Yago's arm candy and the Artful Dodger of cyberspace.'

I looked closer. 'What's this?' With a finger I traced a line up her neck.

'Tattoo,' he said. 'Legend says, it runs uninterrupted from head to toe.'

'It looks like a snake.'

'Snake, or computer cable.'

It reminded me of the tattoo I had seen on the leg of the woman sitting on the balcony at Kenny's house, but I couldn't be sure.

I said, 'Jesse and Adam are the victims in all of this. Brand may have stolen money from this i-heist group, and that's why Yago demanded payment from Jesse.'

'Uh-huh.'

'This is extortion. What are you going to do about it?'

'What do you know about smurfing?'

'Excuse me?'

He watched my face.

I said, 'Smurfing, as in the Smurfs? Those blue gnome cartoon characters?'

Van Heusen stood up. The interview was over.

I said, 'Wait. That's it? What about i-heist?'

He tucked the notebook, photos, and pen back into his coat pocket. 'They've perfected a method of ripping people off one layer of skin at a time. And if I find out you have anything to do with these people, you're in just as deep as your boyfriend.'

Eighteen

I found Jesse and Adam at UCSB, working out in the pool. Jesse looked shark-smooth, the water streaming across his shoulders. The injury had stolen part of his kick, but not all; he had partially recovered what the doctors called ability against gravity, and the buoyancy of the water gave him power he didn't have on dry land. He swam a thousand meters while I watched, finishing with two hundred meters butterfly.

Bringing it home on the final lap, he dug in, accelerating toward the wall, stretching for the touch. He glanced at the timing clock. Pulling off his goggles, he hung on the lane line. I walked to the edge of the pool and crouched down.

'You negative split that last hundred,' I said.

'Great.' He spat into the gutter. 'I told you the wrist was okay.'

That's what he was doing here, I thought, besides burning off stress; feeling competent, in control. Take that, H_2O. In the next lane, Adam flip-turned and pushed off. Jesse cruised to the ladder and pulled himself onto the deck. I tossed him his towel.

'I just had a chat with the FBI,' I said.

I told him about it, and admitted my puzzlement about Van Heusen's final remarks.

Jesse said, 'Smurfing? Did he mean surfing?'

'I don't think so. I've never heard that term, have you?'

'No. It sounds as if it involves unnatural acts with a gnome.'

Adam finished and swam toward us under the lane lines. He bobbed next to the ladder, catching his breath. Jesse told him about Van Heusen, and asked the question.

'Smurfing, yes,' Adam said. 'It's a computer term. A kind of security breach.'

'Computers,' I said. 'Security intrusion, again.'

'I don't know much about it, but come over to my office and we can find out more online,' he said. 'And I know exactly the site to start with.'

I said, 'Don't tell me. Mako Technologies.'

Adam's office in Broida Hall showcased the perks awarded to scientists laboring as postdoctoral fellows: his name on a note card thumbtacked outside the door, metal bookcases, ugly linoleum crisscrossed with scuff marks. And he didn't care.

'View of the ocean,' he said, turning on the lights. 'If you jump out the window, and it's high tide.'

He sat down at his desk and went online, fingers clicking hard and fast.

He hunched forward. 'Here we go. Mako has a library of articles about security threats.'

Jesse pulled close to the desk and I leaned over Adam's shoulder. I could see a list of topics – Computer Crime, Hostile Code, Information Warfare. Adam searched for 'Smurfing' and turned up an article on Denial of Service attacks. We skimmed it.

Jesse said, 'I don't get it.'

'I don't either,' Adam said.

Smurfing attacks were aimed at ISPs. They fooled networks into sending thousands of 'are you there' messages to the ISP, which swamped it. Adam rubbed a hand over his face. How it connected to i-heist, I didn't know.

I said, 'Can I see what else is on the site?'

Adam leaned back. 'My mouse is your mouse.'

I leaned over the keyboard and selected *News*. Up popped a list of press releases.

'Gee,' Jesse said. 'It doesn't lead with "Brand Kills Again." *Quelle surprise.*'

Press releases included *George Rudenski Testifies to Congress* and *Scholarship Benefit Sparkling Success*. There were photos from the costume bash at the museum: Kenny Rudenski dressed as Steve McQueen, and the two Zorros, side by side.

'Uh-oh,' I said.

Zorro Two, who I didn't get a good look at that night, had a trim brown beard and a curly blond ponytail sticking out from beneath his hat.

'It's Mickey Yago.'

'No way,' Jesse said. He and Adam leaned toward the screen.

Adam said, 'What does it mean?'

'I don't know.'

Jesse stared at the photo. 'But it can't be good.'

Jesse rode back into town with me. Halfway home I pulled into the drive-through lane at In-N-Out Burger, joining a line of cars inching along like communicants toward the altar. My Explorer was the only vehicle not toting an In-N-Out bumper sticker cut up to read 'In-N-Out urge.'

Jesse said, 'I had the dream again.'

I glanced at him. 'The same?'

'This time he touched me. Hand's squeezing my arm and I'm staring at the sky, the shadow's right above me.' He rubbed his arm. 'I think I know what it means.'

I pulled up to the menu. 'Brand's getting under your skin.'

'No. I think it isn't a dream. It's a memory.'

The intercom squawked, asking for my order. But I was looking at Jesse.

He said, 'I think Brand got out of the BMW and walked down the hill to see if Isaac and I were dead.' He searched my face for a reaction. 'Think that's crazy?'

'No. It's chilling.'

'I don't know how long I blacked out. Minutes, maybe. He would have had time.'

The intercom squawked again. A horn blared from the car behind me. I ordered, hearing the horn again, impatient. Jesse stuck his arm out the window and gave the driver the finger.

I pulled forward. 'Don't bother. Anybody that desperate for fast food deserves pity, not reproach.'

My window was still down, and I could hear the honker's voice, shouting into the intercom. A sharp, twangy Oklahoma voice. I looked in the rearview mirror.

'It's Taylor.'

'No.' He turned around.

I eased up to the cashier's window and paid, took my food and pulled forward.

Jesse watched Taylor drive up to the window. 'Jesus, look at all those fries.'

I turned into a parking space.

'She's digging straight into them. Look at her go. My God, the woman's a machine. A terrible, unstoppable eating machine.'

I turned off the engine. 'I need to talk to her about stealing my address book.'

'I want to meet her,' he said.

My hand was on the door handle. 'No, you don't.'

'Yes, I do.'

'I'll introduce you another time.'

'She swallowed that last helping of fries whole, including the box. I think she unhinged her jaw to do it.'

'Not now.' I opened the door. 'Stay here. Please.'

'You ask too much.'

His face could look devilish at such times, eyes gleaming, smile so white.

'Don't you trust me?' he said. 'To be sweet to Cousin Tater?'

She was pulling away from the cashier's window. Giving Jesse a look, I got out and waved to her.

The red Mazda braked. I saw Taylor's face through the windshield, fries sticking out between her lips. Her eyes bulged. Recovering, she swallowed, and waved.

She swung into a parking space and jumped out. She was dressed in lemon yellow workout gear, with lines of sweat dampening her shirt. 'What a neat surprise.'

'I'd like my address book back, please.'

'I don't know what on earth you're talking about.' She batted her eyes at me. 'But I do know that tomorrow evening you should plan to be at Nikki's house. Seven p.m. So don't be a party pooper, just – oh, is that Jesse?'

He had stayed in the car, a rare moment of acquiescence. And turned on one of my CDs. The voice of Patsy Cline was now keening from my car stereo. Singing 'Crazy.' He was singing along.

Taylor strode to greet him, wiping grease from her hands onto her aerobics shorts. Approaching the car, she hunched her shoulders and drew in her hand, as though she was going to shake with a Smurf.

'Well, hello there,' she said. 'It's so special to meet you.'

He thrust his arm out the window. 'Taylor, you don't know what a thrill this is.'

'My, aren't you the gentleman.' She took his hand in both of hers. 'You'll excuse the way I look. I must have burned off a thousand calories running on that treadmill.' And she cringed. 'Sorry, I didn't mean to talk about running.'

'You can talk about running.'

'I'm sure it's a sore subject. Not that you could get sore, running. I'm just so sorry. But it's a beautiful day and here y'all are, out for a drive.'

'We were at the pool.'

'Evan takes you swimming? Isn't that sweet.'

I came up behind them, knowing what was going to happen, seeing her sugary smile, and the way she patted his hand, and the look in Jesse's eyes, dead calm.

I said, 'We have to go. Will you put my address book in the mail?'

'Hon, I told you I don't know what you mean,' she said.

She raised up on tiptoe, trying to look through the window at him. After a few seconds she gave up and opened his door. She stood examining him, puzzlement spreading across her face.

'My word, you look perfectly normal,' she said.

For a moment he was silent. Then he said, 'Yes. My work with the faith healer is paying off.'

159

She tilted her head, her eyes blank with amazement. 'Why, that is just wonderful.'

'Yeah, you can't beat Satanism for results.'

Long, long beat. 'What?'

'And you know, since I started tithing I've been getting feeling back.' He popped himself in the thigh. 'Ow.'

She stood with her head tipped, like a punching bag that had taken too many hits.

'The incantations do tend to draw dogs, but what the hell. Oh, here they come.'

He pointed over her shoulder. Taylor spun and nearly jumped into his lap.

She looked wildly around. 'You – where – I don't . . .'

I sighed. 'He's kidding.'

She stared at me, and him, and back at me, and around the parking lot again.

He said, 'Sorry, bad joke. I'm really an atheist.'

My life was over.

Taylor's face surrendered to confusion. 'Then I don't get it. How come you don't look all paralyzed?'

I said, 'Gotta go,' and sprinted around to the driver's side of the car.

Jesse said, 'Court order. I got a permanent injunction against it.'

'Be serious,' she said.

I hopped in and started the engine. Threw it in reverse, not waiting for Jesse to shut the door, backing out, seeing the bewilderment on Taylor's face.

He yanked the door shut. As I dropped into gear, he leaned out and said to her, 'Viagra, and lots of it.'

I floored the car. We bounced out onto the street.

He said, 'Go ahead, give it to me.'

'I wouldn't dream of it. She deserved every word.'

He tried to read my expression. 'But you're worried about the next family reunion. People asking you about marrying a sex-crazed Satanist.'

'Not at all.' I punched the accelerator. 'Because I'm never going to one again. I'm sending you.'

Stu Pyle ran his plumbing business out of the back of a van. It smelled like pork rinds and wet metal, and had a topless hula doll stuck to the dashboard. This late in the day he charged double for a call-out. At about the same time I was jousting with Taylor, Pyle was driving along a back road in the foothills, looking for the house belonging to the woman who called him and begged him to come right now. Her address was scribbled on a Post-It note that he'd stuck below the hula girl. *Miss Jones. Toilet overflowing – freaking out.*

But the houses had died out half a mile back, and he crept along the winding road through overgrown trees and dry brush, chewing on a ham sandwich, trying to find the place. The asphalt petered out into dirt and gravel. Finally, he came to a dead end. Stopped.

Stupid broad gave him the wrong directions. He set the sandwich on the seat, wiped mayonnaise from his hands onto his shirt, and called her on his cellphone.

The mechanical phone company voice came on. 'We're sorry, but your call cannot be completed at this time . . .'

Stupid, stupid broad.

He pulled a three-point turn and was putting the van into gear, when the car pulled up in front of him. A gold car with a rental company dashboard sticker. Driver waving. Asking for directions, getting out, unfolding a map on the hood of the car. The man looked like a rich tourist, wearing that fancy cashmere jacket, maybe up for a polo match. Something familiar about him. Stu Pyle got out of his van to look at the map.

It was his last good deed.

Pyle was big, but he was outweighed. And when the passenger climbed out of the car, he was outnumbered. They grabbed him and he couldn't beat them off. They dragged him around to the back of the van, yanked open the doors, and threw him inside on the floor. The smell was stronger here, wet metal overlaid with sewage. All his tools and supplies were arrayed around him.

They chose the snake.

The metal cable hummed when they extended it. It was aluminum, once clean and shiny but not now. He kicked, knocking washers and pipe fittings out of the boxes in the back of the van. Bolts and pipes and tools flew, ringing down like coins. He stretched his fingers, trying to reach the wrench, but it was too far, so he fought, screaming, but no one was around to hear him. They held his head down, and forced his mouth open.

They cleaned him out.

Nineteen

I didn't hear about it until the next day at Jesse's. It was early morning and I was running on the beach, long and fast, to keep from barking. Fourteen hours left until the deadline.

Sandpipers skittered in front of me, outrunning the breakers. I rounded the point and the coastline flared into light, the harbor a bowl of gold beneath the green rim of the mountains. The waves provided the backbeat to my breathing. Offshore, the Channel Islands rose blue against the horizon. I did two miles and came back, splashing through the waves. I was humming with heat. I saw Jesse swimming out beyond the surf line, his freestyle stroke so smooth it looked lazy. I waved.

I looked toward the house and saw the men in suits standing on the deck.

Correction. Two men were standing on the deck. The third, FBI Special Agent Dale Van Heusen, was sitting in Jesse's wheelchair.

I felt myself tighten. I slowed to a walk, suppressing the urge to charge at Van Heusen, topple him onto his back, and box his ears. I'm told that goes down badly with the Bureau. What he was doing was rude, presumptuous, and intrusive. And from the smirk on his face, he knew it, too.

He set his hands on the wheels. 'Pretty slick ride. Ultralight frame, custom seat – how much does one of these set you back?'

'That isn't a toy, Agent Van Heusen, and it isn't up for grabs. Please get off.'

He talked over his shoulder at the other men. 'What do you guess, Rome? Fiori? Two grand?'

They stood stiffly, their ties flapping in the breeze. To his credit,

Clayton Rome looked embarrassed. Van Heusen shrugged, and took his time standing up. He gazed at the house. His badger nose wrinkled.

'Quite a spread your boyfriend has here.'

'What is it you want, gentlemen?'

Rome stood with arms akimbo, gold cuff links and belt buckle winking in the light, looking at me with calm suspicion. 'Stu Pyle was murdered yesterday.'

Van Heusen said, 'They held him down and drove a plumber's snake into his throat.'

Rome said, 'Where were you yesterday at six p.m.?'

My stomach was jumping, my head abuzz. And I heard the deliberate plural in Van Heusen's description. *They*. I told them I had been at In-N-Out Burger. To prove it, I went out to my Explorer and dug the receipt out of the ashtray.

Rome took it. 'Anybody who can verify this, besides Mr Blackburn?'

'Taylor Boggs.' I looked at Van Heusen. 'You met her the other day.'

'Neat-looking blonde, with eyes that are extremely blue, almost—' Van Heusen wiggled his fingers in front of his own eyes, searching for the adjective.

'Violet,' I said.

Nodding, he took out his notebook. I gave him her phone number. My legs felt watery. This was the final flourish: all at once, I was in Taylor's debt and at her mercy. I needed her to verify my alibi. With the FBI. In a murder investigation. She had just won the gossipers' triple crown.

Rome said, 'Does Mr Blackburn own any other vehicles besides the Audi out front?'

'No.'

'And you?'

'Just the Explorer.' I looked at him. 'What did you do, check our tires against a tread pattern you found at the murder scene?'

He shifted his shoulders. I saw a set of handcuffs glinting on his belt.

164

Van Heusen said, 'Don't get cocky. The only vehicle we've eliminated so far is that one.' He pointed at the wheelchair.

They knew Jesse hadn't been involved. They had to doubt it was me. What was the FBI doing here? The murder was an SBPD matter, not a federal crime. I still didn't know what, exactly, Van Heusen was investigating.

But I knew that everything had spun out of control. Chris Ramseur was dead, and Stu Pyle. Brand was killing off people who knew about the crash. All at once I felt a visceral memory of Brand shoving me to the floor at the motel. Cologne, marbled weight, his words. *You'll see. You'll all fucking see.*

I felt sick to my fingertips. 'Jesse's in danger. You have to protect him.'

Van Heusen said, 'I want to talk to him. Where is he?'

Circling overhead at twenty-thousand feet, jackass. He can fly.

I said nothing. But the other FBI agent, Fiori, nodded toward the water and said, 'That's him swimming. She waved at him.'

'No kidding.' Van Heusen looked at me. 'Go get him.'

I felt a prickle on my cheeks, the flush of abasement. But I walked down to the water and waited for Jesse to swim back. He rode in on a wave and pulled himself out of the water.

Sitting on the sand, he took off his goggles. 'The FBI?'

I crouched down next to him. 'Stu Pyle was murdered yesterday.'

His shoulders fell. 'No.'

He stared at me, and at the men. I could see the strain on his face, the shine of the swim draining into shock.

He said, 'Let's go find out what they want.'

He sculled up the beach, lugging with his arms, pushing with his better leg. Rome and Fiori looked away, discomfited, but Van Heusen stood at the edge of the deck, his mouth creased with impatience. When I walked past him to grab Jesse's beach towel, he said, 'You don't need to be here. Go home.'

I turned my head. 'You should check your sunscreen. I think you may have applied asshole factor forty.'

He sucked on his teeth. 'You don't take direction well, do you? It's not a request.'

'Do you have a warrant?'

'That's beside the point.'

'I thought not. Then you're a guest here. Try acting like one.'

Jesse reached the deck and sat on the edge. I tossed him the towel.

Van Heusen stood over him. 'Stu Pyle drowned in his own blood with a plumber's snake jammed down his esophagus.'

Jesse looked up. 'You must be Agent Van Heusen.'

'When's the last time you spoke to Franklin Brand?'

'When he was trying to beat the snot out of me at Evan's house.'

Van Heusen looked down. 'This needs to be a serious conversation. Get real.'

'I am. What's this about?'

'It's about me guessing that you don't want to end up like Stu Pyle. No matter how bad your life is, it has to be better than having a feces-stained metal cable stuffed down your throat. Though I have to say, your life doesn't look too bad.' He gazed at the house. 'I bet you'd hate to lose all this.'

Jesse squinted at him. 'Evan tells me you're a CPA. Are you with the financial crimes section?'

'What a smart guy. Keep guessing.'

Agent Fiori rubbed his forehead and said, 'Come on, Dale.'

Van Heusen ignored him. 'Here's a hint. Let's talk about Mickey Yago.'

Inside the house, the phone rang. All three cops turned at the sound. Jesse gave me a glance. I took it to mean that he didn't want them to overhear any phone messages, and I went in just as Adam's voice came on the machine.

'Call me, *jefe*. We have a problem. The—'

I picked up. 'Jesse can't talk. What's up?'

'Lieutenant Rome stopped by my place half an hour ago, with the FBI.'

'They're here now.'

'Stu Pyle getting murdered – Lord God, it's horrible. I knew if Brand got out of jail awful things would happen.'

I looked outside. Jesse had pulled up into the chair but Van Heusen was still looming over him, talking down at the top of his head.

Adam said, 'This scares me. Jesse's the only witness left, and the police don't believe the danger. And they seem to have forgotten Isaac was a victim.' Anger edged into his voice. 'That FBI agent, the one who talks with his nose forward, like he's sniffing you – Van Heusen. He asked if Isaac had gang connections.'

I closed my eyes. 'God.'

'Sandoval, that's all he needed to hear. A Mexican name, and he was convinced Isaac must have been a gangbanger.'

'He's a button-pusher, Adam. He tries to set people off. If he comes back, don't talk to him.'

I opened my eyes. Agent Fiori was standing at the sliding glass door, staring at me. Outside, Van Heusen was leaning down, talking into Jesse's face. The hiss of the surf covered his words. He straightened, spread his hands, as if asking a question. Jesse said nothing.

I said, 'Hang in, Adam. I have to go.'

Van Heusen shrugged. He nodded to the other two men and they left the way they'd come, around the side of the house. I walked out onto the deck. Jesse didn't look up. His face, backlit by the glitter of the Pacific, looked stricken.

I started toward him. 'What did Van Heusen say to you?'

It took him a few seconds to speak. 'That I must know what's going on with Brand and i-heist.' He shut his eyes and shook his head. 'He thinks I must have been helping Brand steal from Mako. That's what the two hundred K is about.' He looked at me. 'He said, if I don't come clean, they're going to hook me in with these people. They'll seize my assets.'

'What?'

'Van Heusen thinks I'm part of a criminal enterprise. They can seize any assets I gained as part of that enterprise.'

My toes wanted to cramp. 'That's outrageous. He thinks that because Mako settled with you, he can clean you out?'

'That's exactly what he thinks. And he can do it, if he tries hard. He could take my house, my car, my bank accounts. He could ruin me.'

'What does Van Heusen want you to do?'

'He wants me to snitch on Brand and i-heist. How can I do that? Fucking hell. He could take it all, Ev. I'd spend years fighting it. I could end up on the street.'

We stared at each other, immobile with shock. The surf frothed beyond us.

Franklin Brand almost took Jesse from me once. The thought that he might try to finish the job hit me like a hammer. The fact that the authorities didn't seem to care made me want to beat the hell out of them. I had to do something, anything, find a way to get them to protect Jesse. I needed help, from any corner.

I went inside and phoned Jakarta Rivera.

'What changed your mind?' Jax said.

'I want information. You seem to have it,' I said.

She strode up State Street. The sidewalk vista offered mossy tile roofs, skinny latte, and pierced eyebrows. We passed shoppers, tourists, Spanish-style sushi bars, a demented blues guitarist playing for loose change. Jax's diamonds flashed and her perfume spiced the air.

'Information about us, or about yourself?' she said.

'Both. Foremost, I want to know why the FBI is investigating Jesse. I want to know what's going on with Brand, and this i-heist crew.'

Tim walked next to me, gazing in store windows. 'Tall order.'

'Hey, in the last week I've been robbed and assaulted, Jesse has been beaten up. Franklin Brand has killed two people. He's at large, he's out for revenge, and Jesse's the only witness still alive. The police are treating us like dirt, and a gang of extortionists is demanding two hundred thousand dollars from him in, oh . . .' I looked at my watch. 'A few hours. So yeah, it's a tall order.

Now give me whipped cream and a cherry on top and get your undercover butts in gear.'

They both looked at me.

'Help me get Jesse out of this mess and I'll write your memoirs on spec,' I said.

Tim's cool eyes looked merry. 'When can you start?'

'As soon as you meet my number-one condition.'

'What's that?'

'Prove you're for real.'

He said, 'Certify that we were spies? Ah, there's the rub.'

'The CIA and British Intelligence will neither confirm nor deny whether someone was an agent. So how do you propose to authenticate yourselves?' I said.

Jax said, 'Receipts from the Spy Store?'

'Not funny.'

Tim said, 'Passports? We have them in multiple names, from various countries.'

I shook my head. 'Pay enough, anybody can get a forged passport.'

Jax said, 'These aren't from British Honduras.'

I gave her a sharp look, presuming that was a reference to Brand's phony documents.

Tim said, 'It's tricky. Exceedingly.' His face, so rough and so oddly winning, became reflective. 'Ultimately, verification would come only from an adversary, Evan. The players know each other. You'd have to gain access to an opponent's files and find a name.'

'Well,' Jax said, 'you might also be able to go to a third-party country, someplace on the chessboard. Their intelligence services might know the players.'

'Adversary,' Tim insisted. 'You'd need to go to a broken country and give them the access code. Which is money. Then you might get the proof you're after.'

We walked. That stink of the real was wafting in the air around me.

I said, 'And if I did believe you, what would your story be?'

Tim said, 'Army sniper school, Secret Intelligence Service, flash cars, knives drawn in the souk.'

'You talked about private espionage. Were you a mercenary?' I said.

'No.'

'Industrial espionage?'

'Hardly.'

And with that, he veered into a clothing store. Jax and I followed. Clothes were stacked in earth-toned piles around a giant cactus. Tim chose a pair of brown drawstring pants and held them up to his waist.

Jax said, 'Put those down before somebody sees you.'

He gave her a cutting look. She stepped close to him, and they muttered at each other. Great, just what I didn't need: spatting spies. I turned away, picking up a beige shirt with an iguana stitched on it.

Jax saw me holding it. 'Unh-*unh*. Get your hands off of that.'

'Not my color?'

'These clothes are a crime. Shapeless and clinging, guaranteed to make you look like a lumpy pillow.' She guided me to the door. 'I swear, Santa Barbara is a style disaster zone.'

'Hey, we're casual here,' I said.

'So is an unmade bed, but I wouldn't wear it out to lunch.' She led me outside. 'You need fashion re-education. Repeat after me, slowly. *Prada.*'

I looked over my shoulder. 'Where's Tim?'

'He'll catch up.'

I pursed my lips. 'If you two bicker over something as insubstantial as clothing, how will we get through a manuscript?'

'We're not bickering, we're tempestuous.'

We headed into Saks Fifth Avenue, where the air was cooled to the temperature of crisp French Chablis. She propped her sunglasses atop her head.

'Let me tell you about myself. Father's from Texas, mother's a Cuban refugee. I have a linguistics degree and an ability to lie with a fabulous smile. *Cubano* Spanish accent that went down well in certain South American circles.'

I said, 'Why'd you become a spy?'

'The shrinks at Langley had a theory. As a child, I witnessed the primal scene.'

She headed for the belts and scarves, her fingers brushing over silk and leather.

'You know, peering through a crack in the bedroom door at Mom and Dad. Jax Rivera, spy tot.'

'Why'd you quit?' I said.

'One day I found myself out on a limb in Medellin. I was having an affair with an asset, and he betrayed me.'

She draped a scarf over my shoulder and leaned back to assess the look.

I said, 'What happened?'

'I killed him.'

I couldn't help it; I just stared at her.

She said, 'He was going to shop me to narco-traffickers. It was him or me.'

'You make it sound easy.'

'No, it sent me off the deep end. Thank God I met Tim, or I might have hung myself.' She took the scarf from my shoulders. 'You have potential. Look at you, this wonderful bone structure and lean figure. I should take you to Milan.'

She touched my hair. I brushed her hand away.

I said, 'And what do you plan to title your memoirs, *Kick-Ass in Versace?*'

She raised an eyebrow. 'Catchy.'

She walked on, looking at pashminas. They hung on the wall, blue, gold, and purple, the colors lush behind her brown face.

'Damn.' My head pounded. 'Damn, stop. Jax, what did you do? Shoot him?'

'Gave him a joint laced with heroin, and when he fell asleep put a nine millimeter round through his temple. He never felt a thing. No pain, no remorse.'

I felt as if a golf ball had lodged in my throat. 'Who was he?'

'You don't want to know.' She looked past my shoulder. 'And here's Tim.'

He walked up, cracking his knuckles, looking at Jax. 'You told her?'

'Some.'

He glanced at me. 'You seem displeased.'

'You could say so.'

He nodded toward the escalator and I followed him on, heading up. Jax stayed with the pashminas. He watched her, his expression unreadable.

He said, 'I need to explain something to you.'

'Oh, I think you need to explain a lot of things.'

'Self defense can take many forms.'

'So it can. But to justify killing in self defense, you have to be in imminent danger. You don't drug a man unconscious and then put a barrel to his head.'

'Are you angry that she killed him, or that she slept with him?'

'Excuse me?'

We got off the escalator in the women's department. He said, 'You want proof?' He grabbed a hideous sequined jacket off a rack, handed it to me, and pointed across the store. 'Go admire yourself in the mirror over there.'

'Tim, even Michael Jackson would find this too garish.'

'Humor me.'

Though his face was relaxed, his eyes were sharp. I swallowed the snippy remark, headed to the mirror, and held the jacket up to my chest. The sequins were blinding. In the mirror, I watched Tim walk toward the men's room.

A moment later, I saw a woman get off the escalator. She was young, wiry, wearing gold hoop earrings and a red bandanna over her hair like a 'do rag. She followed Tim. Right behind her came Jax, hands full of accessories.

From that point, it was quick. Tim went in the men's room. Bandanna stopped outside the door. Jax came up behind her, pushed her inside, and shut the door behind her.

I tossed the jacket aside. The bathroom door was locked. I banged on it, hissing, 'Open up,' and the lock flipped. Jax thrust her arm through the door and pulled me inside, slamming and locking it again. I opened my mouth and she held up a finger, signaling silence.

The men's room was splendid. There were flowers on the counter, and Chopin piped in through the speakers, and a shine on the floor, where Bandanna lay face down, hog-tied.

Jax pointed at the scarf gagging the young woman's mouth, and the belts cinching her hands and feet.

'Hermès. Gucci. Don't dis my labels, hon.'

Tim's foot was planted between Bandanna's shoulders. He was going through her wallet. She squirmed on the floor, trying to kick him.

Jax gave her a harsh look. 'Chill. You do not want me to start in on you with a pair of Jimmy Choo stilettos.'

I said, 'What the hell are you doing?'

Tim said, 'I saw her down the street, near that cactus-and-drawstring-trousers shop. Watched her in reflection off the windows, keeping pace with us.'

I felt numb. I got it now. Jax and Tim hadn't been arguing – Tim had dropped back behind this woman to check her out.

I said, 'She was following you?'

Tim looked up. 'No. She was following you.'

I felt my face heating.

He found her driver's license. 'Cherry Lopez. Know her?'

Jax pulled off the bandanna. I saw the cropped black hair and the tattoo climbing up her neck.

I said, 'Yes. She's i-heist. And I think she stole my wallet and cellphone.'

Lopez bucked, trying to get out from under Tim's shoe. He reached down with both hands, yanked her jeans jacket off her shoulders, and wrestled a black club from inside it. He held it up.

'Shock baton. Amazingly unpleasant to be on the receiving end of one of these.'

I felt a chill, like ragged fingernails pulling at my skin. Tim dropped down, put his knee on Lopez's back, and rubbed the tip of the baton along her cheek.

'Tell me, pet. What were you planning to do with this?'

She squirmed, moaning through the gag, trying to shrink from the baton.

'Self defense begins with awareness of the threat against you.' Tim rested the baton on Lopez's ear. 'Then you need the bottle to actually defend yourself. You mustn't shrink from disabling your attacker. Pity will get you hurt.'

The creepy fingernail feeling kept pulling at my skin. And beneath that, anger.

'That's enough,' I said.

His face was harder than a board. 'That's not even a start.'

He removed the scarf from her mouth.

She spat at him. 'Get away from me, you poncy faggot.'

'My, somebody's been watching British telly,' he said.

'You're going to regret this. All of you,' she said.

I squatted down, out of spitting range. 'I saw you at Kenny Rudenski's house.'

She twisted to look at me. Her gothic eye makeup matched the black dye in her hair. 'I'm his au pair.'

I nodded. 'Sure. Babysitting what, his Dale Earnhardt helmet?'

'Woman, you are a bucket of extra-bitchy recipe, aren't you?'

'Why were you following me?'

She spat. It globbed on the gleaming tile floor. 'I'll hurt you worst.'

Tim took her hand in his and bent her thumb back. Her face twisted, and she started to moan. As soon as she opened her mouth he jammed the gag back in it.

I said, 'She didn't attack me. Don't hurt her.'

Weariness crossed his face. 'Jax, have a word with Evan, won't you?'

Jax nodded. 'Come on.'

She led me to the door. A burglar's tool was stuck in the lock. Jax turned it and we went out, heading for the escalator.

'Tim will find out why she was following you,' she said.

'What's he going to do to her?'

'He won't let her come after you with that shock baton, that's for certain.'

'Is this what he meant by private work? Roughing people up?'

'Stop being pissy.'

We trotted down the escalator, marched through the store, and outside.

She said, 'Tim will disable the threat against you, nothing more. Because he's not on the job anymore.'

'Do tell me, Jax. What is this job you keep referring to?'

'Contract assassination.'

Twenty

Driving home, I debriefed myself. *Mission accomplished?* No, there were unexpected difficulties. *Such as?* A purse-snatcher with a shock baton. Prospective clients who took cash to kill people. *Cash?* Okay, maybe a cashier's check. *Did you find out anything about why Jesse's in such a mess?* No. *Did you sign a contract to write the Norths' memoirs?* 'Contract' is not a word I want to use right now.

When I stopped for a light the driver next to me, a cholo in a low-rider Chevy, heard me dishing it out to myself. He locked his doors.

Did you learn one single thing that could help you? Yeah, watch your back. What are you going to do now?

I don't know.

When I swung to the curb in front of my house a man was standing at the garden gate. Holding that clipboard, he looked like an insurance salesman. Excellent, sign me up for a big fat life insurance policy. He walked toward me.

'Evan Delaney? This is for you.'

He handed me a document. I saw SUPERIOR COURT OF THE STATE OF CALIFORNIA and, next to DEFENDANT, my name. Mari Vasquez Diamond had followed through on her threat. She was suing me, Jesse, and Sanchez Marks for intentional infliction of emotional distress.

The phone was ringing when I opened my front door. I let the machine get it. Staring at the complaint, I kicked off my shoes, a bad idea because slip-ons gain velocity like rocket-propelled grenades. One flew onto the dining table and hit the wedding mound. Papers spewed. Jax Rivera's voice came on the machine.

'Evan, it's important that we continue our conversation. Tim learned some things you need to know.'

I didn't move.

'You know how to reach me,' she said. 'Be smart. Call.'

In the depths of my head, *Wipeout* was playing. I had paddled out too far and now the big ones were rolling down on top of me.

I stared at the complaint. *Intentional Infliction of Emotional Distress.* I read: '. . . that under the direction of defendant Blackburn, defendant Delaney subjected Mrs Diamond to extreme abuse intended to cause severe distress. In particular: that in the presence of Mrs Diamond's party guests, Delaney did shockingly call her "old," "cheap," and a "snotty socialite" . . .'

She was going for the hat trick: petty, stupid, and inaccurate. Who, I wondered, was inane enough to file this lawsuit on her behalf? I checked the first page.

I picked up the phone, and slammed it down again. I dug my shoe out from under the wedding pile and headed out the door. To Harley Dawson's law firm.

Harley walked into the lobby at the law firm. In the dove gray suit, with her silver hair shining in the afternoon sun, she looked satiny. She gave me a glossy stare.

She said, 'Uh-oh. You look like you've been drinking gasoline.'

I waved the complaint. 'Since when does this firm take on frivolous lawsuits?'

'What are you talking about?'

I flipped to page three. '"Knowing that her actions would cause emotional distress, Delaney did attempt to serve legal documents on Calvin Diamond in full view of Mrs Diamond . . ." This is non-actionable. It's preposterous.'

'Tone it down,' she said, glancing at the receptionist. 'I don't know anything about this.'

'"Said attempted service of legal documents was committed in a shocking manner; to wit—"' I looked up. '"To wit"? What is this, *Twelfth Night*?'

'Enough.'

'Like hell. I'm just the tip of the iceberg. Wait till Jesse shows up with Lavonne Marks.'

'Whoop-de-doo, get out the party hats.' She put a hand on my back and walked me to the elevator. 'Let's go get coffee.'

I shrugged her off. 'Why do people keep trying to hustle me out of places?'

'Maybe because you're acting like a human air raid siren.'

The elevator came, and we got on.

'When did your firm start representing Mari Vasquez Diamond?' I said.

'None of your business.' She watched the numbers go down.

I said, 'Who referred her, Kenny Rudenski?' Her mouth pursed, and I knew I'd guessed right. 'What is this thing you have with Kenny? He's bad news, Harley. Seriously bad. You should cut yourself off from him.'

'I keep telling you, he's—'

'Yeah. Misunderstood. He's really a sweetheart. You sound like a teenaged girl with a crush on him.'

Her eyes bruised, and her face pinched. The elevator opened and we headed outside. She wasn't looking at me. I knew I'd pushed too hard.

'Okay, I take that back,' I said, 'But what about the lawsuit?'

She held up her hands, looking brittle. 'Obviously, this action shouldn't have been filed. The person who did it is a junior associate. I don't know how it happened, but it shouldn't have . . .' Her voice trailed off.

'Shouldn't have gone this far? No kidding. Sounds like you need to exercise better supervision over your attorneys.'

'My God, will you just back off? You're like a monkey hissing on my shoulder. I'll deal with it.'

'Harley, what's wrong with you?'

She laughed. It was a shrill sound. 'Where shall I start?'

'Is it to do with Kenny?'

'No, it's not Kenny. It's Cassie.' She pushed her hair off her face. 'We're breaking up.' She sighed. 'My life's doing a slow turn on the rotisserie right now. But don't worry, I'll sort this thing out with Mrs Diamond. And I'll talk to Lavonne Marks. We'll be professional about it tonight. No catfighting over the Jell-O molds.'

'What?'

'The bridal shower.' Then she shut her eyes. 'Damn, it's a surprise, isn't it.'

'Not anymore.'

Four hours to the deadline and I had accomplished nothing except to learn how dismally ignorant I was of the dangers surrounding me. I hadn't been able to help Jesse one bit. I ended up at his office, telling him about the encounter with Jax and Tim and Cherry Lopez. Behind him, outside the window, the mountains loomed blue-green in the sun.

'Retired assassins. What the hell does that mean?' he said. 'These people are screwing with you, Ev. Giving you a major mind job.'

'You don't think they're for real?'

'This ghostwriting thing isn't for real. They don't actually expect you to write a book that violates US and UK national security laws, and confesses to contract killings. That's nuts.'

I jammed my hands in my back pockets.

'Whatever they want from you, it isn't your turn of phrase.'

'I don't think they're faking. They're not making this up,' I said.

'I don't think so either. Which leaves two possibilities. One, they really did stop an attack on you this afternoon. Or two, it was a set-up and they were in on the whole thing with this Cherry Lopez.'

'Now you're messing with my mind.'

'You didn't see them take her down. You didn't see them tie her up. And you didn't see what happened after you left the men's room. Maybe North untied her and they sampled the scented soaps and had a good laugh about you.'

'Why would they do that?'

'To scare you, to convince you they were on your side, who knows? That's the thing with mind jobs.' He ran a hand through his dark hair. Under the sun coming through the window, his face was sere. 'Either way it's bad news. It means they aren't retired. They're still in business.'

I felt as though I had a ball of string lodged in my throat.

'Don't call Jax back,' he said. 'Close the door on these people. They're nothing but trouble.'

I leaned against the windowsill. 'I'm not going to the bridal shower. I'm staying with you until we know what Yago's going to do.'

'Absolutely not. You have to go, so that I can hear all the gory details.'

'Jesse, I'm scared.'

'She's just your cousin, Ev. Repeat after me: "The power of Christ compels you."'

'You know what I'm talking about.'

'Yes. And we're not going to cower. So go home and get dressed.' He tapped a pencil against my knee. 'You have to practice looking surprised.'

'It's Tater. No matter how I prepare myself, I'm going to be surprised.'

Understatement of the year.

Twenty-One

Nikki's front door was open and music was rolling out, Alicia Keyes, 'A Woman's Worth.' I walked in and saw the balloons, clown bright against the sunset. I felt glad I was wearing the red dress with gold poppies. I heard voices in the kitchen.

Carl came trotting down the stairs, holding Thea. 'You look lovely.' He pecked me on the cheek. 'I had no idea about your family. You deserve a medal.'

'What—'

He continued straight out the door. 'We're going to the driving range. Remember, you can get through this.' Thea waved at me over his shoulder.

'Well, don't you look darling.' Taylor's voice came at me. 'See what happens when you give it the old college try?'

Her own dress was a screaming shade of orange. She knuckled my wrist and pulled me into the dining room. Finger food was set out on the table.

'I got a little visit from the FBI,' she said.

My stomach dropped. 'What did you tell them?'

'I saw you yesterday at In-N-Out. You had a cheeseburger, fries, and a boyfriend who's a real kidder.'

'Did they explain what it was about?'

'This Franklin Brand and his confederates killed the plumber.' Her blueberry eyes were hot to bursting. 'It's organized crime, right? Or racketeering?'

'Agent Van Heusen told you that?'

'Not in so many words, but it's big or Dale wouldn't be working on it.'

Dale.

'You know, seeing how he's with the Money Laundering Unit.'

Her orange dress pulsed before my eyes. Van Heusen was investigating money laundering.

Nikki came in carrying a tray of antipasti. 'Hi, sweetie.'

Taylor stared at the tray. 'Why don't I see the jalapeño poppers?'

'They're in the oven.' Nikki gave me a hug.

'Bring them out, they're real popular. Come on, we have a schedule.'

'Oven mitt's on the counter. I'm going to present the party girl to her guests.'

Nikki laced fingers with me and led me to the living room. When I started to speak she said, 'Everything's cool. We're going to have a fine time.'

I breathed, trying to rearrange my head, and smiled at the potpourri of guests Taylor had assembled. It looked as though she'd invited anybody whose name she could find on my desk. There was Lavonne Marks, and Harley Dawson. They were looking civil toward each other. Amber Gibbs, and Helen Potts from across the street. And Patsy Blackburn, Jesse's mother. Her ice-pink suit was accessorized with a tumbler of Smirnoff. There was Taylor clipping into the room, saying, 'Girls, scoot in here. We're going to play a game.'

And there by the fireplace, looking as smooth as a string of pearls, was Jax Rivera.

Taylor shoved a notepad and pen into my hand and nudged me down onto a sofa.

Tater, you potato head. You invited a hit woman to my bridal shower.

Patsy Blackburn wriggled her derrière onto the sofa next to me, rattling the ice cubes in her glass. Jax settled onto the sofa across from me, as relaxed as a cat. She looked classy in the black dress, with the gold scarf draped over her shoulders.

I looked closer. The scarf. Hermès. It was the one she had used to gag Cherry Lopez.

I said, 'I need a drink.'

'In a bit,' Tater said. 'I want everybody to write down one fact about themselves that nobody else knows. Anonymously, and we guess who said what.'

I started to stand up. 'Just a drink of water.'

Just air to breathe. An open window to dive through. A SWAT team.

Tater put a hand on my shoulder. 'Nikki, get Evan a glass of water.'

Nikki gave her a look that could have frozen electricity.

Patsy Blackburn said, 'I could use a fresh round, myself.'

Jax was writing on her notepad. Exactly what, I could only dread. *Took out KGB station chief with a single round to the head.* Ooh, neat, you win the home pedicure gift pack. Swerving out from under Tater's arm, I headed to the dining room.

Nikki found me drinking a glass of water. She said, 'We can gut this out.'

'We have a situation.'

'Right. And when the party's over we'll stuff her down the garbage disposal.'

'No, not Taylor, it's—'

Jax walked in. 'Planning a dismemberment?'

I felt the water trying to lurch back up.

She put an arm against Nikki's back, looking big-sisterly. 'I know the woman gets on your last nerve, but keep this in mind.'

She picked up a jalapeño popper, a deep-fried green chili stuffed with cheese.

'Taylor's already eaten half a dozen. So next time she treats you like Prissy in *Gone With the Wind* picture how she'll look at fifty.'

Nikki smiled.

Tater stuck her head in the room. 'Get on out here, we're ready.'

Nikki piled a plate with poppers and handed it to Tater on her way out. 'Here.'

I held Jax back. 'I want you to leave.'

The gentleness sloughed off her face, leaving rock. 'Give me five minutes. It's critical.'

'This is my friend's home. How dare you come here?'

'I was invited.' She stepped closer. 'And you ignore me at your peril.'

From the living room, Tater called, 'Girls, hustle it.'

Jax leaned in. 'Listen well. I don't speak in riddles. I say peril, I mean it literally. You need to hear me out. For the sake of your man, if not for yourself.'

I felt my temples pounding. I heard Nikki call, 'Bring more poppers, Ev.'

I looked at Jax. 'Fine.'

Tater appeared again, an orange banshee, grabbed me by the arm, and hustled me to the sofa. Jax ambled back to her seat. Taylor held a handful of notes and read aloud.

'First off. "I'm helping in an FBI investigation."'

Dead silence.

She waved the note. 'That's me, and wait till I tell you. You won't believe it.'

An hour later I stood at the dining-room table, eating poppers as if they were Tic Tacs and washing them down with wine. I hadn't had five seconds to talk to Jax, let alone five minutes. The music had switched to Wyclef Jean and now Taylor was fighting Nikki for control of the stereo, demanding Shania Twain. Outside, a red sun sagged toward the ground.

Harley came up to me. 'If a party like this doesn't make you swear off romance, you're insane.'

I knew her breakup with Cassie was eating at her, but I wasn't in the mood for sniping. I stuffed another popper in my mouth.

She ran her fingers through her silver hair. 'And by the way, now I understand why you look like death. You and Jesse both. The FBI? When's the last time you slept?'

'It's Jesse who's not sleeping. He's having nightmares about the hit-and-run, flashbacks.'

'Flashbacks.' Her face changed. 'Tits on fire, I had no idea it was hitting him so hard.'

Shania Twain came on the stereo, the country sound popped up, singing that man, she felt like a woman.

Tater called, 'Everybody, it's time for the show.'

'What show?' Harley said.

We walked into the living room. Tater was wheeling in a clothing rack, bulging with lingerie.

'Sit down, y'all. Courtesy of Countess Zara Lingerie, I'm thrilled to present the Dazzling Delicates collection.'

She began handing out brochures that showed a European lady in what looked like Marie Antoinette's bedroom. 'This is party fun, in honor of the bride-to-be, but all y'all are invited to purchase for yourselves.'

People stood where they were. Lavonne looked as though she'd swallowed a hairball. Nikki's mouth hung so far open that I thought her teeth might drop out. Jax stood swirling a glass of wine, her expression inscrutable.

Amber Gibbs clasped her hands together. 'It all looks so elegant.'

Tater said, 'I just need to know one thing, that'll determine which garments we look at tonight.' She supplied a coy smile. 'Are you girls naughty, or nice?'

Jax said, 'No question. We're naughty.'

Tater started tamely, with bra-and-panty sets in pastel colors, lifting each set off the rack and showing us, fingering the fabric. 'Silkesse,' she called it, the miracle fabric used in all Countess Zara garments.

'It has *silkicity*, the patented quality that gives our garments a sleek feel on your skin.'

She showed us underwear with lace, and bows, and ribbons, and flowers. Bras with uplift, and with padding thick enough to stop a .32 slug. The Marvel Bra she called that one, able to create cleavage on *anybody*. Looking at me. She held up panties to lift, shape, separate, or constrain your rear. Teddies, bodysuits, moving now into the black stuff, and the thongs, really getting going.

I gazed around. Everybody looked like guests who've just asked about check-out time at the Hotel California. Except for Amber, who sat transfixed, with a longing on her face that neared the religious.

'And now for our special bachelorette selection. Who's feeling frisky?' Tater twirled a garter on her finger and fired it at us. 'Who likes leather? Who likes toys?'

I stood up. 'I'm getting another drink.'

Harley said, 'Bring the bottle.'

When I came back, the costume show was rolling. Tater was already into the American History line of erotic lingerie: The Hester Prynne, a bustier with a big red A; and the Pocahontas buckskin body-thong, leather strips and fringe. I heard Nikki saying, 'Ninety bucks for ass-floss? I don't think so.' By the time Tater hit the Jackie Kennedy, a pearl G-string and a pillbox hat, my eyes were swimming. She segued into the Heroes line: The New York Firefighter, The Army Ranger, The Paramedic, The Astronaut, The Girl Scout.

'With a special range of sexy merit badges,' she said.

Lavonne, staring at the green beret and push-up sash, said, 'That has to be a trademark violation,' and Harley said, 'I'll file the papers.'

And then we were into the sports lingerie. The Bowler. The Archer. The Fly Fisherman, with green hip waders and a clear plastic bra, for the girl who likes to play with rods . . . until finally, breathless and flushed, Tater reached the pinnacle, Dazzling Delicates' new season premieres: the Rodeo Collection. Not pronounced ro-*day*-o. The Barrel Racer, the Steer Wrestler, the Bronco Buster. When we hit the Bull Rider, I said, 'Tater, where does Countess Zara come from?'

'What did you call me?'

I should slow down on the wine. 'Is she from Tulsa? Muskogee? Bartlesville?'

She tossed aside the spurs and the fleece-lined flank strap. 'The Countess lives in Luxembourg. But she knows her market.'

Was it my imagination, or was she swerving in and out of

focus, doubling and coming back together? Perhaps this was a subatomic fluctuation, and she was about to disappear into a parallel universe. No. She wasn't swerving, I was. Rapidly, I felt ill.

She said, 'Who wants to try on some of our selections? If y'all's purchases total more than two hundred dollars tonight, there'll be a gift of lingerie for our bride-to-be.'

I felt Harley's hand on my arm. She said, 'You look green.'

'Maybe it's the jalapeño poppers.' I put down my glass.

'Come on, ladies,' Taylor said. 'You want to ensure a correct fit.'

I saw Amber standing in front of the clothes rack, pointing out selections. I saw two Ambers. And panties dancing in the air like birds. I stared at my wine. I'd only had a couple of glasses, but I felt woozy.

Harley said, 'You need fresh air.'

'Right.' I closed my eyes, a mistake. My head spun like a centrifuge.

I opened my eyes again and saw a hallucination, I thought – Amber in all her plumpness, standing in the center of the room wearing the Cowpuncher outfit, cowboy hat and chaps, holding the little branding iron in her hand.

'God help me,' I said. It's the last thing I remember.

Twenty-Two

My mouth felt as dry as concrete. My stomach had been tied into a pretzel. I opened an eye and the light hit me like sand, gritty and painful.

I didn't know where I was.

I cursed to myself. Even that made me feel like vomiting. After a minute I eased my head off the pillow and squinted through my lids. The view confirmed my fears. The far wall sloped away from me, and across from the bed stood a row of pillars painted with hieroglyphics.

Meticulously I turned over. The drapes were drawn. I saw gold-painted furniture and more Egyptian designs. Daring to sit up, I inched my feet over onto the floor. The carpet had a bold pattern of gold and red and blue rings that set my head humming. I looked away.

The television had a card on top listing channels. I was in a hotel. Where? And how did I get here? Standing up, I bumbled to the window and pulled open the drapes.

I saw a sky as sharp as a knife, khaki terrain, brown mountains wrinkling on the horizon. I was in the desert. I hated the desert.

Looking down, past the angled wall to the boulevard beyond, I saw hotels, the Sphinx, the Eiffel Tower, hotels.

'Oh, no.'

I was in Las Vegas.

The Strip stared me in the face, swimming with noonday heat. I felt a hot chill, a cramp in my gut. I rushed to the bathroom and threw up.

Afterward I splashed water on my face. I was four hundred miles from home, with no memory of traveling here. I was hugely hung over without having been drunk, and, now that I saw my face in the mirror, looked like I'd lost a fight with a psychopathic hairdresser. I was wearing a T-shirt that said 'Zero to horny in three seconds'.

Heading back into the room, I saw my red dress folded over a chair, my shoes underneath, my purse on the seat. Anxious, I looked inside, found my wallet intact.

Item one: get out of here. If I could remove this T-shirt without taking my head off with it.

A key clicked in the door, and I froze. In walked Jakarta Rivera. She was carrying a cardboard container holding coffee, juice, and bagels. My head pounded.

'What did you do to me?' I said.

She held out an orange juice. 'Drink this. You need to rehydrate.'

'I'm not touching that. You drugged me.'

'It wasn't me.'

I grabbed my dress from the chair and heaved toward the bathroom to change. Jax stopped me, pressing a bottle of aspirin into my hand.

'Brand new. Check the anti-tamper seal, it's fine,' she said. 'And you don't want to put that dress back on.'

I held it up and saw the stain, smelled the greasy salsa.

She said, 'Taco Bell in Barstow, two-thirty this morning. You insisted on stopping.'

I tossed it on the bed and went to take the aspirin. 'Are you holding me here?'

'Honey, I'm not doing anything. I'm along for the ride, just like you.'

I came out of the bathroom. My head hurt too much to make facial expressions, but she caught my confusion.

'You don't remember anything?' she said.

'Fill me in.' I sat on the bed, among the messy covers. 'Just tell me the night didn't involve carnie people, or a video camera.'

'Harley decided to take a road trip, and we came along.' She took the lid off of a coffee and drank.

'Spur of the moment,' I said. 'Middle of the night. To Vegas.'

'Are you saying it's out of character for her?'

'No. Not at all, actually. She thrives on impulse. She had a fight with her lover and this is a typical pepper-upper.' I looked out the window. The light was piercing. 'God, I can hear my hair growing.'

Standing up, I took the coffee from her hand and drank a swallow.

She gave me a sly look. 'Attagirl. Trust no one.'

The coffee was hot and strong. 'What hotel is this?'

'The Luxor.'

'My wine was drugged, wasn't it,' I said.

'I presume. Best guess, someone gave you rope.'

'To hang myself with, you're implying?'

'Rohypnol.'

My head started thumping again. 'The date-rape drug?'

'Yes. Somebody wanted you incapacitated.'

This had to do with i-heist, and the missed deadline. My eyes throbbed.

'Jax, I'm not in the mood for games. Tell me if it was you.'

She got the other coffee. 'Realize something. I am not here to hurt you. I have your back.'

'Why?'

'You couldn't look out for yourself last night.'

'Thanks. But that's not good enough.'

'You'll just have to live with it.'

'Is this what you wanted to warn me about – what I was supposed to ignore at my peril?'

'No, this surprised me.'

I swallowed some more coffee, trying to think. 'Where's Harley?'

'In the casino.' She walked to the window, looked out at the searing day. 'We're all comped. Harley's been here before.'

'She has connections. Her dad was a—'

'High roller. She told me.'

Outside, the Strip was blanched white with sun, mirages sweltering above the asphalt.

Jax said, 'Harley's running away from something. And it isn't a broken love affair.'

'Did she tell you that?'

'You know what I'm talking about. You just need to admit it to yourself.'

In the light her face looked hard, tired around the eyes. My stomach went hollow. For a second I thought I might be sick again.

'You think she's involved in this mess with Franklin Brand,' I said.

'Of course she is.'

Harley was Mako's corporate counsel. She had been warning Jesse and me away from the company since the start. She knew what was happening.

I squeezed my temples. 'She won't talk. Attorney-client privilege.' I felt a bolt of pain. 'I don't mean you should try to make her talk. Forget I said that.'

'Chill, would you? I'm not going to wire her up to a torture machine, Evan.'

I felt unsteady, near shivering. 'Do you think Harley drugged my drink?'

'Most likely. She was around your glass. But so was everybody else. And where did you get that last bottle, in the kitchen? Was it open when you got it?'

'Yes.'

'Did you ever leave your glass in the kitchen?'

'Yeah. Anybody could have come in the back door while we were watching the lingerie extravaganza, and dropped a pill into it.' I rubbed my temples. 'Why would somebody want to knock me out?'

'To do something bad to you, or to keep you from stopping them while they went in your house.'

'But Harley didn't do anything bad to me.'

'Is everything okay at home?'

I didn't know. I got my cellphone from my purse. There were three missed calls, all from Jesse. I phoned back, got his machine.

I said, 'If Harley was behind it, she wouldn't have let our road trip become a threesome, don't you think?'

'That idea has a certain logic to it.'

I drank some more coffee, deciding I didn't have the neuro-transmitters for diplomacy. 'Jax, I think you're screwing with me. I don't know why, but I think you and Tim are playing some twisted game. I don't know what, but this ghostwriting project is a front. Your altruism is a front. And I still think you're the one who drugged me.' I set down the coffee cup. 'I'm getting out of here.'

I turned to go, forgetting to add . . . once I find some clean pants to wear.

She said, 'Check in that sack. It's a goodie bag from the bridal shower.'

It was a big shopping bag with the magenta *Dazzling Delicates* label. I rustled through sheets of pink tissue paper and found a bra and panties with Countess Zara tags. They were an indefinable fabric with a silvery sheen. In the bathroom I changed, putting on my dress, and over it the Zero-to-horny T-shirt, inside out, to cover the stain. The Dazzling Delicates were giving me a special feeling called scratchiness. I came out and grabbed my purse, thinking, let's see if Jax really lets me go.

She was leaning against the window. 'Sit down a minute.'

'I knew it.'

I made for the door. Had she deadbolted it? Or was Tim North waiting in the hall outside? Hand on the knob.

'I know why the FBI is after Jesse.' She was a shadow backlit by the shrill Vegas sun. 'And it all goes back to Mako.'

I walked over to her and sat down.

Jax handed me a bagel and orange juice. 'You need to get back on an even keel. You don't want to be out of it, physically or mentally. Things are deteriorating.'

I did as she suggested.

She said, 'Cherry Lopez has deep and dirty ties to Mako Technologies.'

'And this has to do with the FBI?'

'Listen, and see if you can follow. You have no idea of the shitstorm you've wandered into.'

She paced in front of the window. 'First, background. Lopez works with two men you've seen, Mickey Yago and Win Utley.'

'I know, they call themselves i-heist.'

'They're into online theft and extortion. Preventing that should be Mako's *raison d'être*, but the opposite is occurring,' she said. 'History – Yago was originally a coke dealer, and that's how he got his claws into Mako.'

'You saying he was their corporate cocaine supplier?'

'He was Kenny Rudenski's dealer.'

My pulse picked up. It hurt my head. I drank the coffee.

'It was an ordinary commercial relationship until Kenny screwed up the business unit he was running, and realized he wasn't going to make payroll. He worked out a deal with Yago. He bought large quantities of coke at discount, and sold it to generate quick cash to cover the paychecks.'

'That's – unbelievable.'

She lifted an eyebrow. 'You haven't spent much time around the wilder corners of high tech, have you?'

'Why would Kenny do something so risky?'

'Desperation, lack of morals, fear of Daddy finding out he couldn't run the business unit . . .' She waved a hand. 'The point is, Yago had his hooks in, and Kenny thought he'd found a savior. They now have a deeply symbiotic relationship. When Mako went public, i-heist invested heavily in the IPO. Yago is a significant Mako stockholder. Under the name of shell corporations, of course.'

'And this helps Kenny how?'

'Yago buys and holds Mako stock, supporting its share price and market capitalization. In return, Kenny gives i-heist special access to Mako's security software, under the table.'

I thought about it. 'Kenny's been selling them Mako source code, hasn't he?'

'Yup.'

'And when i-heist gets it, they program in a back door, so they can hack into secure databases to blackmail people.'

'One of Cherry Lopez's favorite things to do,' she said. 'And after she wrings people out to dry, i-heist empties their bank accounts and runs their credit cards up to the limit. Just a little kick in the pants to send their victims on their way.'

I drank my coffee, trying to take in the information. Trying to put this together with the fact that the FBI's Money Laundering Unit was investigating i-heist.

I said, 'There's a Mako slush fund, called Segue. Yago's been running his criminal proceeds through it, hasn't he?'

'It appears so.'

'Kenny Rudenski's been helping Yago launder his profits.'

'That's the gist of it.'

'Damn. And Kenny gets a cut, which he uses to prop up his balance sheet,' I said. 'Who's in on it at Mako, besides Kenny?'

'I don't know. That information, Lopez didn't have.'

Her face was expressionless. I wondered how she and Tim decided that a person was out of information.

'I still know people in Washington. Guy at Treasury gave me a run-down on Win Utley,' she said. 'He was a programmer the IRS brought in to test their security. Try to hack the system, help them plug any holes. He stole thousands of social security numbers and electronically filed tax returns, and used them to blackmail people who were evading their taxes.'

'If your friend at Treasury knows all this, why isn't Utley in jail?'

'Not enough evidence to indict.'

'Then how do we help the authorities get the evidence? It must be in Mako's books, proof that can be untangled.'

Her feline eyes looked bemused. 'What do you think I'm going to do about it, hack Mako's computers? Who do you think I am, honey?'

I stood up and put my hands against the window, looking out at the fulminating day. The glass was hot.

Jax said, 'And don't think what you're thinking, either. You're not going to crack Mako's system, no way, no how.'

I didn't answer.

'Evan, security is Mako's business. You're not going to beat their encryption or reconfigure their routers to grant you access to their net. You wouldn't get through all the barriers they have, multiple levels of admittance to their system. You're not even going to bribe an employee to get the information for you. You don't have the money.'

'How about if I asked them really, really nicely?'

'The only way a rank amateur like you would ever get into Mako's computer system is by getting physical access to a terminal in their office. If somebody propped open the door to a secure room, or taped a password to the bottom of their keyboard, then fancy encryption software and firewalls wouldn't keep you out. But that, my dear, would be a long shot.'

'If I didn't know you better, I'd think you were double-daring me to do it.'

She set her coffee cup down. 'I'm trying to make a point here, and it's that i-heist is a ruthless bunch. They're tight with Kenny Rudenski, and they're not going to back off. If they're after Jesse, my guess is that they want him to set up a new portal for money laundering.'

'Why?'

'Maybe because their present portals are on the verge of collapsing.'

She stared at me, waiting for me to draw the conclusion. I felt sick again.

I said, 'Harley.'

Twenty-Three

I stepped from the elevator, phone to my ear, trying Jesse again. Still no answer. I headed into the casino. Instantly I felt nauseated at the shininess and noise. It was midday, when casinos show their dismal empty heart. Craps tables empty, cleaning crews vacuuming, waitresses hustling free cocktails to the tourists playing roulette.

Harley was playing Blackjack at a table with a fifty-dollar minimum. She had a stack of chips in front of her.

She saw me coming. 'It lives. Feeling better?'

'Take a break.'

'Sweetie, I'm grooving here.'

The dealer busted, and she added more chips to her pile. Her eyes were gleaming.

'We have to talk,' I said.

'Great.' She placed a fifty-dollar chip on the table in front of the empty seat next to her, and nodded to the dealer. 'Deal her in.'

My head throbbed, hot. The dealer was looking at me. I sat down.

Harley said, 'This trip is exactly what I need. And your friend Jax, she's cool. I got tickets to the show tonight over at the MGM Grand.'

The dealer slid cards from the shoe. A nine for me, and then an eight.

I said, 'You've been moving money for Mickey Yago.'

The dealer drew to a twenty-three, and I was up fifty bucks. Harley wasn't looking at me.

'I was drugged. Was it you?'

The cards came again. I hit on sixteen, and on nineteen, and on twenty. When I deliberately busted Harley finally came to life, standing up. She gathered her chips.

'You're not well.' She put the chips in her purse and walked away from the table.

I followed her past fountains and gilt columns out into the sun blinding on the pool.

'Harley, don't ignore me.'

The flint was in her eyes. 'You have some bad juju going. Time to get you out of there before you wreck my luck.'

'What is going on?'

'Did you actually just accuse me of drugging you? You need help.'

'What's happening at Mako? Who's in on it?'

'I'm going to ignore all this, and chalk it up to a major case of the morning afters. I'm here trying to clear my head, and you're going off the deep end.'

'But—'

'But nothing. I've told you before, do not fuck with Mako Technologies. It will only lead to grief. Now, if you'll excuse me, I'm up five thousand dollars. That dealer is good for me, and I want to keep it rolling before she goes off duty.'

Fuming, I headed back toward the room. Jax was right. Harley was dirty. And she was coming unraveled.

I was halfway up the escalator when I looked across and saw Cherry Lopez coming down on the opposite side. She had on the bandanna and gold hoop earrings and was blowing a bubble the size of an orange. For a moment we locked eyes, moving past each other. Then she turned around and started running up the down side, coming after me.

I started running too, up my own side. It was a long escalator, and I wove my way in between fat grannies and Elvis wannabes, aiming for the mezzanine. Behind me I heard a shout, and I looked back to see Lopez jumping over the central divide between the two escalators, now charging up my side.

I got off on the mezzanine and looked around. Ahead, I saw a security guard.

I ran up to him. 'There's a girl coming up the escalator. She tried to pick my pocket downstairs in the casino.'

His head swung around. 'What does she look like, ma'am?'

'Black hair with a red bandanna and big earrings. A tattoo like a snake. I think she's underage.'

'Wait here,' he said, and headed toward the escalator.

I did wait, just until I saw Lopez coming off, right into his waiting arms.

The taxi swept toward the terminal at McCarran airport. The palms sped past in a picket line, making my vision ripple. Inside, I bought a ticket to Santa Barbara via LAX. No luggage to check, it was just me and my Dazzling Delicates shopping bag, and I headed straight for security. I tried calling Jesse again, but the battery on my phone had gone dead. I walked through the metal detector, setting it off.

'Keys, belt, coins in your pockets?' the guard asked.

I said no, and he told me to go through again. The machine buzzed.

He pulled me aside and got out the wand. At the x-ray machine, the screener was frowning at my shopping bag.

The wand waved up and down. Whenever it passed above my bra and panties, it squelched. The x-ray screener opened my shopping bag, rustled through the layers of decorative tissue paper, and took out the bachelorette gifts I should have known were in the bottom of the bag. Tater's party favors included Bondage for Beginners handcuffs and Lickalicious edible body paint.

The screener held up a bag of Gummi Peckers, saying, 'Breakfast?'

The wand bleated over my brassiere. The guard said, 'What's your underwear made of, detonator cord?'

My head started racketing again. How, I thought, could this day get any worse?

The screener handed me the giant dildo labeled T-Rex. She said, 'Would you please demonstrate this?'

★   ★   ★

The flight landed on time at LAX, and I hiked to catch my connection to Santa Barbara. The whiff of jet exhaust contributed to the ache in my head and body. I felt as if railroad spikes had been driven into my eye sockets. I tried not to look down at my clothes. At the Las Vegas airport I'd bought a change of attire and was now wearing royal blue shorts and a matching T-shirt that blared, *I'm winning my grandkids' inheritance!* I headed for the gate where I'd catch a bus to the commuter terminal. It would be a twenty-minute hop up the coast to Santa Barbara.

I was reading a Departures monitor when I felt it, the electric twang of his presence. I looked around and Mickey Yago was standing three feet away, hands in the pockets of his black jeans, gold ringlets shining in the sun, his blade of a face aimed at mine. A crackle went through me.

He hitched the strap of a computer case over his shoulder. 'Let's walk.'

'I have a plane to catch.' I started toward the gate.

He took my arm. 'Your connection ain't for an hour.' His hand was cool, his voice a rasp.

'I'll tell the gate agent you're harassing me. They'll call security,' I said.

'And I'll tell security you're the one who pickpocketed me.' His face was hard. 'Lots of that going around.'

He must have talked to Cherry Lopez.

He said, 'My wallet's in your shopping bag. And a dime bag of coke.'

I looked into my Dazzling Delicates sack. Beneath the tissue paper was a man's wallet and a baggie filled with white powder. My vision turned red. Yago's hand curled around my arm and he led me away from the gate.

How did he know I would be here? Only ticketed passengers had access to this part of the terminal. Was this a show – an exhibition of his ability to find me? If so, he was impressing me.

He walked through the frosted glass doors of the airline's

business class lounge, flashing a membership card to the woman at the front desk. Inside, the leather and pale wood made the place look like a Nordic cocktail lounge. Yago's stride was unhurried. He led me to a sofa by the windows and sat down.

'Blackburn thinks he can ignore me,' he said. 'He's wrong.'

I stared at him. His face lacked any hint of humor, liveliness, or interest in me. This encounter wasn't meant to impress me. It was a message to Jesse.

'He missed the deadline.'

'What do you want?'

'For him to do what I say.' He picked at a bowl of nuts on the coffee table. 'He shouldn't ignore me. Cal Diamond ignored me, and he paid.'

I said nothing, running my gaze over Yago's sharp face. What was he getting at, aside from telling me that he was blackmailing Diamond?

I said, 'Diamond had a heart attack because he was stressed about trying to keep his swindles secret.'

And dammit, one side of his mouth went up, the neat brown goatee curling with it. The smirk was an implication. He meant that Jesse was hiding something.

Do you want your woman to know? Think she'll stay?

I bluffed. 'Don't bother playing the game with me. I know everything.'

He leaned in. His black T-shirt smelled of last night's weed. 'You got balls, but you can't lie for shit. You don't know jack.'

Attitude . . . 'I know Brand was stealing from Mako and he inadvertently ripped off i-heist's slush fund.'

'I love lawyer words. Inadvertently, let me write that down.'

'And Kenny Rudenski covered it up, hid it all from his father and the authorities.'

'He's a scared little boy, Kenny.' He leaned back, stretching out his legs. 'Franklin Brand don't have the money no more. But your dude, he got money out of Mako because of Brand. I'm weighing it up, that money should be mine. I want it.'

I said nothing.

'I told Blackburn, he gives it to me or he pays. He didn't give it to me, so now I need something else from him.'

'What?'

'A million.'

He had to see the shock in my eyes. I didn't know how to hide it.

He pulled out his laptop and casually booted it up. 'But I don't figure he can get it. So I'm giving him an alternative. He does me some favors. That's all, favors. Until they add up to a million bucks. He does that, I'll call it even. I'm an easygoing guy.'

He typed on the laptop. 'I love computers. This is such a better business than blow. Dealing is hard work. You ever been in sales? It sucks. Hustle here, hustle there . . . but this computer shit, you just sit back and watch the bits fly. No inventory, no sales force, it's a dream.'

He was hooking the laptop to a cellular phone with a cable.

I said, 'And if Jesse doesn't do these favors for you?'

'He starts paying in other ways.'

'How?'

'With his friends. With you.'

My throat was dry.

He said, 'I know everything about you. I know where you're going to be at any moment. I can touch you in a dozen different ways, without ever laying my own hands on you.'

He hit a key. I heard the familiar ping of an e-mail message being sent.

'To you, babe. You'll enjoy it.'

He took a white grease pencil out of his computer case and started writing on the table top. 'Blackburn's gonna need this. It's an account name and number, sort code and transmittal information.'

My stomach quivered. He wrote *Segue*. Followed by several sets of numbers.

'I'll need the same kind of information from him, about his law firm's client trust account,' he said.

He wanted Jesse to launder i-heist's money. I said, 'He won't do it.'

'Yeah, he will.'

He picked up one of the desk phones from an end table and punched in a credit card number. 'The call's on me. What's his home phone?'

I said nothing. His face sharpened.

'I can get it in two minutes. Save us both the time, babe.'

I relented, telling him. He dialed, and handed me the phone.

'Give him the information I wrote down.'

Jesse's answering machine came on. I repeated the Segue account information. When I hung up, Yago took a napkin and erased the numbers from the table.

'He has twenty-four hours,' he said.

'What if I take this information straight to the police?'

'You won't.' He put the computer back in the case and stood up. 'Come on. Time for you to go to the gate.'

I sat. This guy was a gamesman. He played with people. He was playing with me now, and I didn't trust his intentions. He had just passed on information without leaving a trail back to himself, and without leaving any evidence that could be found on me by the police. He had something nasty planned.

'If you want your wallet back, you can get it out of the shopping bag yourself. I'm going to dump the coke in the toilet,' I said.

'Dump it? But it's my gift to you.'

I sat.

'Fine.' He reached into the sack and took the wallet. 'You got thirty seconds.'

He followed me to the ladies' room and stood outside the door while I went in. Another woman was at the sink. I waited for her to leave. Using the tissue paper so my fingers didn't touch it, I lifted the baggie out and put it in the trash, pushing it down and placing lots of paper towels on top of it.

Yago was outside the door when I emerged. He said, 'Let's go.'

He walked me to the gate. Before I started out the door, I said,

'You're letting me go. What makes you so certain I won't give this information to the authorities?'

He smiled. It was a hellacious smile, the equivalent of fingernails being drawn across a chalkboard.

'Because of what you ain't figured out yet. So I guess I'd better tell you.' Hands into his pockets. 'That hit-and-run wreck, the one's giving your man a permanent hard-on to see Brand's ass in prison?'

My radar was going. 'What about it?'

'Everybody has the thing backward. All thinking it was about the kid from the startup.'

Over the PA, I heard my flight being called. I didn't move. Yago kept smiling. General Custer, Son of the Morning Star, ghost of a killer.

'Brand didn't care about that kid. He had the stock scam all sewn up. The wreck wasn't about the kid who got killed.'

My vision was pinging.

Yago said, 'You and your man ain't ever figured it. Sandoval wasn't the one was supposed to get dead.'

No. My chest squeezed. 'Why?'

'I told you that, I'd spoil the fun. But if you spill everything to the cops, they're liable to put it all together, and then things will get kinky real fast.' He shifted his weight. 'Know how rough it is for a crip in prison?'

I stared, wordless. His smile broadened and he said, 'Don't miss your plane.'

He watched me go out the door and down the steps to the bus. When I climbed aboard I looked back at the terminal and saw him standing at the window. His gold ringlets buzzed in the sunlight.

I sat like a zombie while the bus clattered toward the commuter terminal, scuttling past the gravid, howling bulk of a triple-seven. I looked at my hands. They were shaking.

Spoil the *fun*?

Jesse, Brand was after Jesse. He had wanted to kill him from the start. The bus pulled into the commuter terminal, a cheap and crowded portable building. Inside a TV was on, and people sat around eating vending machine food.

I heard an announcement. 'Will Santa Barbara passenger Delaney please come to the desk?'

That did it. Mickey had a surprise planned for me, I knew it – whether I got on the plane or not. But what? I went into the bathroom. In the corner stall I dumped out the contents of my purse. My temples pounded. There was a knife.

I took a breath. I had to get out of here. And I had to presume that Yago or his buddies were watching back at the main terminal, in case I came back. I had to get out of the airport without them spotting me.

I needed a disguise. Where's that Diana Ross wig when you need it? I changed out of my bright blue Vegas clothing and back into the red dress, putting the Zero-to-horny T-shirt over the top again to hide the stain. Then, ferreting in the shopping bag, I pulled out the Lickalicious edible body paint. I squirted it on my hand. It was chocolate. I sprayed it on my head and massaged it in, turning my toffee-colored hair a sticky brown. It looked ridiculous, but this was L.A. In L.A. ridiculous earns you a second look but not a third, so you can get away with it.

Covering the knife with toilet paper, I dropped it in the trash. I put on my sunglasses and strode outside to catch a bus back to the main terminal. Somebody would be waiting, I had a bad feeling.

The bus pulled up. My sinews felt tighter than piano wire. I climbed the stairs and headed into the terminal, and there, sitting in a chair eating a Baby Ruth, was Win Utley. He was watching the people coming through the door. As he chewed, his chins flubbered and his ginger chin-beard wriggled. I stared straight ahead and walked past him with other passengers.

Abruptly he stood up. His mouth moved, words. He had an earpiece in, was talking on the phone. I tried not to speed up or look his way.

They wanted to screw me, to get me arrested. Just to pressure Jesse.

Utley tugged the waistband of his jeans and looked around. He had to be looking for me. I saw him humping toward the desk, agitation on his face. I headed toward the front of the terminal.

Two security men trotted past me, heading back toward the gate. I picked up my pace. I tried not to look up at the ceiling, where the CCTV cameras were. Woman with sticky hair, wearing rude shirt and frantic expression . . . a bored guard might look three times at that.

Then came the sound, the alarm, and guards running. I hustled it. Alarm meant security breach. Alarm meant Win Utley pointing his Baby Ruth in my direction.

It meant the guards stopping me outside, and retracing my steps to the ladies' room trash cans, and a bag of cocaine, and a knife. I had to get out or I was hosed. There was a cop at the door of the terminal, talking into his radio, eyeing everybody. I saw him scan the crowd, look my way. My stomach grabbed.

He started waving people outside. I rushed out to the curb and hailed a taxi.

Twenty-Four

Jesse's car was parked in front of Adam's house. I pulled up in the Mustang I'd rented at LAX. I felt dry, dirty, spent. For a moment I stared at the house, my nerves spinning up. How could I break the news, without breaking Adam's heart yet again?

When Adam answered my knock, his face couldn't hide his perplexity.

'What in the world?' he said. 'Is this from the bridal shower?'

'No, honey, I did it to myself. May I come in before the flies settle on my head?'

He gestured me in. 'Do you feel as awful as you look?'

'Worse. I need to speak to Jesse.'

'He's out back.'

On the patio Jesse sat in the sun. There was salsa and barbecued fish and a bottle of wine on the table. Down the hill, the ocean swelled blue. The sun stained the horizon gold.

Jesse looked up. 'Holy crap.'

'I'll explain it in chronological order, except for the parts when I was drugged and blacked out. But first I need to speak to you alone.'

He was using the crutches. He worked himself to his feet and followed me inside to the living room. I stood close and put my hand against his chest.

'The hit-and-run wasn't about Isaac,' I said. 'Brand was after you.'

His eyes held mine. He could see I meant it, knew I had evaluated the evidence or I wouldn't have said it. His chest rose and fell, and a look infiltrated his face, a look of physical pain.

He leaned on his arms. 'Why?'

'I don't know. It came from Mickey Yago, and he insisted that the crash had nothing to do with Isaac. Nada.'

It was sinking in, but not making sense. 'But I don't know Franklin Brand.'

'Think. It's something you know, or saw, or did. Something to do with Brand or Mako. Anything connected with the company, even tangentially.'

His blue eyes clouded. He looked as though he couldn't breathe.

'What is it?' I touched his face.

'No, it's nothing.'

'Tell me. Try to remember. What was going on with you before the crash? Things you did with Isaac, with work . . .'

'It's nothing.'

His shoulders were tight, his eyes focusing on walls, furniture, anything but me. Whatever he had remembered, he didn't want to tell me.

'Jesse, Yago hinted that it's something that could send you to prison.'

'But I haven't done anything that could send me to prison. Christ, Evan, don't you believe me?'

I kept myself calm. 'Of course I do. But Jesse, Mickey Yago screwed with me today.'

I told him about LAX, about Yago's demand that he launder funds for i-heist, and the new deadline. When I said 'a million dollars,' his neck colored. He seemed to shrink.

'He said you need to play ball or you'll pay, with your friends and with me. Today was meant to be a taste of that.'

'Oh, God.'

'So stop being evasive and tell me whatever the hell it is that you're trying to keep me from knowing.'

'I—' He swallowed, and shook his head.

'I repeat. Yago said *your friends* will pay.'

I looked pointedly out the window, at Adam leaning back in a chair at the patio table, running his index finger around the rim of his wine glass.

For a moment Jesse said nothing, then, 'Jesus. I have to tell him.'

I put a hand on his shoulder. 'You're making me nervous. Not to mention pissed off. What's going on with you?'

Wordlessly he pivoted and headed out the back door.

'Adam,' he said.

'No. Tell me that's not true.'

Adam hunched over the table, fingertips on his temples, deadly still. Jesse's hand rested on his back.

'Why would Brand want you dead?' Adam said.

'I don't know.'

Adam looked at him as though he were a stranger. 'You must.'

'Truly, I don't.'

'You're telling me that Brand set out to kill you, but missed and killed Isaac by mistake. And you have no idea what led to this?'

'Not right now, but—'

'I find that inconceivable.'

He stood up, shying away from Jesse's hand.

He looked at me. 'This man Yago didn't tell you why? You didn't insist?'

'He refused,' I said.

He pressed the heels of his palms against his head.

I feared what I was seeing in him. He was undergoing an emotional polarity reversal. Three years of sympathy were blowing away, a new anger coalescing, a new confusion aging his face. He looked at Jesse, disconsolate, his lips trying to form words and failing. His eyes said it. Your fault.

Jesse said, 'I swear to God—'

Adam held up his hands. 'I can't talk right now. Could you just go?'

The sun reflected in Jesse's eyes. I saw hurt and helplessness.

'All right,' he said.

He got up, moving heavily, and headed into the house. I watched Adam. I wanted him to say something, anything. He stared at the ocean as though spellbound.

I said, 'There are people who want to hurt Jesse. These extortionists, i-heist, are threatening to get to him through you and me.'

No response. I felt my own anger kindling. No matter how dazed or grief-stricken Adam felt, he shouldn't take it out on Jesse this way.

He stared at the sun. 'You know about entropy?'

It couldn't be a non-sequitur. With Adam, all thoughts connected.

I said, 'The second law of thermodynamics.'

'It's a measure of disorder in a closed system. It means that chaos always increases.' He put a hand over his eyes. 'Go, please.'

I was halfway to the rental car when I heard the patio table crash, plates smashing, the wine bottle breaking.

Cautiously I pushed open the French doors at my house. With relief I saw that the living room was intact, everything where I'd left it. Whoever drugged me, they didn't do it for the chance to burglarize the place while I was wrecked. I grabbed some clean clothes and headed over to Jesse's place. I didn't want him to be alone.

When I walked into his house, he had the TV on. 'You hit the big time. Fox News. Terminal evacuation after a passenger reported seeing a woman with a knife. No photos, but i-heist will make sure the feds know it was you. If they want them to find you, that is.'

I stared at the screen. 'Very expensive game they're playing.'

'They don't care about the expense. They care about demonstrating their power.'

The sun hit his face. His expression was desolate. I went and put my arms around him.

'I'm sorry,' I said.

He held onto me. I stroked his hair. Gold light infiltrated the room, strangely sterile for a summer sunset.

Finally he straightened. 'You look whipped.'

He was being polite; I smelled like it, too.

I let go of him. 'Let me shower and we'll talk.'

'Sure. I'll call Lieutenant Rome and give him the revised edition. He'll love me for it.'

Ten minutes under hot water washed away chocolate and sweat, jalapeño popper grease and any drug metabolites emanating from my skin. But none of my anxieties. I dressed and went back to the living room. Jesse was sitting at the kitchen table, staring at the sea. It was flat, with a pewter shine.

'I heard your phone message, the Segue information.' He rubbed his leg, as though it ached. 'I have to tell Lavonne. Yago demanding that I move money through the Sanchez Marks client trust account – that's a threat against the firm. Maybe she can talk to the FBI about this, I don't know . . .'

The FBI. My brain, which had been moving all day with the torpor of a salted slug, finally sat up. I remembered what Cousin Taylor had said at the bridal shower.

'Dale Van Heusen is with the FBI's money laundering unit.'

'Damn.' He looked at me. 'He's been angling at i-heist all along. He must suspect that they've been moving money through Mako.'

'And he thinks that you and Isaac were part of their laundering operation from way back. That's why he thinks he can threaten you with seizure of your assets.'

And it came back to me, Van Heusen's seemingly nonsensical remark.

'Smurfing,' I said.

'What about it?'

His computer was open on the table. I sat down and logged on to Google.

I said, 'Van Heusen used that term. Clearly he wanted to pique our interest.'

'But it's a denial of service attack.'

'And it's a blue cartoon character. Maybe it's something else as well.'

I typed in a search request: *smurfing + money laundering*. It was the most basic way I could think of to come up with a connection, maybe the connection I was missing. Let the search engine do the work.

The results popped up in less than a second. I heard Jesse groan out a breath. This was it.

From the Royal Canadian Mounted Police: *Smurfing is possibly the most commonly used money laundering method. It involves many individuals who deposit cash or buy bank drafts in amounts under $10,000.*

From the U.S. Department of Justice: *The Financial Crimes Enforcement Network defines smurfing as a money laundering technique in which the launderer divides large cash deposits into smaller amounts and attempts thereby to avoid CTR reporting requirements.*

'CTR?' I said.

'Currency Transaction Reports. Banks have to file them whenever a customer deposits ten thousand or more dollars in cash.'

He came close to the computer and clicked on another search hit.

For criminals who only want to move a few million dollars a year, 'smurfing' can be the easiest way to launder their cash. They have various people deposit random amounts less than $10,000 in various bank accounts, or less than $5,000 if they want to take the extra step of avoiding a 'Suspicious Activity Report.'

I looked at him. 'So what's the implication here? Does Van Heusen think you're a smurf?'

He stared at the screen. 'Maybe.'

I couldn't tell if he was petrified or unconcerned. He looked frozen.

'Maybe?' I said. 'Maybe the FBI thinks you launder dirty money for a hacker gang?'

'I don't know.'

'The month before the crash. That whole summer. What was going on? Think.'

'Evan, thinking about this is all I do.'

'But back to that summer.'

He closed his eyes. 'Can we let this rest? I don't mean to be a jerk. I'm just fried.'

He pushed himself up to his feet and made his way into the kitchen for a drink. I watched him, thinking, *spoil the fun* . . . Brand had nearly killed him, left him so badly hurt that he'd never be able to get a drink of water without planning ahead how to balance himself at the sink, and Yago was playing the jolly jokester about it all.

Shoot. Yago sent a message from LAX. *To you, babe. You'll enjoy it.* Turning back to the computer, I logged on to my e-mail account.

Cyber-war? It has nothing on the power of words to break the heart. I opened Yago's message, and things fell apart.

Jesse has been a busy boy.

There were photos. I had to scroll down to see them. One at a time.

We warned him. We told him he should behave. He is a bad boy.

At first I thought it was another archive photo. They were available online through the News-Press, Sports Illustrated, or Swimming World. Jesse's face was younger, and he was standing up, tan and shirtless, and as I scrolled down I saw palm trees and a bright blue pool in the background. And the picture kept scrolling.

He turned around at the sink. 'No.'

The photo scrolled, and I saw that he was standing in front of a woman who was stretched out on a chaise. His hands were on her shoulders. Her hands were on his swimsuit, fingers curling beneath the waistband, pulling it down, no question about it.

For a moment I thought this was another doctored picture, like the phony stag-night shot. But Jesse clattered to sit down next to me and reached for the keyboard.

'Ev, stop, don't,' he said.

I pushed his hand aside.

The woman in the photo had her back to the camera, and

now that I looked at it, the photo was taken with a telephoto lens, a long shot into a private garden, where they thought they were unobserved. Scrolling, seeing her legs and freckled shoulders, her face obscured. But I couldn't mistake the hair, all that lustrous silver.

It was Harley.

'Please, Evan, stop,' Jesse said.

My skin felt tight, my vision constricted. I felt his hand on my wrist, trying to keep me from scrolling down. I resisted. The next photo, taken a couple of minutes later, clarified things for me.

'Let me explain,' he said.

'No, this is self-explanatory, believe me.'

'I meant to tell you. I should have.'

I stood up. 'Told me what, that Harley's bi? Experienced at it bi. Athletically, enthusiastically, goddamned wild-for-it bi.'

I wavered across the room to the doors, where the ocean shone the color of tin. Feeling caged, feeling rage, fighting to keep back tears.

'When?' I said. 'How long ago?'

'It was in college,' he said.

And I understood. The rumors, Harley's hints, even the snide remarks directed at me by Kenny Rudenski: Harley had affairs with students.

Jesse was her student.

I felt an inchoate and inflating sense of jealousy, irrational and unstoppable. This happened before I even met him, and I felt like killing Harley. The liar – all these years telling me she was a lesbian, when she plainly loved a good straight romp. With my fiancé.

'It was a fling,' he said. 'I never expected it to come back and haunt me.'

'Just stop talking,' I said.

I went back to the computer. Forcing myself to look at the photos again, I saw that they were dated. Not photo-shop dated, but with the photographer's handwriting in white grease pencil.

I felt as if a match had been put to my head. 'The date. The date's wrong.'

It was more recent than college. It would have been when he was in law school.

'How long did it go on?' I said. 'Where were these photos taken, at UCLA? A fling? You were living in Los Angeles. Who drives a hundred miles for a fling, Jesse?'

'Evan, don't make me talk about this.'

I heard something in his voice I'd never heard before: fear.

'How long?' I said.

'Ev, please, understand. I know it's my fault, but I couldn't bring myself to tell you. And the longer I didn't tell you, the more I thought it would upset you if you ever knew. I should have told you up front, I know. I'm sorry. I'm sorry.'

I couldn't look at him. I stared at the computer screen.

'Don't look at it anymore. Please, delete it,' he said.

'Not yet.' I hadn't even scrolled halfway through the message. 'Is this what Mickey Yago has been threatening to reveal?'

'Yes.'

'Anything else? You'd damn well better say *no*. Or tell me, right this minute.'

I forced myself to look at his face. He was pale, hunched, abject.

'Evan, Harley's your friend. To have all this come out now, right before the wedding – I couldn't handle it. I don't know, I panicked. I'm massively stupid, please, forgive me.'

And I almost believed him. But then I scrolled down into the email message. There was more than just photography on display. There was a credit card bill, from Jesse's account. For dinner, gifts. They were dated the summer we met.

'You were seeing her then? You were doing us both?'

'No, I broke it off with her. I'm telling you the truth. That summer, I broke it off.'

Things were becoming clear to me. Things I knew, things I should have understood. I remembered when we first got together, my feeling that he had been let down by a college sweetheart. I was right, and wrong. He was the college sweetheart. He had just broken up with Harley when we met.

'I was a rebound? I was a consolation prize?'

'Never.'

I felt a crushing in my chest. 'Are you still seeing her?'

'No.'

I slammed the screen down on the computer, just missing his hand, and stood up. Grabbed my car keys and started for the door.

'Wait,' he said.

I kept going. I heard the crutches banging against the table as he got up. Still I didn't stop, and even then I felt the first squirm of shame, at the bald fact that I could outrun him.

'Stop, please, Evan.'

I opened the front door.

'Don't do this,' he said. 'You always do this.'

Now I turned on him. 'Do what?'

'Walk out when you get mad.'

'Sticking around would not be good for your health, cowboy.'

He walked toward me. 'I don't care. I love you.'

'Save it,' I said, and headed for my car.

I left him standing on the driveway, watching me spin the tires as I drove away.

Twenty-Five

'Evan, give me a chance to talk about this.'

I ignored the phone message, the frailty in Jesse's voice on the answering machine. I felt unable to speak to him.

Four thirty in the morning, staring out the window at unknown stars, I felt my charbroiled heart, hardened and hurting. It was illogical. Jealousy, that's what it was, this possessive and hateful feeling.

Before he met me, Jesse had a girlfriend. I couldn't begrudge him that. And yet I couldn't stop seeing the photo, Harley pulling him down on top of her . . .

She had tried to tell me. *This incestuous town.* The sexual metaphor was a message to me. Everybody doing it to each other. Now I knew why Harley was concerned about Jesse's dreams. She worried that he might mention her name in his sleep.

I threw off the covers and jumped out of bed. In the living room I turned on the television and huddled on the sofa in the dark, watching MTV. An N'Sync retrospective; I was in a bad state. Things made sense now, and that scared me.

Kenny Rudenski making snide intimations about the affair? How did he know? He was too tuned in for comfort. How close was he to Harley?

And the photos. Who took them? Why?

Jesse and Harley. My stomach turned. I changed the channel. Evan, you're being a baby.

The photos. No, there was only one reason that made sense. Blackmail. i-heist was blackmailing Harley. And they were forcing her to launder money for them. She was indeed one of their portals.

I got up and phoned Jesse.

No answer.

The sun came up, summer light turning the grass outside my doors emerald, the hibiscus exploding, red bloody mouths. I felt like a husk. I didn't call Jesse again. He could listen to the message I'd left earlier. If he was there.

I sure as hell didn't call Harley.

I worked all day and then drove over to Santa Barbara High and ran intervals on the track. A pyramid workout: 200-400-600 and back down. It felt purifying, like hitting myself on the foot with a hammer over and over. On the way home I stopped at a flower stand and bought a bouquet for Nikki, to thank her for hosting the bridal shower. I was raising my hand to knock on her door when she pulled it open.

'Perfect timing,' she said. Thea was bouncing on her hip.

I handed her the flowers, and thanked her.

'You're more than welcome, sweetie. It's an experience I wouldn't repeat if you promised me eternal youth, but I was happy to do it in your honor. Here, trade.'

She gave me the baby. I followed her into the kitchen.

'We should be back by ten. The Brahms is thunderous, but not long.' She handed me a diaper bag. 'It's loaded. Pampers, wipes, snacks, the full arsenal.'

I stopped still. Thea patted my arm, saying, 'Een.' What was Nikki talking about?

'She didn't nap this afternoon, so she may go to sleep early. Thanks for watching her. You're a pal.'

From the front hallway, Carl said, 'Let's go.' Nikki tucked Thea under the chin and trotted away. I scratched my head.

Back at my house, I set Thea on the rug. If I'd forgotten about babysitting, what else had I forgotten? I checked my desk calendar.

Seven pm – organist/wedding music.

I groaned. It was five after.

Part of me, the nail-his-privates-to-the-deck-of-a-sinking-ship part, said, blow it off. But the rest of me wasn't ready to do that

217

yet. I grabbed Thea and my car keys. Remembered I didn't have a baby car seat in my Explorer. I found Thea's stroller on the back porch at the Vincents' house, piled her into it, and started chugging up the street to the church.

Thea looked up at me. 'Ma,' she said. 'Doon.'

She squirmed, shut her eyes against the evening sun, and put her thumb in her mouth. The walk was uphill, toward mountains burnished green by the light. When we got there I was sweating. The parking lot was empty, the willows swaying in the shadow of the church. I didn't see anybody around. Had the organist given up and left?

I reached for Thea. 'Come on, girl.'

She was tucked into a corner of the stroller, asleep. I hoisted her out, resting her head on my shoulder.

The stairs to the choir loft were in the south bell tower, long flights that corkscrewed up the walls. I hurried up, pressing Thea to my chest. My footsteps echoed on the concrete. Two flights up, a landing led into the loft. Nobody was there. But the organ console was open and a cup of coffee sat on the top. The power was on, too – I could hear air blowing through the organ pipes.

I peered over the wooden railing. The floor of the church below was sinking into dusk. It looked empty, but I heard heels clicking on the stone.

'Hello, Miss Gould?' I called. 'I'm up here.'

The footsteps stopped. The person was out of sight beneath the loft. I heard scuffing below, heels on stone. Two sets of shoes, from the sound. And voices murmuring, the undertones of a male voice.

Worry needled me. Seemingly without anchor to anything, but I stepped back from the railing, listening. Thea stirred and settled again, nestling her soft face against my chest.

It wasn't the organist. Perhaps it was tourists, or parishioners come to pray in solitude. I held still, listening, and heard the footsteps heading in the direction of the stairs to the loft. For a second I stood wondering if I was being paranoid. And I thought: you aren't paranoid if they're really out to get you.

It was time to go home.

I was on the landing when I heard feet starting up the stairs below, and two voices whispering. Then a new, brisk set of heels came clicking, and a woman said brightly, 'Can I help you?'

No response.

The bright voice said, 'I'm the organist. I'm sorry, but the choir loft isn't open to the public.'

And then came a frightening sound: a stunned, animal groan. I heard a thud and a clatter, as if a person had fallen and dropped an armful of books. I pulled back from the stairway.

In the gloom below me, a man muttered, 'It's not her.'

'Shit.' A woman.

'You idiot. She told you she was the organist. What did you zap her for?'

'Get off my case. Delaney has to be in the loft.'

It was Win Utley and Cherry Lopez. Their footsteps came fast now up the staircase, almost as fast as my heart was beating. They were coming after me. Yago's 24 hour deadline had expired and they were going to make me pay . . . I turned back toward the choir loft. There was no place to hide in there, just that low railing and a long drop to the stone floor below. With Nikki's little girl asleep in my arms.

Utley, out of breath, said, 'How long does that thing take to recharge?'

'It's ready to go. Come on, you're slowing down.'

I looked around, frantic. What could I do? Could I brazen it out – charge down the stairs and make it past them? With Cherry jamming her shock baton and maybe hitting Thea? No.

I had to surrender. I'd beg them to let me put Thea in the stroller, take her home, and then they could have at me.

Utley said, 'How many volts you say that thing delivers?'

'Three hundred thousand.'

'It makes a Chihuahua flip like a jumping bean, what do you think it'd do to a baby?' he said. And he giggled.

I squeezed Thea to my chest, my body needling with panic. I couldn't go down, had to get away. Where? The bell tower kept going up, and so did the stairs, narrow and steep. I heard heavy breathing below me. In a second they'd turn the corner and climb high enough to see me here. I had nowhere else to go.

Pressing Thea close, I hurried up. Past the bells hanging in open arches. The stairs turned. The setting sun caught my eyes. I saw hundred-year-old palm trees at eye level, felt the wind whining through the arches. They were screened, but I still felt exposed.

Listening, I heard them under me, paralleling my progress. I told myself to hold it together. If I could keep going at the same pace as them, they couldn't see me, directly above them. They would be expecting me one floor down. They would go into the loft, and when they did I would run back down the stairs, past them, and get away.

Another turn, and I climbed to the top of the bell tower. There was a small landing with a door out onto the roof of the church. I tucked myself back against the wall.

From below me came Utley's voice. 'Go in the loft and check. I'll wait here on the landing.'

No, no . . . if he stayed on the landing he would block my way back down.

It only took a few seconds. Lopez looked in the loft and returned, saying, 'She's not in there.'

Go downstairs, go down.

Utley said, 'Did she get by us?'

'She couldn't have. The stroller's outside the door downstairs.'

There was a horrid quiet. I knew they were looking up.

I couldn't let them catch me up here, on this thin landing. Oh, God, when I had to keep both my arms tight around the baby as it was. I tried the door to the roof, thinking, *no roofs, nobody escapes onto a roof*, and wondering why the hell I hadn't listened to Taylor explain the trick. If Nikki saw me now, she'd tear me limb from limb. But I had nowhere else to go.

My hand trembled. I stepped outside and shut the door, quietly.

The wind caught me. It funneled along the peaked roof of the church and between the bell towers, pushing me toward the drop. Thea squirmed and blinked and grabbed my shirt in her hand. She had to feel my heart jumping. I held her close and stroked her hair.

The view was dramatic, lawn sloping toward the rose garden and across red tile roofs all the way to the ocean. More dramatic was the drop straight down on the other side of the thin railing, a one-second ride to death. I pictured the headline – *Church Plunge: Woman Is Victim of Fatal Irony*. I couldn't stay here. In a few seconds Lopez and Utley would reach the top of the stairs, and would come to the obvious conclusion: stairs plus door equals she's on the roof.

I looked around. There were crosses and stone statues along the front rampart, and a narrow flight of stairs leading up over the peak of the roof and down to the other bell tower.

No way. Not in this wind, not with Thea, squirming now.

I turned, looking along the length of the roof. In the church wall, just below the spot where the roof slanted up, was a small door. It looked as if it might lead to an electrical equipment cupboard. I tried it.

It opened to darkness. Leaning inside, I saw space and a light switch. I ducked in, pulled the door closed, and flipped on the light.

This wasn't a closet. I was on the ceiling of the church, in the rafters just under the roof. It was a long, close space, running a good seventy meters to the back wall of the church, stuffy and spooky. I held my breath and listened.

Lopez and Utley came puffing out onto the roof from the bell tower. I could hear them outside the door.

'Where is she?' Utley said.

'On the far side of the roof,' Lopez said. 'Over those stairs.'

'Fuck more stairs. You go look.'

'You're a sack of *mierda*, Win.'

'Shut up with the cracks about my weight. It's genetic.'

'Right.' Her voice sounded distant now. 'The deep-dish pepperoni gene.'

'The thrifty gene, you bulimic twit. You know, if I stayed as cranked as you, I'd weigh twelve pounds.'

I huddled against the wall, stroking Thea's hair. My arms shook. Who knew that babies were so heavy? She kept squirming, and making a face like a crumpled piece of paper. I rocked her. Don't cry, baby. Don't cry. The air felt hot and dusty. Dust motes jinked in the light that came through dim ventilation windows further down the church.

Heels clicked, running back over the peak of the roof. 'Not there. Shit, she has to be up here somewhere.'

'Maybe she fell over the rail,' Utley said.

A moment's quiet. They were looking. I felt the hair on my scalp rising.

Utley said, 'Okay, Einstein, where'd she go? She went down the stairs.'

The door to the bell tower opened. He said, 'Come on, before she beats it out of here.'

'No. Think about it, Win. She didn't get by us. She's up here.'

'Do you ever admit you're wrong, Cherry? Come on, Mickey's gonna go ballistic if we don't find her. After Vegas, you don't have any credit left with him.'

'After Vegas. After this fiasco. How come it's us up here? How come we're always the ones taking the chances?'

''Cause he's a sadistic head case. I don't care how hot he is in the sack, that's what it comes down to. That and the fact he pays us the money.'

Quiet. Then she said, 'It's all going to blow up. I know it.'

'Maybe for Mickey.'

'For all of us. The FBI is here, for christsake. They're going to find out about Segue.'

'Just a few more days, that's all. We'll have Blackburn, and we can move the rest. Then it's straight to Cancun.'

'Gonna hit the beach? You think Mexican girls go for guys with the thrifty gene?'

'Let's go. Screw Delaney, we'll do the thing with the physicist.'

The physicist . . . they were planning to do something to Adam. Thea turned her head into my chest and closed her eyes again. I felt her little legs relax.

'Okay, we'll go,' Lopez said.

Relief swam over me like a warm wave. I leaned back against the wall. All I had to do was wait here until they were gone.

My cellphone rang.

Utley said, 'You hear that?'

The phone was in my back pocket, where I couldn't reach it without dropping Thea. There was only one thing to do. I started running on tiptoe, across the ceiling of the church. Planks were laid crosswise over thick wooden beams, and I hurried toward the far end of the church, trying to keep my balance. Below the beams was plaster. It held the chandeliers, but might not break my fall if I tipped off the plank and landed hard.

The phone kept ringing. Thea woke up and started crying. I ran. Behind me the small door opened.

'It's her,' Utley said.

Down at the far end of the church was one of the screened ventilation windows. Where did it lead – to steps, a lower roof, a fall? I couldn't tell.

Lopez yelled, 'Move. Move, Win. Let me go first.'

'Then get out of my way.'

I glanced back. They were wedged in the little door together, fighting to get through. I kept going. The phone rang and rang. Thea was wailing. I swung her over onto her stomach and held her like a football under my arm.

Sharp footsteps running behind me, Cherry Lopez coming hard now.

I reached the window. I sat down and kicked the screen out. It clanged onto the tile roof of a side chapel about four feet below me. The roof sloped and the tiles were mossy. I knew now that I wasn't going to survive this evening, because if Cherry Lopez didn't kill me, Nikki and Carl would.

I scooted out the window and picked my way across the tiles to the edge of the roof. It was too far to jump, but near one corner I saw a buttress, a thick adobe support for the wall. It was steep, far steeper than a playground slide, but better than jumping. I sat down on the edge of the roof and swung my feet over the edge.

I tucked Thea against me. 'Hold on, baby.'

I leaned back, flattened my shoes against the buttress, and slid. My feet bounced and squeaked. I accelerated, feeling my shorts heat from friction, my shirt bunch up in the back, plaster scrape my exposed skin.

The lawn was coming up too fast, too fast—

I punched into the grass, crumpling like a skydiver, rolling to protect Thea. I stumbled to my feet. Where were we? In a small garden, surrounded by high walls and old archways, deep in the grounds. Thea wailed, grabbing me with her little fists.

Above me, Lopez climbed out the ventilation window onto the chapel roof. I heard her clattering across the tiles. Turning, I saw an open door. I ran through it and saw that I was in the church sacristy. I heard Lopez thud to the ground outside. I ran through the sacristy, out another door, and found myself on the altar, looking down the length of the empty church. I heard Lopez curse and knew she was coming behind me.

Just her. Win Utley had to be thudding down the stairs in the bell tower. He would be waiting for me at the front door of the church. I cut through a row of pews and ducked out a side door. I barreled out into the cemetery, running past worn headstones with eighteenth-century dates. I looked back and saw a skull and crossbones above the door.

Thea squalled. I ran for the gate, pushed it open, and hurried down the stairs toward the street.

My phone started ringing again. Thea was pistoning her arms and legs. I ran around the front steps of the church, watching out for Utley. Ahead, at the far end of the church complex, I saw people climbing the steps toward the parish office. Off on the side of my vision, in the shadowed archways next to the bell tower, I caught sight of a large figure in black, huffing along. Utley.

I yelled for help. And yelled again, louder.

A woman turned and saw me. I hurried toward her and the others. Utley slowed, turned around, and headed in the opposite direction. They were letting me go, melting away. They were going to cause havoc for Adam.

The cops gave Thea and me a ride home. I wrestled the stroller out of the squad car and thanked them. Thea waved as they drove away. Across the street, Helen Potts peeked through her blinds at us.

I marched up to her door and knocked. She answered, gripping her cardigan tight at the neck.

'Will you watch Thea until Carl and Nikki get home? It's not safe for her to be with me,' I said.

She didn't quaver. She held out her hands. 'Of course. Come here, sweetie pie.'

I was jogging back down the walk when she called to me. 'Evan. Does this have to do with the gold car I saw parked down the street?'

I stopped cold.

'I don't see it now, but it's been there on and off all week. Sometimes there's a man sitting behind the wheel, just sitting, watching your place.'

I felt a shiver. I said, 'Lock your doors, Helen.'

It had to be Brand.

Adam's line was busy, and I was going crazy. I drove to his house.

His truck was in the driveway, the sun glaring off the wind-shield. The wind was rustling the manzanita bushes outside his front door. I knocked and got no answer. Through the door I could hear the television.

I knocked again. 'Adam?'

I peered in a window and saw the TV on in the living room, looked like a sports channel. The door was unlocked. I opened it.

'It's Evan. You here?'

I walked across the entryway, into the living room.

'Adam, are you okay?'

Put that one on my list of Top Ten Stupid Questions. He was sitting on a footstool near the TV, watching a videotape. ESPN sportscasters chatting. Behind them was a pool.

I saw a cardboard box on the floor next to the footstool. Inside were more videos, CDs, odds and ends. The label on the box said *Isaac*.

'Have you come as Jesse's emissary?' he said. 'Because I can't.' Shaking his head. 'I can't talk to him.'

The words gouged me. I, Princess Pedal-to-the-Metal, who twenty-four hours earlier had run away and refused to talk to him myself.

'I came to warn you,' I said. 'i-heist has plans to hurt you.'

He looked up from the TV. 'Jesse sent you to tell me this?'

'No. They're after *us*, Adam. They're using us to pressure Jesse.'

'Pressure him in what way?'

'He should tell you.'

The gloom in his eyes distilled. 'You are his emissary.'

On the television, graphics appeared: Men's four-by-100 freestyle relay. Texas, Stanford, Auburn, UCSB . . . it was the NCAA nationals. The camera panned to the teams walking onto the deck, young men looking intense. The crowd was noisy, cheering and waving banners, stomping on the bleachers.

Adam stared at the screen.

I said, 'Hey. I want you to lock your doors and windows, and keep your eyes open. They have plans to do something to you.'

'They're going to *get* me, is that it?'

I threw my hands up. 'I'll do it myself.' I started walking around the living room, latching windows. 'Please don't be sarcastic. These people are dangerous.'

He laughed. It was an awful, cheerless sound. 'You think I don't appreciate that? They killed my brother. They already got me.'

On the television, the lead-off swimmers stepped up onto the blocks. Rolling their shoulders, adjusting goggles, trying to loosen up. Names flashed on screen. UC Santa Barbara: Matsuda, Sandoval, Sandoval, Blackburn.

I locked the sliding glass door. 'Be careful at home, when you're driving, and when you're on campus.'

'Don't worry, I can defend myself. I have a spear gun and powerheads to load it with, they can stop a white shark.'

I finished locking up and stood staring at him. Finally, as if feeling the weight of my thoughts, he looked up. The light in his eyes was agonized.

'It's illogical, I know. How can I blame Jesse?' he said. 'But I can't seem to stop it. How can I quiet this hissing in my head? Tell me. I don't know if I should pray, or scream, or punch him. How do I climb back out of a gravity well, into rationality?'

From the TV, the starting klaxon. The swimmers burst from the blocks. I turned, wanting to shut off the videotape.

Adam stared at the screen. 'Don't.'

The lead-off swimmers plowed the lanes, racing four laps of the pool. When they charged home the second-leg swimmers leapt, flying over them, and there was Isaac. He was behind but going wild, chasing the leaders with windmill arms and a whitewater kick.

He held on, neither losing nor gaining ground. On screen Adam appeared, stepping onto the blocks, fired-up, waiting. Isaac powered toward him and touched the wall. He sprang. He was a body-length behind the leaders. The noise from the crowd shook the walls. He was flying, clawing back the deficit stroke by stroke, moving up as they turned and came back on their final lap.

Ahead of them the anchor men waited, knowing it was now. Jesse climbed onto the blocks and stood there, a stone statue. Goggles shining, arms relaxed. There was electricity in his stillness. I found myself walking toward the TV, just to see him.

The leaders came into the wall with Adam half a length behind, head down, digging. Jesse bent, went into his roll, and leapt. He looked like a leopard striking. The crowd was thundering, the announcers shouting above them: Texas, Stanford, UCSB. Jesse broke the surface of the water only two feet behind.

On the footstool, Adam rocked back and forth to the cadence of Jesse's stroke, urging him on. I was overcome with the comprehension of how much he loved him.

And finally it was the last lap. At the far end of the pool they flip-turned. The underwater camera caught them, Jesse timing it perfectly, feet hitting the wall and shoving off, gaining another foot on the leaders.

'Go, man,' Adam whispered.

My heart was racing. The announcers were breathless, saying Stanford and Texas but look at UCSB, Jesse Blackburn is experienced, swims on the US National Team, you can't count him out. My throat lumped.

The arena was ringing. Jesse sliced the water, arms wheeling, the effort entirely concentrated. So like him. God, I felt proud. Texas and Stanford were dogfighting each other, and Jesse was inching up on them. And inching. The wall came closer.

The three swimmers dead even, a final lunge, the crowd bringing down the house, and bam, into the wall. Water lapping in waves. Too close to call.

ESPN saying, and Blackburn takes it.

Jesse in closeup now, pulling off the goggles and looking up at the scoreboard, blowing hard, squinting at the times, hoping. He sees it. Neon grin, fist in the air.

In the living room, Adam stared at Jesse's face on the screen. I had to breathe, tingling, thrilled. I watched the tape, Jesse vaulting out of the pool and his teammates mobbing him, Adam grabbing his shoulders and babbling in joy. Isaac leaping on Adam's back, laughing, yelling.

I looked down to see Adam's shoulders heave. He sobbed and plunged his head into his hands. I dropped to my knees and threw my arms around him. He crumpled into my embrace.

'Everything's gone,' he said.

My throat grabbed, and tears stung my eyes.

'Why did he have to die?'

Then he wept without restraint. I rocked him. There was nothing I could say.

Twenty-Six

I pulled up to my house with bluegrass keening on the radio. I could barely rouse myself to get out of the car. Dread enveloped me like dead space, cold and empty. I looked up and down the street, afraid Brand's gold rental car would be parked in the shadows. I saw only darkness.

I was locking the Explorer when my cellphone rang. The display said *Jesse*.

'Can we talk?' he said.

I walked toward the garden gate. 'I'm at home.'

'I'll be there in ten minutes.'

I opened the gate. I smelled green grass and star jasmine. 'You got my message?'

'What message?'

Doubt pricked at me. 'I phoned last night. It was late.'

'I didn't hear the phone ring.' He said, 'Ev?'

She was sitting outside my door, hugging her knees in the blue dusk.

'Harley's here,' I said. 'I don't think you should come over right now.'

'I'm already on my way.'

I hung up. Harley was climbing to her feet, brushing dust from her capris.

'I'll give you this,' I said, 'you have guts, showing up here.'

'No. Call it naivete. Thinking you wouldn't find out.'

'And after years of hiding it, now you want to confront me?' I said.

'No, I want to tell you I've been a big boob.'

I stared. 'Don't say that. You're begging for a bad joke.'

229

Her hard eyes stared at me in the twilight. And then she did not meow. She tossed her head back and laughed.

'You're a peach. Now, ask me in. I have groveling to do.'

My stomach had tied itself into a half-hitch. 'Five minutes, Harley. Jesse's coming over and I'm not up to a three-way chat.' I unlocked the door and held it for her as we went in.

She said, 'The photos were intended to blackmail Cassie. These people thought they'd catch us in a clinch, threaten to wreck her endorsement deals.'

'These people – you mean i-heist. I have to talk to you about that.'

She ran her fingers through her hair. 'Jesse looks like a whipped dog.'

Stomach into full-hitch. She'd seen him.

She said, 'I'm talking serious misery, gal. I haven't seen him look this bad since rehab.'

I didn't need Harley arguing his corner, but that's not what yanked my chain so hard. 'Rehab. I didn't know you were still seeing him—'

'Oh. He didn't tell you.' She cast her gaze down. 'Of course he didn't. I behaved carelessly.'

I couldn't find words to answer. I felt as if someone had poured gasoline on my tender little heart and lit a blowtorch.

'Okay, I was a shit,' she said.

She was misunderstanding my reaction, but I was caught in my own jealousy and couldn't speak. Rehab was when I started spending time with him. That she was still seeing him then . . .

'The whole thing was winding down before he got hurt,' she said. 'And I was seeing Cassie, and – Jeebus wept, will you stop looking at me like that? He was paralyzed. I acted selfishly, but I couldn't handle it.'

I squeezed my eyes shut.

'Evan.' She grabbed my arm. 'You're the better woman here. I treated him bad. But things weren't the same as before, and I couldn't pretend they were.'

I opened my eyes. 'You might want to keep your voice down. He'll be here in a minute.'

'He's not afraid of this conversation. He and I have made our peace. It's you who's the emotional firecracker.'

My head was humming like an electrical transformer. Everything I wanted to ask her, all the questions about i-heist and Mako, were drowned in the buzz.

She put her hands on my shoulders. 'We had an affair. That's all. It was a rush, like skydiving, or heroin.'

'This is what you call groveling?'

'I'm trying to say it was a physical thing, not love. Girl, get a grip.'

Harley on the chaise by the pool, fingernails clawing his back . . . yeah, *get a grip* was the operative image, all right.

Out on the street, a car door slammed.

'That's him,' I said.

She stared at me. It was her game face, her hardball face. 'I thought you were tougher than this.'

'I'm a rusty nail. But you've heard about camels, and straws?'

I heard the latch lift on the gate. If I had to watch her be with him in my house, I would puddle.

'Goodnight, Harley.'

Her shoulders dropped. The hard light in her eyes dimmed.

'You know I love you, kid,' she said.

She walked out, leaving the door open. I listened to her footsteps, sandals on the flagstone. They stopped. Her voice murmured, and I heard Jesse's voice in reply.

Don't look, don't.

This felt like a bad flashback to puberty, but that would be crediting myself with too much maturity. I had turned into a full-grown two-year-old. I walked into the kitchen and got a glass and filled it with ice. And then with Glenfiddich. They don't make baby-bottle nipples to fit cocktail tumblers, so I drank it straight.

A rap on the door, two taps, his code.

'Ev?' He was in the doorway, looking uncertain. 'Harley said you're ready to throw knives at me.'

I went into the living room and sat on the couch, pulling my knees up to my chin. 'You can come in.'

He approached the far end of the couch, but no nearer. 'What is it?'

I drank, trying to bring myself back to adulthood. Say something mature. 'I just wish you had been honest from the start.'

'So do I. You have no idea how much I wish that.' He was trying to read my mind, my face, my body language. He couldn't like what he was seeing.

I said, 'The affair. I can't hold that against you.'

Liar liar pants on fire.

'But you still haven't been open with me. About you and Harley. And . . . about after the hit-and-run.'

'What?'

'If there's more, I want to hear it from you, not from her. Or from i-heist.'

'All right.' He took a risk, moving onto the couch. 'What did Harley tell you?'

'About breaking it off when you were in rehab.'

'She did?'

'It wasn't a pretty story.'

'No.' He looked strangely fretful. 'She really told you?'

'It's okay. I'm sorry for you, that's all.'

'Sorry . . .' The question mark was in his voice.

'Her attitude. She was honest about it, but what can I say?'

'You've lost me.'

'She said—' I looked away. I loathed talking about this. 'She broke it off because you were paralyzed.'

A strange expression began forming on his face. 'Hold it. *She* broke it off?'

'I'm sorry—'

'Jesus, I hate that word. Stop saying it.'

My mouth snapped shut. Neither of us spoke. *He said, she said . . .* in my book of bad conversational techniques, rerunning the gritty details of a breakup is right up there with burping *Jingle Bells*. I did not want to get into it.

'Jesse, I don't care who ended it. But the other night I asked you how long it went on, and you didn't tell me this.'

'In rehab, Harley said?'

'Yes.'

'You sound hurt.'

'I feel hurt.'

His blue eyes were chilly. 'What's really bothering you? You're sorry. You're hurt. What's got your goat about the idea that Harley saw me in rehab?'

'When did this turn into a cross-examination?'

'You want honesty. So do I. Tell me why it bothers you so much.'

He was supposed to be cowering before me. Instead, he was trying to drag my unconscious onto the witness stand. I looked at the coolness in his eyes. Deep in my brain the worker ants sensed danger, and started scurrying in all directions.

'What are you getting at?' I said.

'You sound like you want to keep rehab all to yourself. Why, would that give you special status as the only woman valorous enough to keep dating me?'

'No, never.'

'Selfless Evan, willing to put up with my injury and with the stigma of being seen with a gimp. You like thinking you're the only one, but now Harley's told you she was seeing me in rehab.'

I went stiff as a door. 'Are you saying she's the one who—'

'Right, I knew it. That's what this is about. You think she broke my cherry after the crash, when all this time you've been counting on it being you.'

He stared at me, his eyes glacial. 'Didn't mean to disappoint you. Spoil your chance for brownie points. How many do you get for screwing a crip, ten thousand?'

'You've got it wrong.'

'Dear Diary, what a special day. I helped Jesse—'

'Stop it.'

He pulled the wheelchair close and hopped on. 'You're sorry, always so sorry. What is it, you get off on pity fucks?'

233

He could not have hit me harder if he had used his fist. 'That's low.'

'I'm feeling low.'

He backpedaled, spun, headed for the door. I went after him and put a hand on his shoulder.

'Stop being such a jackass,' I said.

He jerked away. 'I'm not a project, Evan. I won't be your damned cause.'

'How can you say that, even think that?'

He stopped, looked up at me. His expression was beyond anger, beyond hurt. It was astonished and broken.

'Take a look in the mirror. A hard look, and think about what you see.'

I didn't answer.

'Until then—' He shook his head. 'No, I can't do this. There is no until. I can't be with you. All bets are off.'

He left.

Twenty-Seven

Two days, no word. It finally hit me when the dressmaker phoned.

'Miss Delaney, you missed the appointment for your fitting. If you want the gown to be ready for the wedding, you need to come in.'

'Yes,' I stammered. 'It's just, I don't know if . . . I can't tell you when—'

All bets are off.

There wasn't going to be any wedding.

Jesse was hurt. I had battered him in a place I had no right to.

Do you trust me? How many times had he asked me the question? But he'd never had to assert his trust in me – that had been a given. Not anymore. I had squandered that trust. I had hurt him in the worst way. I made him think I didn't respect him.

After the crash, I was the one who treated him normally. I was the one who didn't cringe or patronize or let him get away with things. I knew, because he'd told me so. And now I had made him feel small and weak, made him think that he was a cripple in my eyes. Made him think that I wanted it that way.

My stomach turned. Did I feel that way – did I consider myself virtuous for staying with him? No, I couldn't believe it.

I looked at his photo on the mantle. That wicked grin, the sun on his face. My God, how I loved him. I couldn't lose him. I had to fight to recover his belief in me. Even if I had to beg, or crawl. Being an optimist, I felt sure I could do it. And, being an optimist, I thought things couldn't get any worse.

Walking toward the courthouse, I had my face in a legal pad. The day was balmy and bright, the sunken gardens vibrating green across the street, tourists wall-to-wall in the clock tower, taking in the view. I had a meeting, actual work, but with my mind full of marbles I was struggling to think in two-syllable words. I crossed the street, distracted.

I didn't pay attention to the car idling at the light. But when I stepped onto the sidewalk it pulled to the curb next to me. The driver honked. I looked up. It was a white Jaguar XJ8, so new that you could practically smell the English accent . . . *Jag*-u-ahh. Mari Vasquez Diamond got out.

'You,' she said. 'Don't walk away.'

She picked the wrong moment to jab at me.

I said, 'My God. You take offense if pedestrians passing on the street don't stop and kowtow. Have you informed NASA about the size of your ego? They'll want to add it to their GPS system, so jetliners can avoid it.'

From the expression on her face, she'd just swallowed straight pins. Her bony bronze legs tottered on stilettos. She looked like a human swizzle stick.

'You've been libeling me,' she said.

'You're off your perch, parakeet.'

'That's a second count. I'm adding it to the lawsuit.' She hitched her bag up on her shoulder. It bore a photo of her Chihuahua.

'You have several misapprehensions about tort law,' I said. 'First, spoken defamation is slander, not libel. Second, denting a prima donna's feelings doesn't give rise to a cause of action. Third, get your ass out of my face.'

I walked past her.

'You told Kenny Rudenski I'm a slut,' she said.

Turning, I gave her a quizzical look. 'Not remotely close.'

'You interrogated him about my sex life. You insinuated I sleep around, and that I married Cal for money.'

'No I didn't. But Kenny did.'

Her lips parted. 'You tricked him. You're a reporter, I know you.'

'Where's Franklin Brand?' I said. 'Is he staying at your place? The police would like to know.'

She rocked back. 'You're a liar.'

'You were with him the night of the hit-and-run. You were in the car when he ran down Jesse and Isaac. You're the one who called the cops and turned him in.'

Her face puckered. 'You sent Cal the photos, didn't you? You left that envelope at our gate. You're the person who screwed my marriage.'

Oh, baby. 'What photos? Of you with Franklin Brand?'

'See. See. It was you. I knew it.'

'Photos of you with him from the night of the hit-and-run?'

'Print that, anything close to that, and I'll take you for every penny you have.'

I had a flash, and I fired at her. 'Why did you turn Brand in? You couldn't take the idea of him getting away with it, not a second crash, after your sister died and the driver ran away.'

I saw the gooseflesh rising on her arms. She started shivering. The bag on her shoulder was shaking. Her Chihuahua popped its head out of the bag and yapped at me, all teeth and frantic eyes. It was joined by barking from the Jaguar. I glanced past Mari's shoulder and saw two Dobermans in the back seat, faces to the window, chewing the air.

I said, 'I'm sorry about your sister. But maybe you should think about Adam Sandoval, who lost his brother in similar circumstances.'

'You leave Kenny out of this.'

I stepped back mentally, wondering at the non-sequitur.

'He had nothing to do with this. Dragging his name into this won't help anything,' she said.

'I don't—'

'Throwing Kenny in my face is as base as you can get. You make me sick.'

She really had lost me now. The dogs kept barking. I took a harder look at her, and saw real pain in her eyes.

'Mrs Diamond, if I've overstepped, I'm sorry. Kenny told me about the car accident, and your sister. I—'

'He was sixteen years old. He was afraid. Comparing what Kenny did to this other accident, it's crazy.'

What Kenny did. The negative developed.

'Kenny was in the car with your sister?' I said, and saw her mouth crimp. She thought that I already knew. 'Kenny was driving the car?'

'He had a concussion. He was in shock. He went looking for help.'

He left Yvette to die.

'Back off,' she said. 'Back off of me, and off of Kenny. If I hear his name in connection with this again, I'll ruin you.'

The Chihuahua lunged, scrabbling out of the shoulder bag and diving at my arm. I ducked back. It fell to the sidewalk.

'Caesar!' Mari gasped and bent to grab it. 'Look what you've done. You bitch. You bitch!'

I walked away. I didn't think she was talking to the dog.

I went to Sanchez Marks, but Jesse wasn't there. Lavonne said, 'I sent him home. The Fibbies are throwing their weight around, and it isn't good for the firm to have federal agents arguing with Jesse here in the foyer.'

I rubbed my eyes.

'He's overwrought. Go talk to him,' she said.

When I got to his house the stereo was pounding. Hendrix, a portentous sign. Taking a long breath, I knocked on the door and waited until he called, 'Come in.' He was stretched out on the couch staring at the television, remote in one hand, beer in the other, one in the afternoon. Watching NASCAR.

He said, 'I've been sent to the corner.'

'Lavonne mentioned it.' I walked into the living room. 'Was it Van Heusen?'

He pointed to a letter on the coffee table. I picked it up, saw FBI letterhead and a lot of jargon. *Under Title 18 of the U.S. Code, section 981, any property, real or personal, traceable to proceeds obtained from money laundering activities is subject to forfeiture to the United States.*

'Van Heusen's leaning on me,' he said.

He raised the remote, upped the volume. The whine of stock car engines clashed with 'Purple Haze'.

'Want to talk about it?' I said.

'No. Talking got me the afternoon off.' He drank from the beer bottle. 'And now I don't need any more suggestions. The meter's pegged. I'm at maximum shit-bearing capacity.'

He wasn't telling me to leave, but he wasn't asking me to stay, either. The chill couldn't have been colder. I knew we were both nuked to the point of emotional meltdown, but I couldn't walk out the door and leave this.

'Jesse, I don't want us to fall apart like this. I respect you more than anybody I know. I don't care what happened with Harley.'

'I didn't keep it going on with her after the crash. That's not what happened.'

My inner brat did a somersault, chirping *hooray*, but I looked at him, seeing the gravity in his eyes, and my stomach dropped.

'What did happen?' I said.

He stared at the ceiling as though weighing something heavy. Finally he said, 'I would never do this, break a confidence, if Harley hadn't just taken you to Las Vegas.'

A confidence? He had a deep and heavy confidence to keep for Harley? But of course, he was a person people confided in, and trusted.

He said, 'I broke it off with her because she's an addict. A compulsive gambler.'

The room seemed to refocus.

'You don't look surprised,' he said.

'I don't think I am.'

Her dad the high roller, the trips to Vegas and the track at Del Mar . . .

'How did you find out?' I said.

'When I was in law school she'd call, say she was in L.A., could she stop by. It was never business, it was always days out at Hollywood Park. After a while, it became obvious that things were getting out of control.'

'That's how i-heist got their hooks into her. They found out,' I said.

'Listen, I broke it off because of this, but I promised not to expose her problem if she got help. She started going to Gamblers Anonymous,' he said. 'That's why she came to rehab, to tell me she was getting straightened out.'

'But she never stopped gambling,' I said. 'And i-heist used it against her, to get her to launder money for them.'

The chill had turned into a fear creeping up my neck. 'So why are they asking you to launder money for them, if they've got her?'

'Harley's cracking up, that's why. She's going to pieces.'

And she was the link to Brand. Somehow, it all tied in. The money, her work for Mako and i-heist . . .

He said, 'It's only a matter of time before they decide she's too much of a liability. Kenny, and i-heist. And when they do—'

'They won't see any reason to keep her alive.' She was in danger.

'I've been trying to contact her but she's out of the office,' he said.

I drew a breath. 'I'll see if I can find her.'

A new Hendrix track came on the stereo. 'All Along the Watchtower,' his favorite. I felt discomfort congealing in the air between us.

'Jesse, I know this is a terrible time, but I need to talk about us.'

He looked away. 'Harley lied to you about rehab, and you believed it. That just . . .'

He meant, why did I believe her instead of him? Did I have so little faith in him? I felt sick.

'And why was it so important for you to be the only one after the crash?' He looked at me. 'You are, by the way. There hasn't been anybody but you, since then.' He looked reproachful. 'I just can't get it out of my head that you . . . does it make you feel big to stick with a crip? Are you glad that things have turned out this way?'

'My God, no. Jesse, don't think that.' I felt a pounding between my eyes, tears starting to form.

He spread his hands. His eyes were a storm of anger and confusion.

He said, 'You should probably go. If I say anything else right now, there may be no going back.'

I found Harley three hours later. I convinced her secretary to tell me she had driven to a meeting in Santa Ynez. I headed north over the mountains, across the long span of Cold Springs Bridge, past woodlands and wineries and Arabian horse ranches and rolling golden hillsides, to the only place in the Santa Ynez valley where Harley would, at this stage in her collapsing life, take a meeting: the Chumash Indian casino. She was playing video poker, propped on a stool with a bucket of silver dollars on her lap, shoveling coins into the machine. When I walked around to face her, I could see the machine's display reflecting cards in her eyes.

Pair of threes, a losing hand. She glanced at me.

'Come outside,' I said.

'The machine's due.' She fed it silver dollars. 'I'm not going to leave and let someone else get my payoff.' She scowled, and slapped the machine. 'Come on, you bastard.'

But it didn't pay off. She fed in more coins.

I grabbed the bucket from her lap. 'Come on.'

'Hey.' She spun off the stool and followed me outside. 'Damn you, give that to me.'

It was hot, the sun unvarnished, a perfect vacation day. The casino parking lot was shiny with tour buses. Harley's hair looked white under the blue sky.

I said, 'When did you start laundering money for i-heist?'

'I don't know what you mean.'

'What happened, did they find out you were in debt to bookies? Did they offer to pay off your creditors before the cops or the repo men came around?'

She stared at the bucket of silver dollars, dazzling in the summer light.

'Well.' She ran a hand through her hair. 'It turns out Jesse Blackburn doesn't know how to keep his promises.'

'Jesse ain't the problem here, kid.'

'There is no problem here. I'm fine. I'm just taking the edge off.'

'Gamblers Anonymous? Do they recommend that you relax by playing the slots?'

'You have no idea.'

'Tell me, then. Explain it to me.'

'My life's in the crapper. I just need a day to get myself together.'

I shook the silver dollars. 'Looks like you have a big bucket of togetherness here.'

She snorted. 'That's not gambling, that's like a box of candy, or a glass of wine at the end of the day. It's entertainment. Relaxation.'

'Expensive box of candy.'

'You can't understand. You'd buy a church raffle ticket and think that's gambling. What I do is different, it's professional, it's analytical. Shit on a biscuit, woman, I had five thousand on War Emblem when he won the Kentucky Derby, a twenty-to-one longshot. I had Goran goddamned Ivanisevic to win Wimbledon at a hundred-twenty-five to one. I earned a quarter of a million dollars thanks to a tennis wager.'

'Oh, my God. Harley.'

She mistook my shock for admiration. 'Damn right.'

If those were the amounts she was winning, how much was she losing?

'How badly are you in debt?' I said.

The light was doing unkind things to her face. Her skin looked papery, the freckles blotchy.

'Everything's under control.'

'No, it's not. Harley, how much are you into i-heist for?'

'I can cover it. One win and that'll be it. My old man may have been a prick, but he taught me that. You're only ever one win away.'

'A million?' I said. 'Two?'

Her mouth opened, and closed again. She stared at the bucket as if the silver dollars were amphetamines.

'Harley, are you skimming from i-heist?'

She didn't answer.

'Did you use Segue?'

'How do you know about that?' She grabbed my arm. 'How much do you know?'

'I know about Mako.'

'Jesus, you can't tell anybody this. Mako – they'll kill you. Oh, shit, they'll kill me.'

'Who at Mako – Kenny?'

'Who else? He's been in on it from the start. Got my firm to buy Mako's security software. Then his pals hacked our system to find out everything about the firm's finances, and my own. Figured out a way to screw me. He has a noose around my neck.'

'You have to go to the police.'

She laughed. 'And be prosecuted? Disbarred, go to prison? I'd rather die.' She put a fist over her lips, gave a bitter laugh. 'Maybe I should.'

'What?'

'They're going to try to get me, you know. And you and Jesse. We're toast. Maybe I should save them the trouble.'

'What are you talking about?'

'Getting it over with. Drive off the Cold Springs bridge, maybe. End of story. No more worries, everything off my back. Including you.'

She turned away, hugging herself. When I put a hand on her back she shrugged it off. I glanced toward the casino. A bus was parked near the door, partially obscuring the sign on the building. I saw CASI. I had one of those little *well, duh*, moments.

I felt my face heating. How long had Harley been counting on my gullibility?

I said, 'This is Cassie, isn't it?'

Cassie was her lover, all right: gambling. The one she adored, the one who was always there for her . . . The one Harley could never leave, because i-heist was using her. Forcing her to take cash to casinos and scrub it clean for them.

'You need help,' I said.

'Jesse tried that one on me. GA, it didn't work. Bunch of blue-haired women who lost their Social Security checks playing Bingo and sat around wringing their hands. They didn't have anything to do with me.'

'This is out of control.'

She laughed, loudly, loosely. It was like watching a downhill skier head too fast toward a turn.

'Oh,' she said. The laugh kept going. 'You are the cat's meow.' She bent over and put her hands on her knees, as though I had told the funniest joke in history.

I set a hand on her back again. She straightened, shoving it away. Her eyes looked as hard and bright as the silver dollars.

'Maybe you should stop meddling in other people's lives,' she said.

She grabbed the bucket from me. The coins flew, bouncing and ringing on the asphalt. The last I saw, she was on her knees, picking them up, one by one.

I drove toward home, feeling blank. I couldn't stop Harley from self-destructing. And, as much as she had misled me, the thought that I couldn't help her – that she refused even the hand I offered – depleted me. I turned the corner onto my street. My cellphone rang.

'Evan?' It was Taylor. 'Can I stop by? I want to drop off the lingerie you ordered.'

I couldn't take Tater tonight, not even a small helping. 'I won't be home all evening.'

'Not home at all? Are you sure?'

'Positive.'

'Can't I use the spare key? You keep it in that drainpipe, right?'

Had she snooped into every corner of my house? 'Taylor—'

The battery on the phone cut out momentarily, breaking off the call. It didn't matter. I'd rumble with her later.

Adam Sandoval's Toyota pickup passed me going the other way. I honked. He U-turned and parked behind me. I was stepping out of the car when he came stalking toward me. He clutched papers in his hands. His face looked rough.

'What's wrong?' I said.

He held out the papers. His voice was a whisper.

'They loaded when I went online tonight. And when I tried to delete them, they printed.'

I took them and looked. The dizziness was immediate.

They were photos of Isaac's autopsy. Adam slumped against my car.

'Oh, God,' I said. 'Oh, Adam. You should have never had to see this.'

He had identified Isaac's body after the crash, I knew. He saw the brutality done to his brother. But he also took comfort from seeing the embalmer's reconstruction. He chose the clothes Isaac was buried in. And the night before the funeral he stayed awake next to Isaac's casket, praying. He ensured that Isaac was put to rest, with dignity. It had been a sacred thing.

Now undone. By photographs of Isaac's corpse lying naked on a steel autopsy table, with the Y-incision open on his chest, and his skull half off. This was the final violation, images to destroy Adam: a desecration of Isaac's memory.

'They're going to publish the photos,' he said.

I shook my head. 'No.'

'On the net. Pervert sites, for twisted—' His head dropped, and he fought for control. 'Necrophiliac sites. Holy God, he was my *brother*. And they're going to put these up for freaks and monsters to get excited about. *Madre de Dios*—'

His words dissolved into a lament. He raked his fingers into his scalp.

'Is Brand taunting me? Is this a horrific game?'

'It's i-heist, this guy Mickey Yago. And it's no game.'

'Why is he doing this?' he said.

Because he's a sadistic head case . . .

'It's a tactic. They're using these photos to get at Jesse,' I said.

He recoiled. 'They're defiling Isaac's memory to hurt Jesse Blackburn's feelings? That's too much.'

'Listen to me. They want you to lose it, to go to Jesse and—'

He held out his hand. 'Give me the photos.'

'No.' I shook my head.

'I want Jesse to see them. To know what happened to Isaac because these people have an argument with him.'

If he confronted Jesse right now, the explosion would be in the megaton range.

I said, 'Don't.'

'You've been begging me to talk to him. Why are you shielding him now?'

'I'm not. Mickey Yago is using you, trying to drive you over the edge. If you have a knock-down-drag-out with Jesse, you're playing into Yago's hands.'

'Too bad. Where is he?'

'I don't know.'

'I'll call him. Can I use your cellphone?'

Evan would flash on Jesse's display. 'He wouldn't answer it.'

'Why not?'

My scalp felt tight. 'Things are going badly with us at the moment.'

His brow beetled. 'Oh, I'm – damn. I didn't know.'

I leaned against the car next to him, staring at the mountains. They glowed in the sun. It was heading toward six. Happy hour.

'Is there anything I can do?' he said.

Even stressed to the point of fracture it was still there – his innate decency and compassion. I put a hand on his arm, shaking my head.

He reached for the photos and I let him take them.

'I'll deal with this,' he said.

'How?'

He folded the photos and stuffed them in his back pocket. 'Decisively.'

Gravel flew from beneath his tires when he drove away.

They were closing in.

* * *

To obtain the autopsy photos, i-heist had either broken into the Coroner's files, bought them from a clerk, or breached security and found them online.

My third phone call, to the hospital IT department, hit paydirt.

'Sandoval, Isaac. Date of death?' the woman said.

I gave it to her. I had already explained that I was Adam Sandoval's attorney.

'I need to know if the autopsy photos are in your computer database.'

I heard her hitting keys. 'Yeah. We have them.'

'One more question. Which Mako security software are you running?'

'Just a sec.' Quiet on the line. 'Hammerhead, version six.'

I thanked her and hung up. I went looking for Kenny Rudenski.

Twenty-Eight

Almost everybody was gone for the day when I walked through the door at Mako Technologies. Cars were sparse in the big parking lot. The black-and-white photos on the walls hung in shadow, and a janitor was pushing his cart across the lobby. The front desk was unmanned.

But a second later, Amber Gibbs came bustling out of the women's room.

She beamed. 'How's the lingerie?'

'Scratchy. Yours?'

'I feel like royalty.'

She hummed around the desk, looking brisker and more purposeful than I'd ever seen her. Maybe Countess Zara had powers I didn't appreciate.

'I'm looking for Kenny Rudenski,' I said.

'I don't know if he's still here.'

'Could you call and find out?'

Her face twitched. 'I'm kind of in a hurry.'

'Please.'

'It's just, Pop Rudenski needs some papers—'

'Amber.'

'—and he asked me to bring them to his office before he leaves.'

'Come on, I'll walk back with you,' I said.

She looked flustered. 'Okay.'

Grabbing a folder, she unlocked the keypad on the security door and we headed down the corridor. A security guard stood at the vending machine, dropping coins in. He nodded to us.

Outside Kenny's office, his secretary's desk was unoccupied.

How lucky would I be if Kenny was gone as well? I stopped and Amber kept hustling down the hall.

I knocked and opened the door. The lights were off. I went in and shut the door behind me. I looked around. The office smelled like aftershave and tennis balls. The computer monitor was dark. I sat down at the desk.

Okay, now what? I opened a few drawers. Pencils, rubber bands, a bottle of rum. This was fruitless.

There was a jangle of keys outside the door, and I jumped. The door handle turned. It was the security guard.

'What are you doing in here?'

My pulse was knocking against my temples. *Attitude, Delaney.*

'I'm trying to find a piece of paper so I can write Kenny a note.'

I rustled through his desk, and behold, found a notepad. I took a pencil from a holder on the desk. The guard watched, not moving. Shoot.

Behind him in the hall, Amber came bustling back. He turned. She smiled at him, and his posture straightened. He hitched up his belt.

She glanced over his shoulder at me. 'Oh, Junior's not in?'

'I'm just writing him a note.' Lie, rinse, repeat.

'Okay.' She looked at the guard. 'Len, help me get some stuff in my car?'

He said, 'You bet.'

They walked off, leaving the door open. Their voices receded. Len's keys jingled down the hall.

How long before he came back? Forget the desk. Whatever I wanted would be on Kenny's computer. I tapped the keyboard and the screen bloomed awake.

Enter Password. Damn. The cursor blinked *ha, ha.*

I stared, thinking Kenny wasn't stupid, but he was arrogant. I picked up the keyboard and looked underneath, hoping he had taped the password there. Nothing.

If I wanted to access Kenny's files, I was going to have to guess his password. Fortunately, I knew from writing about cyber-security, password-guessing is likely to succeed. Passwords usually have six to eight characters, and people tend to pick bad passwords – children's names, pets, hobbies – because they can remember them.

However, I had to presume that Mako would limit login attempts, probably to three tries. How could I narrow down my guesses? If at least I knew how many characters the password protocol called for, I might be able to do it.

Kenny, however, wasn't going to leave that information lying around. He was too crafty.

But Amber wasn't.

Did I have time? I would have to run.

Don't just sit here. Go.

I dashed out. Sticking a piece of paper in the security door to keep it from locking, I hurried to the front desk. Looked out the front door, and saw the guard flirting with Amber in the parking lot. Did these two have any clue how close they were to unemployment?

I lifted Amber's keyboard, ran my hand along under the monitor, under the desk, and under her chair. Nothing. I looked outside again. Amber was getting in the car.

And then I saw Mr Frog, her stuffed animal, propped next to her monitor. Success. A Post-It was stuck on his little bottom. *Dazzl*ng*. I hurried back to the computer.

Kenny's password was going to contain eight characters. And it would probably require a numeral or at least one character other than a letter of the alphabet.

Think. Think about Kenny. What did he like? Himself. Cocaine. Dirty money, sex, cars.

I put my fingers on the keyboard and typed *McQueen*1.

Incorrect password.

Come on . . . *Carrera**.

Incorrect password.

The Porsche, he loved that Porsche . . . the image returned to me, of his vanity license plate. I counted the number of characters on my fingers. Typed it.

2KPSECUR.

The screen cleared. I'd done it.

A new prompt appeared on the screen, and I remembered that Jax had mentioned multi-level security – the first password gives you nonprivileged access. A second password is then required for higher level, privileged access.

The prompt remained, the cursor blinking at me.

Okay, Kenny. I vote for hubris. I think you believe nobody would get this far, and so you've made the rest of the trip easy for yourself. The prompt waited for me to type the password.

I touched one key: *return.*

I was in. A message on the screen said *90 sec timeout returns keyboard to 10 min nonpriv mode.* If I stopped typing for ninety seconds, the computer would automatically revert to nonprivileged mode for ten minutes before I could get back in again.

I went to *Search* and typed *Segue.* Three files appeared.

The first folder was full of documents – letters, memos, correspondence – and spreadsheets. I opened them as fast as I could, listening for Len's keys to jingle in the hallway. I skimmed the documents. Incorporation papers – from the Cayman Islands. Lists of company directors – Kenneth Rudenski, Maricela Vasquez de Diamond, and Mikhail Yago . . .

Then I found the financials. Hundreds of thousands of dollars were running through this company: to Mako, from Mako, to a variety of other entities. They had techie names, venture capital names, and I bet that if I could access them, they would show the same directors as Segue.

I breathed. Segue was indeed a shell corporation, attached to Mako. A slush fund for i-heist money. This was the stuff the FBI was after. The stuff Jesse needed.

i-heist had plainly sunk their claws into Kenny Rudenski, deep. They were partners now, or maybe parasite and host. Was he doing it willingly, or under duress?

I had to get this evidence to the police. Tonight. Once Kenny touched this computer, he would see that somebody had been looking at this file. And when he did that, he'd make sure that these files disappeared. Or maybe he'd make sure that the somebody disappeared.

But I didn't have a mini-disk, or a CD burner. And wouldn't it be charming for the security guard to find me at Mako's printer, collating and stapling confidential corporate documents.

But I did have e-mail, and so did the FBI. I fished through my purse for Dale Van Heusen's business card, but had left it at home. Plan B.

Three cheers for web-based e-mail. Punting caution aside, I connected to my account. I could delete the connection from Kenny's browser history afterward, but any one of a dozen geeks down the hall in engineering could find it as easily as if I'd written my name in peanut butter across the screen. I didn't care. Let him know it was me.

I accessed my account, chose *new message*, and attached the Segue file.

Jingling in the hallway again. Keys, and now I heard Len whistling. Could Dazzling Delicates lingerie truly be accounting for his and Amber's happiness?

The jingling stopped. Uh-oh. And I hadn't had time to send the e-mail.

Under the desk. Kenny's executive model looked like a solid cube of walnut from the front, so I dove off the chair to hide beneath it.

And saw my blunder. This big tank of a desk didn't sit on the floor; it was raised about six inches above it on clawed feet. Someone standing in the doorway would be able to see my rear end on the carpet.

Does my butt look big in this?

I pressed my feet against one end of the well under the desk, pressed my back against the other, and shimmied off the ground. I heard the door open. My breathing echoed off the wood. The lights flipped on. Footsteps approached. What was he doing? My thighs started shuddering.

Leave, I thought. Go away. Now.

How long had I been away from the keyboard? After ninety

seconds, the computer reverted to nonprivileged mode . . . if Len didn't get out of here soon, I would be locked out of the system for ten minutes. And I hadn't sent the e-mail file.

Noise above. He was standing over me, punching buttons on the phone.

'Harry? Len. You see a gal leave by the back door? About thirty, light brown hair . . . no, she came in without a visitor's badge, was snooping around Junior's office. She ain't here now.'

I willed him not to walk around the desk.

'Yeah, I'll meet you by the loading dock.' He left without closing the door.

I lowered myself to the floor. Scooted out, saw the screen still active. Staying crouched, I reached up to the keyboard and hit *Send*.

No time to stick around. I hoped this would get the ball rolling with Agent Van Heusen.

I quit the browser program, ready to dash, and a new window popped open on the screen. It was labeled *Mistryss Cam*. It was a view from a webcam. In grainy black-and-white, it showed a desk, and behind it picture windows opening onto a Spanish-style courtyard and driveway.

It was a view of Kenny Rudenski's study at home. Why had it unexpectedly appeared, of its own volition?

A message appeared on screen: *Front Door.*

I stared at the screen. Outside Kenny's picture windows, somebody was at his door. I saw a Toyota pickup on the driveway, bright in the evening sun.

Adam, get out of there.

I heard the keys coming back.

I rushed to the door. The only thing to do now was to get out ahead of him. I zipped into the hall and didn't look back.

Len's voice. 'Hey. Hey, you—'

I kept going, through the security door into the lobby. Behind me the keys rang like wind chimes. I hustled outside and ran toward my car. Squealing out of the parking lot, I checked the rearview mirror and saw the guard writing down my license plate number.

Screw it. I was in all the way now.

I had to get to Kenny's house. Kenny was in bed with i-heist, and if Adam confronted him, he was going to get hurt. Bad. I sped through Goleta, onto the freeway, and toward the elegant houses of Kenny's foothill neighborhood. After twenty minutes, my hands tightened on the wheel. I braked around the switchback. Mistryss was golden in the sunset, with the mountains rising beyond.

Adam's truck was gone.

I slowed, about to turn into the drive. But the *Mistryss Cam* system alerted Kenny he had visitors. It showed up on his screen at the office – what about other screens? Perhaps on a laptop he kept elsewhere? I didn't want him to know I was here. I idled on the road. And lookie there, the garage door was up, and the Porsche was gone.

In all the way. Why not do a water ballet, with fountains and an orchestra?

I turned the Explorer around and drove back downhill until I found a turnout, and a footpath that ran up the ravine behind Kenny's house. I parked and jogged up the path toward Mystriss. After a while I angled up the side of the ravine, climbing a slope so steep I had to lean forward against the hillside, holding onto handfuls of tall grass to pull myself up. I was panting when I got to the top. I crouched behind a tree near the lip of the hill and peered across Kenny's lawn.

I saw no motion in the house, just lights on in the kitchen. I trotted across the lawn, past the pool, to the kitchen door. It was unlocked.

Considering the extent of Kenny's security system, I thought he had either run out on a quick errand, or an emergency. Otherwise he wouldn't have left the house unlocked. If it was an errand, he'd be back soon.

I crept into the kitchen, grabbing a dishtowel off the counter, and headed on down the hall until I found Kenny's study. I draped the dishtowel over the webcam. Sliding the blinds shut, I sat down and turned to his computer.

Search. *Segue.*

Two items. I tried the first and the computer connected to the Internet, and from there to an auction site. I felt as if a bug were crawling up my spine.

This wasn't an ordinary auction site. It was a morbid corner of the Net, specializing in the souvenirs of death. Bids, time left in the auction . . . it had all the earmarks of a legitimate site, except that the items being bid on were mementos from celebrity deaths. The movie star found drowned in his pool. The football player who took the curve too fast. The R&B singer whose plane crashed in a hailstorm. It was macabre.

On screen, a section called Bid Tracker automatically kept pace with Kenny's bids. My stomach shrank when I read it.

Yazminh/personal effects from crash site . . . $47,500
Bobby Kleig/Ferrari brake disc . . . $29,650
Alaska Air/misc . . . $74,900

These were more than celebrity mementos. They were death relics, pieces left from the violent accidents that killed the singer, and the quarterback, and the passengers and crew of the Alaska Airlines jet that plunged into the sea off Point Mugu, fifty miles down the coast.

Kenny was a ghoul.

The walls around me seemed to shiver. The air felt like cold breath on my neck. I thought of him kneeling next to Yvette Vasquez's grave, pressing his fingers along her name in the stone. I thought of the way he looked at Jesse, and how his fingers worked when he stared at the wheelchair, and his certainty that disability was my turn-on. I thought of the way he grabbed me at the cemetery, and my skin wanted to shrivel. My head was thumping.

But what did all of this have to do with i-heist? The auction program had opened when I searched for Segue. Segue was a shell corporation, set up to run i-heist's money through the high tech markets . . . it was a laundering facility. And some of that

255

money was running out again from Segue to this freakish online auction outfit.

Was i-heist compensating Kenny for his services by helping him buy crash relics? My knees wanted to shake. That was their hold on him. Willing? He was an eager partner.

I left the auction program. I searched again, for a name that should have been obvious from the start. *Jesse Blackburn.*

The screen lit up with search hits. My mouth felt like cotton.

Jesse's life spread out on the screen before me: his financial records, mortgage balance, credit report. His medical records from the hit-and-run. His chart from the ER, admission records at the Rehabilitation Institute, even a psychological evaluation. *Patient is 24-year-old male, T-10 incomplete para . . . survivor's guilt and adjustment issues . . . possible clinical depression; coping mechanisms include sarcasm . . .*

There was enough information to rob him or manipulate him for years to come.

Okay, in all the way. New search. *Evan Delaney.*

I felt as brittle as cracked porcelain. Here were my own financial records. Here were credit card purchases and websites I visited from my home computer. I felt ill, clicking through the list. Here was an icon labeled *D Cam.* Delaney camera? I hit *View.*

I leaned toward the screen, and gasped.

On the monitor were split-screen pictures of my house. Live. One feed looked out at my living room. Another, slightly warped, peered down on my bed. It had to be a fiber optic camera hidden in the smoke detector in my bedroom. A third peered from above the medicine cabinet in my bathroom. Anger and understanding crawled through me. Kenny had set this up to watch me in the shower, and in bed.

I remembered his leering face. *Corporate America is Big Brother.* Telling me he'd like to see me when I was really turned on. How did he install these things? When?

I hunched, staring at the screen, clenching my jaw. 'Oh my God.'

The bedroom camera was focused on my grandmother's patch-work quilt. It was moving.

Writhing, in fact. Rhythmically. I leaned closer, and heard sound. I heard the silky voice of Marvin Gaye, singing 'Let's Get It On.' I gaped at the humping quilt. Marvin Gaye, that was Jesse's album. My head was pounding. He couldn't, he wouldn't. I squinted at the screen. Please, no, don't let it be Harley, no—

The quilt quivered and someone gave a little shriek. The blanket flew backward. A woman reared up onto her haunches. She arched her back and her breasts swelled into view, warping before the tiny fiber optic camera.

She shouted, 'That's it, baby. Buck me.'

I said, 'Tater, you bitch.'

'I'm a broncobuster. Give it to me, you great big stallion.'

She wore a bandanna neckerchief and a pair of six-shooters. Nothing else. It was the Billy the Kid outfit. She raised an arm in the air like a rodeo cowboy hanging on for those eight seconds out of the chute.

'Buck me, big man. Taylor loves your bucking!'

A grunt. I moved my eyes from the spectacle of Taylor's gyrating breasts to the man pinned beneath her, laboring for breath. He was roped and tied to the bedposts, a sight that gave me a bizarre flush of relief. It couldn't be Jesse, because he would never submit to bondage, would never let his arms be tied. No, it had to be Ed Eugene, and oh, lord, why couldn't I tear my eyes away from this?

'Oh. Oh—' Taylor whooped, bouncing on the saddlehorn, so to speak . . .

The man panted with effort. 'Ride 'em, cowgirl. Dig in those spurs. Dale's been a *baaad* horsey.'

My jaw dropped. It was Special Agent Dale Van Heusen, FBI. The man who wouldn't bend his knees for fear of wrecking the crease in his trousers.

Taylor rose up and pounded down again. 'Red Rover, Red Rover, you are a naughty boy, let Taylor *come* over—'

Red Rover – Dale – Agent Van Heusen – bucked beneath her. And then . . .

He whinnied.

I put my hand over my mouth. Then over my eyes. Then I grabbed the computer mouse and swirled it around the screen, pointing and clicking, hoping to do . . . what? My God, how could I stop this?

'That's it, baby. That's it. Don't make me draw my six-shooters.'

And I heard a sound I recognized. It was a doorbell. My doorbell.

On screen, Taylor jerked upright. 'Ssh.'

But Dale was . . . in the moment.

'Hitting – the finish line,' he wheezed. 'Taylor, don't stop—'

She slammed a hand over his mouth. The doorbell rang again. A moment later I heard pounding on my front door.

A man called, faintly, 'Taylor? Open up.'

Wham, the quilt went sailing, and Taylor flew off of Van Heusen as though she'd been bucked right in the butt.

Dale said, 'What's wrong?'

Taylor was running around the bedroom, grabbing her clothes. 'It's Ed Eugene.'

'Your husband?'

The pounding continued at the front door. 'Taylor, I know you're in there.'

Van Heusen said, 'What's he doing here?'

'Fixing to kill you, if I don't get out there.' She unbuckled her holster and threw it in the corner.

The front door rattled. 'Woman, get your ass out here.'

Van Heusen pulled against his restraints. 'Untie me.'

'Quiet.' She pulled on her shirt, wriggled into panties and her skirt.

'Let me loose.'

'Will you hush? If he finds you, he'll go off.'

Van Heusen said, 'Oh, God, get my gun out of your holster. It's loaded—'

Taylor exhaled, a sound of disgust, and knelt on the bed.

Ed Eugene was roaring. 'Taylor!'

She dashed from the room, slamming the bedroom door behind her. I heard Ed Eugene shouting at her. I had to get over there before he killed Van Heusen. I saw the look in the FBI agent's eyes: desperation. Taylor had left him tied to the bed, with a horse bit jammed in his mouth.

The sound of an engine brought me back to Kenny's house. I peeked out through the blinds and saw Mari Diamond's white Jaguar parked on the driveway. She and Kenny and her dogs were climbing out.

Adam walked toward his front door, keys in hand. He wracked his brain. Kenny Rudenski wasn't home – where else could the bastard be? Inside, the phone started ringing. He rattled the keys into the lock, went in. The answering machine picked up.

A woman's voice came on. 'Dr Sandoval, we've never spoken, but I know you've had a truckload of shit dumped on you. I want to tell you it's gotten too heavy, and—'

He grabbed the phone. 'Who is this?'

'Never mind. I'm calling to say I'm done with this game.'

'Is this—' the name, her name. 'Cherry Lopez?'

'It doesn't matter. The autopsy photos were too much. I'm out.'

'You're working with Brand, aren't you? I know it.'

'Not anymore. Not since he ripped us off. That's why I'm calling you. To say he can have whatever's coming to him. He is one sick fuck.'

'Where is he? Tell me where he is.'

'You want to have a crack at him? Do tell.' A humorless laugh. 'What's it worth to you?'

What was it worth to him? To find Isaac's killer? It was worth everything.

He gripped the phone. 'Tell me what you want. Tell me what I have to do.'

*   *   *

259

I was in Kenny's kitchen when I heard them open the front door.

'—getting out of hand. I'm worn out,' Mari said, her voice moving across the atrium toward the living room.

Kenny said, 'Won't be long now. Want a drink?'

I darted out the kitchen door and ran across the lawn, past the pool. At the lip of the gorge I jumped, ready to slide down the slope. The trees and boulders looked ghostly, as if they were shifting in the twilight.

And one of them spoke. 'Mind the rocks. It's treacherous out here.'

Electricity seemed to crack through me. I landed crooked, and tripped, going down on my knees. I scrambled to my feet, swearing, because that's all I could do to keep myself from screaming.

Tim North was standing half-shadowed behind a tree, holding a tiny pair of night-vision binoculars. For God's sake, was there any moment of my life when people weren't watching me? If I ever got the chance to sit down and think about how bizarre this evening was, I would probably blow a lobe out my ears, but at the moment I had to stop Dale Van Heusen from being turned into patchwork samples by a jealous husband.

'What are you doing here?' I said.

'Taking in the show.'

'I have to go,' I said. My skin was still prickling.

He leaned against the tree. 'Do you recall what I told you about self defense?'

It began with the awareness of the threat against you . . . 'What about it?'

He pointed toward the house. 'There's a Doberman behind you, and I think it's on your scent.'

I looked and saw, rushing across the lawn, fur and teeth and sleek bunched muscle. I sprang past Tim down the slope, sliding and stumbling. I heard growling. Panting, too – but that was me, arms flailing, legs spiking into the hillside, flinging up pebbles and dust, fighting for balance.

Where was Tim? No sound, nothing – had the dog ripped his throat right out?

I didn't even pause. Because the barking was much louder now. I jolted down the hill and onto the trail. The dog flailed behind me. I heard it coming, heard the slobber and gnarl. I accelerated, saw the Explorer ahead. The dog lunged for my leg. I felt it bite into my jeans, and I stumbled, hands hitting the dirt. I felt hot breath, saliva, wetness on my leg. I fought to break free. My jeans and leg jerked in the dog's mouth.

I cocked my free leg and kicked. I knocked the dog's mouth loose from my jeans and scrambled for the Explorer. The teeth clamped again, around my foot. I pulled. The dog pulled back, yanking the shoe off. I scrambled onto the hood of the car, my hands clawing at the metal, legs slipping.

Two feet swung down from the roof, and a hand reached out for me.

'Grab hold,' Jax said.

She pulled me onto the roof of the car next to her. We looked down at the dog, thrashing my shoe back and forth in its mouth.

She said, 'That dingo's got your baby, mate.'

My jeans were soaked with drool. I stuck my fingers through the rips and was astonished to find my skin intact underneath.

The dog dropped the shoe and began sniffing the bumper.

I said, 'Figure five seconds before it jumps up here. Any suggestions?'

'Make it two seconds.' Putting two fingers in her mouth, she whistled.

The dog reared and leapt onto the hood. I jerked my feet up, horrified. Jax held up a little canister and sprayed the dog in the face. It squealed and tumbled off the car.

'Pepper spray,' she said.

We jumped down and got in the car. The dog was on the ground, rubbing its face in the dirt, whimpering. I started the car and went backing down the trail, fast. I bounced out onto the road, spun the car around, and stopped.

I looked at Jax. 'Out.'

'You're welcome,' she said.

'Thanks. Out.'

She opened the door. 'Tim's up there, and he's going to find out what you saw.'

'Great. Call me. We'll do lunch.'

I left her by the roadside and went tearing toward my house. I hoped Dale Van Heusen would still be alive when I got there.

I ran along the flagstone path toward my cottage. The lights were off in my living room, and the front door was closed. There were no sirens or flashing lights, no neighbors crowding the lawn. So at least there hadn't been gunshots.

I opened the door, stopped, and listened. The house was silent. The living room showed no signs of a struggle. I headed to the mantle and picked up a vase. The video bug was stuck to the front. I threw it on the sofa and went to the bedroom door. From the other side came thumping sounds. God, was Ed Eugene in there beating Van Heusen to death? I opened it.

Inside, the FBI agent was alone, spreadeagled, arms and feet bound to the four posts of the bed. He was sawing back and forth, trying to break the restraints, but Countess Zara had defeated him. He had merely marched the bed away from the wall.

He saw me and snapped still. His eyes shrank with relief and horror. I grabbed the bedsheet and covered him up. He mumbled through the bit in his teeth, shaking his head back and forth on the pillow. I put a finger to my lips.

Setting a chair beneath the smoke detector, I climbed up and removed the cover. Inside, I found the tiny fiber optic video cable. I yanked on it, pulling two feet of it out of the ceiling. Van Heusen lay frozen on the bed, staring, his chest starting to heave. Jumping down, I went to the kitchen and got a pair of garden shears. I came back and cut the cable.

I found the third bug in the bathroom, above the medicine cabinet. I pulled it out of the wall and cut it. When had Kenny's henchpuppets wired the house, when I was in Las Vegas? Walking back into the bedroom, I took the bit out of Van Heusen's mouth.

I said, 'What happened to Taylor? Did Ed Eugene drag her away by the hair?'

'They argued, and then they left.' He pulled against the restraints. 'Untie me.'

'He didn't come in here? Didn't even open the door?'

'No. Release me, this instant.'

'How on earth did she dissuade him?'

'She told him you were in the tub with me. Now let me loose.'

I almost laughed. Taylor was smarter than I'd thought.

'How did she justify being in the bedroom, herself?' I said.

'She took the quilt. She told him she came here to get it without you knowing.'

I shook my head. 'You just dodged a bullet or six.'

He was breathing with the rapidity of a small mammal. I turned on a lamp, pulled the chair to the bedside, and sat down. I flexed my hand, opening and closing the blades of the shears.

'Let's chat,' I said.

He thrashed. 'Untie me or this will go down as a hostage situation.'

I sighed. 'Right. Let's call in the Hostage Rescue Team. I can see them now, rappeling down from the chopper, kicking through the window, radioing headquarters. "Quantico, we have a problem. Dale's been a bad horsey."'

He closed his eyes, grimacing.

'Let's review the evening's discoveries.' I picked up the severed fiber optic cable and started cutting bits off the end. 'I learned that my house was bugged with surveillance cameras. And that a federal agent was using my bed to re-enact the Calgary Stampede. This agent has questioned me, and insinuates that my boyfriend is involved in the criminal matter he is investigating. I find him out of uniform, having placed his weapon beyond his control and available to others.'

'You can't—'

I leaned toward the bed and nickered. His lips quivered.

'Moreover.' I whacked another inch off of the cable. 'The surveillance cameras, it turns out, were transmitting this agent's rodeo performance to the computer system of another suspect in the investigation.'

'Oh, Lord. Who?' he said. 'Who installed the bugs?'

I leaned toward him. 'Stop threatening Jesse.'

'But he's a person of interest in the investigation.'

'You know he's innocent of all allegations.'

'I can't just—'

'What is wrong with you? You're in my bed, uninvited, boinking a married woman, and it hasn't even occurred to you to say *sorry*.' I rested my hand on the bed next to him, with the shears pointing toward his armpit. 'What were you doing, using my house for your tryst?'

'Taylor said we couldn't go to her place, her husband would know.'

'Does the word *motel* ring any bells?'

'I'm on Bureau business, I couldn't possibly submit a motel bill in an expense report . . .'

I exhaled, and dropped my head. 'Back off. Stop threatening to seize Jesse's assets. Start protecting him from these thugs who are after him.'

He looked at the ceiling. From the way his nostrils were flaring, I guessed that he didn't want to admit defeat. I guessed that he was trying to think of a way to screw me the minute he walked out of my house.

I said, 'Dale?'

'Fine. Blackburn gets a pass.'

'You'll call it all off.'

'Yes.'

'Truly call it off. No screwing around, no trying to turn this around on me once you leave here.'

'Why would I do that?' he said.

'Because you're a power-tripper and a bully. But you won't do it this time, because you not only owe me. You need me.'

'After tonight, we're done. I never want to see you again.'

'No. I can direct you to evidence against i-heist. And I can tie it to Mako.'

Now he looked at me, his eyes sharp. 'How?'

'Keep your word to stop harassing Jesse, and I'll tell you.'

He blinked. 'Yes. Yes. Okay.'

'Bottom line, Dale. I watched the video on a computer screen. And I captured the image, and e-mailed it to several people. Their e-mail addresses end in things like navy-dot-mil, cia-dot-gov . . .'

'You didn't.'

I didn't. But I didn't tell Van Heusen that.

'And don't forget that at any time of the day or night, I can send it to others, as easy as typing the name Ed Eugene Boggs.'

I gave him a long, sour smile, and watched him bite his lip.

'Yippie kay-yay, Dale.'

I cut him loose.

Twenty-Nine

When Van Heusen shot his cuffs and straightened his tie and scurried out my door, I dropped onto the sofa, drained. Waiting. I was counting boomerangs. How many things had I thrown out that might come back to hit me?

Start with my intrusion into the Mako computer system. My foray into Kenny's house. I knew his secrets now. Don't forget Mari Diamond, who had sworn to ruin me. And her Doberman, who may at that moment have been trotting the streets of Santa Barbara with my shoe in its mouth, hunting for the foot it came from, to give me an ending from the AntiCinderella story. Jax and Tim? I didn't know where they fit, except that they crawled out of every crack.

And I was looking in the wrong direction.

The message light was blinking on my answering machine. Adam had called, twice.

'Evan, please, it's urgent. I need – just please call. I'll try your cellphone.'

My cell had run down again, but when I plugged it into the charger and checked my messages, I felt a sharp twang of alarm.

'Evan, I would never ask this except in an emergency. I need to borrow some money. Please, please, phone me the instant you get this message.'

What the hell was going on? I phoned him back. No answer at home, or his office. I tried his physics lab and reached one of his colleagues.

He said, 'If you can tell me what's going on with Adam, I'd be grateful. He was here earlier, asking to borrow money.'

I hung up. I heard my heartbeat, pounding in my temples.

266

I phoned Jesse. The coolness in his voice killed me, but I pushed through the brambles.

I said, 'Have you seen Adam in the past few hours?'

'No. What's the matter?'

'I think i-heist is making a move on him.'

I told him about the autopsy photos, and my phone messages.

'Jesus,' he said. 'I'm going over to his place.'

'I'll meet you there.'

It was dark when I got to Adam's house. His truck wasn't in the driveway. He didn't answer the door, and the house was locked. I walked around to the patio, tried that door as well. The curtains were open and the living room was empty. I went from window to window, standing on tiptoe and peering into various rooms. I heard a car door slam and headed out front. Jesse was coming up the driveway. Under a streetlight, his face looked severe.

I said, 'House is locked. No sign of him.'

'The spare key should be under that planter by the kitchen window.'

I found the key and unlocked the door. We went in, calling Adam's name. He wasn't there. I let my gaze wander across the house. A bowl of soup sat on the kitchen counter, half-eaten. The phone was in its cradle.

The message light was flashing on the answering machine. I pushed *play*.

'*Dr Sandoval, we've never spoken, but I know you've had a truckload of shit dumped on you. I want to tell you it's gotten too heavy, and—*'

'*Who is this?*'

The hairs on my arms started rising. It was Cherry Lopez. I listened, and said, 'Jesse.' He came into the kitchen, heard Lopez's voice.

'*You want to have a crack at him? Do tell. What's it worth to you?*'

A long pause, and then Adam sounded as if he was walking onto shifting ice.

267

'*Tell me what you want. Tell me what I have to do. Do you want money?*'

'*Five thousand.*'

'*Dollars?*'

'*Cash, baby.*'

He breathed heavily into the phone. '*My bank opens at nine thirty tomorrow—*'

'*I won't be here tomorrow.*'

Another heavy pause. '*I can get a thousand. Tonight.*'

I felt watery. Jesse's hands were knotted in his half-fingered gloves.

Adam's voice again. '*Where?*'

'*Downtown, there's this place near the train station.*' Lopez described a chancy part of town.

'*When?*' Adam said.

'*Couple hours. Say eleven thirty.*'

Jesse spun toward the door. I was close behind him. It was eleven twenty-five.

'The address sounds familiar.' He stopped. 'Suck.'

He was looking at the hall closet. It was open, and inside it I saw sports equipment neatly lined up. Scuba tank, fins, and, next to a tennis racket, an empty space.

I said, 'What's missing? Did he take the baseball bat?'

'No. He took the spear gun.'

We barreled down the hill on Cliff Drive. Jesse pushed the Audi up to seventy.

'A thousand bucks,' he said. 'That's loose change to i-heist. Why would Lopez try to wring that money out of Adam?'

I felt my legs starting to quake. 'It's a set-up.'

The road curved, the car slewing, rubber whining.

He said, 'Setting Adam up.'

'They've driven him to the edge and now they're pushing him over. By making him think he can get Brand.'

What was waiting for Adam downtown – a beating, or worse? Or even a confrontation with Brand – who might be armed as well? I got out my cellphone, and Dale Van Heusen's business card, and started punching numbers.

'Who are you calling?' Jesse said.

'The FBI.'

'The hell you are.'

'Adam could need serious help.'

'Van Heusen – are you nuts? No.'

He reached out to grab the phone. I tried to stop him. The headlights swept over the hillside dead ahead. I jammed my hands on the dash, feet against the floorboards. He jerked the wheel. We swerved, straightened, kept going. Fast.

'Slow down,' I said.

'Hang up the phone.'

'Ease off the damned gas. Adam needs real back-up.'

'And if we find Brand shot with a spear gun? You want the FBI to take Adam down?'

We hit the bottom of the hill, screeched around the corner onto Castillo, heading toward the beach.

'You don't know what's happened tonight. You're off the hook with Van Heusen,' I said. 'And he owes me. His career, and possibly his genitalia.'

He gave me a disbelieving look. 'What—?'

'Later. It involves Cousin Tater, bondage toys, and a spy camera.'

He stared at the road, his mouth half-open. 'Delaney. Will I ever live through a day when you don't shock the shit out of me?'

We ran the red light at Cabrillo and raced along the beach. Out in the harbor, the lights from Stearns Wharf shimmered on the water. Jesse's face was pale under the sweep of streetlights.

He said, 'What if it's Brand they're setting up, and they want Adam to take the fall? We have to get him out of there before it goes down. Hold off. Let's assess the situation when we get there.'

'What if that's too late?'

The engine growled. We roared along.

'Dammit. Fine, call.'

I dialed. He turned into an industrial neighborhood near the train station.

He slowed. 'This is it. Here we go.'

The street was dark. A single streetlight shone at the end of the block. The light in front of the warehouse was out, looked as if it had been broken. We were only two blocks from the beach but it felt like the middle of an urban wasteland. Around us were warehouses, all locked, many behind chain-link fencing. Adam's pickup was parked in front of the address, the only vehicle on the street.

Jesse coasted to a stop behind it. I called Van Heusen, wanting some federal muscle to know we were here. His number was busy. I pressed redial. Still busy.

I said, 'Why would Adam come down here by himself?'

'He thinks he doesn't have anybody else.'

'But to this neighborhood.'

He looked at the building, its filmy windows, the big rectangles of whitewash covering up graffiti.

'Isaac worked here.'

I followed his gaze. On the building were signs for several companies that had space here. Garnett-Horner Medical. South Coast Storage.

Mako Technologies.

'That's why it sounded familiar. Isaac's company, Firedog, this was their office. Cheap space for six guys and their startup.' He killed the engine, opened the door. 'I didn't know Mako kept it. Maybe they're using it for storage.'

We got out. I heard a freight train clacking in the distance. Following Jesse along the sidewalk, I looked at the building. It was creepy in the darkness, three floors of gloom. Van Heusen's phone was still busy.

'I'm calling Lieutenant Rome,' I said.

'Yeah. Good.'

I started dialing the police department. Jesse reached the door and pulled it open. The building was black inside. He leaned forward, trying to see in. I grabbed him by the shoulder.

'Don't go in. Wait for the cops.'

'Adam's in there.'

'With how many opponents? Jesse, you can't go in blind and unarmed.'

'I can't just let it happen to him.'

From above us came crashing sounds, wood splintering. Jesse shrugged loose from me and went through the door. For better or worse . . . I ran through the door behind him.

Inside, the building was half warehouse, half loft space for offices and mom-and-pop manufacturing. It was dark. The street-light cast sharp shadows. I found a bank of switches, flipped them. No light.

'Power's off,' I said, knowing what that meant: no elevators.

He headed for a metal staircase. It led to a series of walkways and lofts – an upstairs building within the building, where office windows overlooked the cavernous ground floor. He reached the bottom of the stairs and grabbed the rail, looking up, as though he was going to try to pull himself to his feet and climb them. No way, I thought.

He said, 'Screw it, I'll go up on my butt. You bring the chair.'

I was still dialing the police department. 'Let me go first and look.'

He hitched up his jeans. 'If my Levis fall off, bring them too.' He swung onto the staircase and started bumping up. 'Come on.'

Listening to the phone ring at the police department, I started climbing behind Jesse, pulling the chair. We were noisy, and slow, and my teeth were on edge. The building was a maze, dark and sinuous and full of places to hide. Directly above, an office window reflected the streetlight.

Finally Rome came on. 'What's the problem, Ms Delaney?'

How could I phrase this, without coming off as a nut, or a scaredy-cat?

'I'm downtown, trying to stop an assault. Can you send a patrol car?'

Jesse climbed, working hard.

'Assault. Could you be more descriptive?'

Something shiny whistled past my ear, skiing through the air. It sailed over Jesse's head and landed in the wall with a thwack. For a stupid second we both gaped at it. It was one of Adam's fishing spears.

Rome said, 'Ms Delaney?'

I spun. Below me, Cherry Lopez emerged from the shadows and started up the stairs. The spear gun gleamed in her hands. She was reloading.

I backed up the stairs toward Jesse. He was a sitting duck. Lopez paused on the stairs, muscling the rubber bands on the spear gun into firing position.

She looked at me. 'Well, shit. Have I finally found a way to shut you up?'

A sound shattered the air: glass bursting, directly above us. The office window above me erupted. A mound came flying through it. A human mound, limbs flopping. It was Win Utley, plummeting toward us.

Jesse turned his head and raised an arm against the bright foam of glass. Utley dropped like a boulder. I dove toward Jesse, trying to get out of the way, and heard Utley hit the stairs with a thud.

Panting, gritting my teeth, I looked back down the stairs. Utley lay heaped near the base of the staircase. Beneath his body lay Cherry Lopez. I could see her leg twitching. It looked as if her snaking cable tattoo had electrocuted her. Getting to my feet, I walked down a couple of steps. Glass crunched under my shoes. I looked at Utley. My stomach kipped, bile jumping into my throat.

Utley was dead. Blood was pouring from his head, dripping through the metal grating of the stairs, pattering on the floor below. So much blood, my God – had he landed on the spear? Beneath his gargantuan mass, Lopez stopped twitching. She looked as though she'd been crushed by a falling block of cement.

My arms and legs felt like yarn. I turned to Jesse. 'You okay?'

He looked up at the shattered window. 'Adam, can you hear me?'

From somewhere above, Adam called back. 'Here—'

I jammed the wheelchair against the wall and ran up the stairs. My heart was going like a big band in my chest.

Jesse kept climbing, saying, 'We're coming.'

'Stay back,' Adam said.

Top of the stairs. Adam's voice had come from the room with the shattered window. I pressed myself against the wall and inched toward the door.

From inside came Adam's voice. 'Jesse, no. Get out of here.'

'Hang on,' Jesse said.

I squatted down against the wall, getting low, hoping that if anybody was in there with Adam, they'd be expecting me to show up at eye level. I leaned around the corner and peeked inside.

It was a loft space, taking up this whole side of the building, smelling of dust and wood. Light trickling through the windows shone on disused office equipment, desks and chairs stacked in a corner. I didn't see Adam, or anything capable of propelling Win Utley through a window. Behind me, Jesse labored up the stairs.

In the shadowy loft I heard a scraping sound. My eyes refocused. I saw Adam on the floor, slumped against a desk. He was in trouble.

Now what? Go in, and get hit with whatever blew Utley through the window? I pulled back from the door. Jesse was hauling his way upward, with six or seven steps to go. When he got to the top he wouldn't wait, wouldn't huddle at the doorway while Adam was inside. Never. Even if Adam told him to go to hell. Even if that room was hell itself. He wouldn't leave Adam in there alone.

He hadn't been able to reach Isaac on the hillside in Mission Canyon. He would get to Adam or die trying.

I leaned back against the wall. 'Adam. Are you alone?'

'I— I'm . . .'

'Adam, where are they?'

'I don't know. I don't, can't see anybody.'

My synapses did a quick crackle. I dove through the doorway, onto my hands and knees, and skittered toward him.

He raised a hand. 'No, go back.'

'Oh, God.'

He sat slumped against an old wooden desk. He had been shot through the shoulder with the spear gun. The back of the spear protruded from below his clavicle. From the way he hung in front of the desk, I could tell that the spear had gone clear through and lodged in the wood, pinning him there. His shirt was dark with blood. It glistened in the dim light. I scrambled to his side. I was afraid to touch him.

Tears shimmered in his eyes. 'Get out. It's a trap.'

My deepest fear. They were setting Jesse up. Adam was the bait to draw him here.

My limbs shook. 'How many are there?'

'Maybe two, three.' His head rolled. 'They disarmed me when I came through the door. Stupid, I was stupid . . .'

'What happened to Utley? Did you knock him through that window?' I said. No answer. 'Adam, stay with me.'

He leaned his head back against the desk. I took his hand in mine, squeezing so he wouldn't know how frightened I was. Tears of pain fell down his cheeks.

His voice was almost gone. 'They're out there.'

Noise from the hallway, Jesse thudding up the stairs. I turned and saw him in the doorway, looking at Adam. The shock on his face was horrible to see.

Adam squeezed my hand, and coughed. His face was pale. The spear, I thought, must have hit a vein. All those old westerns, where the hero gets shot and says it's nothing, ma'am, just got one in the shoulder – garbage. Shoulder wounds can lead to a quick death.

I heard Jesse struggling to get through the door. He said, 'Adam . . .'

I held Adam's hand, clammy, weak. The shadow of Beyond crossed above me, a presence I had known but not seen before.

Jesse crawled toward us, breathing hard. 'I'm sorry, buddy, I'm sorry.'

'Get out,' Adam said.

Jesse reached Adam's side. He looked at the spear, and at me.

I said, 'We have to wait for the police and paramedics.'

'No. We have to get him out of here.'

'How? We can't remove the spear.' I tried to put emphasis in my voice, to get the point across: because the spear is all that's keeping him from bleeding to death.

'Maybe we can get him loose from the desk,' Jesse said, his hand hovering above Adam's shoulder. 'Go get the wheelchair, so we can put him in it.'

Mister common-sense, the clear-eyed cynic, who would shrug and say 'Shit happens' at the worst televised carnage, sounded pleading. I had never heard such wishfulness in his voice.

'We're getting him out of this building,' he said.

Behind us, the floor creaked. We looked around. Mickey Yago was strolling into the loft. He had a pistol in his hand.

Thirty

I started to stand up and Yago waved the gun.

'No, stay where you are, that's a nice tight target grouping,' he said.

He sauntered toward us. In the dingy light his gold ringlets looked ashen. His face was a hatchet.

He approached Jesse. 'You, my friend, are a major dipshit.'

Jesse tried to put himself between Yago and Adam.

Yago said, 'It would have been real simple for you just to do what I told you. But no, you had to be a yahoo and hold out. And look what happened.'

'Adam has to get to a hospital,' Jesse said.

Yago stepped forward and nudged Adam's leg with his foot. 'You ain't kidding.'

'Let me get him out of here and I'll do whatever you want.'

'Too late, amigo.'

'You've made your point. I'll move the money for you.'

'No. I don't think you get how stupid you been, not yet. You need more convincing,' he said.

He looked at me. And rubbed a palm against his shirt, as if wiping off sweat.

Jesse said, 'Touch her and I'll kill you.'

Yago snorted. 'You haven't told her, have you? She don't know . . . wait, *you* don't even know, do you?'

He smiled. Pretending to pout, he put on a falsetto voice. 'Oh, babydoll, I've been so bad, I can't help gambling, boo hoo . . . I'm so sorry about everything, thank God you saved me, Jesse . . .'

Yago laughed. Jesse shrank back, trying to stay in front of Adam.

Yago said, 'You really think you know how to protect and save a woman?' He eyed me. 'Come here.'

I said, 'The police are coming.'

'Yeah.' He wagged the gun. 'Can they get here faster than a speeding bullet?'

I saw the flash. It was a snap of light in the shadows somewhere beyond the doorframe. Sound followed, a crack. Yago flicked forward and dropped to the floor like a sack of corn. A dark flow spread from beneath his head.

Jesse stared at him, eyes huge. 'Fuck.'

I was shaking. I felt it again, the feeling of Forever, of something coming toward us out of a rift in the air, a black presence pressing on me.

'Jesus,' I said. 'Oh, Christ—'

Then they were in the loft, sliding through the shadows, and I knew why Win Utley came crashing through the window with no warning, pouring blood. He'd been shot. Jax and Tim moved toward us, Jax holding a pistol with a suppressor screwed on the end, Tim carrying the scoped rifle that had just emptied Mickey Yago's brain onto the floor.

They were coming for us. Right now. Everything Jesse had feared, should have been feared. It had been them all along. And I'd ignored him, and now we were next.

I felt bile climbing up my throat. I tried to stop myself from throwing up, covered my mouth with my hands. I looked at Jesse. He was looking back, the confusion on his face clearing into understanding.

He said, 'It's them, isn't it?'

From between my fingers I said, 'I'm sorry.'

Jax went to Yago. She kicked the pistol away from his hand and stopped to take a good look at him. I tried not to do the same, because I could tell that Yago's face had become an exit wound. Jax nodded at Tim and made a slashing motion across her throat with her thumb.

Tim came toward us. He held the rifle tight to his side, index finger outside the trigger guard. He was wearing gloves.

He gestured for Jesse to move away from Adam. 'Out of the way.'

'You'll have to kill me,' Jesse said.

Tim's dog-pound face registered surprise, but he didn't slow down.

I said, 'Don't do this, Tim.'

He said, 'For christsake, move. Let me take a look at the wound.'

'What?' I said.

And I felt Jax's hand pulling me out of the way. Those ballerina arms were stronger than steel cable. Tim knelt next to Adam, set the rifle down, and peered at the shoulder.

He put his hand around Adam's wrist. 'You all right, mate?'

Adam was sweating. 'Been better.'

Jax pulled me away from the men. I felt stunned, relieved, embarrassed. Jax held the pistol at her side. Her black gloves looked stylish.

She said, 'You thought we came to kill you? You are the most distrustful person I've ever met.'

'I—'

'Be quiet and listen. The building is now secure.'

'You mean they're all dead.'

'Yes.'

I rubbed my hands across my face. 'Did you follow Jesse's car? How did you know what was going down?'

'Another time. What matters now is getting out of here.'

She glanced toward Tim. He was talking to Jesse.

'We can't sanitize the site,' she said. 'We'll have to leave the bodies.'

Ridiculously, I found myself nodding, as though I faced such niggles every week.

'We can get you and Jesse away from here, but any halfway-decent crime scene team will be able to figure out you were here,' she said.

Another glance at Tim. He looked back this time. He tapped a finger against his wrist and shook his head.

Jax's expression didn't change, but she lowered her voice. 'Tim can't find a pulse. If Adam doesn't get to a hospital soon he's liable to lose the arm. If he makes it that far.'

I stared at Adam. He was gritting his teeth, trying to maintain consciousness. Tim spoke to Jesse, who maneuvered to get under Adam's good shoulder, to lift him up, take the weight off the side that was impaled.

I said, 'The police and paramedics should be here soon.'

Her face hardened. 'You called them? How long ago?'

'Maybe five minutes.'

'Tim. We're going,' she said.

He said, 'Right.'

She put a hand on my arm. 'When I say going, I mean far gone.'

'You know the police are going to interrogate me and Jesse,' I said.

'Yes.'

'I won't be able to keep all this from them.'

'I know. You're hardly an accomplished liar. What will you tell them you saw?'

'A flash in the dark. Yago falling. I presume it was a gunshot, but I didn't see who fired it.'

She nodded. 'Fine. But expect to spend the night in jail.'

In the distance, sirens.

Tim said, 'We can't stay.'

I turned back toward Adam. Jax stopped me.

'Listen, i-heist is dead, but this isn't over. And we can't protect you any longer.'

'I don't understand.'

'i-heist wanted to keep you and Jesse alive. They thought they could manipulate you to get money and access. But now they're dead. And the people who are left only want to shut you up. Irrevocably.'

The big band was starting a new tune in my chest. 'What people are you talking about? Franklin Brand? I thought – wasn't he here tonight?'

'No. He wasn't here.'

Tim looked at me, and at Jesse. 'If you want to go, we have to get you out right now.'

Jesse said, 'Can you get Adam out of here?'

'No.'

'Then I'm not leaving.'

The sirens drew nearer. Jax went to the window, peered up the street.

'Two squad cars, SBPD. We're gone,' she said.

On the floor, Jesse struggled to prop Adam up. The sirens wailed outside. Lights kaleidescoped across the windows, blue and red. Jax and Tim made for the door.

I said, 'Thank you.'

Then they weren't there anymore.

I heard doors slamming out front, voices raised, cops talking. Adam breathed raggedly. Jesse spoke to him.

'That's it, breathe, hang in there, just a minute longer, they're coming now.'

Adam turned his head to look at Jesse. His lips moved, but his words were inaudible.

Jesse leaned toward him. 'I can't hear you, buddy.'

Adam tried again. 'Last leg.'

Jesse swallowed. 'No. Come on, stay with me.'

'Can't. It's up to you, anchor man.'

'No. Open your eyes, come on.'

'Not your fault.' He looked at Jesse. 'I'm so cold.'

Jesse listened, and watched, his face inches from Adam's.

He said, 'Ev, get the cops. Get the paramedics. Now.'

I ran to the stairway. At the bottom of the stairs I could see flashlights. The cops came through the front door of the warehouse, guns drawn.

'He's not breathing,' Jesse said. 'Adam. Son of a bitch.'

'Up here,' I shouted. 'Hurry.'

Jesse said, 'Breathe, Adam. Come on, do it.'

I raised my arms. 'We need the paramedics. My friend's not breathing.'

Jesse said, 'Get up here!'

And I knew what had to happen. The lights and muzzles swung my way. A voice shouted, 'Face down the floor. Hands behind your head.' I did it, immediately.

The cops spread out, fanning across the ground floor. I knew they wouldn't come upstairs, across open ground, until they thought they were secure. And they wouldn't send in paramedics, either.

Jesse shouted, 'He isn't breathing. Help me.'

I turned. Jesse was trying to support Adam's head, and fighting, impossibly, to give him CPR. He couldn't lay Adam flat, couldn't clear his airway, couldn't get him in a position where he could give him chest compressions that made a difference.

I called down the stairs, 'Hurry.'

The cops were coming up the stairs, stopping at Win Utley's body, checking it for signs of life. I heard one say, 'Jesus, there's another one underneath him.' The flashlights zigzagged up the stairs. In the loft, I heard Jesse pushing on Adam's chest, three compressions and silence when he breathed into his mouth.

Feet above me now, a sharp voice saying, 'Don't move,' hands grabbing my wrists and pulling them back. I felt the cuffs snap around my wrists. They turned to the door into the loft, and one said, 'Whoa.' Beyond Mickey Yago's corpse Jesse held Adam's face in his hands.

The officers said, 'Move away from him and lie down.'

'Help me,' Jesse said.

'On the floor, face down. Move it.'

He kept doing compressions. 'Take over.'

'*Now.*'

That's when the buzzing started in my head. The officer crossed the room in two steps, grabbed Jesse by the collar, and dragged him away from Adam. Another cop talked rapid-fire into her radio, calling for medical assistance. I saw Jesse face down on the floor, the policewoman kneeling at Adam's side, and Adam hanging limp, soaked in blood, eyes wide.

More feet came running up the stairs, and I heard Lieutenant Rome telling me to keep cool. He hurried into the loft.

The policewoman got on the radio again, calling for bolt cutters, urgency in her voice. Jesse was saying, don't stop the CPR. Rome hovered above them, and I saw him give the cops a look. Jesse said breathe for him, come on – and Rome went to his side. The buzzing in my head got louder. Rome was on one knee, his hand on Jesse's back, talking, and I didn't hear his words, refused to hear them.

Jesse said, 'You're wrong.'

Rome called to the cops, said, uncuff this guy.

Jesse said, 'Don't stop.'

The cuffs came off and Jesse crawled back to Adam's side. He gripped Adam's hand, calling his name. Rome knelt beside him.

'Son,' Rome said, 'he's dead.'

Thirty-One

The sun was out, red light seeping through the afternoon haze. My eyes felt as though they'd been scrubbed with steel wool. I felt drained to the point of numbness, sitting in the interview room at the police station, waiting for Lieutenant Rome to come back and tell me it was time to take the drive to the county jail. An entire day of questioning hadn't gotten him whatever answers he hoped to get.

The doorknob turned. I looked up and my spirit shriveled.

Dale Van Heusen stood in the doorway. He was pulled together with origami neatness, the suit stiffly pressed. An indecipherable look rode his face.

'Let's go,' he said.

I stood, and accompanied him through the station. I didn't see Rome, didn't speak to anybody, received only a cursory glance from the man at the front desk. We walked out into the late afternoon.

He put his hands on his hips. 'You're free to go.'

For a second I squinted at him. 'How—'

'I'm not as useless as you imagine, Ms Delaney.' He sucked his teeth. 'This is now a Bureau matter, that's all you need to know. Should there ever be a prosecution in regard to the deaths at the warehouse last night, you can expect to be called as a witness. But you're under no threat of criminal charges yourself.'

I tried to assess him. I was feeling faint. 'That's good to hear.'

He buttoned his suit jacket. 'And we're square. From this point forward, we owe each other nothing.'

'What about Jesse?'

'He won't be hearing from me.' He smoothed his tie. 'Conveniently for him, the people I was after are dead.'

'Adam Sandoval's dead, too,' I said.

His hand hesitated, stroking the tie. 'Yes. I'm sorry about that.'

A erratic light roamed his eyes. It may have been sincerity, or regret. Either way it was too little, too late.

He looked over his shoulder at the door. Jesse was coming out. Van Heusen said, 'I'll leave you two alone,' and headed back into the station.

Jesse looked wrecked. His hair was lank, his face pale, his eyes sunken. His shirt was smeared with blood. I wanted to throw my arms around him but held back, not sure how he'd take it. He stopped, facing the red sun, staring someplace distant.

He looked as if he wanted to speak but was waiting to catch the moment when his voice wouldn't crack; as if a rough syllable would throw the master switch and blow everything to shreds.

He said, 'I have to go back and get my car.'

I knew there was no way he could cope with returning to the warehouse. I said, 'I'll get it.'

'No, I need it, I have so much to do.'

'You don't have to do anything, Jesse.'

'I have to call Adam's priest. And his relatives, he has cousins in New Mexico.' He closed his eyes. 'I have to tell them he's dead.'

At that last word, his shoulders dropped and he pressed his fingers against his eyes. And I did put my arms around him, cradling his head in my hands. He leaned against me, and I felt him start to shake. But abruptly he pulled back. Maybe it was me, or being outside police headquarters, but he didn't want to relent, give it up.

'Come on,' he said.

He crossed the street and kept going along the sidewalk in front of the courthouse. The big building was tinted coral in the light.

'What Yago said last night, right before he got shot. I know what he meant.' He stared straight ahead. 'When he said I hadn't told you, that I didn't know myself. I do now.'

I kept pace with him, waiting for him to say it.

'It's about Harley.'

'Her gambling?'

'That summer, before the crash, it was getting worse and worse. Stints in Vegas, losses to bookies. Until one day I stopped by her office and found her with a lot of cash.'

'How much?' I said.

'Thousands. I walked into her office and found her stuffing it into envelopes,' he said. 'I thought she was stealing it from her firm's client trust account to pay off her gambling debts.'

But she wasn't. I knew now, she wasn't. 'What did you do?'

'Confronted her. Told her I'd go to the head of the firm and turn her in.'

'And what happened?'

'She broke down. It was pathetic, Evan. She was on her knees begging me not to expose her. Such a tough woman, falling at my feet, wrapping her arms around my legs and weeping.' He shook his head. 'I told her I wouldn't turn her in if she put the money back and went to Gamblers Anonymous. That night. I said I'd drive her to the meeting.'

'And?'

'She clung to me, thanked me, said she'd do it.'

'And?'

He looked at me. 'You see where this is going, don't you?'

'What happened to the money?'

'I put it in the bank for her.'

'How much?'

'Ninety-five hundred dollars.'

He stopped. We looked at each other.

I said, 'You smurfed.'

It was a structured transaction, meant to keep under the Treasury's $10,000 reporting limits.

I ran my hands through my hair. 'Oh, Jesse.'

'I thought I was helping her. Thought I was keeping her clients from getting ripped off, too.'

His gaze drifted. Not, I thought, into the distance, but into the past.

'Harley did come to see me in rehab. Told me she was going to a recovery program, meetings three nights a week. Proud of herself, saying she was getting straight. She thanked me for shocking her into it. That's what Yago was making fun of. Imitating her, and he knew everything she'd said to me. She scammed me, Ev, to keep me from turning her in. She never stopped gambling, never stopped laundering money for Yago.'

'Did you tell the police?'

'Yes.'

'Do you think Brand is the one who helped Yago get his hooks into her?'

'The cops can find that out.'

His voice was flat. He wasn't trying to shade his words, wasn't trying to protect my feelings anymore. He didn't care.

I looked at the sun sinking toward the rooftops, reddening the western sky. 'Jesse, what Adam said to you – about the anchor leg.'

The anchor man was the final member of the team, the one who was counted on to bring home the victory.

He stared at his hands. 'He meant it's up to me to get Brand.'

He didn't say *find*. He didn't say *turn in*.

'I know what I have to do,' he said.

And I knew what he meant. It turned my heart to ice.

Thirty-Two

I heard the phone ringing. I had fallen asleep on top of the covers, face down on my bed. I fumbled to my feet, knocking a glass of water off the nightstand, grabbing the phone. By the light coming through the window, I could tell it was evening. My hair was still damp from the shower, so I couldn't have dozed for long. The scent of jasmine hung lush in the air and hibiscus flowered outside, violent red.

Amber Gibbs's voice brought me awake. 'Oh, Evan, it's awful.'

'Yeah.' I pressed the heel of my palm against an eye.

'Is it true you were down there when people were shooting?'

'How'd you find out, Amber?'

'Things are crazy here.'

'Crazy how?'

'Junior went nuts. Tearing up his office and screaming at people. We had to call Pops in Washington, D.C., and finally Mrs Diamond came over to calm him down.'

I was now wide awake. 'Amber, back up. Why did Kenny get so upset? Because he heard about the shootings at the warehouse?'

'No, your boyfriend.'

When did I grow an apple in my throat? 'What about Jesse?'

'He came rolling in here saying he had to see Junior. He set him off like a bottle rocket.'

Not again. 'Is he still there? Do you need me to come over and break it up?'

'No, Junior went tearing out of here with Mrs D, and Jesse left right after them.'

She may have kept talking, but I didn't hear it. I hung up and tried to reach Jesse. No answer at home, on his cell, or at the office. A breeze swirled through the windows. I felt a presence again, the way I had the night before, the shadow of death. *The people who are left only want to shut you up. Irrevocably.*

Grabbing my keys, I jumped in the Explorer and floored it toward Jesse's house. Pulling into his drive, I saw that his car was gone. I went in, calling his name, but he wasn't there. I stood in the living room looking around, trying to find any evidence to tell me where he'd gone. The breakers cartwheeled up the beach in the red sunset. The Yellow Pages were open on the kitchen counter, and I saw at which page. Firearms.

He couldn't have bought a gun. Not this evening, not from a licensed dealer.

Who was I kidding? He was resourceful, and relentless, and . . .

And a good shot.

Somebody was either going to get killed tonight, or go to prison. I couldn't let it be Jesse. Think, I told myself. Where would he have gone? Only one place.

I phoned Dale Van Heusen. 'I'm going to Kenny Rudenski's house.'

'I can be there in twenty minutes. I'll meet you outside,' he said.

I got in the Explorer and gunned it toward the foothills.

At Kenny's house, the only car in sight was Mari Diamond's white Jaguar. No Porsche, no Audi. The setting sun turned the mountains a sharp blue, threaded with gold seams of rock. I was feeling déjà vu. Had it been only twenty-four hours since I was up here looking for Adam?

I pounded on the front door. Nobody answered. I stared into the security camera and said, 'Kenny, open up.'

They had to be here, I thought. I left the door and walked to the window of Kenny's study. The blinds were open, and his computer was on. The screen was displaying video footage – I could see motion. Trying to get a better look, I pushed through the bushes bordering the window. That's when I stepped on the dog.

One of the Dobermans was lying in the bushes. I jumped, ready to run, but the dog didn't move. Pushing the bushes aside, I bent down and saw that the dog was dead. It head was crushed. It had been hit with a hard, heavy object and dragged out of sight into these flower beds. My throat constricted. Fearfully, I touched its fur. It was warm. The blood on its head was wet. This had just happened.

Mari would never have done this. Frightened, I looked around again. Heard nothing, saw nothing outside. Took another look through the window at Kenny's computer screen: the video on screen was from the *Mistryss Cam* system. Oh my God. I saw Mari, somewhere inside the house, banging on a closed door. I heard no sound, but her mouth was working frantically, and I could read her lips. *Help.*

Where was Van Heusen? I couldn't wait for him.

The front door was locked. I ran around the house to the patio. The lawn was emerald in the fading light. The patio doors were locked. Finally I found an open bathroom window. I leapt and grabbed the sill, pulled myself up and shimmied through. I opened the bathroom door and listened for a burglar alarm, or footsteps, anything . . . I crept out, looking around. I heard Tim North telling me *self defense begins with awareness of your surroundings.*

Well, rightie-o. Surroundings: house of weirdo who may want to kill me. I crept along the hallway, hearing my shoes scuff on the wood.

Mari was locked up somewhere in here. Where? I looked in the living room. Everything was in place: Steinway gleaming, glass memorabilia cases in mint condition. Into the kitchen; the big refrigerator hummed, but the room was still and clean.

I heard a sound, a cry coming from further back in the house. I picked up a skillet from the countertop. Tim's voice again, lecturing me . . . *Pity will get you hurt.*

I put the skillet back and took a meat cleaver from the magnetic knife rack. The biggest thing on the rack, with a thick handle and a gleaming blade that looked sharp and heavy enough to decapitate a pig.

I started toward the sound, down the hallway past Kenny's

office. I held the meat cleaver flat against my leg. The noise again, the crying, behind me now. I turned. It was coming from a door in the hallway, the door to Kenny's wine cellar.

Scratching and whimpering, the sound of fingernails scraping wood. Raising the cleaver, I pulled the door open. And as soon as I did, I knew the scratching was not the sound of fingernails. It was the sound of claws. I slammed the door.

Right on Mari's Chihuahua. The dog squealed, I pulled the door open again and it skittered to its feet, eyes bulging. I jumped back.

It glared at me, the Chihuahua Terminator, then turned tail and ducked back into the doorway. Holding the cleaver higher now, I pulled the door all the way open.

There was no sign of Mari. Instead, a staircase went down into the cellar. The yelling was coming from beyond another door at the bottom of the stairs.

This was without doubt a human voice crying for help, accompanied by the sound of a hand beating on wood.

I called, 'Hello?'

The pounding intensified. So did the crying. The Chihuahua tottered down the stairs, claws ticking. At the bottom, it pawed at the door, whimpering.

Banging, frenzied now. 'Open the door. Open the door.'

'Mari?' I said.

'Let me out. Open the door.'

Should I wait for Van Heusen? I checked the hallway, saw nobody. I ran down the stairs. The door at the bottom had a deadbolt lock; the key was in it. I turned it.

The door blew open and Mari Diamond tumbled out. Her eyes looked like cue balls. Her red nails flailed against my chest. She clattered into me and started climbing the stairs on all fours, grunting and squealing.

I staggered back against the stairs, hitting my butt, and grabbed her leg.

'Wait. Who locked you in?' I said.

She sawed her leg back and forth. 'It's him, let me go—'

'Where's Jesse? Was he here?'

'You stupid – move! In there. Kenny took a shovel, you know what he's going to do with it? Get out. Let me out of here—'

She saw the meat cleaver.

'Jesus, you crazy bitch. Oh, God.'

And she kicked me in the chest with a dainty, spike-heeled confection of a shoe.

I gasped from the pain, flinching backward down the stairs. Mari skittered up the stairs and out into the hallway.

I started up after her. Somebody locked her in, and that was probably Kenny. And I didn't want to be locked in after her. I got three steps up the stairs and heard the dog going the other way, into the wine cellar. And that's when I smelled it.

The odor was faint, an undercurrent in the air. But it was unmistakeable. It wasn't the bouquet of old wine. It was the smell of decaying flesh.

The Chihuahua disappeared into the cellar, barking and moaning. Instinct, revulsion, the urge to self preservation, told me to haul my butt up the stairs after Mari and keep going. Except for one thing. I'd asked her where Jesse was. And in her babblings she had said, *in there.*

I felt the meat cleaver in my hand. I walked down the stairs.

I stepped through the doorway. The air felt cool. The smell was almost subliminal. Like a nightmare. My shoes scuffed on the concrete floor. I took the key from the deadbolt lock and put it in my pocket.

The wine cellar looked normal. At the far end of the room, however, was another door. I crept to it and looked in. My heart was trying to climb up my throat.

Beyond the door was a museum. This was where Kenny kept his most valuable collectibles, the memorabilia that meant the most to him. My skin started slithering.

The display cases were installed with the same care as the ones upstairs in the living room. More care, perhaps, because this was where Kenny's heart lay. His dirty, worm-eaten, fetid heart.

I had seen a hint of this on Kenny's computer, with the bidding on off-the-books crash memorabilia. But seeing it in person was different. It closed in on me, though encased behind glass. This was a cathedral, a cesspit, a museum of sudden death.

I walked between the displays, holding my breath. On the walls, flat-screen displays played footage of famous air crashes. The United Airlines DC-10 going down in Sioux City. The Concorde streaming flames as it struggled toward Le Bourget, fighting its doom. Air show catastrophes: Ramstein, Paris, Lviv. I kept walking. Bizarrely, I was aware that this was arranged with the care of a good museum exhibit, leading the visitor through the experience to greater understanding.

Here were the fruits of Kenny's bids in underground auctions: *mementi mori*. A lovingly tended, dirty collection of death souvenirs. Some . . . *pieces*, I supposed he called them, came from everyday fatal accidents, but some were from famous events. Princess Grace, one display was labeled. Buddy Holly, said another.

After visiting the cemetery with him, watching him at Yvette Vasquez's grave, I thought I understood. This obsession had been developing since Yvette died in the car wreck. This, not her headstone, was his memorial to her.

Literally. Because directly ahead was a case with a black velvet pillow, and inside was a relic. It was nothing but a piece of twisted metal, stained with brown streaks that I knew were blood. Her blood. I read the label on the display case.

Yvette Vasquez.

This, for Kenny, had become the embodiment of the girl's death, a stand-in for her crushed body. The start of his collection. Kenny the thrill seeker. Here was where he kept all his fear, and his lust, hidden. And the biggest secret he hid was that he had stolen a piece of the car in which Yvette died.

No wonder Mari pounded on the door to be let out. Here was Kenny's inner life: death.

That was what I was smelling. And it didn't come from the

display cases. I followed the keening of the dog, around a corner, and stopped.

The Chihuahua was standing in front of a wrapped package, growling, lunging and darting back, tiny hackles up. The package was wrapped carefully: in a blanket, and then in trash bags, all secured with duct tape. It was a body.

I stood without breathing, watching the dog dart back and forth. Who was it? What should I do? I seemed as disconcerted as the pooch.

The dog dashed in again. It bit through the trash bag and started tearing at the blanket underneath. I backed up a step. I didn't stop the dog. I wanted to know who it was. I took out my phone to call Van Heusen, but couldn't get a signal.

Horrified, I watched the dog wrangle its way through the blanket and sink its teeth into flesh beneath. It wagged, ripped, tossed its head back and forth. Finally it backed off. Protruding from the blanket was a gray waxy hand. On the hand was a diamond pinkie ring as big as a computer chip.

It was Franklin Brand.

I backed away. The dog darted in and rolled on the body.

Brand, dead, here. Not freshly dead, either. And what had Mari said – he took a shovel? Kenny had murdered him.

I backed into a display case, felt it rock on its pedestal behind me. Turning, I steadied it. It was a small Plexiglas case, unadorned, set at the end of the display. No lighting, no explanatory notes. None were needed.

Inside the case were a gear cog and derailleur from a bicycle. And a damaged pair of bike shoes. And a crucifix of Mexican silver. The display was labeled *Mission Canyon*. They were mementos from the hit-and-run.

For a second I held onto the case, staring. What the hell was this doing here? Had Kenny bought it from the police or scavenged it from the dump? Why?

I felt my head thudding. My knees felt soft. The bike parts could have been scavenged, but not Jesse's shoes, or Isaac's crucifix. They had disappeared from the scene of the crash, before the paramedics arrived. Jesse was right: his dream was a memory, a memory of the killer standing over him. Stealing bits of his handiwork. I looked around at the museum, the entire display, and realized that it was arranged so that two pieces had pride of place. They were the pillars upon which the exhibit rested. They were relics from the two death scenes in Santa Barbara – Yvette Vasquez's crash, and the hit-and-run.

They were the two scenes where Kenny was present. Where Kenny was to blame. Where Kenny was at the wheel.

I hissed through my teeth. Franklin Brand had been telling the truth all along. He was not the driver. He did not run Jesse and Isaac down.

Kenny did. And he'd taken trophies.

Was he planning to turn Brand himself into his newest exhibit? Gagging at the thought, I staggered toward the door. I ran back through the wine cellar, up the stairs, and out into the hall, gulping fresh air.

Van Heusen, where was Van Heusen? I ran through the front hall, into the atrium. The front door was wide open. It was almost dark, stars appearing in the eastern sky. I dashed outside. Mari's Jag was gone.

But Kenny was home. His Porsche was parked behind my Explorer. He had the hood up on my car, and was ripping wires loose in the engine.

I stopped on the porch, still holding the meat cleaver.

He wiped his hands on a handkerchief and gave me a solid stare. He was sweaty and his shirt was covered with dust. It was the *Great Escape* look all over again, but I didn't think he'd been digging a tunnel. Rather a grave. I felt the handle of the cleaver in my palm. My hand was sweating.

I said, 'The FBI is on the way.'

He smirked and nodded at the cleaver. 'You might get in a half-hearted swing at me, but I'll take it from you. I'll hack off your arms, and then I'll bury it in your face.'

Don't move, don't back up, don't give him encouragement. I pulled out my cellphone. Screw it, call 911.

No signal.

Kenny walked toward me. 'You can't get reception this far back in the ravine. Sorry, Gidget, you're fucked.'

I stood on the porch, my quads shivering. And out of the dusk a car swept into the driveway. Relief lit me up like a klieg light. Van Heusen was at the wheel.

Kenny looked at me with a sneer on his face. Van Heusen was getting out of the car. Kenny called to him.

'She's armed. Watch out.'

Van Heusen looked from Kenny to me, saw the cleaver.

'Dale, don't listen to him. He killed Franklin Brand,' I said.

Kenny started toward him. 'She's whacked out of her head. She chased me out of my own house with a meat cleaver. The bitch is freaked, man.'

Van Heusen raised a hand. 'Stay where you are. Both of you.'

Kenny kept walking. 'She's been in my face since the beginning, she and Blackburn. They won't go away. They're like a bad case of herpes.'

Van Heusen reached under his jacket, hand going to his holster. 'I said hold still.'

Kenny stopped, next to my car.

Van Heusen looked back and forth between us. He still hadn't drawn his gun.

'Put your hands on the grill of the car, Rudenski. Evan, set the cleaver down and step over here.'

'Dale, he's lying,' I said.

'Do it.'

Kenny leaned on his hands against the grill of my Explorer and stared under the open hood at the engine, as though he were a mechanic. Van Heusen kept his gaze on me.

I set the cleaver on the driveway. My relief had fizzled.

'The body's in his basement,' I said.

'Jesus Christ,' Kenny said. 'She breaks into my house, goes for me with a kitchen ax, and you're going to listen to this shit?'

'Franklin Brand is dead, wrapped in trash bags and duct tape,' I said.

295

Kenny shook his head. 'That's not a body, that's a mannequin. Come in and see, man.'

'Don't, Dale. I know a dead body when I smell one.'

Kenny guffawed. 'It's for my sports memorabilia collection, stupid, to display the new driving suit I bought.'

He started to turn and gesture to me. Van Heusen drew his weapon.

'Both hands on the car.' He walked toward Kenny.

Kenny made a point of drawing a deep breath, giving an appearance of calming himself down. Quieter now, he said, 'She's desperate to blame this on me. She's over the edge.'

Van Heusen gave me a glance. He looked intent, and confused, and over his head.

He pointed his gun at me. 'Go sit over on the driveway and lace your hands behind your head.'

I felt the ground seeming to drop away beneath me.

The Chihuahua trotted through the front door and skeltered up to Van Heusen, moaning for attention. Clenched in its teeth, diamond ring shining, was Franklin Brand's finger.

Thirty-Three

Van Heusen gawped at the little dog, and the trophy in its mouth.

'That's not . . .'

Caesar reared onto his hind legs and put his paws against Van Heusen's shin. Van Heusen shied backward, stepping toward my car.

Kenny charged at him.

Van Heusen looked up, but Kenny slammed against him and slapped his head sideways across the open engine block. Van Heusen cried in surprise and fumbled to regain his balance. Kenny reached up for the hood of the Explorer and slammed it down on him.

I yelled, 'No!'

Once, twice, Kenny smashed the hood on Van Heusen's head and upper body. Van Heusen staggered, tried to straighten up, threw his arm toward the car to keep from falling. He got his head clear and Kenny rammed the hood down a third time. I heard bone crack, metal slam, the hood latch shut, Van Heusen screaming, feet sliding out from under him. The dog skittered around his feet.

Kenny had smashed the hood closed on Van Heusen's hand. His gun hand. He was trapped. His arm was broken, his pistol lost down in the engine.

Kenny's shoulders were heaving. He watched Van Heusen struggle, and then he turned toward me. The meat cleaver was on the ground in between us. We looked at each other, and we both lunged for it.

I saw it gleaming on the ground, the blade so promising. I reached for it.

Kenny ran straight at it, kicked it out of my reach, and picked it up. He hoisted it and turned back toward me.

Van Heusen hung on the car, pale, barely holding on to consciousness through the pain. Kenny stood between us. There was no way for me to get to Van Heusen, or even to get into the car and pop the latch to release the hood. Kenny stepped back and glanced at each of us, as though deciding who to go for first.

Van Heusen reached his free hand into his jacket and pulled out his cellphone. He looked at me. The pain was striating his face.

'Run,' he said.

My legs didn't move. How could I leave him here? But he gave me a look that made me understand. He wasn't being selfless. He was captive prey. I was the fox the hound would have to chase. The only way to buy him time was to get Kenny away from here. And the only way Kenny would leave was running after me.

I lit out toward the street.

About eighty yards along the road I looked back. I knew what Dale Van Heusen didn't: his cellphone wouldn't work up here. He couldn't call for help. Only I could do that. I had to get out of the microwave shadow of this hill and call for backup. I had to draw Kenny away from Van Heusen, and I had to keep him away until the cops could get here. I had to keep him on my tail, but not close enough to bury the cleaver in my face. If I got away, he would go back and finish Van Heusen off. I had to run, but not too fast. I was fit. Dear god of running, please let Kenny be out of shape. I turned and looked. He was fifty yards back, chasing me.

In his Porsche.

Neighbors, I needed neighbors. Or another driver. I pounded down the hill, seeing no driveways, no other cars. Hearing that German engine. I had to get off the road.

I pumped my arms, running hard. I heard the Porsche shift gears. Just off the road, the hill descended through tall grass toward a line of sycamores, that looked as if they lined a creekbed. Beyond the trees an avocado orchard climbed the far side of the gully.

Jump. I careened down the hillside, running toward the cover of the sycamores. Racing into the shadows, I ducked behind a tree trunk. On the road above, the Porsche rumbled, slowing to a crawl. I got out my cellphone. I had a signal. I punched 911.

Access denied.

Gaping at the display, I redialed. *Access denied.*

This was impossible. My phone was guaranteed to reach the emergency number anywhere, anytime, even if I hadn't paid my bill. Maybe the signal was too weak . . . but it didn't matter. I had to draw Kenny's attention again.

Calm down. Listen. In front of me, through the trees and blue shadow, I heard water slurring over stones in the creekbed. Behind, I heard Kenny revving the engine of the Porsche. I peeked around the tree trunk, up the hill. In the drawing dusk, the car idled on the road above.

I ran back into the open where Kenny could see me. Heard him jam the Porsche into first gear. The creek flowed parallel to the road, and I ran downstream, toward the city, toward Foothill Road, the main street at the bottom of the hill. The Porsche kept pace above me.

I tried the phone again. *Access denied.*

The foliage thickened, grass and trees and dammit, that was poison oak I just ran through. I looked up. Kenny had rolled down the window and was staring at me.

I crossed back into the treeline. For the fourth time, I tried 911. Hell. Running in the deepening darkness, sidestepping rocks and gopher holes, I tried another number, one my fingers could speed-dial by feel alone.

Jesse.

I called his cell, and ran. I heard clicks and static, and the phone ringing.

Above me, the Porsche accelerated, drawing ahead. I heard the engine rev, and saw it round a curve and edge out of sight.

The phone rang. I veered back into the cover of the trees.

Jesse, answer the phone.

Because I knew what Kenny was going to do: get ahead of me,

park, and wade down the hill to cut me off. Literally, with the cleaver.

Finally, in my ear, I heard Jesse's voice. 'What's up?'

'Call the police. Send them to Kenny's house, tell them a federal officer is down and will die if they don't haul ass over there.'

'What? Jesus, Ev—'

'Do it now.'

Silence; I could virtually hear the shock crackling through his mind. He said, 'I'll call you back.'

Again I peered out from the trees. Where was Kenny? I stopped and listened. I could no longer hear the engine. Sweat trickled into my eyes. A breeze shivered the leaves, a chill taunt.

The phone chirped. I answered, 'Yeah.'

'They're rolling. Are you hurt?'

'No.'

'Are you safe?'

'No.'

'I'm coming to get you.'

Jesse, my love, my sorrow, my heart. 'I'm downhill from Kenny's house, and—' I looked around. 'I can't see him.'

'I'm in the car, don't hang up.'

I pressed myself against the bark of an old tree. The leaves stirred in the breeze.

I said, 'Did you get the gun?'

Quiet. 'No.'

'Shit.'

The light had dimmed to a blue glow in the west. I heard creatures scurrying, and water licking in the creek. I listened for signs that Kenny was approaching. He was now downstream; I couldn't keep heading that direction.

Jesse said, 'You there? Head toward the cops.'

'Right.'

Once more I listened. I thought I heard, skating on the wind, the sound of voices up on the road. My nerves were playing pachinko, pinging and chattering. Keeping to the shadows under the trees, I started upstream.

I said, 'Brand's dead. Kenny killed him.'

Static, no reply.

'I saw the body.' I ran. 'Brand wasn't the hit-and-run driver. Kenny was.'

Here's what stunned silence sounds like: my own hard breathing, the catch in my throat, oleander rushing as I push past it.

He said, 'How—'

'He stole things from the crash scene. Isaac's crucifix.'

'Oh, fuck.'

'I—'

Behind me, a snapping sound. I spun around. Downstream Kenny slid out from the shadows. He saw me.

'Oh, God.' I ran harder. 'He's coming.'

'Don't hang up.'

I didn't. But I took the phone away from my ear to pump both arms as I ran, upstream, back toward Kenny's house. Going flat out. But now that he was on foot, I could return to the road. The police were coming. If they found him chasing me up the street with a meat cleaver, great.

I started angling up the embankment toward the road. From the phone came Jesse's voice, shouting, 'Evan. *Evan.*'

I climbed. I heard a car driving up the hill.

To Jesse, Kenny, the darkening sky, I said, 'It's the cops.'

But as I said it, I knew I was wrong. No sirens, no lights, no urgency in the sound of the engine. The car curved into sight. It was a Mercedes, cruising slowly. The windows were open and the driver was shining a flashlight across the hillside. When the car drove past, the beam swept over me.

The car braked. The beam swung back. Spotlight. My legs went rubbery.

The driver shouted, 'Kenny. She's here.'

Kenny had help. It was Harley.

I had to get out of here. And I couldn't go forward to the road, couldn't go back toward Kenny. I ran straight down the hill toward the creek. I pounded through the tall grass, into the sycamores, onto the sandy stream bank. I heard the water slurring. I skittered over mossy rocks and into the creek. The water soaked my shoes, splashed cold on my legs, and I was across.

Jesse shouted, 'Delaney, talk to me.'

I raised the phone. 'Kenny has help. I'm running.'

'Mari?'

'No, it's Harley.'

I broke from the trees into tall grass. Ahead, the avocado orchard blanketed the hillside, spreading up the slope and over the crest. I looked behind me. The sycamores shivered in the breeze. I heard Kenny splashing across the creek.

I ran into the orchard. The trees were mature, with slick greenery hanging low to the ground. I glanced back. Kenny was coming. Walking, the cleaver dangling from his hand. He seemed unhurried, looked calm and determined.

Running, I talked into the phone. 'I'm going over a hill into the next ravine. If there's a road, I'll head toward town.'

Here in the hills, roads got scarce. They meandered up the canyons toward the mountaintops, dying out into trail heads or dead ends. I reached the top of the hill and kept running through the orchard across the summit, until the land started descending again. I had no idea where I was.

Ahead, I saw moonlight shining beyond the edge of the orchard. I came out of the trees above a road.

'There's a street. I'm going to run downhill toward Foothill,' I said.

The hill crumbled sharply toward the asphalt. I turned sideways and approached the drop, planning to scoot down.

Harley's car was idling on the road, dead ahead. She had cut me off.

How the hell did she figure out to double back and get here? Did Kenny call her from a cellphone to tell her where I was heading? I stopped, crouched down by a tree.

'Ev, talk to me.'

I held the phone against my leg and crept through the trees. If I could get behind the car, I had a chance of crossing the road without her seeing. I scuffed down the dirt embankment and dashed across the road, ducking into brush on the other side.

I looked around, seeing that this was the V of another gully. The hillside rose in front of me, covered with live oaks. I found a trail and ran up it. I'd made it.

'I think I outfoxed them. I'll head over this rise and meet you down on Foothill.'

Jesse said, 'You're sure it was Kenny driving the car that night.'

'Yes.'

'Brand's BMW.'

'Positive. He keeps Isaac's crucifix in a museum in his cellar.'

He was quiet. I wove up the trail.

'My nightmare. The man is Kenny,' he said.

'I know.'

'He crashed into us and came back to see if we were dead. He walked down the hill . . .' A pause. 'In the dream I'm always face up, staring into the sun. He flipped me over.'

'He thought you were dead.'

'Or the girlfriend heard Stu Pyle's plumbing truck coming and—'

I got it. 'Mari was with Brand that night.'

'If Brand wasn't in the car, neither was she.'

'The anonymous call,' I said. 'They set Brand up.'

I was climbing up the trail now, trying to watch my step over the ruts and rocks.

Back on the road, Harley's voice rang through the dusk. 'Kenny, I've got her heading up the trail.'

Got me? How? I looked back. She was U-turning. How did she know where I was? The car swung around and she aimed her flashlight at my side of the road, sweeping the bushes until she spotted the path.

'Kenny!' she said.

I started running again, up the trail. 'Jesse, she's tracking me.'

'Tracking, how?'

How indeed? I thought about it. There was only one thing it could be: my cellphone.

'Oh, dammit.'

My phone had a mobile positioning system. It could alert police or rescue crews to my location. Or anybody else with an emergency scanner.

'My phone's a beacon,' I said.

'What?'

'They rigged my phone to send a locator signal. That's why it runs down all the time. It's been constantly transmitting my location.'

They'd probably also programmed it to deny 911 access, I realized – and another thought snapped me between the ears. 'They may also have a cellphone scanner.' They could be listening to our conversation right now.

I heard the car roaring. Harley wasn't waiting, knew I wasn't standing still.

'I have to get rid of the phone,' I said.

I kept running up to the top of the ridge. I was breathing hard now.

'I've probably come a mile east from Kenny's house,' I said.

Jesse's voice changed. 'Okay. You know where to go.'

I didn't.

'There's only one place.'

Hearing the solemnity in his tone, I understood. He was right.

'I'll be there,' I said.

'So will I.' His voice turned hard. 'Rudenski, are you listening? Your time is up. You're done, you sack of pus. Finished, cocksucker. You shit-eating, rat-fucking—'

I threw the phone into the bushes and ran. Toward Mission Canyon.

Thirty-Four

Scraping through the tall grass, I hurried down the slope toward the road. Ahead I saw eucalyptus trees gleaming silver under the moon. Below, where Mission Canyon spilled open at the foot of the mountains, I glimpsed city lights. This was the crash site.

Running across the road, I edged over the drop-off and lay down below the lip of the shoulder, out of sight. The grass rasped at me.

Come on, Blackburn, throw that big-block engine into high gear and take these curves.

I knew he hadn't called the police again. If his cell calls were being intercepted, telling the cops to come to Mission Canyon would have given Kenny my location and a head start.

Besides, Jesse wanted to kill him.

I had to get out of here, and I had to make sure that Jesse didn't turn tonight into an exclamation point on his own life, a fast trip to prison.

An engine droned in the distance. I raised my head. Headlights arced around the curve below me. Come on, Jesse. Anchor leg. Bring it home.

It wasn't him. By the shape of the headlights I could tell that it was the Mercedes. I crabbed backward down the slope. The car slowed to a creep and the flashlight brushed the hillside, white light bleaching the shoulder of the road and the tree trunks above my head, but missing me. I held my breath. The light lingered.

And moved on. The car drifted up the hill.

She didn't know I was here. I put my head down in the dry grass. My temples pounded. She was gone, but the road dead-ended 400 meters uphill. She'd be back. At most I had a few minutes.

And Kenny was out there in the dark.

305

Flattened in the grass on the steep slope, I thought: this is where Isaac died. I felt no sense of him, no pain, no lingering spirit. Only my own dread. Not least because his brother's rage, Adam's star-bright fury for revenge, was coming in the form of Jesse Blackburn.

I thought about the hit-and-run. How we hated Franklin Brand all these years for a crime he didn't commit. Thought about Kenny driving Brand's car – he could have stolen Brand's keys and taken it from the Mako parking lot. Or from Brand's house, or Mari's. The mechanism wasn't important. The real question was: why did Brand flee? Why didn't he turn Kenny in? Why did he agree to take the rap?

Because Kenny had something on him.

Brand was embezzling from Mako. Kenny must have discovered that; must have found out that Brand plundered the Segue fund, stealing money earmarked for i-heist. After the crash, did Kenny convince Brand it would be better to take the blame for manslaughter than to be charged with grand theft, securities fraud, and have a pack of hyenas like i-heist on his tail?

Vehicular manslaughter. That had been the charge. That's why Brand left the United States for the length of time he did. The statute of limitations for manslaughter was three years.

Brand came back to Santa Barbara three years and three weeks after the crash. Because he thought he was free and clear, that he could no longer be prosecuted for the crime. But he hadn't studied the law carefully enough. The statute didn't apply, because a warrant had been issued for his arrest, and charges filed. He should have gotten legal advice.

Rather, he should have gotten good legal advice. Not counsel meant to deceive. Like a rockslide, the pieces tumbled in my mind. Of course. Harley had misled him.

I heard a car coming up the canyon. The engine was whining, had to be redlined. I scuffled toward the lip of the slope and saw the Audi curving along the road. Relief splashed over me. I scrambled up the bank and started waving.

Kenny was standing on the far side of the road. When he saw me, he charged.

I was screaming when he hit me, my skin, bone, muscle shivering, seeing the blade. But he slammed me with his chest, threw his arms around me, and pushed me toward the drop-off.

He wanted to get me off the road and down into the darkness that would camouflage his hacking. I had to stay in sight, right here. I squirmed, tried to plant my feet, and he kept pushing me toward the shoulder. *Pity will get you hurt.* I clenched my hand into a hitchhiker's fist and flailed my arm around. My thumb hit him in the eye, the nail sinking in.

He howled and grabbed at his face. I ran.

He came at me again. Tackled me around the hips. I went down, elbows and chin cracking against the road. He landed on my back. I heard the cleaver scrape against the asphalt, felt his breathlessness and sweat. I writhed beneath him. Sounds poured from my own throat, growls and cries.

Jesse's car came screaming around the bend. The headlights were blinding white. I was shouting and Kenny was clutching at me. We were face down on the center line.

Jesse braked hard, tires squealing. He spun the wheel and the car skidded.

Yelling, I turned my head away and tried to shrink into myself. Thinking so loud, big damn engine and all that momentum—

And the tires shut up.

I peeked. The car had stopped sideways on the road. It was five feet downhill from us, back end toward the drop-off, engine guttering and the tires wafting scorched rubber.

Kenny lay on top of me, sweaty and hot, his breath scratching in and out.

I said, 'Ding dong. Herpes calling.'

From the car, Jesse shouted, 'Rudenski, this is done. Throw the hatchet away and get off of her.'

'I'll kill her,' Kenny said.

'Not with me watching. Even you aren't that stupid.'

'Like you can stop me?' He grunted to his feet, pulling me up by a fistful of shirt. 'You and the paralympic team?'

'You won't get us both,' Jesse said. 'And I'm the one you want.'

Kenny wrestled me toward the car, pushing me down onto the hood and leaning on me. The metal was hot, painful on my chest. I squirmed and kicked.

Kenny struggled against me, shouting at Jesse. 'Get out of the car.'

'I'm the last eyewitness to the hit-and-run. Let her go,' Jesse said.

'How'd you like her with fingers missing? How's she gonna look without a nose?'

Jesse's voice kicked up. 'Let her go and I'll get out.'

I fought. 'No, Jesse, don't.'

The car was all he had, his only weapon. If he got out, that was it.

Kenny said, 'Turn off the engine.'

Jesse did it. I could see him through the windshield, face like a steel beam.

'Rudenski, I know you took trophies from the crash,' Jesse said. 'I know about your museum, your little toy stash. What do you do down there, you necrophiliac cumwad? Do you go down and jerk off?'

'Shut up,' Kenny said.

'You think about dead race drivers and burned bodies and you slap your dick around? Look at you, I can see it in your face right now. You're hard just thinking about it.'

Kenny's voice got louder. 'Shut up, I'll do it, I'll kill her.'

'You're so wound up about it you don't even know where you are, do you?'

Kenny pressed against me. I tried to get leverage, to get out from under.

Jesse said, 'This is it. This is the place where you killed Isaac.'

I felt Kenny hesitate, take a breath.

'You're done taking trophies. Let Evan go,' Jesse said.

I heard, in the distance, the sound of the Mercedes coming back.

Kenny shuffled his feet. 'Get out of the car!'

'On one condition.'

'No conditions.'

'Tell me the truth. When you got out of Brand's car and came down the hill to check on us, was Isaac already dead?'

Kenny laughed. 'That's it? You want closure?'

'I need to know that there wasn't anything I could have done for him.'

Kenny's laugh was almost hysterical. 'Christ, you are such a fucking Boy Scout.'

'Tell me.'

'Let me make you happy, yeah. The dude was dead. His head was smashed flat on one side. It was just gone, caved in, he looked like a Picasso painting.'

Jesse said nothing. I could see him through the windshield, his eyes dark. He gripped the steering wheel, staring at Kenny, his face starting to crack.

'Out of the car, now,' Kenny said.

Jesse lowered his hands from the wheel. His shoulders dropped.

'Don't,' I said, struggling, kicking ineffectively at Kenny. 'Jesse, don't trust him.'

Jesse reached toward the dashboard, I thought to take the keys out of the ignition. I heard a clicking sound.

He pulled his cellphone out of the hands-free mount and put it to his ear.

'You're off the speakerphone now,' he said. 'Did you get all that?'

'What are you doing?' Kenny said. 'Get out.'

Jesse held up the phone. 'It's for you.'

Kenny laughed again. 'Hey, mister slick-ass lawyer, you know the cops can't use that as evidence. You record somebody without his permission, the court has to throw it out.'

'It's not the cops,' Jesse said. 'It's your father.'

★ ★ ★

It must have taken less than five seconds, but Kenny's breakdown felt as if it lasted a year. He began shaking, groin to fingertips, so hard that the cleaver tap-danced against the hood. His voice melted into a bray.

He went for Jesse. Straight for him. With animal frenzy he elbowed me aside and attacked the Audi's windshield with the cleaver. One blow, two, huge thunking swings, the cleaver ringing as it cracked down.

The safety glass spidered but didn't break, and I reeled back, hearing Jesse fire up the engine. I heard the Mercedes coming down the hill from above us. This was it, my last chance to escape. I had to get into the Audi. But as soon as Jesse started the engine, Kenny gave up on the windshield and grabbed for the passenger door's handle. It was locked.

'You're dead, Blackburn, you're fucking dead.'

He swung the cleaver into the passenger's window and the glass collapsed like a wall of ice.

The Mercedes came back down the hill. It purred around a bend, coasting toward us. Braked to a stop about sixty yards away. Pausing, idling, perhaps wondering what was going on. The headlights lit up. High beams, full effect, showing Kenny center stage: screaming obscenities, chopping away at the crumbled safety glass that clung to the window frame.

Now playing: My Heart Belongs to Daddy.

Jesse pushed his door open, shouting, 'Ev, get in.'

Kenny cleared the glass from the frame and reached inside, fumbling for the door lock. Jesse, trying to stop him, threw the car in reverse. I ran around the front end of the car, trying to figure how to jump into a moving vehicle onto the driver's lap while he was steering and Kenny was—

Kenny was climbing headfirst through the passenger's window.

I heard it, the growl of the Mercedes accelerating as Harley floored the gas pedal. The headlights swelled. I had time to think *she wouldn't*, and the Mercedes roared past me and smashed into the Audi.

Steel and glass sang. The Mercedes T-boned into the Audi's

passenger's door and shoved it sideways. The cars stopped, and the Mercedes backed up.

I expected to see Kenny crushed against the door like a fruitfly, but he wasn't there. The Mercedes backed up about twenty meters. One headlight was out, the hood bent, the grill squashed. The wheelwells shrieked.

Kenny was in Jesse's car. I could see his feet – he must have dived through the window right before she hit. The Audi's engine had died and I could hear Jesse working the ignition, trying to restart it.

The Mercedes stopped backing up. She put it in drive and accelerated toward the Audi again.

I said, 'Stop—'

I saw Kenny now, fumbling up, looking out the window at the onrushing Mercedes, raising his hands against the coming blow.

She was trying to kill him.

She rammed the Audi again. They slid further downhill, toward the far edge of the road. I ran toward them. She was trying to push Jesse's car over the drop-off.

They stopped. The Mercedes's horn was blaring. Its engine had died. Jesse was still trying to start the Audi.

Kenny was shrieking. 'You bitch, you crazy miserable bitch.'

In the Mercedes, Harley slumped unconscious over the steering wheel. In the weak light from her remaining headlight, I could see Kenny shaking the Audi's door, trying to get it open. The crash had smashed it shut.

I stood in the center of the road, hands limp, head thumping. The back end of the Audi was over the lip of the drop-off. I could hear rocks and dirt clods dropping out from beneath the rear axle and tumbling down the escarpment. Each time Kenny rattled the door handle, the car trembled and more debris let go.

I walked toward the Audi, stopping short, as if my breath might send it over the edge. I stared through the windshield. Kenny was squirming around inside but Jesse was sitting perfectly still, hands on the wheel. He had a cut on his forehead but looked focused.

'Get me out of here,' Kenny said.

Jesse said, 'Hold still or I'll punch you.'

'Get me out.'

Jesse called to me, 'What's it look like?'

Kenny started to climb out the passenger's window. He got his arms out. He was still holding the meat cleaver. He began pulling his head and shoulders through. The shift in his weight unbalanced the car, and it started hinging like a seesaw, the front tires rising off the ground.

I ran and threw my upper body onto the hood of the car, adding weight. I felt the balance slowly, slowly come back in my direction, the car hinge down, but only by inches.

I looked at Kenny. 'Don't you move. Don't you damn move.'

But he couldn't control himself. He tried again to shimmy through the window, and again the car shuddered and started to swing. I felt my feet leaving the ground.

He shrank back, and the car tilted down. My toes found earth.

'Help me.' Kenny's voice had risen to the pitch of the Chihuahua.

Jesse's door was still open, and I could see him looking oh-so-carefully out.

Kenny said. 'Get me out of this fucking car.'

Jesse locked eyes with me. He didn't look scared. He had a wry expression on his face. I didn't want it to be the last thing I ever saw of him.

'Can you make it out?' I said.

'No.'

Kenny said, 'Okay. Right. Here's the deal. I'll get back inside the car. If I see Gidget coming around to help me, I'll throw the cleaver out. If not, I'll use it on Blackburn.'

Jesse said, 'Don't listen to him.'

'Help me or I'll swing it right into his neck. One blow, I'll kill him,' Kenny said.

Jesse said, 'That's not what you're going to do, Ev.'

'Yes it is. She has to. She has no other choice.'

Jesse's gaze pinned me. He pulled the seatbelt tight against his shoulder and gripped the wheel with both hands.

'I'm counting to three,' Kenny said.

I checked my inner radar, trying to understand what Jesse was telling me. I knew that if I did what Kenny told me to, either Jesse or I would die. Kenny wouldn't give up his weapon. He would use it.

'One,' Kenny said. 'Help me and I'll make it worth your while. We'll both get Blackburn out.'

'He's lying,' Jesse said.

'I know.' I looked at him.

Kenny said, 'Two. You stupid cunt, it's the only way.'

Jesse was waiting for my answer.

I held his gaze. 'Do you trust me?'

'With my life,' he said.

'Three,' Kenny said.

I leapt backward off the hood.

The Audi hinged up, front wheels rearing into the air. Kenny screamed, a weightless howl. The car hesitated for an instant, and slid backward over the edge. All the rest was noise and darkness.

Thirty-Five

The dust was thick. In the beam of the flashlight it whitened the silence in front of me at the bottom of the hill. I pounded down the escarpment, following the trail of flattened grass.

The flashlight was Harley's. I'd grabbed it from the Mercedes, found it on the floor below the cellphone scanner and mobile positioning monitor. Harley was still unconscious.

Kenny was lying in the grass in the middle of the fall line. One look, and I knew that the car had rolled over him.

He was alive. I shone the flashlight on his face. His nose was spewing blood and his jaw hung crooked but his eyes were staring back at me. He raised a hand. Not a pleading hand, but a claw, wanting to tear at me one more time.

I left him there. Running across uneven ground, I reached the car. It was upside down, roof crushed on one side, wheels spinning at the sky.

'Jesse?'

I dropped to all fours and shone the flashlight through the shattered windows. The first thing I saw was the blood, blooming red under the flashlight. It covered his face.

'Jesse, can you hear me?'

He was hanging from the seatbelt, his head an inch off the crumpled roof of the car.

He blinked, and grimaced. 'Where's Kenny?'

'Up the hill. It worked.' My hand quaked as I reached through the window. 'You're hurt.'

'It's only a cut. Is he dead?'

My voice was shaking. Everything about me was shaking. 'Alive, but he isn't going anywhere.'

'Help me out.'

I shone the flashlight into the car. From what I could see, he was tangled up with the steering column in the smashed interior.

'Maybe we should wait for the paramedics.' Tears were pushing their way into my voice.

He braced an arm on the roof of the car below his head. 'When I unbuckle the seatbelt, pull me through the window.'

You can't argue with a mule. 'Let me clear out the glass.' With the flashlight I knocked away the beads still clinging to the window frame. 'Ready?'

He reached up, pressed the buckle, and bumped down onto the roof.

'Okay.' He stretched his arm out the window.

I clasped it, braced my feet against the chassis, and pulled. Got his head and shoulders through the frame, and he wrenched his other arm out to help push. Huffing, I pulled, he shoved, and he came free, sliding out.

He wound his arms around me, spread his fingers into my hair, and fell back on the grass, holding me.

He said, 'Remind me never to come here again.'

I put my head down on his chest. His heart was knocking as hard as my own. I listened to it, a blessed sound, wanting never to let go of him.

He breathed, shifted. 'I want to see Kenny.'

'Why?'

He worked his elbows underneath himself and sat up. 'I'm not finished with him.'

'No.'

He looked at me. 'I'm not going to kill him.' He angled himself toward the car. Rolling onto his side, he reached inside and pulled out one of his crutches.

Above us on the road, I heard a car stop. I looked up and saw headlights.

'Honest. I'm not going to touch him.' He held out an arm. 'Give me a boost.'

I crouched by his side. He put his arm over my shoulder and I helped him get to his feet. With him leaning on me and on the crutch, we picked our way across the ground. From the road came the sound of voices.

Kenny hadn't moved. We halted along until we could look down at him. I aimed the flashlight over him. He was twisted and swollen in a dozen ways. But he managed a sneer.

'Unbelievable. Blackburn is the last man standing.' He turned his head and spat. A bloody glob trickled down his chin. 'You win.'

Jesse looked at him. 'No I don't. But you lose, Rudenski.'

'It was the dyke's fault. She screwed it from the second she left the money out and you found it. Never trust a woman.'

From above, a man called out, 'Is anybody down there?'

'Here,' I said. 'Call the paramedics.'

Kenny said, 'No, no ambulance. I want – get me out of town. I have money. Get me to a private airfield and I'll—' He coughed. 'Millions. I can pay you millions.'

Jesse shook his head. 'Ev, let's go.'

'I'm talking seven figures. You'll be rich.' Kenny said, 'What is wrong with you? Don't you want to be rich?'

Jesse stared down at him. 'You're going on trial. And then you're going to prison.'

'My father won't let that happen.'

The voice above said, 'Does one of you have the keys to the Mercedes? We should move it out of the road.'

I called to him. 'Don't touch the driver. She could have head or neck injuries.'

'What driver?'

Jesse and I looked up the hill.

Kenny laughed harshly. 'Never trust a woman.'

Jesse said, 'I think I'd better sit down.'

I felt his hand. It was cold and clammy. I said, 'Come on.' We got five feet before he passed out.

The surf was up, breakers scintillating as they rolled in. I walked around the side of Jesse's house and onto the deck. He was sitting in the sun, watching the ocean.

'Quite a shiner,' I said.

He looked around, touched his black eye, and shrugged. He had stitches running up his forehead into his scalp, and bruises from head to toe. Otherwise he was all right. Thank seatbelts, airbags, guardian angels, maybe sunspots.

Pulling up a deck chair, I sat down next to him. 'They found Harley.'

He leaned on his knees, wove his fingers together. 'Where?'

'Cold Springs.' I felt a snag in my throat. 'The bridge.'

'She jumped?'

I nodded, trying, impossibly, not to picture that long, irrevocable drop into the gorge below.

'Jesus.' He closed his eyes. 'What a waste.'

I listened to the roll of the waves, watched the seagulls swaying above the water.

'Lieutenant Rome came by. He gave me this.' I took the photocopy from my pocket and handed it to him. 'The original—' Another snag. 'It was on her body.'

He unfolded it and started reading.

The word 'sorry' cannot begin to express my regret. I have turned my life into a bonfire and burned down the lives of people I care about. Everything I touched is reduced to ashes.

George, you trusted me to keep things shipshape and I screwed it. Sorry.

Evan, you were my friend and I fed you to the wolves. Sorry.

Jesse, you were the one true thing, and fear set me out to destroy you. Sorry.

Sandoval family – there are no words.

He looked up, eyes the color of sky, staring out past the horizon. Looked back at the photocopy.

I make the following statement fully aware of my constitutional rights and the laws of evidence of the State of California—

He turned the page over. 'There's no more.'

'Rome's keeping the next two pages confidential. The prosecutor will want it as evidence at Kenny's trial.'

'And you didn't wangle a look?'

'Of course I did.' I saw a look of appreciation brush his face. I said, 'It's a confession.'

'Was it what we thought?'

'Yeah. Harley and Kenny were laundering money for i-heist. Harley would take it to casinos. Kenny let them invest in Mako. In return, Yago let Harley skim a percentage so she could keep gambling. And he helped Kenny build his secret museum.'

He looked again at the suicide note. 'Did she admit to being with Kenny when he ran me and Isaac down?'

'Yes.'

He pinched the bridge of his nose. 'Did she say why they did it?'

'Because you saw her with the cash, Yago's money. She told Kenny, and he decided to eliminate you.'

'I thought I was helping her. I thought . . .'

'Jesse, you don't get to feel guilty.'

'I know that, but—'

'No. You're blameless. You're in a state of grace. And that is an FFL.'

He breathed. 'Why'd they blame Brand?'

'He was the perfect patsy. If he refused to take the blame for the crash, Kenny could have turned him over to the feds, or to i-heist, for embezzling money from the Segue fund. So Brand agreed to take the fall. He thought if he fled he could come back scot free when the statute of limitations expired. And then Harley made the anonymous call, setting him up.' I stared at the surf. 'But when he came back he tried to blackmail both Kenny and Harley. Which started the whole thing unraveling.'

'What about Chris Ramseur?'

'They're charging Kenny with his murder. And with Stu Pyle's, along with Brand's,' I said. 'They found Brand's gold rental car in Kenny's garage. He'd been driving it, trying to make it look like

Brand was still alive. They think he was the one who parked it down the street from my house.'

He glanced again at Harley's note. 'Why did she turn on Kenny at the last minute?'

'That I don't know. Kenny helped Yago get his claws into her, and was holding her feet to the fire. Maybe she finally just had enough, and saw the opportunity to get him off her back, once and for all. Maybe she just hated him.'

Kenny was in intensive care. His recovery would be spent in unpleasant places. So would the rest of his life.

Jesse put his hands on his push-rims. His arm was shaking, a sign of taking too much weight for too long. 'Then it's over.'

Over? I looked at him. Thinking how his friends were gone, his body savaged, how his life had been torn apart and could never be restored.

'Yes,' I said. 'It's over.'

Tentatively I put my fingers on his. He looked at my hand.

'And you're here. As always.' He laced his fingers with mine. 'What are we going to do?'

Join the circus? Take our act to Hollywood? For the love of God, why didn't he ask an easy one? *Contestant number two: the plutonium bomb in front of you has just reached supercritical mass. How will you disarm it?*

'Do you love me?' I said.

'Without reservation. Do you love me?'

I took his hand in both of mine. 'Jesse, you are my lover, my sparring partner, the angel on my right shoulder and the devil on my left. You are the very air I breathe. Yes, I love you.'

He held my gaze, and those blue eyes undid me.

'Do you think we're good for each other?' he said.

He was deadly serious, but now it was my turn to look wry.

'We seem to be responsible for keeping each other alive. Let's put that one in the *yes* column.'

'Do you think we should start over?'

'From the beginning?' I sighed. 'Yes. But without the tryst in the truck bed.'

'Wedding?'

I managed to hold his gaze. 'That'll have to come later, won't it?'

'I think so.'

I realized I was squeezing his hand as though trying to crack a nut. I loosened my grip. Looked out to sea.

He said, 'You okay?'

I thought about it, expecting to feel sad. But a mountain was lifting from my shoulders. 'I feel good.'

'So do I.' He exhaled. 'The invitations?'

'I never got around to mailing them.'

'The dress?'

'Will still fit me if we reschedule within the next . . . ten years.'

'Optimist.'

'I've been told.'

'The tickets to Hawaii?' he said.

'Cancel them and I'll wring your neck.'

Now, after what seemed like a lifetime, he smiled. 'The five hundred canapés you ordered?'

'Oh, shoot.' I ran my hands through my hair. 'I'll give them to Cousin Tater.'

'God, I've missed you.'

He took my face in his hands. I leaned in and kissed him.

When I left Jesse's, I drove out to Goleta. I had a final stop to make, a final question to ask, a final measure of self-protection to see to.

Security guards were posted outside Mako Technologies. No surprise. The media were on Kenny's arrest like flies on rotting meat. The press was clotted along the sidewalk, reporters and a TV news van with its dish antenna extended. When I approached the door, a guard stepped up, keys jangling. It was Len, Amber's flame.

He crossed his arms. 'I'll have to ask you to state your business.'

'I want to speak to George Rudenski,' I said. 'And yeah, Junior really chased me with a meat cleaver. So let me in before I give the gory details to the media gang over there.'

He let me in. When I approached the front desk, Amber waved.

'Call Pops,' I said.

She got on the phone. Her curls looked disheveled, and her mascara was caking. When she smiled at me, her eyes scuttled around like beetles. That cinched it. I knew my suspicions were on the money.

I said, 'Last night, when you called me—'

And her lip started quivering.

'Junior told you to do it, didn't he?'

'I didn't mean to. I mean, I didn't think . . .'

'That's a nice new car you have out there, Amber.' I nodded toward the parking lot. 'I saw it when I came in last time. It must be great to replace your bike.'

Her mouth quavered.

I leaned over the desk, close to her face. 'Kenny gave it to you, right? That's how he paid you.'

Blink, blink. The phone rang but she didn't answer it.

'I can see how it looked like a good deal. You put a couple of pills in my drink at the bridal shower, and in return he bought you a new car.'

George's secretary appeared in the lobby, calling my name. Ignoring Amber's sniffling, I followed her down the hall. She knocked on his office door. He said, 'Come,' and she melted away. I went in.

George sat behind a desk the size of an M-1 tank. His white hair bristled and his suit had steak-knife creases, but he looked gray and deflated.

'Sorry to butt in,' I said. 'I promise, this is the last time I'll pull my command-performance act. I'll never bother you again.'

'Say your piece.'

'I know that you brought in Tim North and Jakarta Rivera.'

He stared at me from under bushy eyebrows. His gaze was opaque.

'You asked them to get to the bottom of i-heist's involvement with Mako. You knew something was rancid in the company, and you wanted it rooted out.'

He began lining up fountain pens on his desk, precisely parallel. They looked like a missile battery.

'You wanted an investigation, on the quiet. I understand that. You wanted to sever the links between the gang and Mako before they brought Mako down. If the FBI found out that your source code had been sold to a criminal gang, Mako people would go to prison. If they found out about the money laundering, they'd seize Mako's assets. Either way, your company's goose was cooked. But George – bringing in a hit team? What the hell were you thinking?'

He aimed the pens. 'You don't know what you're talking about. You don't think outside the box.'

'Which box is that? The one holding Adam Sandoval's body?'

Saying it, I felt a twist of pain. I forced myself not to blink. George looked away from me.

'You chose well, George. Jax and Tim cleaned house for you. i-heist is gone, for good. You only had one bump in the road. You didn't know that it was your son who was conspiring with them. Now your goose is cooked, and Mako's, and Kenny's. Burned to a crisp.'

'I have nothing to say to you.'

'But don't you want to know that you got your money's worth? They were terribly clever. They got me to do a lot of their snooping for them, and they're remarkably personable, compared to my admittedly limited circle of contract-killer friends.'

'This is all speculation.'

'Jax opened my eyes, in so many ways. Look here.'

Walking to his desk, I put one foot up on the edge. My knock-off boots weren't as pricey as Jax's Jimmy Choos, but the heel spike was just as sharp.

'This heel can put your eye out. Bitchin, huh?'

His face reddened, all the way up into his hair. 'You should go now.'

I drew my foot down. 'Two more things. One, do you know who they were really working for?'

For the first time, his reserve started to chip. I had caught him off guard.

'The way I put it together, when you decided to bring in outside – security consultants? – you got in touch with your contacts in Washington. Some of those old boys in the photos that hang on the wall in your lobby. What, NSA, Defense Intelligence, CIA? Am I on the right track? And you asked them to recommend people with the skill set you were looking for.'

I could hear the air whistling in and out of his lungs.

'And Tim and Jax contacted you, perhaps anonymously. You arranged to pay them through their account in, I'm guessing Zurich, and they sent you untraceable progress reports. So my question is, were they working for you, or for the spooks at Langley, or both?'

The redness was leaching down his neck and under his collar.

'Here's the thing, George. Considering how you like to think outside the box, I figure I should watch my back. Because I know about this.'

'If you're frightened of me, why are you laying all this out?'

'So you'll know that I know how it works. Because there's one other thing – Jax was watching my back, and she gave me her business card. I'm guessing that means whoever she's working for was watching my back too, and still is. If I ever have the slightest bit of trouble, they'll be on you like fleas on a dog. And I have to say, you don't want to see Jax shoot. Believe me, the results aren't pretty.'

I started for the door.

'Good luck, George. If you need a lawyer, I know a good one.' I stopped and hit myself in the forehead. 'Wait, what am I thinking? You can't hire him. He's going to be too busy suing your sorry ass into the ground.'

★   ★   ★

Coming out, I passed the front desk without looking at Amber. She clattered off her chair and came around, shoulders hunched, hands up, as though she were a leper in a passion play, beseeching me.

'Please, let me explain. He said it wouldn't hurt you. I didn't think—'

'Start thinking, Amber. Do it every day. It can get to be a habit.'

'He said—'

'He wanted me unconscious so he could wire my house with video bugs and program my phone to track me. He used it to spy on me. In my shower, Amber.'

She put a hand over her mouth.

'Quit Mako. Get out of here,' I said.

She was crying.

'Right now,' I said. 'Just tell them you're going, for the sake of your immortal soul.'

I started to walk past her.

'But I already did. Don't hate me. I already gave my notice.'

'Great. Good luck getting a reference.'

'It's okay, I have another job. I'm going to work for your cousin Taylor. Selling Countess Zara lingerie.'

Examination of that night's news footage shows me coming out the door, laughing so hard I nearly fainted.

Thirty-Six

Adam's funeral mass was packed to the rafters with colleagues and grad students and former swimming teammates, big men crowded into the small, sunny church. Jesse gave the first reading, from the Book of Wisdom: But the souls of the virtuous are in the hands of God, no torment shall ever touch them. It was a sight that would have astonished Adam, left him shaking his head. Jesse Blackburn in a Catholic church, with the Lectionary open in his hands.

'Their going looked like a disaster, their leaving us, like annihilation; but they are in peace.' His voice was strong, and he almost got there, until he read: 'Those who are faithful will live with him in love; for grace and mercy await those he has chosen.'

It was beyond him: Adam, belief, his grief. His hands touched the words on the page, and he looked up at us. His eyes, afire with tears, gave the eulogy.

Later, we went with Adam's uncle and cousins on a charter boat to scatter his ashes on the ocean. The shore was low on the horizon, the Pacific swelling blue in all directions. The ashes drifted away on the sea, surrounded by flowers, and sank into water glittering with light. I thought about Adam, his passion for the wonders of existence, his curious understanding that for light, time does not pass. He was with the light, I hoped, with the shine of forever, ageless and eternal.

It was the next weekend when thunder woke me, an exotic rumble for a Santa Barbara morning. The breeze lifted the curtains and blew papers off my vanity. Smelling rain, I opened my eyes to see black clouds bunched outside. Lightning blanched the sky, and fat drops came falling. I got up to close the windows.

Jesse pulled the quilt over his head. 'I thought they passed an ordinance. No rain on Saturdays.'

The quilt was back, for good. Taylor hadn't fought me for it. In fact, when she saw me coming up her walk she met me at the door and handed it to me, without a word.

I went to the living room to close more windows and grab the morning paper from the front step before it got soaked.

The package was sitting next to it. It was a padded manila envelope several inches thick, addressed to me. I brought it in, set it on the kitchen counter, and stared at it. After a minute I ripped it open. Inside were clippings, reports, handwritten journals, memoranda. They went back two decades, and told the story – stories – of Jax and Tim and their adventures in the dark realm of espionage. They seemed to sting my hands.

There was a note.

Read up, and let us know your price. Come on, you know you want to.

Outside, the thunder cracked and the clouds cut loose.

I called to Jesse. 'Hey, Blackburn, get out here. Have I got a rainy day project for you.'